CH00822329

FREE THE DARKNESS

KING'S DARK TIDINGS

TIDINGS

BOOK 1

KEL KADE

BOOKS BY KEL KADE

ACKNOWLEDGMENTS

Thank you to my family and my most patient and understanding daughter who have encouraged and supported me throughout this writing process.

www.kelkade.com

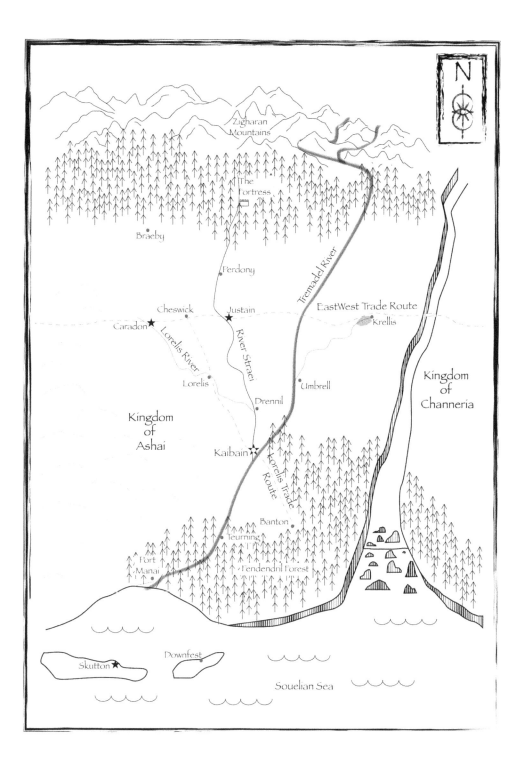

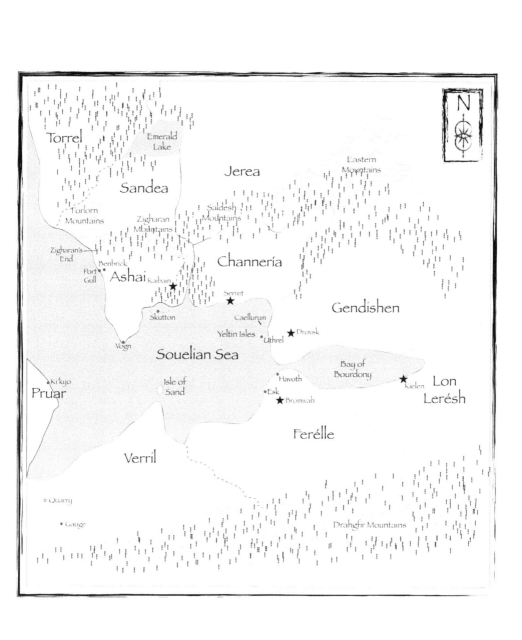

PROLOGUE

"Good men want only the power to make things right. Great men seek to make things right and gather the power to do so. Great leaders find those who are worthy of wielding power and set them to the task of making things right."
- Coroleus, J.E. 1,067

Relief washed over the weary rider as his destination finally emerged from the gloomy, moonlit darkness. He had not at all been certain of the success of this mission, and if he had failed, he would not have lived to regret it.

Tree branches creaked at the night's gentle exhale. It was soft and passive, so unlike the aggressive sucking pops and sloughs of the mud pulling at his mount's hooves. He shivered beneath his damp cloak and shifted the bundle that was carefully tied about his torso as he repositioned the various weapons worn both openly and secreted beneath his padded leather armor. He reminded himself that if these people had a mind to end him, his weapons and all his years of training and experience would be worthless.

The brief respite he felt only moments ago for having reached his goal was short-lived as the persistent doubts that had plagued him from the mission's onset resurfaced. A flash of heat surged through his blood as an overwhelming anxiety breached his carefully constructed defenses. Loyalty and honor could only take a man so far. His gut churned like a twisting rope winding back upon itself. *A noose.* But no, these people would not bother with a noose. He would not even see it coming. One moment he would be alive and breathing and thinking, and then he would cease to exist. The rider did not even consider that he might meet the Maker. There was no glory of an afterlife—not for men like him. Any oath-bound who caught the attention of his liege could not hope for his soul's redemption. After all, loyalty and honor could take a man only so far.

As his horse plodded closer to the foreboding fortress, his future's fortunes once again flashed across his mind. How might he be received? Would his success simply go unremarked as a natural expectation of having fulfilled his duty, despite the trials and transgressions he had suffered? Could he dare hope to be congratulated for his courage and unwavering dedication to his liege? He released a soft grunt. *About as likely as me ever meeting the Maker*, he thought sourly. If they did not kill him here, it was just as likely he would die upon his return to his liege, having fulfilled his duty.

Had his liege finally drawn him into his greatest confidence in assigning him this mission, or was he a loose end, destined to perish in an unfortunate *accident*? Never did he consider not returning—at least not for more than a breath. If he ran, he would be hunted, and it would not be long before one of *them* would snuff out his life. The brief days—*hours?*—of freedom would be filled with terror and dread as he waited for the bleak blackness of the void to consume him. No, running was never an option. Even had there been the slightest chance of success, he could not consider it. He had loyalty and honor, after all.

The lone rider took a deep, shuddering breath, steadying his nerves as he covered the final few paces before the solid iron gate. He pulled his mount to a stop and waited. There was no need to pound or call out his presence. They would have known he was here long before he set eyes on the dark citadel. A clank and groan reverberated through the metal goliath that posed as a door, and then it swung open in eerie silence except for the soft swoosh of air being drawn through the passage as it curled around the monstrous structure.

Nudging his horse with his heels, he passed through what he was certain was the darkest, blackest shadow he had ever encountered and could not help the shiver that rocked him as he considered the implication of crossing such a veil. A moonlit figure emerged from a shadowed recess before him. Others might call the recess the door to the main hall. To him, it was perhaps a portal to H'khajnak, the demon realm.

The restless warrior took a steadying breath and forced his hands to release their tension on the reins. He was not successful in dispelling the tightness in his shoulders or the rest of his body, for that matter. The battle charger snorted and stomped, no doubt picking up on his rider's anxiety. All the dread and struggles against the dangers he suffered to get here had finally pooled together and were threatening to overcome him. This was not the way an experienced veteran behaved. Perhaps he had finally cracked.

Despite the gloom, the moonlight was bright, and the rider could make out most of the features of the approaching figure. He was a middle-aged, stern-faced man whose only two facial expressions appeared to be *blank stoicism* and *scowl*. The moonlight reflected off his slightly balding crown but was absorbed into the coarse, dark material of his robe that fell to mid-thigh. The robe draped over a plain tunic and pants of dark color and fastened with a leather belt. If the belt had a buckle, he could not see it, for nothing the man wore reflected any light. With his head covered, he could probably disappear altogether, which was most likely the point. Although no weapons were visible, in this place, it was certain the man was well armed. The man stopped within a few paces but did not invite the rider to dismount.

"You brought it?" spoke a quiet, harsh voice.

"Yes—" the rider croaked. He cleared his throat and tried again. "Yes, I brought *him* to you."

The man grunted. "It matters little what you call it—*him*, if you prefer. It is no longer relevant."

A sliver of the warrior's terror receded, replaced with indignation. "Regardless of your intentions, you would do well not to forget who he is. You will regret it otherwise."

The robed man nearly chuckled—*nearly*. "I was unaware you had a gift for prophecy. You had best remember that *this*,"—he pointed a gnarled finger at the wrapped lump resting against the warrior's chest—"is not a person. It is a weapon, newly forged and as yet without an edge. Any who meet him will not live to remember it."

"Does that include you?" snarled the rider. His concern for his own welfare was quickly dissipating as the reality of the situation dawned on him. Perhaps he should have run. They certainly would have found him, but surely he could have hidden one small babe somewhere, perhaps with a loving family, before he died. After securing the child's future, he could have fallen on his own sword to prevent them from torturing him for information. He lightly squeezed the small bundle, eliciting a slight gurgling *coo*.

A cruel smile played across the man's face as he replied, "I will live to serve my purpose, same as you. Neither of us can expect much more than that. Now, hand him over. He is no longer your concern."

1

Bone snapped and flesh parted as hot blood spewed from a jagged wound. A gut-clenching wail echoed off the stone walls and startled the ever-present black sentries into flight. As the alert subsided into moaning sobs, the sleek, black ravens resettled on their perches, the grey twigs of the sorry excuse for a tree that occupied the courtyard.

"Silence!" The command was followed by the crack of a whip and a slight, strangled cry. "You cannot afford to be heard even when you are injured —*especially* when you are injured. Silence! Always. Be. Silent."

The deep sobs were slowly replaced by tiny, sniffling whimpers as young Rezkin pulled himself together. At six years old he knew full well he should not have shouted. He was stupid, so stupid. He had to think quickly. Any moment now, Master Jaiardun would begin to ask questions, and he needed answers, or he would suffer even greater punishment. How could he have fallen? He should have been more careful. If he had set his weight properly as he streamed across the battlements, he would not have slipped on the loose stone. Always, he was supposed to be prepared to compensate for uneven or treacherous footing. He had become careless in his mad dash to make up for time lost getting tangled in the rope. It was not the fall that doomed him, although that would have led to severe enough punishment as it was. No, it was the shout that sealed his fate.

Finally managing to draw a complete breath, his vision started to clear. For several moments the sheer intensity of the pain had robbed him of sight as his mind flooded with heat and light. The spinning in his head had threatened to rob him of consciousness … or his breakfast, but he managed to hold on to that much at least and thereby escaped *those* dire consequences. That would have been much worse than what he was facing already. To shout was to draw attention to one's presence, but at least one could still defend oneself or commit suicide to prevent capture. To lose consciousness meant to face discovery *and* be taken alive. *That* must never happen, *Rule 117*. Rezkin knew these truths already. Still, he had not been able to control the involuntary noise that emanated from his small lungs.

A shadow fell over him as Master Jaiardun towered above. His face was red, and his eyes were blazing with fury beneath an intense scowl. "You failed! Explain."

Rezkin swallowed the lump in his throat and took several shuddering breaths through his nose before containing his nausea enough to speak. "Master, I failed to set my weight and slipped on the loose stone. I fell."

"I can see that you fell," snapped Master Jaiardun. "You are still too weak. You could not contain your pain. You will work diligently to master it. You can be sure of this. Now, set that," Master Jaiardun said as he waved his hand in the direction of the injury.

The injury in question throbbed with a pain so overwhelming that Rezkin still was not sure he would remain conscious. As soon as his eyes fell on the bloody off-white edges of bone peeking from flesh and wool, his head swam, and he lost his breakfast after all. When he finished retching, he sobbed, "Master, I cannot."

Master Jaiardun scoffed, "Then, you die. Do you think someone will always be there to help you? No! You must be *one*. Alone. No one will help you. No one will care. If they find you, they are more likely to kill you immediately or torture you for information and then kill you."

Rezkin sniffed and whimpered as he reached tentatively toward his leg. The break was halfway down his left shin. It could have been much worse. A twenty-foot fall could easily kill a man. He was aware that he had most likely sustained other injuries as well, but the pain stabbing his leg overshadowed anything else. He tugged on his pant leg to expose the injury, and the sickening dizziness filled him once again. "I-I cannot do it, Master," he sobbed.

"Men must care for their own injuries," Master Jaiardun stated as though it were that simple.

"But, I am only a small-man," replied Rezkin. "I do not know how."

"That is no excuse! You are still a man. You will never be a big-man if you do not learn this *Skill*," Master Jaiardun rebuffed.

"Jaiardun, enough." The soft but firm voice came from somewhere behind Rezkin.

He jerked his head around in surprise only to feel a sharp pain shoot through his body from his leg. He should have heard Master Peider approach. He should have known *exactly* where the old man was. Rezkin began to worry about his mind. How could he be failing so much?

Master Peider scrutinized Rezkin with a critical eye. Seeing the apparent panic on little Rezkin's face he stated, "It is the pain, Rezkin. It addles the mind. It makes a man unable to think clearly, and he can easily lose track of his surroundings, sometimes even forgetting who he is or his purpose. The injury is damaging. The pain can be deadly."

Master Peider turned to Master Jaiardun with calm surety. "I will take him. Without proper treatment by a skilled healer that injury could negate all of our teaching. He would be a cripple, useless."

Unsatisfied, Master Jaiardun countered. "He must learn to treat such an injury. If he never fails so miserably in the future, this will be the only injury of the sort, and he needs the experience. Plus, it will teach him not to be so careless."

Master Peider frowned. "I am sure he is already regretting his carelessness. I will not sedate him during treatment. He will watch how it is done so that he knows what to do in the future. Still, I will have to use a bit of power to stimulate and speed the healing unless you want him unable to train for the next six months. Obviously, that is something he will not be able to do for himself."

"Fine," Master Jaiardun huffed. "Just make sure he learns from this. It would be a waste for him to sleep through the treatment and gain nothing." He turned his brooding glare back on Rezkin. "You will face me again when you are healed. You will not enjoy it."

Enjoy? What did that mean? Rezkin frowned as his eyebrows pulled together on his tiny face. He was not sure what this *enjoy* was, but perhaps it was a big-man thing. He would have to ask Master Peider about it later. He knew he had much to learn of big-man things. The masters had explained to him how men came into this world very small and knowing nothing. In order to become a big-man, he had to learn the *Rules* and *Skills*. *Ignorance*, (that meant not knowing the *Rules* and *Skills*), was no excuse for failing. Small-men

7

were always punished for *infractions* (that meant breaking the *Rules* or failing the *Skills*), and as the men grew bigger, they were punished less because they learned the *Rules* and *Skills*.

Rezkin wanted to become a big man fast, so he worked very hard to learn all of the *Rules* and *Skills*. Unfortunately, he had just failed in his *Skills* miserably. He had also broken *Rule 6—Do not get injured* and *Rule 12—Do not make sound*. As Master Peider bent to pick him up, Rezkin sucked in a breath and spied the blood and vomit on the cobblestones. He was about to break *Rule 10—Do not leave evidence* as well. Just as Master Peider lifted him from the ground, a searing pain ripped through him, and all went black.

Rezkin reached for the swaying branch, just barely managing to grip the rough bark with the tips of his fingers. As soon as he caught hold, he used the considerable strength of his wiry frame to pull himself up. He perched in the bough as he surveyed his surroundings once again. He was still honing his observational skills. Master Jaiardun assured him that once he was a full-grown bigman he would no longer need to concentrate so hard on his environment. The *Skill* would be so infused in his mind that he would do it automatically without thinking. Until then, he had to concentrate. Striker Farson and Striker Adona were both here somewhere, and they were looking for him. This was by far the most difficult task he had been assigned yet. Not only did he have to enter the fortress by stealth, but he had to do it during the day with the "inhabitants" having been forewarned of his coming.

There was no movement in the courtyard or on the balcony across from him. He took a moment to peer into a shadow to one side. He saw nothing to indicate anyone was hiding there. Averting his gaze, he reexamined the area with his peripheral vision. One could often see things in the periphery that one could not see directly. Still, nothing appeared.

He took a deep breath and then stood, balancing his weight on the balls of his feet. Normally, he would turn his feet to the side to walk about a swaying tree, but what he was about to do required speed and power. Without a moment's hesitation he darted forward, his feet barely touching the sturdy limb, and then launched himself into the open space beyond. Just as he began to think he had misjudged the distance, he closed in on the balcony's railing. Strong hands gripped the carved stone, and he swung his legs forward so that his feet impacted the wall below. His legs coiled with his momentum, and like a viper, he sprung back from the wall while pushing slightly downward with his toes. He shot upward and over the railing to land softly in the shadow of the stone wall.

Soft boots settled lightly on the stones making neither sound nor mark. The balcony doors would surely be locked, but that would be no problem—not anymore. He had achieved his *Lock Mastery Skill* last year. Now, at twelve years old he was focusing on a number of other *Skills*, the present most important one being *Daylight Stealth Invasion*. His task was to enter the fortress and retrieve an item from a predetermined location and then return said item to the master waiting in the stables. Not only was he required to succeed without getting caught, but also without anyone knowing the item was missing before he finished the task. Five strikers were assigned as regular guards at stationary posts, four were on roaming patrols, and two, Farson and Adona, were actively seeking him. The strikers were permitted to check on the artifact only once in twenty minutes, so he had to time the acquisition just right.

Rezkin had to plan the entire invasion without assistance, which was part of his *Stealth Strategy and Tactics Skill*. What made it even harder, though, was that in this particular exercise, he was not permitted to kill or even engage any of the guards. It was truly meant to test whether he could get in and out without anyone ever knowing he had been there.

Rezkin slipped through the balcony door and closed and locked it after him. He would not be using the same route to exit, so he made sure to leave no trace of his presence. An unlocked outer door would be a dead giveaway. He had decided on this particular entrance because it was so obvious and open. If the inhabitants had not been aware of his intent to break in, he would never have taken this route. Since they were looking for him already, they would never assume he would choose such a vulnerable entry.

Crossing the sitting room as quickly as possible, he crouched low just in case anyone glanced through the plethora of bright and open windows. Prostrating himself at the door leading to the corridor beyond, he pressed one hand and ear to the door. He watched the light that peeked through the slit at the bottom and felt for the slightest hint of a breeze. When he was sure no one was skulking on the other side of the door, he very carefully eased it open just enough to slip through. He looked up and froze, his heart beating wildly, his attention riveted on the armored guard standing stoically at attention across from him.

Armor. He sucked in a deep breath to calm his racing heart. Full plate armor. None of their guards wore plate armor. This was just a suit. Never had there been a suit of armor decorating a corridor before. They had placed this here for the purpose of confusing or alarming him. He realized he needed to hurry. If they had placed this here, they had considered the chance he would choose this entry. There was no telling how many other things they might have changed to confound him.

Rezkin knew he only had moments before the next roaming guard wandered down this corridor. He padded quickly and quietly to the end where it met a second corridor at a T-shaped juncture. This is where it got tricky. Thirty paces to the left, the second corridor ended at another corridor. A guard would pass by just as the roaming guard entered the corridor in which he was currently standing. He would have to slide into the second corridor at exactly the moment the second guard passed out of view or the first guard would see him. The guards were using time dials to coordinate their efforts. Rezkin did not have a time dial of his own, but he had been given a copy of the guard rotations two days prior to simulate the event that he had a spy in residence. He had memorized the guard patterns and relative movements to the point that he had actually dreamt about them the previous night.

His ears perked. *Was that a scuff?* Rezkin strained to hear the eventual passing of the guard in the third corridor. *There.* He was certain he had heard a creak. Two more breaths would give the guard enough time to pass. He silently exhaled and peeked around the corner just as the brown hair disappeared. Jerking his body into motion, Rezkin thrust himself around the corner into the second corridor just as he heard a shuffle of feet in the passage he had just vacated.

He listened a moment. No running footsteps. He let out another silent breath. The guard had not seen him. Luckily he did not have to worry about avoiding *all* of the guards since they were stationed throughout the fortress. If he could keep out of sight of the second guard and the standing guard near the target, he would be okay—at least until he had the object. Then, he had to get out before they knew he had trespassed.

Reaching the end of the next juncture, he peered around the corner. The second guard was heading away from him. Rezkin did not have time to wait for the guard to vacate the corridor, so he would have to silently follow behind and hope the guard did not turn around. Twenty-five paces farther was an alcove that led to a supply room with an entrance to the disused servants' passages. Of course, the fortress had no servants, but he had been told that long ago the fortress served some other purpose. No one had seen fit to tell him what that purpose was. It did not matter. Today, he would use those passages.

Silently slipping along about fifty paces behind the guard, Rezkin suddenly felt a prickling on his skin, and the hairs on his neck stood on end. He knew someone was approaching from behind. He shot forward as fast as possible hoping he did not make any sound and slipped into the alcove. His heart pounded, and the sound of blood rushing through his ears was making it difficult for him to hear if anyone pursued him.

Rezkin took several deep breaths as he reached into the pouch at his belt with shaky fingers. He quickly pulled out a small clay jar with a cork stopper. Digging into the jar, he drew out a clump of thick grease made from pig fat. With jerky movements, he slathered the grease on the old hinges of the storage room, replaced the stopper, and held his breath as he pressed on the heavy door. It swung inward with a gentle glide, and he let out a quiet sigh. He ducked through the door and closed it just as a booted foot came into view of the alcove. There was no guard scheduled to be there at that time, so it must have been Farson or Adona. He had to move quickly. If one of the strikers chose to investigate the storage room at this moment, he was done for.

After greasing the hinges on the next door, he gave it a push, but it did not want to open. He realized he was going to have to put his weight into it, and he hoped it would not be so loud as to alert the guard. It took three tries, but finally the door burst open with a thud. Rezkin winced at the sound. Of course, he broke *Rule 12* ... again. That had to be the hardest one. Some of them were much easier, like *Rule 156—Do not die.*

Rezkin started down the corridor and came to a sudden halt. He looked behind him and suddenly realized he had made a mistake. Another *Rule* broken. *Rule 10*, again. *Do not leave evidence.* The floor of the corridor was covered in dust, and he was leaving footprints. Considering his options, he decided he had only three. First, he could try to find a way to cover the tracks, which would be difficult and time consuming. Second, he could clean the entire corridor, which would erase his tracks but could potentially alert people that someone had been here recently. That method was also time consuming, not to mention he did not have a broom. It would also be noisy. The young man decided the third option would have to do. He would continue on and hope that the disuse of the corridor would suffice for the purpose of the test. It was unlikely anyone would come through here and find his tracks.

The servants' corridor turned several times and branched off twice before Rezkin stepped through another door into a privy. One inhale set him to gagging, and he realized that this particular privy needed some attention. Rezkin absolutely did not want to be the one to do it. He cracked the door of the privy open and peered down the corridor. The target room was only ten paces to his left on the opposite wall. The masters had not set a guard directly outside the room because that would have made the test impossible. Instead, a roaming guard would pass by the room every two minutes.

Rezkin pushed the door closed as a guard came into view around the corner. It would be so much easier if he could just kill the guards, but that was not the assignment. He waited several tense moments for the guard to pass and then counted to fifteen before checking that the guard had turned down the other corridor. Closing the door behind him, Rezkin silently rushed to the target room. He pressed the latch, and of course, it was locked. This was not a problem for a lockmaster, and he had the door open quickly, but almost not quickly enough to avoid the next guard.

Once he slipped into the room, he sighed. No one would enter this room for another twelve minutes. He would have liked to have made it inside the room immediately after the last check so that he could have the full twenty minutes to exit the fortress and return to the master, but they would be looking for him to be near this room right before or after a check. Thusly, he decided to enter the room late and give up a bit of his escape time.

The masters had not told him what to expect upon entering the room. He thought he might have to search for the object, but to his relief, it was displayed on a stand atop the dressing table. It was a necklace with a fine silver chain and a green stone the color of fresh leaves in spring. Rezkin held the necklace up to the light. He appreciated the shimmer and reflective qualities, which could be useful for signaling a partner during a mission, but otherwise he saw no purpose in the item. He understood from his studies that some people decorated themselves with jewels in an attempt to appear important or desirable. He did not see how putting metal and rocks around your neck could improve your quality. Perhaps they had some hypnotic affect. He had learned in survival training that one could use shiny objects to lure fish, so he decided it was possible this necklace had the same effect on people.

The young man shook his head and stuffed the necklace into a pouch at his belt. He frowned as he glanced down at the empty stand. It was obvious something was missing. He surveyed the room and had a sudden inspiration. He would have to move quickly since he was running out of time. Reaching the bed, he selected a long tassel of braided silver thread. He pulled out a few strands and twisted them together as he crossed to the side table. Upon the table was a decorative oil lamp with multicolored glass beads dangling from the top. He tilted the lamp so that he could remove a green glass bead from the back and threaded it on to the silver strands as he moved back to the dressing table. He hung the counterfeit jewelry on the stand and stepped back toward the door. A close inspection would reveal the necklace to be a fraud, but if the guards simply peered into the room, they may not notice the necklace was gone. The ploy could give him extra time if he was too slow in his escape.

Pressing his ear to the door, he listened carefully for the guard to pass and then flew out of the room. He rushed down the hall in the opposite direction from which he had come and, after a brief inspection, darted around the corner. He had planned for time to hunt for the item, so making the replacement had not really put him behind. He was still pushing the limits, though, because he now had only eight minutes to get back to the master before someone checked on the object.

Twice more the young man had to wait for guards to turn corners, and as he entered the solar, he was preparing himself mentally for the most daring … or reckless, but certainly the most dangerous part of his plan. The windows in the solar were already open, so he approached with caution, knowing that he still had no idea where Farson and Adona were located. Hiding in a shadow, he peered out into the garden below. He saw no movement or manlike shapes. Taking a necessary risk, he stuck his head out of the window and examined the rooftops above and around him and again saw no one.

Stepping onto the windowsill, he examined his escape route. It was thirty feet to the ground, and he was not sure the fates would allow him to survive another such fall. The garden was surrounded by a ten-foot stone wall, atop which stood a five-foot high iron fence. At twelve years old, he stood at just over five feet tall, so if he hung from the windowsill, he would drop only ten feet to the iron fence. The top of the iron fence, however, was lined with foot-long metal spikes, so he would have to land with his feet on the crossbars between the spikes, and he could not crouch too far in the landing, or he would be impaled. Additionally, the crossbar was a little more than an inch wide, so it was going to be a balancing act.

Maneuvering himself into position, Rezkin dangled from the windowsill, and without hesitation, let himself fall. He immediately regretted his decision. He struck the iron fence and produced a muffled clang that reverberated along its length. *Rule 12, again.* While he managed to land his feet on the crossbar as planned, one of the spikes caught in his pant leg and sliced into his calf. *Rule 6 broken.* His arms pin wheeled as he wobbled before regaining his balance, and then he dropped to grab hold of the crossbars. Once he planted his feet on the stone wall, he released his grip and caught himself once again on the lip of the wall. With one final release, he dropped to the ground in a crouch nearly tipping forward when his calf screamed in pain.

Rezkin took in a deep breath through his nose and drew a strip of cloth from another pouch at his belt. After wrapping his calf, he scanned to see if he had left any noticeable blood behind. Satisfied that he had not broken *Rule 10* again, he crossed the garden, looked for guards, and then passed through a gate. He darted across the yard toward the stables then ducked behind a hedge only to run into a massive wall of flesh. Dark eyes peered down at him above a cruel smirk. *Striker Adona.* Rezkin's heart skipped a beat just as a meaty fist connected with his temple and all went black.

"*Method 16?*" queried Master Peider.

"A thin blade, such as a stiletto, directly to the base of the skull in an upward thrust. If done properly, it causes instantaneous, silent death with little blood. The blood and wound can be hidden if the target has long hair or bulky garments. Most effective if left in a position and situation appropriate for feigning sleep," explained Rezkin as another arrow came hurtling toward his face. His blade flashed up, snapping the arrow in two and turning it aside. The rest of his body remained still so as not to spill any of the water in the bowl balanced on his head.

They had been at this for over two hours already, and Rezkin was getting tired. Master Peider had required him to recite the list of deadly and harmful poisons and had moved on to kill methods. The strikers shot arrows at him randomly, sometimes several at a time and then with long breaks in between. Then there was the water, which could not be spilled.

At seventeen years of age, he knew better than to protest. To do so would mean breaking *Rule 17—Never complain* and *Rule 43—Fight off fatigue,* which did not mean he could force his body not to need rest. Rather, it simply meant that he should avoid becoming fatigued in the first place through rigorous training and planning ahead. If he became fatigued under dangerous circumstances, he was supposed to push through until he was safe. Of course, he also had to observe *Rule 258—Obey your masters*. Rezkin had managed not to break a single rule in three days, and he was not going to start now, especially for something so mundane.

"Good," said Master Peider, "you may stop. You have a task to perform."

Rezkin nearly sighed but just managed to stop himself before he broke *Rule 14—Do not revel in success*. That was an important one he had learned the hard way. If one became overly satisfied or relaxed after a success, it could lead to disaster. Master Peider quirked an eyebrow at him as though he had read Rezkin's mind and knew he had almost broken the *Rule*.

Rezkin sheathed his sword then poured the water into the fountain before returning the bowl to the bench for later use. He followed Master Peider to the main courtyard where Striker Farson stood over a kneeling man. The man was filthy and wearing rags covered in blood. Master Jaiardun stood off to one side examining a lengthy scroll.

He glanced up and asked, "*Method 32*?"

"No," replied Master Peider. "He performed thirty-two yesterday. He has not yet performed sixteen."

"Very well," grunted Master Jaiardun.

Master Peider turned to Rezkin and explained, "Rezkin, this man has been found guilty of multiple crimes including robbery, rape, and murder. He has been sentenced to death."

Master Jaiardun rolled his eyes and huffed, "He does not need to know all that. Just tell him to do it and let us move on. I have other things to do today." Rezkin had to agree. He was tired, and he did not need to know all of the details. They needed to tell him what to do so he could be done with this task, but Master Peider always insisted that Rezkin possess all of the information, so he listened carefully.

Master Peider scowled and turned back to Rezkin. "You will carry out his sentence using *Method 16*. Remember, one quick thrust upward." He handed the young man a thin, silver blade. Rezkin took it and walked to the criminal. He had used this type before for *Methods 14* and *27*. It was optional for several other methods, but it was not his weapon of choice. His favorite for close-range attack was a broad, slightly curved, double-edged dagger with a hook catch on the back side near the hilt that could be used to tear flesh, disembowel, or simply catch and lock an opposing blade in a fight. It was a highly versatile weapon that would have been utterly useless for this task.

Rezkin grabbed the smelly man's hair and jerked his head forward.

"No! Please!" The man lurched as he cried out.

Rezkin ignored him. He pressed the tip of the stiletto into the man's neck. "Yes, that is correct. Right there," stated Master Peider who was watching closely.

"Wait!" begged the vermin at his feet. "H-How can you be so cruel?"

Master Peider stilled Rezkin's hand. "Cruel?"

"Y-yes, you talk about killing me like it's just another job. I am a man, damn it!" The man struggled against his bonds but stilled when Rezkin pressed the blade into his flesh.

Rezkin frowned in confusion. "Master, what is *cruel*?"

Master Peider shook his head, "No, Rezkin, we are not cruel. Cruelty is when one takes pleasure in the pain and suffering of another."

"Ah, I see," Rezkin said as he felt his face relax. Then he jerked the man's head back by the hair and spoke clearly as he looked into the terrified man's eyes. "Cruelty is how you felt when you raped and murdered your victims." He shook his head. "No, I do not feel pleasure in this. I feel nothing."

The shivering man's eyes widened. "No, n—"

The sound was cut off as Rezkin thrust the blade upward into the skull. The dead criminal slumped to the ground as the young man released him. Rezkin looked at his hands and noted the lack of blood with a satisfied nod.

"Well done. You may go for now. Be at the main hall in two hours," Master Peider said over his shoulder as he and Master Jaiardun walked away.

Rezkin made his way back to his quarters as he pondered the dead man's words. Why did the man seem so offended that Rezkin might be cruel when the criminal himself had been cruel? He shook his head. Of course, Rezkin had not been cruel. *Rule 37—Separate from one's emotions.* If he had felt any pleasure, it would also have been a breach of *Rule 14*, which stated that he should not revel in his success. And, breaking any *Rule* was an automatic breach of *Rule 258* to obey his masters, so he could never break fewer than two *Rules* at any time. Master Jaiardun had told him long ago that people who failed to adhere to *Rule 5—Master your fear* would often say or do anything to preserve their lives. *Yes, that must be it.* He nodded to himself satisfied that he had solved the mystery and promptly put the whole matter behind him.

It was still early, barely midafternoon. He had been up all night tracking the strikers through the woods, so he could use a couple of hours of sleep. As he entered his quarters, he checked for hidden traps and poisons. His room consisted of a small, windowless square, no more than eight feet wide and ten feet long. It contained a bed with a straw-filled mattress and plain wooden wardrobe. There were few places to hide treachery, and that was how he liked it. When he was satisfied that his room was secure, he placed his own traps and alarms. If anyone attempted to enter his room while he slept, the intruder would get a nasty surprise, and the clanging glass and metal shards would be more than enough warning.

While Rezkin knew he was not quite a full-grown big-man, he was expected to be cognizant of his surroundings and prepared to defend himself. The masters and strikers would often set traps and ambushes for him. If he failed to avoid them or fend off his foes, the results were less than desirable. The young trainee slumped into his bed, let out a deep sigh, and sunk into blackness

2

Rezkin stood patiently before his two masters with fifteen strikers arrayed around him. His muscles were loose but ready to coil into action at the slightest provocation. He no longer thought about *Rule 24— Always be on guard* or *Rule 96—Always be prepared*. These rules required little consideration since they were ingrained in his mind. When he was a small-man, those *Rules* were necessary because he did not know any better, but now that he was nineteen and close to fully grown, he realized many of the *Rules* were superfluous. It dawned on him that this was the entire reason for the *Rules* in the first place. If he adhered to all the *Rules* and learned all the *Skills*, then he would grow into a big-man at which point the *Rules* and *Skills* would simply become a part of his being.

"Rezkin." Master Jaiardun's voice had become even more coarse and gravelly over the years. It sounded almost like he was chewing on rocks all the time. "You have learned all of the *Rules* such that you rarely break any, and since you passed your final *Skills* test last week, we have little more to teach you. You have done so well, in fact, that you completed your training at least three or four years ahead of our predications." Master Jaiardun paused at the perplexed look on Rezkin's face. "What is the source of your confusion?"

"Master, you said I know all the *Rules*, but I still do not know *Rules 1* and *2*," Rezkin replied.

"Hmm, yes, you will learn those as well. They are your final lesson, which you will learn when you leave here," replied Master Jaiardun.

"Leave, Master? Am I not to stay here?" Rezkin asked. This was the first he had heard that he would not be staying in the fortress where he had lived his entire life.

Master Jaiardun huffed, "What did you think we were doing here, Rezkin? You have learned the *Rules* and *Skills*. It is time for you to put them to use. You have a purpose, and that purpose is not here."

"I have a purpose?" he asked with surprise.

Master Peider stepped forward and spoke in his usual quiet, sure voice. "We are men, Rezkin. All men need a purpose. Our purpose, and that of these strikers, has been to train *you*. Our purpose is now at an end. You must now go into the outworld."

"So, what is my purpose?" Rezkin asked. Curiosity was one characteristic of Rezkin's natural personality the masters had actually encouraged. He was never punished for asking questions … unless they were something he was already supposed to know.

"That, Rezkin, will become clear when you learn *Rules 1* and *2*," replied Master Peider.

Rezkin knew that men played different roles in the outer society. He had been trained to understand the workings of many of them. First, there were the average commoners. He was familiar with many of their *Skills*, but he otherwise did not know much about these people. His masters had always said they held little importance to him. Then, there were the thieves. The minor thieves held about as much importance as the average commoners, but the thieves' guilds had been a major point of discussion. Rezkin certainly had the necessary skills for a thief, but to act as such would render much of his knowledge wasted.

Rezkin thought of his other *Skills* and compared them with what he knew about society. He could become a soldier or guard, but most soldiers and guards would never need the majority of his *Skills*. None of the strikers in his own fortress were masters of all of the *Skills*, which had been confusing to him since they were obviously grown men. How had they grown without knowing all the *Skills* and *Rules*?

What else was there? He could pass for a merchant. Although he had never been to a market, the masters had described them in detail and made certain he was knowledgeable in matters of currency and bartering. On a greater scale, he was qualified to broker trade deals between merchant houses, evaluate supply and demand, determine trade routes, and he understood (and could undermine) levies, tariffs, and taxes. The masters had even brought in a master of one of the great merchant houses, Lord Butrand, for a few years to teach him from firsthand knowledge. Lord Butrand had been a rather nervous man who sweated profusely and always seemed on edge. After Rezkin passed his *Merchant Skills* test, he had never seen Lord Butrand again. He briefly wondered what had happened to the man. Redirecting his thoughts to the present, he wondered how his training in poisons and battle tactics would be useful to a merchant.

A noble might need any one of his *Skills* but would probably never actually need *all* of them, and from what he understood of the nobility, one had to be born into it. Rezkin had never thought much about his birth, but he was fairly certain he was not a noble. He had been thoroughly trained in court etiquette and intrigue in case he ever had to pass as a noble, but he was certain he lacked the long-term social skills necessary to endure such a position. Furthermore, no one in the fortress had ever treated him with the carefully choreographed illusion of deference that was supposedly the thing to do among nobles.

Rezkin supposed he could become a spy, but anyone could be a spy. From what he understood, outworlders valued gold and power more than anything, and with promises and payment anyone could be bought. Average commoners made excellent spies because nobles rarely took notice of scullery maids and footmen. Of course, what a maid might think was important information might not be the same as what a merchant or lord would.

Well, Rezkin knew he would find out soon enough. He had no more time to ponder his purpose now, so he pushed it to the back of his mind. "Masters, when will I be leaving, and will any of you be coming with me?"

"There is one task you must complete before you leave, Rezkin," Master Jaiardun solemnly stated. The master's dark eyes bored into his own, and Rezkin realized for the first time that he was no longer looking up at the master. In fact, he might even have been looking slightly down.

Master Jaiardun was a tall man at a few inches over six feet. Now, his shoulders slightly stooped with age, but he was no less imposing. His hair, once dark, had thinned so that he was completely bald on top, and grey and silver strands hung long from the sides past his shoulders. He wore the same brown short robe with grey tunic and pants that Rezkin donned every day. Today, Master Jaiardun wore a sword at his hip.

Both masters were considered masters of the blade, but Jaiardun rarely carried one. In fact, several of the strikers were swordmasters. All of the strikers were required to be masters of at least one *Skill*, and several were masters of two or three. Strikers Farson and Adona were each masters of five *Skills*, which was the most of any of the strikers. Still, none of them were masters of all of the *Skills* like Rezkin.

Rezkin had been told to come to the courtyard fully armed. It was an unusual request. Of course, Rezkin always had weapons secreted about his person unless he was told otherwise, but he was expected to know how to make anything a weapon, even mundane objects such as a comb or drying cloth. For years he had been trained in the knowledge that *he* was the true weapon, and he could forgo any other accouterments, needing only his own body and mind to prevail.

Rezkin bowed slightly. "What would you have me do, Master?"

Master Jaiardun held his gaze and said, "You will kill the strikers."

There were several gasps and shouts as the strikers leapt back. Steel sang as they drew their swords. The hairs on Rezkin's neck pricked, and he spun to the side just as a dagger shot through the air where he had been standing. The quake of battle energy abruptly surged through him. He had to get to a more advantageous location. The masters had set him up in the worst position possible when they surrounded him with opponents. He had no idea why he was supposed to kill the strikers, and it did not matter. The masters had said it was so, and he must obey. It was a moot point, though, since now that the strikers knew his objective, they would do everything in their power to prevent him from accomplishing it. The strikers were now trying to kill *him*.

Rezkin launched two throwing knives ahead of him at the two strikers who blocked his escape. One of the knives was deflected when the man on the right caught it with his blade, but the other sunk deeply into the shoulder of the striker on the left. Rezkin had known these men all his life. They had been his trainers and sparring partners as long as he could remember. Of course, he knew their names, but his training told him to put all personal considerations aside. The strikers were no longer men. They were targets—targets that were trying to kill him.

Rezkin drew a dagger to catch the blade of the striker on the right and threw his weight into the man. As the striker fell, Rezkin grabbed the man's face and smashed the back of his head into the cobblestones. He did not wait to see if the man was dead. Rezkin knew he would not be getting up again.

Spinning around, he kicked out at the man who had been on the left and swiped his legs out from under him. When the man fell, Rezkin stabbed the striker in the throat. Jerking the blade out just as quickly, he leapt over the dying man and ran toward the next foe. A loud snap made him veer to the side as a crossbow bolt whipped by his ear. In a movement faster than thought, he launched a throwing knife at the source of the bolt and heard a strained yelp as reward.

Rezkin feigned a slashing attack with the dagger, and the man he was closing in on raised his blade to deflect the attack. This left him open for what Rezkin truly intended. He dropped to the ground and skidded across the stone under the man's guard to crash into him. As Rezkin tumbled forward, the striker flew over Rezkin's back. It was unfortunate for the striker that the crossbowman had recovered and chose to launch his attack at that instant. The striker took a crossbow bolt to the face, but the bowman must have gotten closer because the bolt continued through the man's head to burst free from his skull, casting blood and grey matter across the cobblestones.

Three strikers had now converged on him, but one backed off when he saw what had happened to the last man who had gotten between Rezkin and the crossbowman. Hearing a *shnick*, Rezkin knew the crossbowman had reloaded. He counted to three and then dove to the side just as the bolt was released. The two strikers nearest him were forced to dive out of the way as well.

Rezkin reached forward and grabbed one man's ankle, dragging him closer as Rezkin clambered over him. As he reached the man's torso, Rezkin gripped his shoulders and rolled over so that the man was on top of him. The striker's eyes nearly popped out of his skull as a long silvery blade impaled him through the chest. Blood poured from the wound followed by more blood sputtering up through the man's lips on his dying breath.

Tossing the man aside, Rezkin kicked up into the groin of the striker who was now standing over him. The striker cringed but seemed to use the pain to power a downward strike of his sword. Rezkin kicked out with his other foot, bashing the man's hands free from the hilt. He must have lost some of his grip on the sword with the groin impact. Rezkin clenched his abdominals and lurched up, ripping through the man's intestines and stomach with his favorite curved dagger. At that moment a throwing dagger sliced through Rezkin's right bicep and imbedded itself in the suffering striker's shoulder. The young man jerked the striker around and threw him toward his rear attacker.

Rezkin ran toward the nearest striker, who happened to be the crossbowman. The bowman realized too late that he would not be able to reload in time. Before he was able to draw his sword, Rezkin grabbed him, spun the man around, and impaled him through the kidney with a stiletto. The excruciating, searing pain from such an injury would be so intense that the striker's muscles would lock up, and the man could move no more than a statue—at least, that is what Rezkin had been taught would happen. Luckily for him it worked, and Rezkin was able to hold the man in front of him while he assessed his surroundings.

All of his opponents were now located in front or to the side, so he did not have to worry about his back for the moment. He was surprised and dumfounded when his eyes landed on the masters. The men who had worked together diligently his entire life to instruct and guide him so that he could grow to be a big-man, were engaged in a bitter duel, and it appeared to be to the death.

Nine more. In the brief seconds Rezkin had taken to assess the situation, his attackers had launched several daggers and bolts at him, all of which were ingloriously caught by his makeshift shield. Rezkin scowled. These men should be better than this. It was such a waste of long-range weaponry to launch it without a sure shot at the target. Everyone could see he was hidden. The young man scanned the faces of the strikers and realized with disbelief that these men were terrified. They had all failed *Rule 37—Separate from one's emotions.* Now, he understood. They were unable to fight like big-men because they were breaking the *Rules.* The solution was simple, then. He simply had to follow the *Rules,* and he should prevail.

With grim determination, he released his grip on his shield. The man teetered before him for a few seconds before falling to the ground. It was just enough time for Rezkin to launch a series of his own attacks against the strikers. He managed to catch one man in the throat and another in the eye with his throwing knives. A third received a knife in the chest, but the man was not yet ready to give in. Rezkin ignored him for the moment and took out the man to his left while he was still surprised. Rezkin's hands were empty when he engaged the sword-wielding striker. After a brief flurry of strikes and blows, Rezkin prevailed. He managed to get inside the man's guard to punch the striker in the throat. Rezkin reached up and jerked the man's head around snapping his neck.

From his right, the monster of a man with the knife protruding from his chest was bearing down on Rezkin. Without looking in his direction, Rezkin lurched to the side, spun around, and grabbed the knife embedded in the striker's chest. He drew it out with a *slurch* and slashed across the man's throat. Blood surged forward, some of it spraying across Rezkin's face, the rest pouring down the man's chest like a crimson waterfall.

Rezkin shoved the burly man out of the way. He drew his longsword with his right hand and a short sword with his left before he dove into the group of three strikers who were attempting to organize an attack against him. The strikers leapt back. Two of the strikers, Adona and Gant, were swordmasters. The third was renowned for developing a method of fighting with daggers that was unmatched—except by Rezkin, of course.

He had been required to practice until he could best each of these men regularly. At times, he fought multiple strikers, and he was successful most of the time, although he did at times take injuries. None of those previous fights were to the death, though. As he gained *Skills*, the men were ordered not to pull their strikes. If they *could* score an injury or even kill him, then they should. Rezkin had never tried to kill any of these men, though. It turned out to be less difficult than he thought it would be.

Once Rezkin's full *Skills* were unleashed, he seemed unstoppable. He no longer had to worry about *accidentally* killing one of his training partners. Still, it was not his normal style in training to actually land a mortal blow to any of these men. Blades sliced through the air with deafening clashes. Rezkin met each strike and slash when necessary and dodged others. One opponent sliced high, while another struck low. When one would attempt to back away to gain room for a ranged attack, Rezkin would pull him back into the fray or dance his partners around so they stayed between him and the third assailant at all times.

Like maneuvering playing pieces on the Queen's Gambit board, Rezkin finally arranged his opponents exactly where he wanted them. With encouragement from his own blows, each one struck at him in just the right way. In one quick motion he spun, lashing both blades outward, and two heads toppled to the ground followed by their bodies, which crashed into the third from either side. Before he could recover, Rezkin ran him through.

As Striker Adona fell to his knees, he looked up into Rezkin's pale blue eyes. His voice was strangled and weak, but his words were clear. "Long live the king." His lips curled into an ironic smile, and he laughed, which was cut short when a bubble of blood slithered out of his throat. "May he forever dwell in this darkness he has unleashed." Adona pitched forward and breathed no more.

Darkness? What darkness? And what has the king to do with this?

Rezkin spun around seeking and searching, high and low. Something was wrong. One was missing. He had kept track of his opponents at all times, but one had managed to disappear while he was battling the others—Striker Farson. He was nowhere to be seen. Since Farson had apparently run away, Rezkin doubted the man would come back to face him in the open now that his comrades were dead. Rezkin hoped the striker was not secreted away somewhere waiting to take a shot at him from afar.

As Rezkin surveyed the courtyard, he noted that both of the masters were also down. Master Jaiardun was obviously dead. He had been nearly cut in half from shoulder to hip. Master Peider was lying not far from him. The master struggled to breathe and suffered from a fatal gut wound. Rezkin rushed over and knelt beside him.

Master Peider grabbed his arm in a firm grip on his wrist. Rezkin continued to glance around as he kept in mind that Farson was still a threat. Peider strained to deliver one last message.

"You … are the only one … the only one now who knows of you … except …" His words were garbled and clipped as Master Peider coughed up blood. Rezkin could not understand what he said, but perhaps the old man knew that Farson had survived. Peider's grip on Rezkin tightened as if it was all he could do to cling to life.

"*Rule 2—kill with … conscience.*" The coughing and wheezing made his words come out in fits. Master Peider's head spun in a vortex of ever encroaching darkness as he tried to remember what he had been saying. *Yes, kill without conscience.* He continued, "*Rule … 1—Protect and … honor … your … k—*" His words were cut off by another round of coughing. *King! Say it!* Peider thought to himself. His world spun, and suddenly Peider was surrounded by people from long, long past. He was a young boy. Other boys were all around him. He was laughing, and they were laughing with him. Benson and Teyry were there. It had been so long. *You are all here!* He smiled, *All of my …* and somewhere far, far away in the waking world he said, "*Friends.*"

Rezkin frowned as Peider released his last breath. *Friends? What are friends?* It was not that he had never heard the word. Peider and Jaiardun had taught him about many relationships between men. There were partners, associates, allies, comrades, peers, lieges, and vassals, to name a few. A contract between a man and a woman was called *marriage*, which resulted in the titles of *Husband* and *Wife*. All of these relationships tended to be based on some written or oral contract of mutual interest. A few, such as those pertaining to slaves and indentured servants, were decidedly one-sided. Then, there were the familial relationships of blood into which one had to be born— mothers, daughters, sisters, brothers, fathers, sons, etc.

He had heard the term applied—so-and-so was a *friend* of so-and-so, but he never understood what the word meant or how one obtained such a status. He looked around again. Everyone he knew was dead, except for Farson, and Rezkin knew enough that he was certain an enemy was not a *friend*. How could he have *friends* if he and Farson were the only ones left who knew of him?

Rezkin was more confused now than ever. Perhaps he truly was not yet ready to be a full-grown big-man. He could not even understand what *Rule 1* meant, much less put it into practice. For that matter, *Rule 2* did not make sense either. *Kill with conscience.* What, for the sake of the masters, was *conscience?* It did not sound like any weapon he had been trained to use. And, why would there be a *Rule* to use only one weapon when he had been trained to master *Skills* using many weapons. *Rule 233* clearly stated that *he* was the weapon, and anything else was actually just a tool. So, maybe this *conscience* had something to do with *him*. Maybe it was a type of knowledge. *Yes, that would make sense.* But, where was he to gain this knowledge with the masters and strikers dead?

Farson might know. The masters had been secretive about *Rules 1* and *2*, but it was possible that Farson had been allowed this knowledge. The only way to get Farson to talk would be to torture him. Farson certainly knew *Rule 3—Reveal nothing.* Any amount of torture Rezkin could inflict upon him would probably be for naught, and if Farson *did* talk, it was unlikely he would be truthful. How could Rezkin ever know if what he was told was accurate? No, he could not ask Farson.

Rezkin wandered among the bodies to make sure they were all truly dead. This whole situation made no sense. Why did he have to kill the strikers? Why did the masters kill each other? In the end, he decided the only way to get answers would be to adhere to *Rule 1—Protect and honor your friends.* Now, he just had to find these *friends*. Perhaps he could ask *them* what *conscience* was. Surely, if they were the subjects of *Rule 1*, they would know.

Rezkin headed back into the fortress to get some help with disposing of the bodies. The only people left would be the cook, his two assistants, and the healer's two assistants. Peider had been the true healer in the fortress, but he kept two others who provided healing when he was busy. Upon entering the kitchen, Rezkin realized he would be getting no assistance. The cook and his two assistants were dead. Rezkin knew the healers would be dead, as well, but he went to check anyway. Once he confirmed his suspicions, he headed to the washroom. He had already concluded that he could not take the time to bury everyone since he did not know Farson's intentions.

Rezkin had never thought Farson a coward, but this disappearance was curious. He thought about it in terms he understood. Farson had failed to kill him or even engage him as far as Rezkin could remember, which would go against *Rule 258—Obey your masters* and *176—Finish your tasks.* But, had Farson been ordered to attack him?

Rezkin had been told to kill the strikers, but he did not know if they had been ordered to kill him in return. So, Farson seemed to have adhered to *Rule 245—Retreat when you cannot win*, in which case Farson had not broken any *Rules*. He had acted like a big-man by holding to the *Rules* and *Skills,* and therefore, he had prevailed by staying alive. Yes, Farson's actions made sense now. It was as it should be. If the other strikers had remembered the *Rules* they would be alive too. Well, maybe some of them ... for a while. Rezkin *had* been ordered to kill the strikers, so he would have to hunt down the missing striker.

If Farson left the fortress, which Rezkin was fairly sure he did, then the striker had gone into the outworld. Rezkin could not go to the outworld covered in blood. It would raise alarms and draw attention. He would need to clean himself and don outworld attire. He would also need money, food, and supplies. Since he had practiced these *Skills* over and again, he knew exactly where everything was located. As for where he would go, he would start by following Farson's trail. Farson would not risk an open confrontation at this point, so Rezkin knew the man would keep running.

It was a week's ride to the closest village, and Farson left on foot. The fortress had three packhorses and a battle charger, but Farson would not have had time to go to the stables and obtain one, nor would he have been able to open the gates in the courtyard and make his escape.

Rezkin was familiar with the battle charger from his training. There had been times when each of the strikers had used one in training scenarios, but after he passed the *Skills* tests, the other horses had been sold or returned whence they came. At the thought of the other strikers, he felt a sudden pang in his chest that he did not understand. He was sure he had never felt it before. Perhaps he had been injured during the battle, but he did not remember taking any hits to the chest.

After bathing, Rezkin applied a healing salve and wrapped the minor flesh wound on his bicep. He stood before the costume wardrobe trying to decide his strategy. What should he wear? Should he pose as a tradesman or merchant? Posing as a noble might be difficult since he did not know where he was going and could not set up a suitable cover story. Hmm … a landless noble maybe? The third cousin of a minor lord? Rezkin shook his head. Farson was not a noble, as far as he knew, so it would do him no good to use the pretense. A trader perhaps? Not so wealthy as to attract attention but well enough to command respect. No, then people would wonder about his lack of goods, and traders did not ride battle chargers. He certainly did not want to drag the packhorses around just to satisfy the image. Farson was a warrior. It held to reason that he might seek out other warriors for protection or assistance or simply for a crowd in which to feel comfortable.

Rezkin could easily play the part of a warrior. Well, it would not be a role, actually, since he *was* a warrior. At his age, though, according to his masters … (again he felt that tightening in his chest) … no one would believe he was an officer unless he was a noble, which brought him back to the problem of playing a noble. Rezkin could not afford to get caught up in a draft or some lords' boundary feud, so he could not be a regular soldier. Hmm … a mercenary it was, then.

Rezkin threw on a simple but well-made green tunic of fine linen and brown wool pants with a heavy leather belt. He decided to be a successful mercenary and don good quality, but not ostentatious, leather armor and heavy boots. He used a leather thong to tie his shoulder-length, slick, black hair into a queue at his nape. Lastly, he pulled a heavy, dark blue cloak about his shoulders and secured it with a decorative silver clasp embossed with a black raven.

Master Jaiardun had said that all mercenaries kept loot from their exploits, so even poor mercenaries could be found wearing accessories too rich for their station. Most of it was sold to pay for drink and women, from what his master said. It sounded like a waste of money to Rezkin. Drink and women were so fluid—there one moment and gone the next—at least from what he had heard. It did not seem like a sound investment.

After stuffing several changes of clothes into a bag, including one ensemble fit for a noble and one for night stealth, Rezkin headed down to the armory. Not having known what he would be doing earlier that day, he had selected weaponry used for practice. The weapons were kept sharp and in good repair, but they were not the best weapons in the armory. Since Rezkin doubted he would be coming back anytime soon, he took his time to select the best assortment available. At first, he wondered if he should collect his masters' swords from the yard, for surely they would be the best quality, but then his eyes landed on a pair of swords that he had never before seen in the armory.

There was a longsword and a short sword, a matching set similar to those he used most often. The scabbards were polished black with lacquer and unadorned. Pulling the longsword from its sheath, he was nearly blown over with the splendor. The blade was streaked with blue swirls that looked like melted topaz flowing in liquid silver, but it had an edge finer than he had ever seen. The hand-and-a-half hilt was wrapped in dark blue silk cord that matched his cloak, and the cross guard and pommel were both silver. The center of the pommel was slightly raised to a point like a teardrop.

Rezkin held the blade in awe. He plucked the short sword from the rack and found it to be the same as the longsword. These were Sheyalin blades! He had never thought to see one in his life. Sheyalin had been a master sword-smith who lived and died over two hundred years prior. He had produced the most exquisite blades ever created, and no one had been able to match his technique or quality in all the years since. The silver-blue swirls were unique to the Sheyalin blades. These blades were quite literally worth a king's ransom.

All the remaining Sheyalin blades in the Kingdom of Ashai were property of the crown. As such, the blades could only be bestowed by the king, in great honor, to the recipient. Each blade was catalogued and named, and their bear-ers' names were recorded much like the records of a family bloodline. It was required by law for the blades to be returned to the crown upon the bearer's death. Ownership of the blades could never be revoked within a bearer's life-time, even by the king, but neither could it be passed to the bearer's heir. It was a death sentence for any but the rightful bearer to carry a Sheyalin blade. The few remaining blades were precious, and already too many had been lost or secreted out of the kingdom.

Only a swordmaster would dare to carry such a blade, anyway, for fear of drawing unwanted attention. Anyone returning the blades to the palace after the bearer's death would receive a hefty reward. The reward was meant to encourage people to return the blades, but the unfortunate side effect was that the sword bearers were often targeted so the killers could claim the rewards for the weapons. In response to this threat, a long-dead king had issued a law stating that anyone who returned a blade and was found guilty of killing the bearer would receive the worst possible punishment. The murderer would be tortured endlessly for years without hope of death.

Rezkin was suddenly wary of carrying these blades. He was not concerned about thieves, but he did not want to attract the attention of the Royal Guard or the king. Without the proper papers of ownership, any guards who recognized the blades would be required to take him before the king. If he resisted, they would kill him—or at least *try*. Rezkin did not want to meet the king. At least, not unless it was required of him to fulfill his mysterious purpose. He could not leave the blades here, though. He would need to hide them.

Looking back at the scabbards, he noticed a small parchment tied to the one belonging to the longsword. Rezkin pulled the parchment free from the sheath. He unrolled the small note and read.

Certificate of Authority

By Honor of the Great King Bordran of Ashai, these two Sheyalin blades, Kingslayer the Longsword and Bladesunder the Short sword, are hereby bestowed upon Rezkin (black hair, pale blue eyes, six-feet three inches), and with them all the rightful authority of a Sword Bearer of Ashai.

Rezkin was astonished. These blades were meant for *him*! The certificate was signed and sealed by the late King Bordran. No date was given, and his name and description seemed to have been written by a different hand. Equally strange, no title or surname was provided.

Even commoners were referred to in legal documents as Master or Mistress so-and-so. In lieu of a surname, the town of birth, current residence or the person's occupation would be used—Master Jarin of Spokeburrow or Mistress Evana Baker, for example. Rezkin had no occupation and no idea where he was born. He assumed he was not born at the fortress since there were no women. He did not even know if the fortress had a name. Rezkin was just … Rezkin. Anyone reading these documents would have no idea how to treat him. The lack of title was legally binding, and without one, he could be a smith or the king, as far as anyone knew.

After contemplating the conundrum for a few moments, Rezkin decided he understood. The masters must have arranged for him to have these weapons, and because he would not always be filling the same role or living in the same location, they simply left it blank. The fact that he owned these weapons at all was a source of confusion for him, though. There should have been additional information after his name. It should have listed some accomplishment of his or reason the king bestowed this honor upon him. The document *should* have explained his role or rights as a sword bearer, as the bearers of these weapons were known.

Anyone carrying a Sheyalin by right had to have earned some amount of trust or recognition by the king, and therefore, should have a specified amount of authority. For example, he might be authorized to act as a magistrate or carry information sealed by the crown. Rezkin's certificate did not specify any authority. With this type of document, however, that did not automatically imply he had no authority. It could equally mean that he had *every* authority. Even the king could not argue successfully for one interpretation or the other.

Rezkin would have to keep this information to himself unless it became absolutely necessary to provide the documents, per *Rule 123—Do not seek praise or acknowledgement* and *Rule 57—Remain in the shadows when possible*. This latter *Rule* was meant both literally and figuratively, depending on the situation. Rezkin could not afford to attract undue attention to himself, lest it interfere with his purpose.

After strapping the swords to his waist, he selected several daggers, a set of throwing knives, a stiletto, a boot knife, a small crossbow and quarrels, and a recurve bow and quiver of arrows. The bow he would use mostly for hunting or shooting from horseback if he must.

Next, he went to the healer's stores where all of the remedies and poisons were kept. Rezkin could make his own, but this would save him a lot of time and effort. He was not sure when he might have the time or supplies to make more. He packed away as much as he could along with bandages, suturing materials, and other healing necessities.

Before heading to the kitchens for food supplies, Rezkin stopped in the masters' office. He disabled the traps on the safe and picked the lock. He collected all the gold, silver, and copper, which was much more than was safe to carry at one time, but he would find a place to hide much of it when he had a chance. A number of bank notes and account books were also in the safe, and he stowed those in his pack as well.

After collecting his food, Rezkin made his way to the stables where he saddled a horse and strapped down his pack. He also collected a bag of oats for the horse, although there would be plenty of grazing opportunities. His route should more or less follow the river if Farson was headed toward the town, which was the only place the man could go. The fortress was at the very edge of the settled part of the kingdom, and he did not imagine for an instant that Farson would suddenly decide to become a hermit and live in the wilds. No, Farson would head toward civilization in hopes of losing Rezkin among the masses.

Rezkin opened the other stalls so that the horses could wander at will. Eventually, they would get hungry enough to leave the gates in search of food or water. Taking the reins, he led the battle charger out of the stables toward the gate. The tangy, sour stench of blood was heavy in the air, and the horse balked, but being a trained battle charger, he pushed forward anyway. Glancing around, Rezkin realized he could not leave things the way they were. There were seven swordmasters dead in the yard along with the other strikers who were masters of various other weapons. Their swords and weapons would be masterpieces, and it would be a terrible waste to leave them to the harsh forces of nature.

Rezkin spent several moments collecting weapons and other valuables from the dead men and stored them in the armory. None of the weapons were as exquisite as his own, but he did select a few knives and a throwing ax he particularly admired for himself. He secured the armory with the double inter-locking iron doors and multiple heavy master-level locks. Since most of the lockmasters in the kingdom were dead in the yard, anyone else would require a catapult to bust through the stone walls and get into the facility. He doubted Farson would come back for anything.

Finally, around midmorning Rezkin was on his way. Farson had a two-hour head start, but Rezkin hoped he could catch up to him quickly since Farson was on foot. Just as Rezkin suspected, Farson's trail led to the river heading south toward the village of Perdony. After following Farson's tracks along the river for less than an hour, Rezkin spotted something unusual. He dismounted to examine the perturbed mud. Farson's tracks ambled all around the site indi-cating he had stopped here. That was not what disturbed, Rezkin, though. It was the drag marks leading into the water. Farson had boarded a boat. It would have been a small boat, big enough to fit only three or four people, but it was more than enough to get one man down the river quickly.

Rezkin felt disheartened now that he realized this was not going to be a simple track and hunt. He had no doubt Farson would use the boat to get as far away from Rezkin as he could as quickly as possible. Rezkin was going to have to hunt him through the cities and across the kingdom.

A tiny voice in the back of his mind begged for attention. It wondered why he had to hunt Farson at all. Until today, everyone Rezkin had been ordered to kill had been some kind of criminal, as far as he knew. Master Jaiardun did not always tell him why he had to kill someone, but Master Peider did, and they were always terrible people. Farson though, had always struck Rezkin as an honorable and loyal man who adhered to the *Rules* as much as possible. In fact, all of the strikers could fit that description. Again, he felt a slight tightening in his chest when he thought of the other strikers.

Rezkin shook his head. He could not afford to think like this. His master's last order was to kill the strikers, and that was what he was supposed to do. *Then why were the masters fighting each other? What if Master Jaiardun's order was wrong? Stop it,* he told himself. He could not afford to question the orders, now. Maybe, when he caught up with Farson, he could ask the man what was going on before he killed him.

For the next seven days, Rezkin followed the river to Perdony without incident. During his training, he had spent quite a bit of time in the wild learning survival skills and hunting and tracking. About a half day from the village, he encountered the first signs of people in the outworld. A small cottage was set upon a clear hill covered in thick grasses. Milling across the hill were fluffy, white sheep. A barking dog ran around the sheep nipping at their heels. Rezkin had never seen such a dog before. He had learned to use dogs for hunting, but this dog did not seem to be trying to kill the sheep.

At midafternoon, Rezkin got his first look at an outworlder village. It was much like what he imagined, only everything was more colorful. The homes were decorated with flowers in planters, and a few stalls where produce and other general goods were sold had been covered with bright cloth that provided shade. None of the men appeared to be armed, as far as he could tell, with the exception of a few belt knives. One man carried a hoe propped on his shoulder, but it was rusted and bent. The scruffy man was trudging toward the smithy.

Rezkin suddenly yanked on the reins and pulled his charger to an abrupt halt as a small-man ran right in front of him. The small-man was chasing a round ball. As soon as he caught up with the ball, he kicked it to another small-man. Several other small-men and a few small-women were running alongside, laughing and calling out for the small-man to kick the ball to one of them.

Rezkin frowned. These small-men and small-women should know better than to run in front of a battle charger. And, none of them were carrying weapons, nor did they take note of him or his weapons. They seemed completely oblivious to their surroundings. They were currently breaking at least half a dozen *Rules*, not the least of which were *Rules 8—Know your surroundings* and *24—Always be on guard*. He could not see how any of these small-men and -women would live to see the next year of their lives.

He watched the small-men and small-women for a few more moments, taking special care to keep the rest of his surroundings in mind. He had never seen other small-men, aside from himself in the looking glass when he was young. He had not imagined there could be so many together in one place. He could see the advantage in training them in this way, though. Learning to fight opponents of similar size would be much easier than having them fight against big-men as he had. The small-women's garments were completely unacceptable, though. He could not see how draping one's body in so much loose material could be beneficial. Even now, as the small-women ran, their legs were tangling in the fabric, and they had to keep their hands occupied with holding the material out of the way. If their hands were filled with clothing, how could they hope to carry a weapon?

Rezkin tore his attention away from the small-men and small-women as he noted that more of the villagers had stopped their chores to stare at him. Why were they giving him their attention? He was not moving or making any threatening gestures. If anything, they should be paying attention to the movements of the small-men in case they decided to launch a surprise attack during their chaotic fury. Some of the big-men stepped in front of the big-women, apparently prepared to serve as guards should Rezkin choose to attack.

He could not see any advantage in attacking these people. They did not seem threatening or hostile. If anything, they looked terrified. The hidden women must have failed to learn their *Skills* since they were apparently unable to protect themselves. Considering the fact that the grown women were wearing the same ridiculous garments as the small-women, it was understandable that they would have difficulty during battle even if they had the *Skills*.

Noting that several villagers were eyeing his horse, he decided these people might think he had hostile intentions since he was the only mounted man. Rezkin swung down from the saddle, glad for the chance to stretch his legs. As he started toward one of the produce stands, an anxious middle-aged man stepped forward from the crowd. He hesitated a moment, presumably to gauge Rezkin's reactions. Rezkin stopped and nodded to the man politely, waiting for the man to speak, as the masters had taught him.

The stranger let out a pent up breath and said, "Good afternoon, sir. I am Mayor Jorge. We haven't seen you around here before. Is there something I can do for you … sir?"

Rezkin would not have guessed this man was the mayor of the village. He had been taught that mayors were of elevated station, often pompous and vain. This man looked no different than any of the other villagers in his muted, brown homespun tunic and pants. His hair was clean but disheveled, and he looked to have worked up a sweat. Rezkin held out a hand in polite greeting by commoner standards and replied, "I am Rezkin. It is a pleasure to meet you. I seek only to resupply, and then I will be on my way." Rezkin stretched his lips into one of his practiced smiles that Master Peider insisted belonged with the pleasantries.

Rezkin knew he had performed correctly when Mayor Jorge's shoulders relaxed, and the man smiled in return as he clasped Rezkin's hand. "Well, sir, we have some fine produce just harvested this morning. Carlon, here, is the butcher," he explained and pointed to a man over his shoulder, "and he can get you some decent cuts of meat. Hay and oats are stored down by the smithy. Is there anything else you might be needing while you're here?" While the man acted pleasant enough, it was obvious from the anxious stares and fidgeting of the villagers that they would prefer for Rezkin to leave the town as soon as possible.

Rezkin shook his head while maintaining his smile. "No, that should be fine, thank you. Oh," he said as though he had just remembered some minor detail, "I am looking for someone who may have traveled through here. Has anyone not of the village come around in the past week?"

The mayor's smile slipped, and his eyes darted around the gathered crowd in query. People shook their heads, and the mayor turned back to the him. "N-No, sir. Not that we know of, aside from you, that is. Should we be looking for someone?" he asked nervously, as though he thought he might be failing a test.

"No, you need not be concerned. If you have not seen him then he has probably passed by," Rezkin replied.

Mayor Jorge eyed Rezkin's swords and asked, "Is the man dangerous? Should we be concerned?"

Rezkin pondered the question for only a moment before he replied, "No, I do not expect he would be any kind of threat to you good people. He is … a comrade of mine." That tiny voice in the back of Rezkin's mind whispered, *Of course he is not a threat to the innocent villagers. He will try to kill me*, he answered himself.

"I see," the mayor said, but he did not look convinced as his gaze fell once again on Rezkin's swords. Rezkin nodded his thanks and then headed toward the produce stalls. By this time, the gathered crowd had finally attracted the attention of the oblivious small-men, and they were gawking at the massive battle charger as Rezkin bartered for his goods. The deals seemed a little *too* good, and the young man was once again reminded that these people wanted him gone.

Upon leaving the village, Rezkin paid close attention to the bank along the river just in case Farson *had* left his boat in search of supplies. Rezkin might have been able to find someone in the village willing to sell him a boat, but then he would have to abandon the battle charger. There was also the possibility that Farson had left the river on the other side and headed west toward Caradon, rather than continuing south to Justain. In truth, Rezkin knew that he had probably already lost Farson for good.

Rezkin decided to continue south to Justain, and if he found nothing there, he would continue all the way to the capital city of Kaibain. Farson was a striker, and while the masters and strikers had never really explained who the strikers were relative to the rest of the kingdom, Rezkin always had the impression they were, or had at one time been, soldiers. With their levels of mastery, it was likely that these particular soldiers had belonged to the king, rather than some lord's estate. If he needed to look for the king's soldiers, the best place to do that would be the capital.

That thought made him pause. If the strikers *were* part of the military, did that mean there would be more strikers than the ones he knew? If so, was he supposed to kill *all* of the strikers or only the ones who had been at the fortress? And, if he was supposed to kill strikers and they *did* work for the king, did that mean he was a traitor against the crown? But, if he was a traitor against the crown, why had he been given the Sheyalin blades?

Maybe Rezkin was supposed to work for the king, and the king had found out that the strikers were traitors. Perhaps it was only the small faction at the fortress that was composed of traitors. But why had the masters killed each other? And, why would the traitors help to train their own killer if they had known he was supposed to work for the king?

Rezkin shook his head to clear his thoughts. He was getting ahead of himself. He did not even know for sure that the strikers actually worked for the king. It had only been an impression of military bearing on his part, and truth be told, he was not really familiar with any other style of bearing. He had learned how to discern much about a person by his or her appearance and behavior, but he had not had much opportunity to put those skills to use since he had grown up isolated from the outworld.

3

Rezkin decided to follow the road to Justain rather than continue along the river. The road, pitted and overgrown, was not far from the river as it was, and he thought it was unlikely Farson would make the mistake of leaving an obvious trail if he did abandon his boat. It took four long days in the saddle to reach the city. Rezkin was surprised how worn he felt considering he had done little but ride the entire way. His saddle soreness was already dissipating, but his body wanted more action. Rezkin had never gone so many days without endless hours of training. Whenever he would stop, at night, midday, and just before dawn, he would work his muscles and go through various weapon forms. Still, it did not feel like it had been enough.

Justain was supposed to be a large city, strategically located both on the River Straei and the East-West Trade Route that stretched from the western coast all the way to the Kingdom of Channería in the East. Merchants flocked to the city to sell their wares, and all kinds of unusual items could be found. At least, that is what the masters had told him. Rezkin, of course, had never been to a city, so the vision in his mind was based completely on paintings, the diagrams he had seen when learning the *Siege Skill*, and the descriptions of items, dress, and customs learned from his instructors. Absolutely nothing he had learned could have prepared him for the sight before him.

Standing upon the slight hill just north of the city, Rezkin could finally behold the might of human ingenuity. Perdony was a speck of dust compared to this fantastical monolith. On the rise in the center was what once was an old fort that dated from the days of the Conquering. The fort had been modified and built upon until it resembled what his masters had called a grand estate.

The estate was surrounded by a fifteen-foot wall that enclosed a meandering series of gardens and courtyards. On the far eastern side of the grounds, a row of hedges towered over the boundary of a sprawling garden as if to conceal what was hidden beyond. On the other side of the hedges were several practice fields, two rows of barracks, and stables. Rezkin knew from the maps that this area also contained an armory, smithy, and healers' quarters, but he could not see them from where he stood now. The original towers and battlements of the old fort no longer stood, having been destroyed during the Conquering, and all of the additions since were primarily decorative for the intent of showing off the wealth and success of the city.

Beyond the walls of the estate, the city appeared lopsided and disjointed to Rezkin's critical eye. The western end of the city was limited in its ability to expand by the river, so the buildings closest to the docks were built one upon the other with no space in between. The warehouses and merchant halls looked sturdy enough, but some of the residences leaned precariously. The layout made little sense where a few roads came to an abrupt end when, seemingly in desperation for space, people decided to simply build more structures across the road. Rezkin mentally grunted at the city planners' carelessness. The current layout impeded the efficient flow of goods and services, isolated key structures from infrastructure support, such as the fire brigade, and created niches that acted as havens for gangs and thieves' guilds.

The eastern side of the city, having no landforms limiting expansion, sprawled quite a way into the countryside with large mansions and minor estates surrounded by wooded paths and carefully sculpted gardens. The area between the eastern and western districts was where the average commoners, craftsmen, merchants, service providers, and anyone else with enough money to get out of the dockside slums lived and worked. The non-craftsmen and women who were lucky enough to find employment in a lord's household would live here as well.

In line with the northern and southern gates of the city was a wide boulevard that held the shops, stalls, taverns, and inns. While this certainly made trade and travel for visitors easier, Rezkin thought it was a strategically bad idea to provide this kind direct route for enemies to access the main estate.

But, since the city's planning was not up to him, he decided to push the concerns to the back of his mind.

At least the entire city had a decent wall around it, with the exception of the break around the docks, of course. It was thirty feet high and made of stone, but was sparsely manned with guards. The masters had told him the guards were mostly for show since the kingdom was not at war, and Rezkin could easily believe it. Rezkin thought he might be able to get an entire battalion across those walls without anyone noticing. Still, the only violence the kingdom saw was feuds between lords over borders or honor or some such, and those battles never came to the cities.

Upon reaching the northern gate, Rezkin noticed that everyone who approached did so on foot. As he dismounted behind the last person in line, he watched the proceedings ahead. A pair of guards stood on either side of the gate, which was wide open, and a second set of guards stood to one side speaking with the people who were entering and making notes on a scroll. An old man driving a cart pulled by a donkey entered the line behind him. A very young small-man, with perhaps four or five years, sat on the bench next to the older man and was chattering excitedly. Rezkin turned so that his back brushed up against his horse, and he could see the pair in his peripheral vision. He did not like having people at his back.

"Gampa," said the small-man, "what kind of horse it that?"

"Shush," replied the withered old man. "I don't rightly know. I ain't never seen one like it, myself, but I'd say from the stories, it's a warhorse of some sort."

"Squeee! Does that mean he's a hero?" asked the small-man excitedly pointing at Rezkin.

Hero? Why does he think I am a hero? I would have to have done something notable to be a hero.

"Bah, Braen, not everyone who has a warhorse be a hero. Not every warrior or soldier be a hero neither. Don't you go thinkin' men with swords is good men 'cause most of 'em ain't," replied the old man.

The small-man looked back at Rezkin and caught his eye. He must have seen something that frightened him because his smile fell, and his face went a little pale as he clung to the old man. Rezkin frowned at the small-man's reaction. He had not done anything to intimidate the small-man. He had not made any threats or hostile gestures. He just stood there. Rezkin thought back to his teachings. The small-man would have few *Skills* at his age, and that, combined with the old man's words, might make Rezkin seem intimidating. He had no desire to seem intimidating. Neither the old man nor the small-man had done anything to him, nor were they breaking any laws as far as he knew. He had not been ordered to kill either of them, so they really had no reason to fear him.

Rezkin did not think that going around intimidating people with his sheer presence would help him in his purpose. Fitting in with these outworlders was going to be more difficult than he originally thought. Based on the villagers' reactions and those of the old man and small-man, here, Rezkin was beginning to think that none of these commoners had bothered to practice their *Skills*. If they had no *Skills*, then they would be filled with fear and break many of the *Rules*. How had any of them ever grown big if they had not learned their *Skills* and *Rules*? Rezkin brought his attention back to the old man and small-man. He pulled the corners of his lips up into his practiced smile. The small-man immediately loosened his grip on the old man and gave him a tentative smile in return. The old man looked at him speculatively and then nodded in greeting.

Hmm, Rezkin thought, *the smile seems to reassure others that I intend no harm.* Smiling was not a normal facial expression for Rezkin, and simply holding it for the short time he was in the village had made his cheeks hurt. He would have to practice it more often.

When Rezkin finally made it near the front of the line, he listened carefully to what the guards were saying to those in front of him. They asked for each person's name, place of origin, and business in the city. Once the information was provided, the guards waved the people through. Rezkin frowned. What was the point of this? Anyone could give any name and say whatever town and purpose he or she chose. The guards would never know the difference. It seemed like a waste of time and parchment to him. These guards could be doing something useful like practicing their *Skills*.

Rezkin thought about giving a false name, but he was not hiding from anybody. If Farson came to find him, that would make his life much easier. Besides, if the guards noticed his Sheyalins and asked for proof of ownership, it could create greater problems for him. These guards did not appear very observant, but perhaps they were both masters of deception. If *he* were selecting guards for a city gate, he would definitely post a couple of masters of deception.

The first guard was lean with brown hair peeking from under his helm and

41

had a wiry mustache. The second was at least a hand shorter than the first and had a ruddy complexion and bright green eyes. Rezkin stopped before them and waited to be acknowledged. The first finished his scrawling on the parchment and then glanced up. His eyes widened for a moment, as though in recognition, and then he shook his head and continued.

"Name?" the guard barked.

"Rezkin," he replied. The guard glanced up at him again with a critical eye. He grunted as he took down the name.

"From?" the man asked.

"Perdony," Rezkin answered calmly.

Both guards' eyes locked on him as they took in his attire, weapons, and gear. They examined the magnificent battle charger and then looked back at him with suspicion and disbelief.

"You don't look like anyone from Perdony," the second guard accused with a hint of hostility.

Rezkin's icy-blue eyes fell on the second guard as he replied, "I am not from the village proper, but it is the closest named settlement to my home."

The first guard grunted and nodded in understanding, "You're a wilder, eh? You'd be better off saying you're a wanderer than claiming Perdony. No one here will believe you."

Inclining his head, though still staring the second guard in the eyes, Rezkin replied, "Very well, then, I am a wanderer." What was the point in asking if they were just going to tell him what they wanted to hear?

The first guard grunted again and made a note on his scroll. The second guard could no longer hold Rezkin's gaze and looked away quickly as though he had seen something interesting farther down the line.

The first guard said, "State your business."

Rezkin, satisfied that the second guard had been cowed, looked back to the first and replied, "I am passing through on my way south. I am expecting a comrade of mine, though. He may have arrived sometime in the last week. Is there a way I can find out if he has entered the city?"

"You'll have to go to the main guardhouse for that. The city's travel records are public information, but you'll have to look through them yourself," the first guard informed him.

"Thank you, sir." Rezkin nodded courteously. "You have been most helpful. May I now enter?"

"Yes, yes, go on. Don't cause any trouble," the guard said as he waved

Rezkin through. The second guard was determinedly *not* looking at Rezkin as he studiously examined the old man in the cart, which was in turn making the old man nervous. Apparently, elderly farmers with noisy small-men required more scrutiny than a warrior covered in weapons and riding a battle charger. Rezkin shook his head. What good was a guard who was too scared to confront a possible threat?

Rezkin guided his horse down the main boulevard, taking in all of the new sights, sounds, and smells, all the while developing plans for a quick escape and identifying the most defendable positions in case people decided to attack him. He had been expecting the foul smell. The masters had told him that cities, almost in their entirety, smell like a latrine, and they had been right.

The one thing Rezkin had not been prepared for in his studies was the noise. The masters had told him that cities were loud, but he never realized how loud people could be. Small-men were squealing or wailing, merchants were shouting out their wares, and men and women alike were hollering to each other or having boisterous conversations on outside patios. Carts groaned and clanked over the cobblestones, hooves clopped against the hard ground, dogs barked, and doors and windows creaked and slammed as people opened and closed them. Somewhere not far away, Rezkin could hear a blacksmith's hammer slamming down on an anvil seemingly in concert with the clanging of pots and pans from a nearby inn overlaid by a woman's voice, not quite in tune, singing a bawdy melody. Never had Rezkin thought to hear so many sounds all at once.

Rezkin had learned of all of the inns in the major cities and knew, which would be best to stay in depending on his need. Today, he decided to head to the Golden Cockerel. It was supposed to be a moderate establishment that was clean and well managed. Overall, it was simply average. It was located near the market and was one of the closest to the main guardhouse. Rezkin doubted that Farson would have given his real name upon entering the city, but he could check the records to be certain. If he constantly assumed that Farson would know better, then he would never be able to catch the striker's mistakes.

After five crossroads, Rezkin turned to the right and continued halfway to the next street. There, on his right, was the Golden Cockerel. He examined it closely, taking in all of the small details and ensuring he completely understood the layout of the building and those surrounding it in order to plan his escape routes. A small-man of about fourteen years approached him with a cheeky smile and bowed with a flourish.

"Good evening, sir! The Golden Cockerel is the nicest inn on this side of the city. People come from all over to taste our fare. Our stables are dry, and our floors are clean. You couldn't ask for a better stay." The small-man paused in his obviously practiced speech and eyed the massive battle charger. With less certainty he asked, "Shall I take your horse?"

Rezkin smiled in return, not wanting to scare the small-man off, and considered the question. It had taken him some time to learn the *Skills* necessary to handle a hardened battle charger. Even now, the horse was huffing and stomping as he eyed the small-man. The small-man's lack of confidence would get him nowhere with the disgruntled horse.

"No, I think I had best see to him, myself," Rezkin replied. The small-man's relief was evident, but he also looked as though he was not sure if he should be offended. "I mean no offense, but this horse can be aggressive, especially toward anyone but me."

The small-man smiled and nodded. "Will you be staying with us, then, sir?"

"Yes, if you have a room available," replied Rezkin.

"Oh, yes, sir. It is still early enough that they have not filled up. If you bring your horse around, I'll show you to the stables. I'm Pot, by the way," said the gangly small-man.

"Pot?" asked Rezkin. He had never heard of anyone named Pot.

"Yeah, well, it's short for Potkinally. It's just easier to say Pot. I don't know what my ma was thinking when she named me." The small-man laughed.

"Your mother named you?" Rezkin asked with interest. He had never really thought about where he got his name. He wondered if his mother had named him.

Pot yanked open the gate to the yard and closed it again after they had gone through. "Yeah, my da was off on the trade route somewheres when I was born, and my ma got tired of calling me the babe, so she went ahead and named me. My da wasn't too happy about it when he got back, but he couldn't really say nothin' since he'd been gone a lot longer than he was s'posed to."

"I see. I am Rezkin. It is a pleasure to meet you, Pot."

"That's kind of a funny name. Why'd they name you that? Is it cause of your hair?" asked Pot inquisitively.

"A man named Pot is saying *my* name is funny?" asked Rezkin, although he had no idea what his hair had to do with his name.

The small-man looked surprised for a moment and then straightened proudly as he said, "Ah, sorry, sir. I didn't mean offense. There's an open stall here. You can lock your tack over there in the cupboard. The key's in the lock. Please, don't lose it. It's a hassle to find a lockmaster to get into it and make a new one. There's only one in the city, you know … the lockmaster, I mean. Everyone wants him to take a few apprentices, but he refuses. He doesn't want anyone stealing his business, you see?"

As the small-man rattled on about various happenings, Rezkin unloaded his belongings and brushed down the horse.

"What's his name?" the small-man finally asked.

"What is whose name?" asked Rezkin.

The small-man pointed at the battle charger, "Your horse. What's his name?"

Rezkin looked back at the horse in surprise. He had never considered naming a horse. He was not sure why a horse needed a name, but the boy seemed to think it was the normal thing to do. He thought quickly. Just as he was about to speak, the horse lifted his head high and rolled his eyes around to look at Rezkin as if daring him to come up with something strong and proud.

"Pride," Rezkin said. The horse snorted and went back to chomping on the oats and alfalfa the small-man had poured into the feed bucket. He felt a slight tug at the corners of his lips, as if his mouth was about to twist into a smile all on its own. That was odd.

"That's a good name," said the small-man. "He does seem really proud."

Rezkin gathered his things together and motioned toward the inn. "We can go in, now. You had best stay away from him. He could injure you. I would suggest keeping other horses away from his stall, as well, if possible." Rezkin then remembered he was supposed to give the small-man a gratuity for his assistance. He pulled a silver from his purse and handed it to the small-man. Pot's eyes lit up, and he smiled grandly.

"Thank you, sir! I'll keep a good eye on him, but I won't bother him at all," Pot said. "I should help you with your things."

"I would prefer to carry them myself," Rezkin replied.

Pot's face fell once again, and he looked put out. Rezkin wondered what he had done to upset the small-man this time. Not knowing what else to do, he decided to give the small-man additional information in case he was confused.

"Some of my things are not safe for a small-man to handle if he has not yet learned the *Skills*," Rezkin stated.

Pot eyed the swords and dagger at Rezkin's waist and then took in the bow and arrows and crossbow that were strapped to his pack. The rest of the weapons were either hidden on Rezkin's person or inside the pack. Finally, Pot nodded in resignation and led the way toward the building. Rezkin was satisfied that at least this small-man recognized his own limitations. He was a smart man.

They entered the inn through the rear door and headed toward the front common room. Rezkin's eyes roved over every inch of the establishment, resting on each individual momentarily to assess the threat level. Pot practically skipped up to the bar where a heavyset man wearing an apron stood wiping down mugs.

"Master Nol, we have a customer. We took care of his horse already. It's amazing, Master Nol. I've never seen such a horse. His name is Pride. The horse, I mean. The man's name is Rezkin, and he wants a room." Pot said all of this in a single breath.

"Pot! Stop talking, boy, and let me greet the fellow," the barman replied. "Greetings," he paused as his gaze finally landed on Rezkin, "ah … sir. I am Nol, the owner of this fine inn. I understand you would like a room?"

Rezkin reminded himself to smile as he replied, "Yes, Master Nol. I will be staying for two nights, perhaps three. I would prefer a room on the east side of the building with a window, if one is available."

Master Nol's brow furrowed. "I have such a room available. You are young, but I don't think you wear those swords for show, do you? It's not the first time I've had such a request—always from the warrior types, soldiers and such, you know? It'll be eight silver per night for the room. That includes dinner and breakfast. It's another four silver for the horse. A bath will be two silver. We can have your clothes laundered for an added cost, depending on what you have."

"Perhaps we can call it an even twenty-five for everything, including the laundry, for two nights, and I will pay you up front," Rezkin suggested. His masters had taught him to always haggle the price, even when it was already a good deal, or people would become suspicious.

Master Nol nodded and said, "That'll do. I'll show you to your room, if you'll follow me." Good, it did not seem like this man wanted to quibble over a few silvers, which was just as well because Rezkin did not want to either.

The room was just as Rezkin had suspected although a little larger than that to which he was accustomed. It was clean and tidy with a few decorative touches. Rezkin cared little for the adornments. He was more concerned about the ease of setting traps or escaping from such a room.

The innkeeper waved him in saying, "This is the room most of your type prefer. They're always muttering about defensibility and escape routes and such. I don't know anything about that, but if you do find yourself in a pickle, please take it outside and try not to break anything."

Rezkin forced a smile once again and replied, "You have little need to worry, Master Nol. I have no intention of causing any problems. It is the training, you see." As he was speaking, he dug through his purse and counted out five silver pieces and two thumps, which were named after the sound they made when dropped on a table and were each equivalent to ten silver pieces.

"Yes, well, I hope you enjoy your stay. We will begin serving dinner in about an hour. Shall we have your bath brought up?"

"I would be much obliged," Rezkin stated through his practiced smile.

The innkeeper left, and Rezkin set down his pack. He checked every corner and nook of the room for traps and poisons. He searched through his bedding and even pulled back the mattress covers to stab at the straw underneath. Just as he finished replacing the material, he heard a soft knock at the door. He gripped his dagger with one hand and swung the door open with the other, standing off to the side so as not to present an easy target. The young woman waiting in the hall gasped at the abruptness and stood staring at him wide-eyed as a frightened doe.

"Move, Roxie! This is heavy," the small-man behind her said with a huff. Pot beamed at Rezkin from behind the young woman. "Hi, Rezkin! This is Roxiella. She's the maid and helps out in the kitchen. We've brought you your bath."

Rezkin smiled down at the young maid, and her cheeks turned pink as she quickly looked away. *What did I do wrong?* Had he made her angry? The smile seemed to work on the others. *Perhaps it only works with men.* He motioned them to enter. They placed the heavy tub in the center of the room and then headed back out saying they would bring up the water. Inside the tub was a basket containing a few bottles of oils, cakes of soap, a scrub brush, and a drying cloth.

Waiting patiently while the two scampered up and down the stairs with pails of water, Rezkin began unloading his pack. He piled his dirty clothes next to the door and pulled out his comb and shaving kit, setting them next to the tub. After several long minutes, the tub was sufficiently filled, and the maid turned to him and curtsied. Her face turned pink again as she almost whispered, "Sir, if you leave your laundry outside the door, I'll see that it's cleaned."

Rezkin bowed slightly to the young woman and gave her his best court smile as he said, "Thank you, Mistress Roxiella. I will do as you say."

Her pink cheeks turned a darker shade of red, and her lips broke into a giddy smile of her own. She nearly ran from the room. From the doorway came a sudden burst of laughter. Pot grinned back at him.

"She likes you," he said before scurrying off to his own chores.

She liked him? When men's faces turned red, it usually meant they were angry. Then again, he vaguely remembered a lesson on human behavior in which his master told him that men sometimes turned red if they were embarrassed. Was the young woman embarrassed? Why would she be embarrassed to like him? And how could she know if she liked him when they had not even interacted or tested their *Skills* against each other.

Rezkin had always felt it was much easier to gauge a man's worth after he had sparred with him. This had been his first interaction with a woman who was not a target of his blade, and if she had gone away liking him, then he must have succeeded somewhere. It seemed that women needed a better smile and a softer voice to make them feel comfortable. He would have to remember that in the future.

Rezkin stripped off his armor and gathered up the remainder of his dirty clothes into a pile before placing them outside the door. He would have to find something else to put on after his bath. People wore nicer clothes in the city, so he could get away with wearing his dark grey night stealth breeches. He was left with a dark blue silk shirt and a simple white linen tunic. Since he did not want to appear too wealthy and attract attention, he decided to wear the tunic. Few people in the city wore armor, aside from the guards and city watch, and he did not wish to stand out. He could clean and oil the leather gear tonight and forego the armor. It was a risk to expose himself so, but he had to get used to blending in with society. He had known there would be many times when it would not be considered appropriate to don battle gear and had trained for such instances. His masters had made him wear ridiculously flamboyant court dress while dueling, battling insurgents, or conducting stealth operations.

Once he was finally washed and dressed with his damp hair combed back into a queue, he strapped his swords to his hips, tucked his dagger into his belt, and secreted a number of knives about the rest of him. The room had a long mirror in one corner, a luxury he was surprised to find in this moderate inn. He surveyed himself to make sure he was fit for his role.

After a moment, he realized he no longer knew what role he was playing. When he first left the fortress, he thought he would play the role of a mercenary, but thus far no one had asked for his occupation. Perhaps he did not need to play a role. *But, if I am not playing a role, then what am I?*

Considering his reflection in the mirror, he wondered what he would think of the man in front of him if he were to see him on the street. The man in the mirror looked like someone who had money but did not care to show it. His clothes were of excellent quality but simple enough that most people would not notice. His weapons were plain and unadorned, despite being priceless masterpieces. The man's silky black hair, pale skin, and pale blue eyes might have been startling if he had not been used to seeing them all his life. His above average height, broad shoulders, and cut physique made him look older than his nineteen years, and he could see why he might appear intimidating to smaller folk.

Rezkin was suddenly surprised to realize that the man before him looked *dangerous*. He had an air of wealth, power and authority but also a confidence and self-assurance such that he did not need to flaunt it. This was the kind of man that people respected simply because his presence demanded it. *Is this who I am?* He did not think so. He realized that he must have settled into a role on instinct, not even realizing what he was doing.

Gathering himself and hiding away the absurd amount of wealth he was carrying around with him, he headed down to the common room for dinner. In his absence, the room had become quite full with patrons enjoying food and drink. It smelled like herbs, roasted meat, and fresh bread. Rezkin's stomach grumbled, and he realized that he was hungrier than he thought.

"Ah, Lord Rezkin, I am glad you could join us for dinner," Master Nol called out from a few paces away at the bar.

The young man nodded and replied, "Thank you, Master Nol, but please, just call me Rezkin."

Master Nol's smile faltered at the odd request, as if he hoped he had not offended the young man. "Of course … ah … Rezkin. Please have a seat, and I will have a meal brought out to you. Would you like an ale, perhaps?"

Rezkin had only had ale, wine, or spirits for training purposes because they were appropriate to consume in certain social situations, but he had never developed a taste for any of them. Glancing around quickly, he realized this was one of those situations when he would be expected to imbibe. "Yes, thank you. Your best, please," Rezkin replied with a tight smile. He would have preferred water.

Upon entering the room, he had immediately taken stock of the occupants and available seating. Now, he strode toward the far side where a small table sat near the hearth. It was not the most ideal seating in the room, but it would suffice. He could observe most of the common room from his seat, and no one was sitting behind him. None of the people around him seemed threatening. An older couple sat with a middle-aged couple on the other side of the hearth, and a young man and woman were seated directly in front of him. A lean man in a flashy silk robe was strumming a lute to his left.

The young couple across from him caught his eye again. He had never seen two people behaving in such a way. The man was holding the woman's hand, and Rezkin wondered if he was restraining her. The woman did not appear to want to get away, though, since she was laughing and smiling. All of their attention seemed to be focused on what the other was saying and staring into each other's eyes.

How could they possibly be watching for threats or listening to subtle changes in atmosphere if they were completely oblivious? And, after one had examined the other's eyes for a moment, why would he or she possibly need to continue to examine them? It was not as if they were going to change. But, perhaps that was why the man was holding the woman's hand. Perhaps he was staring into her eyes to gauge the truthfulness of her words, and he kept a grip on her hands to keep her from accessing a weapon. Perhaps this was an interrogation. He had never seen anyone enjoy an interrogation so much, though, and both of the young people's behaviors did seem to fit the definition of enjoyment.

Rezkin realized he was focusing his own attention in one place for too long and went back to surveying the room. After a few moments, a cloaked young woman who entered the bar while he was seating himself turned to survey the room. When her eyes landed on him they widened, and her jaw fell just enough to part her lips. Realizing he had seen her staring, her face flushed, and she quickly looked away.

Rezkin mentally kicked himself for forgetting to smile. He did not necessarily want to catch her attention, but he did not want to seem unfriendly or intimidating to people, either. He was, after all, trying to fit in. He kept an eye on the woman as he continued to observe the room for any threats. Finally, she gathered herself and sauntered in his direction.

"Excuse me," she said in a soft but cheerful voice, "I don't mean to intrude, but there are no more tables available. Might I sit with you?"

Dark brown eyes like molasses in the firelight looked at him imploringly from beneath thick black lashes. She had a heart-shaped face and pale skin with just a few freckles dusting her nose and upper cheeks. Wavy brown hair hung past her shoulders over a pale green tunic. Rezkin was surprised to see that the woman was wearing dark brown pants rather than the ridiculous layers of fabric worn by the other women he had seen. She had a long dagger tucked into her belt, but he could see no other weapons.

Mentally kicking himself again he plastered on the same courtly smile he had given the maid earlier and said, "Of course, you are welcome to sit with me. I do not believe that I will need both seats for myself."

The woman actually laughed, although he did not know why. Her eyes roved over him for a moment, presumably to assess the threat. He appreciated her observational skills and was relieved to find someone who could at least follow *some* of the *Rules* in this strange society.

"No, I don't believe you would. You seem very fit." Her eyes widened, and she laughed, "I mean, you seem to fit … um … in your seat, that is." Her face flushed again, and Rezkin remember his *Etiquette Skills*. He was supposed to stand and assist her in seating herself. He could see why most women needed assistance with even the most basic physical actions with all those layers of fabric in which to get tangled, but this woman was not wearing anything restrictive. Well, the masters had never said this particular rule of etiquette was dependent on the attire, so he stood and pulled her chair out, anyway.

The woman smiled up at him and said, "Thank you, you're such a gentleman."

Well, he supposed that was true. He *was* attempting to be gentle. He did not want to frighten anyone away, especially if the person did not pose a threat to him.

"You are welcome, my lady. My name is Rezkin," he said as he took her hand and laid a soft kiss across her fingers. The masters had taught him that when in doubt, assume a higher station. Since this woman seemed to be following more of the *Rules* than the other people he met, he decided she deserved more respect, so he would treat her as a lady until he learned otherwise.

"Oh," the young woman breathed, "I … um … I'm …" She blinked several times as her face flushed again. Was she trying to think of a name? Perhaps she did not want to give him her real name, and she was obviously becoming flustered about it. It did not really matter to him, since they were just sharing a table. He had only introduced himself because it was protocol. Still, he felt a bit disappointed, and he was not sure why. *Perhaps it is because I failed at performing to expectation?*

"It is all right, my lady. You do not have to tell me if you prefer to keep it to yourself. I understand," Rezkin bowed slightly to show he was not offended. The masters had told him that to not introduce himself properly could be considered an offense, but that did not mean *he* had to feel offended. He felt a slight tightness in his chest, again, and furrowed his brow in confusion. It had been nearly two weeks since the battle at the fort. Surely he was not still experiencing pain from an injury.

"Oh, no!" the woman gasped. Her eyes widened in alarm as she grabbed his hand. He slipped a dagger into his free hand beneath the table and nearly jerked away in defense but managed to stop himself just in time. Outworlders were prone to more nonviolent physical contact than he was used to. "I did not mean to offend you. I'm sorry. It's just that you surprised me is all."

Rezkin frowned in confusion. He *knew* it. He *had* done something wrong. "I surprised you? Did I act inappropriately in some way, my lady?"

"No, not at all. Quite the opposite, really. I mean, I'm not a lady. Just Frisha. My name, I mean, is Frisha."

Rezkin smiled, once again relieved that he had not caused her distress, although he still did not know why she had become flustered. "It is a pleasure to meet you, Mistress Frisha."

"Oh, please, don't call me Mistress. It makes me feel old, and I am only twenty, after all," she replied just as the maid, Roxiella, brought them their food. Rezkin was actually surprised to hear that the young woman was a year older than he. Roxie smiled shyly at Rezkin and completely ignored Frisha as she set the plates and goblets before them. "We are friends after all," Frisha continued.

That caught his attention. *Friends?*

"We are friends?" he asked.

"Well, of course we are! Here we are sharing a meal and having pleasant conversation," Frisha replied with a soft smile. "It's a start, right? Being friends, I mean." Her expressive face communicated both hope and fear.

Rezkin mulled over the question in his mind. *Rule 1* was to protect and honor his *friends*. Logically, he would have to start by finding these *friends*. Perhaps Frisha was a member of a select group, and somehow she managed to identify him as a part of it. Somehow, she knew she was his *friend* before he did. Had Frisha known he was here or was it just happenstance that they managed to find each other in this big city? No matter how he looked at it, this was certainly a start. He felt a tension release from his shoulders that he had not realized he held.

"Yes, it is a start," he replied.

Frisha smiled again and looked down at her food. She suddenly realized she was still gripping Rezkin's hand and pulled it away quickly in embarrassment.

Rezkin slipped the small dagger in his other hand back up his sleeve.

The pair ate in silence for several minutes. Rezkin was a little wary of eating the food since it was the first meal he had eaten prepared by someone other than himself since he left the fortress. He mentally went through the list of poisons and antidotes and reminded himself where he had stored each in the pouch at his waist and his pack upstairs. All of the other patrons were eating seemingly without concern, but he hardly considered this to be evidence that it should not concern him.

"So," said Frisha, breaking the silence, "are you staying here also or just enjoying the meal?"

"I have a room," the young man replied.

"We're staying here, as well," Frisha said as she took a bite of buttered bread.

"We?" asked Rezkin.

"Oh, yes. Tam and me. Tam is another friend. He's escorting me in my great quest," she said with a smirk. "Well, *I* am staying here, I think. They only had one room left when we arrived, so Tam went to see if any other inns had two rooms. He really doesn't want to leave me alone, which is understandable since he's supposed to be my escort."

"You cannot just share a room?" asked Rezkin. The rooms were plenty big enough to fit several people if they did not mind sleeping on the floor.

Frisha was aghast as her face turned bright red. "No! No, it isn't like that. He and I, we're just friends. He's my escort, nothing more."

Rezkin was confused. If the man was her escort, then would it not be prudent for him to stay as close as possible in case there was an attack? He thought back to his cultural lessons and recalled that, in many circles, it was inappropriate for a man and a woman to be left alone unless they were closely related or had entered into a contract of marriage. With this thought, he realized he had inadvertently offended the young woman.

"Forgive me," he bowed, "I did not mean to offend you. I thought perhaps he was your relative or husband since he is serving as your escort," Rezkin said in explanation.

The woman *did* look embarrassed now, and she would not look him in the eye. "Oh, no, you didn't offend me. I just didn't want you to think that … well … that he and I … Anyway, no, we are not related, and I am not married." At this she glanced up into his eyes through thick lashes and then looked away again. "He and I have been friends since we were born, and my father trusts him. He has sworn an Oath of Protection for me, and he will honor his word."

"So, he is in service to your father as your protector?" Rezkin said. Now, this made sense. It seemed Tam's duty was also to protect his *friends*. He now felt more confident that he had met the right people. They seemed to understand his duty better than he.

"Well, no," she said, "not normally. He is the carpenter's apprentice, actually, but he wants to be a soldier. I have to go to Kaibain and needed an escort. Tam convinced my father to let him take me so that he could enlist in the army."

Rezkin considered what he knew of craftsmen, which was not much. He did not think that craftsmen such as carpenters typically trained in the martial *Skills*. "So, this Tam, he is capable of protecting you? He has weapons and combat training?"

The young woman shrugged, "No, I don't think so. He's never said that he did, and he doesn't own a sword. We traveled to Justain from Cheswick with a merchant caravan that had guards of its own. We had planned to travel the rest of the way to Kaibain by riverboat, so we didn't think there would be any problems. Really, I guess he's just here to make sure strange men don't wander into my tent," she said as her cheeks turned pink again.

Rezkin held her in his steady gaze. He did not like to think that someone would swear to protect another person when he knew he was completely incapable of doing so. "And, if a strange man *did* wander into your tent? What would this Tam do?" he asked.

Frisha's eyes widened, "Oh, he's not completely incapable. I mean, he's gotten in fights before with some of the other boys, and he can hold his own."

She bit her lip and furrowed her brow in consternation. "I mean, I guess if he were really up against any skilled fighter or swordsman, then he probably couldn't do much, but there are always other people around to help. And, not that I would want him to, but I know he would probably die fighting if he was trying to protect me." Frisha's face was scrunched up with worry, and it was obvious the thought of this Tam dying on her behalf was upsetting to her.

"And, you? You are able to protect yourself?" he nodded toward the dagger hilt that he could see poking over the top of the table.

Frisha worried her lip again. "Well, it's better than *not* having it, but no, I've never learned any fighting skills. My father insisted I have something with which to protect myself, just in case."

With a shake of his head, Rezkin realized that this was exactly his purpose. He had managed to find his *friends*, and they needed his protection. He applied what he hoped was a disarming smile and said, "I am also going to Kaibain. It would be my honor if you would allow me to travel with you and provide additional protection."

Frisha's face lit up, and for a moment, Rezkin thought perhaps the sun had risen again. She smiled widely, and her eyes sparkled. Rezkin had been monitoring his surroundings throughout their conversation, and now he noticed that the young man who had just entered the inn was heading in their direction. As he waited for the new arrival, he took the opportunity to study him carefully. He was just under six feet tall and had short-cropped, messy brown hair and brown eyes. His muscles were toned but not bulky, and he walked with a confident, playfully arrogant gait. None of his movements had the careful coordination or grace of a trained fighter. His only visible weapon was the dagger at his waist, which looked nearly identical to the one Frisha carried.

"Frisha!" the young man called out from several steps away. Frisha jumped from her seat and grabbed the young man's arm, pulling him forward.

"Tam! Did you find any?" she asked quickly.

Tam shook his head in the negative and glanced over at Rezkin.

"Oh! Tam, this is my friend. He has agreed to travel with us to Kaibain and provide extra protection!" Frisha rattled off quickly with excitement.

"Has he, now?" Tam's gaze had not left Rezkin since he approached the table. His smile and tone were friendly enough, but there was a glimmer of warning in his eyes. Rezkin might have thought the young man had a chance at being intimidating if he did not know it was all bluster.

Rezkin rose from his chair like a viper uncoiling moments before a strike. "I have," he said, his powerful frame towering over the young travelers.

Frisha's smile fell, and she froze with wide eyes staring at the two swords and dagger strapped to the handsome young man's waist. When he had helped her to her seat earlier, she had been so completely caught up in his striking blue eyes and courtly manners that she had not even noticed them. Tam must have noticed, as well, because he suddenly gripped her arm tightly as though doing so would somehow protect her.

Tam's eyes darkened, "You make interesting friends quickly, Frisha. Can I not even leave you alone in a crowded inn for less than an hour?"

Frisha shook herself and, with feigned confidence, pulled her arm from Tam's grasp. She smiled brightly. "Don't be silly, Tam. Rezkin, this is my friend and escort, Tamarin Blackwater. Tam, this is Rezkin."

Rezkin held out his hand. Tam did not take it. He crossed his arms over his chest (a ridiculous stance since he could now no longer reach his weapon), and his eyebrows arched as he asked, "Rezkin … is that a joke?"

Rezkin frowned. "Excuse me? I assure you, I do not jest."

Frisha smacked Tam's arm. "Tamarin Blackwater! Don't be rude!"

Tam turned to Frisha exposing his left flank and placing his only weapon within Rezkin's reach. "Frisha, I am sworn to protect you, and you have just agreed to travel with a complete stranger without consulting me. We don't know anything about him!"

Frisha scoffed. "Of course we do. He's …. well, he's …"

Tam interrupted her sputtering. "Where's he from, Frisha?"

"Well, um …"

"Why is he in Justain?" Tam queried.

"Uh …"

"What does he *do*? What is his job?" he asked with frustration.

Frisha thought back over their conversation. She couldn't think of a single detail about the man she knew as Rezkin except that he was going to Kaibain, and he had only told her that after she mentioned that it was her own destination.

Her face flushed in embarrassment as she meekly peered up at Rezkin through dark lashes. She said in a hushed voice that he could obviously hear, "Shush, Tam, you will offend him."

Tam looked back at Rezkin suddenly aware that his behavior probably *had* offended this very formidable-looking man carrying multiple deadly weapons.

Far from being offended, Rezkin was relieved that at least Tam's mind was in the right place, even if he was completely devoid of martial skill. He had withdrawn his hand after Tam's slight, so this time he performed a shallow court bow and said, "It is a pleasure to meet you, Tamarin Blackwater. I am pleased that you show such concern for your charge. If you care to sit, we can get better acquainted, and perhaps I can allay some of your fears."

Tam was momentarily taken aback by the scary man's uncommonly good manners, but after glancing at Frisha's pleading face he finally relented. "Yes, very well."

Rezkin nodded and then strode to a nearby table with a few extra chairs. "Pardon me, master, mistress, might I borrow one of these chairs?" Rezkin was fairly certain his evaluation of this situation as nonthreatening was accurate, but he would be remiss to let his guard down, which would also break *Rule 24*, so he maintained complete concentration the entire time his back was turned.

Once he had returned with the chair, the three sat down at the table. He placed Tam on his left, but recognized that the young man would not understand the significance of the gesture. Since most swordsmen were right-handed, their swords were strapped to the left hip. Placing a potential opponent on the left meant that the opponent was closer to the sword and could, therefore, interfere in drawing the weapon. Of course, Rezkin was equally skilled in using both hands and carried two swords in addition to a number of other weapons, so the gesture was largely symbolic as a sort of goodwill gesture.

Roxie returned looking a little happier now that Tam separated Rezkin and Frisha. She brought a fresh round of ale and asked if Tam would like a meal.

Frisha, still embarrassed, avoided looking at the handsome warrior. When she had first seen him, she was completely mesmerized. She had never seen anyone so striking and powerful looking as Rezkin, and he had just a hint of danger about him that made her blood heat. She wanted to run her fingers through his silky black hair and thought for certain that she could drown happily in those crystal blue eyes.

Now, after seeing Tam's reaction and realizing Rezkin was *very* well armed, she acknowledged that he had much more than a *hint* of danger. She worried that she had made a huge mistake, but he seemed so kind and courteous. No man had ever treated her like a true lady, and it was not only toward her. He had been polite and gentlemanly toward everyone so far. He had even brushed off Tam's rudeness with cool grace.

"So, Master Rezkin ..." Tam started.

Rezkin held up a hand, "Please, just Rezkin."

Tam nodded, "I'm curious about your mannerisms. Are you a noble?"

Rezkin smiled but gave neither affirmation nor denial, "Just Rezkin."

Tam shifted in his chair and glanced back at Frisha who was doing an admirable job of examining every nuance of the table in front of her. "Rezkin, then. Frisha says you wish to travel with us. Why?"

Nodding, Rezkin replied, "Yes, first of all, we have the same destination, and are traveling at the same time. Secondly, there is safety in numbers. Third, and most importantly, is because it is *Rule 1*."

Tam was nodding in acquiescence up until the last one. He furrowed his brow. "What is rule one?"

Rezkin cocked his head to the side and studied Tam anew. "I thought you knew. *Rule 1—Protect and honor your friends.*"

Tam's face relaxed. "Well, of course, one should always protect and honor one's friends. But, what makes you think we are friends? I mean, no offense, but we've just met."

Rezkin forced himself to smile again and nodded toward the oddly silent young woman. "Frisha told me so." Frisha glanced up and smiled weakly.

Tam looked at Frisha, who lowered her eyes back to the table. "You accept that just because she said so?"

Rezkin cocked his head, again as he studied Frisha. Her cheeks flushed under his scrutiny, but she still said nothing. "I have no reason to doubt her. She is a surprisingly open and cheerful individual. Nothing she has said or done leads me to believe her to be duplicitous or conniving. Thus far, her most grievous flaws seem to be that she is entirely too trusting and is unable to protect herself. Both are problems for which I can be of assistance."

The carpenter's apprentice was staring at Rezkin with his mouth hanging open. "You seem to have a firm grasp of Frisha's character, but you still know little about us. By the looks of you, you could easily make it to Kaibain on your own much faster and without the extra effort. Why would you take on the burden of two more people, even if we are *friends*?" His last words were heavy with skepticism.

"You are Tamarin Blackwater, a carpenter's apprentice who wishes to be a soldier. You have little to no knowledge of combat and no martial or weapons training. You carry only a dagger at the waist, although you probably do not know how to use it. You swore an Oath of Protection for Mistress Frisha with full knowledge that you will probably end up dead if you ever have to uphold it against an enemy. I do not believe you thought that one through. I am quite certain Mistress Frisha did not." Tam gave Frisha a sidelong look.

Rezkin continued, "I think you will find that she is less willing to allow you to risk your life on her behalf than either of you thought. I believe you were both excited about traveling to Kaibain for your own reasons, and about traveling *together*, and you both accepted the oath without considering the consequences. I would be remiss in my duties under *Rule 1* if I allowed you to continue on your journey under such conditions without my protection."

Both his new acquaintances stared at him wide-eyed. It seemed neither could think of anything to say.

Tam recovered first with heated indignation. "Say, now! How dare you claim I am incapable of providing protection! I am every bit as capable as the next man." Tam's face was hot with anger and embarrassment, but all three of them knew it was all bravado.

Rezkin leveled his stare at Tam. "Very well, let us go into the yard. We will spar with daggers, since that is all you have. If you can defeat me, I will leave you both alone, and you will never see me again. If I win, we will travel together to Kaibain."

Tam immediately snapped his mouth shut as his face lost some of its color. Staring into cold blue eyes, he nearly started shaking. Swallowing hard, he cleared his throat and said, "No, I think you'd best leave us alone. Just because you're the stronger fighter doesn't mean you can bully your way into our lives."

Frisha gasped, "Tam!"

"No, Frisha, I won't let him threaten us," replied Tam.

Rezkin was taken aback. He had not expected Tam to interpret his words in such a way. He felt the tightening in his chest, again as he reached into his purse to retrieve a few coins. He placed them on the table and stood. Bowing low toward the two companions he said, "I beg your pardon. I truly meant no offense, nor did I intend to threaten or frighten either of you. I apologize if I have dishonored you. I only meant to offer my protection to my newfound *friends*. Master Tam, if you were unable to find suitable lodging for your stay, I am willing to vacate my room so that you can stay near to Mistress Frisha. Do not worry yourselves that I will cause you problems, for you will not see me again."

Rezkin turned and, staying cognizant of his surroundings, made his way back to his room. The bathing tub had been removed, but nothing else seemed to have been disturbed. He roved over the space, once again looking for traps and poisons, and after finding none, he began to pack the few items he had left out. He would need to pick up his laundry later. *Rule 1* was going to be harder than he thought. Protecting and honoring seemed like easy things to do, except when they conflicted with each other. In trying to protect his new *friends,* he had dishonored them.

Rezkin was sorely disappointed in himself. He had only found his *friends* little more than an hour ago, and he was already failing miserably. Now, in order to protect them, he would have to follow them at a distance, staying unseen. That is what he promised them, after all … that they would not *see* him. How would he secretly protect them on a riverboat? Surely they would know he was aboard. Riverboats were not so large, after all. He would have to disguise himself. Neither of them had seen his horse, so *Pride* would not give him away. But, was it dishonoring them to mislead and pursue them in secret?

Communicating with outworlders was so much more difficult than the masters had said. He tried using the lines he had been forced to memorize and mimicked the gestures and pleasantries, but it was tiring and confusing at times. When he thought he had performed a gesture just perfectly, people would stare at him with confusing expressions.

The men had seemed easy enough, until Tam, anyway. It was the women who were so confusing. He knew it was an unavoidable tactical error that he had met Frisha first. By the time he met Tam, the young man's protective instincts had kicked in, and he was less willing to see reason. If he had somehow met Tam first, he might have found a way to convince him of his sincerity.

Swinging his pack over his shoulder he stepped quickly to the door and pulled it open to reveal Tam standing on the other side with his arm poised to knock. Rezkin released the hilt he had grasped in surprise. He could not believe he had made such a mistake as to not check the door before opening it. His mind was muddled with his missteps, and he knew he had to get it together before he failed completely.

He stepped aside to allow Tam to enter and said, "I have gathered my things and will inform the innkeeper of the change upon my departure." He stepped toward the door to make his way out but was stopped by Tam's hand on his shoulder. He resisted his instincts to grab the hand and twist until the young man submitted. He calmly turned toward the young man instead.

"Wait, please," Tam requested.

Rezkin simply stared at him, willing the young man to get to the point.

"I-I'm sorry," Tam said while wringing his hands awkwardly. "What I said was uncalled for. I didn't mean to offend you, nor did I mean to be ungrateful." He let out a heavy breath, and his shoulders slumped. "You're right. I don't know what I'm doing. I'm in over my head. When I made the oath, I thought it was no big deal. I would just stand up for Frisha when she needed me."

The uncertain young man scratched at his scruffy jaw as he thought and continued, "On the way here from Cheswick, I spoke to several of the caravan guards. Some of the things they described ... attacks along the roads and even on the river, well, they scared me. I know I'm supposed to protect Frisha, and I want to, but if it comes down to it, I know I *can't*. So, if you could possibly forgive me, I would like to accept your offer to accompany us to Kaibain."

Tam looked up into Rezkin's eyes, almost pleading. The vulnerability that Tam was trying so hard to hide earlier was obvious to anyone who looked. Rezkin inclined his head and said, "It was my fault. I failed to communicate my purpose properly. You had every right to be defensive and protective of your companion."

"No, I should not have spoken to you in such a disrespectful manner," Tam replied. "Your behavior has been above reproach. I just didn't like having to face the truth, and I was ashamed to do so in front of Frisha. It's better this way, though. It was wrong to let her think she was safer than she really was."

Rezkin smiled to soften his words. "I do not think Mistress Frisha is a fool."

Tam barked a self-deprecating laugh. "No, no she's not."

"When were you planning to leave," Rezkin said.

"We were going to see if we could purchase passage on a river boat tomorrow. From what I hear it takes a day or two to reserve a space, so maybe the day after?"

Nodding, he said, "That will be fine. I can go with you in the morning to make arrangements, but I will need the afternoon to complete a task."

"After breakfast, then?" asked Tam.

"Yes, good night, Master Tamarin," he replied. He shifted his pack and turned to leave.

"Wait!" Tam nearly shouted.

Rezkin turned back to him with sad blue eyes. At least, Tam thought they looked sad. "I don't have any intention of kicking you out of your room, although I do truly appreciate the gesture. The innkeeper said I could sleep in the common room once all the patrons have gone, so it worked out after all. It turns out it's a lot cheaper that way, too."

Rezkin could tell that Tam wanted to escape the room but was blocked by Rezkin's own large frame. He frowned at the thought. The common room would not be secure by any means. Anyone could sneak up on the unsuspecting young man. It was one of the most vulnerable places he could think of, only one step above sleeping out in the street. Tamarin would presumably be protected from people outside the inn, but anyone from within could sneak down upon him. In addition, Rezkin imaged that all of those patrons below had no intentions of leaving until very late.

Rezkin cocked his head to the side in the way he did when he was considering something deeply. "This room is plenty large enough for two people. I see no reason why we cannot share. At least in here you only have one person to worry about. In the common room you have the entire inn's worth."

"You would do that? You would share with me?" Tam asked.

Rezkin lifted a brow and replied flatly, "I was willing to give you the whole room. From my perspective, this is a better deal."

Tam finally smiled, "So it is. I wonder if the innkeeper has an extra cot. I'll go check and let Frisha know what's happening. You take the bed since it was your room in the first place. And … thanks."

Rezkin stepped back into the room, shaking his head. Were all commoners this difficult? If he was supposed to protect and honor commoners, why had his masters insisted they were too inconsequential to study? Perhaps this was one of those difficult lessons he was supposed to learn on his own. He set his pack on the bed and dug around for some items with which to make an alarm.

A short while later, Tam returned with Pot, each lugging one end of a mattress. Roxie followed close behind carrying bed linens. The young woman gazed at Rezkin, smiling shyly and fluttering her lashes. Since she was not paying attention to her surroundings, Roxie found herself crashing into Pot who was bent over settling the mattress. Bed linens flew into the air. Tam stared at the scene mouth agape, while Rezkin simply tilted his head and said, "Perhaps you both need to review *Rules 8, 24, 84,* and *96.*"

Pot snickered and, untangling himself from Roxie, asked, "What are those?"

Rezkin recited, "*Know your surroundings, always be on guard, do not let your attention linger,* and *always be prepared.*" Tam could no longer contain himself and burst out laughing. It was clear now, why these two ended up in such a predicament. They had not even bothered to *learn* the *Rules*, much less follow them. How *had* these people grown?

"Have you managed to break *Rule 6* as well?" Rezkin continued.

Pot grinned as Roxie hid her face in her hands. "Which would be …?" the small-man asked.

"Do not get injured," Rezkin stated in a quiet, steady voice while looking at Roxie who was peeking between her fingers. These two should know at least *that Rule*.

Roxie slowly lowered her hands to reveal her bright red face. She smiled shyly again and replied, "No, I am well. Thank you for your concern, my lord. You're so kind."

Rezkin cocked his head to the side. He was not particularly concerned. The woman was not bleeding all over Tam's bed, and she was certainly well enough to be removed from the room when he wanted to turn in for the night. Any discomfort she might be feeling would not hinder him in any way nor affect his purpose.

Pot regained his feet and reached down to help Roxie recover hers. Rezkin nearly intervened but held himself back since he was neither of these people's master. *No wonder these people never learn the* Rules, he thought. If someone assisted them every time they failed, how would they ever learn anything? If anything, both of them should be punished for their failure. Roxie had managed to cause the incident, but Pot failed to recognize the danger and avoid it. He was certain that a week of pain and suffering and a trip to the infirmary would impress upon them the importance of the *Rules*. Then again, with these two, a week might not be enough. None of them seemed to expect any kind of punishment to be administered, Tam included, so he held his own.

Roxie went to retrieve the linens from Tam, who had already collected them. The young woman turned to make the bed, but Tam refused saying he could do it himself. Tam was simply trying to save the girl from further embarrassment, but Rezkin only saw it as encouraging disobedience. Tam was not doing the young woman any favors. Then again, maybe Tam no longer trusted the hapless woman to perform her job. Rezkin nodded. This made sense. If she could not be trusted to follow the *Rules*, what other anarchy might she instigate?

As soon as the duo left the room, Tam burst out laughing again, "On the Maker, Rez, you're funny! I couldn't think of anything good to say fast enough, but you're quick. That was hilarious."

Rez?

Rezkin was utterly confused. He did not know what humor had to do with anything, but he let it go since Tam was obviously in a much better mood than he was earlier. Rezkin retrieved the supplies he had been tinkering with before all of the commotion and began setting the alarm around his bed.

Tam watched Rezkin quizzically. "What are you doing?" he asked.

"Setting an alarm," Rezkin replied.

"Why?" Tam inquired.

"To wake me in case someone attempts to attack," he stated.

"Why would you need that? Who is going to attack you in here? Wait … am *I* the someone?" Tam asked with round eyes.

Rezkin glanced at him with a look of contrition. "There are two ways to enter this room—the door and the window. There are any number of people outside who could intend harm, and perhaps a few inside. It is prudent to keep an alarm set where one is sleeping."

"You worry about that kind of stuff? This has happened to you before?" Tam asked. He was no longer sure he wanted to share a room with someone who attracted that kind of attention.

Rezkin shook his head. "Where I grew up, the men were always sneaking in to test me. They did all kinds of things to teach me the *Skills*, particularly when I was most vulnerable."

Tam visibly relaxed and nodded as he said, "Yeah, I understand that. My brothers and I were always pulling pranks on each other. One time, my oldest brother, Caineth, convinced Perrin to help him sew Connin's bed linens closed around him like a sack while he was sleeping. Then, they put a mouse and a snake inside with him. I'm pretty sure you could hear the screams from the other end of town. Ma and Pa were *really* angry. Plus, ma made Cainith and Perrin pay for the ruined bed linens."

Rezkin considered this attack, *prank*, as Tam had called it. He could not see any practical use for such a technique except perhaps to teach the victim to be vigilant even in his sleep. Still, if it was effective, then who was he to judge?

Tam put his linens on the bed while he spoke, and Rezkin finished adjusting his alarm. He looked back at Tam who was removing his boots and asked, "Have you any more need to leave the room tonight?"

"No, I'm good. I'm exhausted after traveling and running from inn to inn looking for a room," Tam replied. "I really do appreciate you offering to share. It put Frisha's mind at ease, too."

"How do you expect to protect her in her room from in here?" he asked curiously.

Tam was surprised, "Well, I don't expect anyone to attack her in her room. It's not like people are after us. Besides, her door will be barred."

Rezkin shook his head and then grabbed a small pouch from his pack. "I will be back in a moment. Bar the door."

"What? Why, if you're going to be right back?" asked Tam.

"Just … bar the door … please." His masters had said that many people found it difficult to deny a request if one said "please," especially if the request would have no direct impact on them.

Tam got up and barred the door after Rezkin left. Rez was a strange man, calm and commanding at all times, but he had a wicked sense of humor. Tam began to wonder if Rez was really as dangerous as he seemed. He was so polite and courteous, and he spoke like a learned man. Tam did not doubt that he had had some weapons training. Anyone carrying around two swords would have to or be an idiot otherwise. It was just asking to be challenged to a duel, especially if he was a commoner, since many lords were arrogant enough to want to put a commoner in his place.

Rezkin stalked down the hall to what he knew to be Frisha's door. He rapped softly against the hard wood. A moment later, the door swung open to reveal Frisha wrapped in a silky, cream robe. Wavy brown hair framed her face, and her cheeks were slightly flushed from rushing to cover herself.

"Rezkin!" she said in surprise. Her mind worked quickly wondering where this late night bedchamber encounter might go. Would this smooth, devastatingly handsome man push his way into her room, take her in his arms, and ravish her? The young woman's cheeks turned deeper red as she realized her thoughts stemmed less from concern than from fantasy.

"Mistress Frisha," Rezkin said as he bowed slightly. "I apologize, again, for the incident in the common room earlier. I meant no offense."

"Oh, no, you have nothing to apologize for. Tam was out of line, but I understand you two worked out your differences," she replied.

"Just so." He nodded in affirmation. "You should probably inquire as to whom is at your door prior to opening it, though."

Frisha looked a bit chagrined as she replied, "Yes, you're right. I didn't think."

Rezkin inclined his head and said, "Very well. If you have no more need to leave your room tonight, then I will place a trap on your door. Anyone who attempts to open it will be rendered unconscious. Does this suit you?"

Frisha's eyes widened. "Do you really think that's necessary?"

"I do, unless you would prefer to sleep in my room where I can better protect you," he stated with surety.

Frisha's cheeks reddened, again. She knew he was not propositioning her —at least, she thought not. He was simply stating a fact, but her mind had other ideas. "Uh … no … um, I do not think that would be wise."

Rezkin cocked his head at her reaction. He thought it would be the wisest move. A single room would be much more defensible. Plus, he would not have to concern himself about what was happening two doors away while he slept. Frisha said that she and Tam were both his *friends,* so he needed to protect them both. He could not do that as effectively if either of them were separated from him.

This society seemed to value the rules of propriety over safety, though, and he could not change that. The thought made him pause. Was *propriety* another set of *Rules?* Were they *Rules* he was supposed to abide by now that he was in the outworld? His masters had taught him about propriety but always discussed it as though it was a role to play when appropriate rather than something by which to live.

"Very well," he said. "Do not open your door until morning unless you absolutely must. If you do, then stand behind it as it opens."

"O-Okay, then. Thank you. Um … goodnight, Rezkin," she said with a small smile.

After setting the trap on Frisha's door, Rezkin stalked back to his room. He listened carefully with his ear pressed to the door then drew Bladesunder from its sheath and slipped it between the door and frame. With one quick flick, the bar blocking his entry flipped into the air. He shoved the door open quickly and caught the beam before it could strike the ground.

Tam jerked up from his bed wide-eyed with shock, mouth agape. He looked at Rezkin, then at the bar in Rezkin's hand, then at the open door, and then back to Rezkin. "I had no idea …" was all he could say. "Frisha?"

"I spoke to her and set a trap on her door. Do not try to open her door until I have disabled the trap in the morning," Rezkin said as he closed his own door and put the beam back in place. He drew one of his daggers and jammed it into the wood just above the bar. He turned to see Tam looking at him questioningly. "If someone slips the bar up, the dagger will fall and clatter on the floor, warning us that someone is entering."

"Oh …" Tam replied, still watching Rez move about the room.

Rezkin strode to the window and balanced a long-handled dagger on the sill, the tip just barely settled into the groove between the frame and sill. "If someone raises the window, the dagger will fall."

Rezkin removed his sword belt and propped Kingslayer against his bed. He tucked his belt dagger under his pillow and removed his boots. He did not want to disarm completely, nor did he wish to reveal his hidden weapons to Tam, who was still a stranger if also a *friend*. While he was supposed to protect and honor his *friends*, there did not seem to be anything in the *Rules* stating that his *friends* could not harm *him*. Even if there were, none of these outworlders regularly adhered to the *Rules*, anyway, so he would not trust them to do so in this.

Tam and Rezkin settled into their beds, and Rezkin snuffed the lantern.

4

When the sun finally breached the horizon and the twilight stars faded from view, Rezkin decided he had waited long enough. He strode over to the well and hauled up a fresh bucket of cool water. He pulled off his sweat-soaked tunic and poured the refreshing liquid over his hot head. The water streamed down his sculpted torso dampening his pants and pooling around his bare feet. He shook his long, black tresses, squeezing out the dripping water. The wet strands hung loosely about his head, and several fell forward around his face. Grabbing his tunic, he strode to the back entrance of the inn. Roxie was standing on the stoop mesmerized.

Rezkin nodded as he passed by and said, "Good morning, Mistress Roxiella."

With wide-eyed fascination, she reached out and gripped the tunic in his hand. "I can wash that for you, my lord."

Rezkin glanced at her in confusion. *My lord?* It was not the first time someone had referred to him as such. He released his grip on the tunic and thanked her. When he returned to his room, Tam was having a serious conversation with Frisha. Both stopped speaking immediately and stared at him as if he had just turned into a pink dragon. Rezkin froze.

"What?" he asked hesitantly.

"Your muscles ... *shirt*! I mean, ah, where's your shirt?" asked Frisha stumbling over her words and blushing furiously. Even as he spoke, she could not take her eyes from the perfect lines of his exquisite form. She almost checked to see if she had drool running down her chin.

"Mistress Roxiella has it," he said as he closed and barred the door and then sifted through the pile of laundered clothes that had been left on his bed.

"What!?" Frisha shouted. Her face went from pale disbelief to flushed fury in less than a breath. Rezkin furrowed his brow in confusion. He did not know why Frisha would suddenly become angry. Did she think Roxiella robbed him?

"It got dirty … while I was training. She said she would wash it."

Frisha was overcome with relief and utter embarrassment. Tam eyed the young woman speculatively. She averted her eyes and refused to meet her friend's gaze.

Tam turned back to Rez and said, "The sun has barely risen, and you've already been training? How long were you out there?"

Rezkin shrugged, "A couple of hours."

"Do you do that often?" asked Frisha.

"I am accustomed to practicing my physical *Skills* most of the day and night when I am not studying other subjects or sleeping. Since I have been traveling, I have been lax in my physical training.

"Ah, that explains it," said Tam.

"Explains what?" Rezkin asked perplexed.

Tam waved his hand around in Rez's general direction, "All of … *that*."

Rezkin looked down at himself and could not see to what Tam was referring. The healers had done an admirable job over the years, so he bore few scars, and those he had were barely visible. There was nothing particularly notable about his appearance. Rezkin shrugged off his confusion and changed the subject.

"If you wish to be a soldier, Master Tamarin, it would behoove you to become accustomed to rising and training early. You will be required to do so during your basic training and will probably continue doing so during the majority of your career," Rezkin stated as he began dressing.

Frisha, knowing she absolutely should leave to allow Rezkin to dress in private, found that she could not, for her life, force her feet to move.

"Ugh," Tam moaned, "are you serious? I hate getting up early."

Rezkin noted that Frisha was still silently staring at him, so he asked, "Mistress Frisha, are you alright?" He glanced down at himself and said, "Is something amiss?"

She jerked her eyes away from his chest that was now fully covered with a dark green tunic and met his eyes. "Ah, yes. I'm great. Um ..." Her eyes widened as he began untying his black pants.

Tam nudged her with his elbow, "Frisha, perhaps you could go order us all some breakfast. We'll meet you in the common room shortly."

Frisha's eyes darted to Tam as though she had just realized he was present. Her cheeks flushed at realizing she had been caught ogling the amazingly fit warrior. She hurried from the room slamming the door just as Rezkin dropped his pants.

Tam snickered, "You really had her going. I don't think I've ever seen her so flustered. She was being rude by not allowing you your privacy."

Rezkin thought the statement ironic since Tam had not offered him any privacy either, but perhaps this was part of the *propriety* with which he was supposed to be concerned. He cocked his head in thought.

"She should not have been locked in this room alone with two men in the first place," Rezkin said. He meant it as a question, but it sounded more like a statement.

"True, and as her protector, I guess I should have insisted she leave earlier, but I really didn't think about it. I grew up with three brothers, not sisters. You're much better at these things than I am, so maybe you can remind me when I forget," Tam stated.

Rezkin lifted a brow, "If *I* am to be responsible for our group's propriety, then I am afraid we will have little of it. I am more concerned with safety. There will be many situations while traveling when it would be best for us all to stay together rather than take the risk of separating simply for appearances. We will have to be satisfied with knowing that we will treat each other with honor."

Tam studied Rez closely as the young man tied on his boots. "You really mean that, don't you?"

"What?" asked Rezkin.

"That you will treat her with honor," Tam stated.

Rezkin was surprised that Tam would have to ask. "Of course. I will treat you both with honor. It is *Rule 1*."

"Protect and honor your friends?" asked Tam, remembering Rez's words from the night before. Rezkin nodded. Tam said, "You truly follow a code ... like a Knight of the Realm."

A code? He pondered the question. Well, a code *is* a set of rules. Rezkin stretched his lips into the smile everyone seemed to like and said, "Always."

Both young men descended the stairs in a hurry. Tam was simply hungry and eager to get on with the day. Rezkin was concerned about Frisha being left alone in the common room. Just as the men sat down at the table with her, Roxie arrived carrying a tray with three platters of breakfast. It was a modest but tasty meal of eggs, sausage, and fresh-baked rolls. Roxie filled Rezkin's tea three times before he finally had to politely inform her that he had consumed enough.

Rezkin noticed that Frisha was oddly quiet, and he was concerned she might be ill or uncomfortable with his presence. "Mistress Frisha, is everything well? You *do* still desire my assistance in your travels?"

"Oh, yes!" she said as she met his gaze. Her thoughts seemed to scatter as soon as she looked into those crystal blue eyes. He looked at her with genuine concern. "I do desire you …" Tam sputtered and coughed as he choked on his food, which refocused Frisha's attention. Realizing what she had just said, she practically shouted, "to come with us!"

Tam was still trying to clear his airway as she scowled at the young man and kicked his shin under the table. Rezkin's attention was on Tam, now, and she hoped he did not take notice of her embarrassing blunder.

Frisha continued anyway. "Please, Rezkin, just call me Frisha. I told you we're friends. There is no need for formalities."

Tam, finally getting himself under control, said, "Yeah, Rez, you can just call me Tam. *Master Tamarin* sounds so *old*. Besides, we're friends, too."

"Thank you, Frisha, Tam." Rezkin stood and said, "I think it is time to head to the docks. You know, it is not necessary for us all to go. I could make the arrangements while the two of you stay here. The district near the docks is filled with seedy people who are more than willing to cause trouble for unsuspecting travelers."

"Well then, we're not really unsuspecting, now, are we?" Tam asked. "Besides, I don't want to stay here all day. I want to see the docks, and you know we can't leave Frisha here alone. We'll all go together," he said as Frisha nodded her approval.

Rezkin inwardly sighed. These two outworlders were determined to make his job difficult. "Very well. Let us depart."

The three travelers toured a winding circuit of roads and footpaths between buildings on their way through the western part of the city.

"Um, Rez, are you sure this is the way?" Tam asked. "A lot of people use the docks, and I don't think most travelers would go this way. I must admit I'm completely turned around. I have no idea where I am," he said, and Frisha nodded in agreement.

Rezkin simply shrugged. "The main thoroughfare to the docks is rife with thieves. Neither of you would make it to the docks and back with your purses. In addition, those people will know you are looking for passage on a ship, which means you will have to return via the same route with the rest of your belongings when you depart. It would be an ideal situation in which to arrange an ambush. And while this route seems confusing because we have made so many turns, it is actually the most direct route with the exception of a few detours I took to avoid thieves who were lying in wait."

Frisha's eyes widened. "What? There were thieves waiting for us?"

Rezkin nodded. "We have already avoided three such traps plus a few pick-pockets I deterred."

"How did you scare off the pickpockets? I didn't see you do anything," asked Tam.

"I looked at them," Rez stated. "Once you identify a pickpocket, he or she would have to be an idiot to try, so they look for another target."

"How did you know there were thieves waiting for us?" asked Frisha.

"It is a learned *Skill*. You see up ahead and to the right"—he tilted his chin —"next to that stand with potatoes? There are several men who look like they are performing their duties but are actually waiting for people to approach. When we get there, they will start a confrontation with each other. Many people would be uncomfortable with such a situation and choose to cut between the buildings over there to get to the next street. There will be several thugs in that alley ready to rob anyone who takes that route."

Tam looked at Rezkin skeptically. "How can you tell any of that?"

"The man on the left, there, in the brown tunic, has moved those same four barrels twice already into the same places. The one in the grey shirt is wringing the wash and hanging it on the line, only he keeps taking the same rags from the line and throwing them back into the wash. That potato merchant is probably not a part of the scheme, but he does not want to interfere either. He is avoiding looking at any of the men and keeps nervously glancing in our direction. There is a small-man playing lookout on that roof over there above the alley. He is signaling how many people are approaching and the level of risk," Rezkin explained quietly to the two as they approached the intersection in question.

Tam's eyes took in all of the sights Rez pointed out and realized he *could* tell something was amiss. Frisha whimpered and grabbed onto Rezkin's arm.

He forced his muscles to relax a little as he suppressed his natural instinct to protect himself from the physical contact.

"Are you sure we should be going this way?" she queried barely loud enough to be heard.

"Tam, could you please take charge of Frisha? I would like to keep my arms unhindered in case I need to draw my weapons," Rezkin requested. To Frisha he said, "Do not worry. If we choose not to take the alley, there is little chance anything will happen to us. The locals are familiar with the ploy and would know how to avoid it. We will do so by simply continuing straight ahead."

Tam took Frisha's arm and held her as they walked. He tensed when they reached the intersection and found himself gripping the handle of his dagger. He tried to appear calm and avoid looking at any of the thugs but knew he probably failed miserably.

Rezkin, on the other hand, blatantly glared at each of the members letting them know he was aware of their plot and would not be fooled. The man who had been moving the barrels nodded in acknowledgement, and the three travelers passed beyond the intersection without incident.

Frisha and Tam each let out a breath as the tension eased, and they smiled at each other in relief. Tam laughed and said, "You must be from the city to know so much about these things. I'm really glad you're with us, now. If these things are normal, we would be in major trouble."

Rezkin shook his head, "This is my first time to the city. I arrived yesterday, not long before you. But, do not be overly concerned. This is not necessarily normal except in this part of the city. Most of Justain is relatively safe, although you will find pickpockets everywhere—even in the affluent areas, fewer there since stealing from a noble is a hanging offense."

"I hear they cut off the hand of someone caught stealing from merchants and other commoners," said Tam.

Rez nodded, "Yes, but the thieves must be caught. If you have not noticed, there are few guards or city watch patrolling this area."

"So, you were trained as a soldier, then?" Tam asked.

Rezkin considered this. He had been trained as many things. A soldier was just one of them. "Yes," he said, "and more."

"When I'm a soldier, I'll be able to figure these things out, too?" asked Tam.

"Perhaps," said Rezkin. "There are many kinds of soldiers, and it is dependent on whether you master your *Skills*. If you joined the city guard, I imagine you would learn most of it if you worked hard."

Tam shook his head. "I don't want to be a city guard. I want to travel the kingdom. Maybe even go to other kingdoms. Do you think I could do that?"

"If you join the regular army, you may be posted at a fort somewhere in the kingdom, but it is unlikely you will transfer more than a few times in your career—depending on how long you serve, of course. We are not at war, so most positions are fairly stagnant, and few are ever sent beyond the borders. You would have to join the navy to get beyond the kingdom, and even they rarely make calls to foreign ports. Your best bet would be to become an escort for an ambassador, but you would have to be an exceptional soldier, at least a sergeant with notable accomplishments, to acquire such a position."

Tam's face fell. "But, that's not at all what it sounds like in the stories. They always talk about great battles and travels and unusual places around the world."

Rezkin shook his head. "Stories are rarely accurate. Those that are not pure fiction are embellished. Sometimes bards will take the adventures and accomplishments of many different soldiers and tell it as though it all happened to only one. The truth is, soldiering is not about excitement and glory. If you were to become an officer, you might have a better chance at experiencing the things you want. They have more freedom and ability to request transfers. Since you are not a noble and are therefore unable to purchase a commission, it is highly unlikely you will ever become an officer. Few commoners ever receive the honor, despite their hard work and dedication."

"Is that why you haven't joined the army?" asked Tam.

Rezkin glanced at Tam and shrugged. "My *Skills* would be wasted in the army." Rezkin nearly came to a halt when the next thought crossed his mind. "Although, if you join, I may have to as well."

"Why?" Frisha exclaimed in surprise. Tam was startled as well.

Rezkin shook his head once again looking at Tam as though the man was completely dense. "*Rule 1*, Tam, remember?"

"Wait, you would join the army just to protect *me*?" asked Tam. He was flabbergasted. He had just met this man, and the idea seemed a bit ... obsessive.

Rezkin rubbed his jaw thoughtfully. "I cannot think of how I could protect you in the army and Frisha at the same time, though."

Frisha laughed, "Rez, you cannot expect to protect *both* of us *all* of the time. We have our own lives, you know. And, we're not your responsibility, anyway. Besides, you only said you would lend your aid on our journey to Kaibain. After that, we will each go our own way." Frisha's tone was soft and understanding, and the last was said with a note of sadness.

Rezkin felt the tightening in his chest again. They would each go their own way? But, if that happened, then what would be his purpose?

"I must protect and honor my friends," he said with distressed confusion.

"Don't get me wrong, Rez. It's an honorable code to live by, but I think it should be more of a general sense of protection," Frisha said as she waved her hands around. "It doesn't mean you have to stay with us at all times. Besides, what happens when you find *new* friends?"

New friends? He had not thought there would be more of them. How many of these *friends* did he have? And, how would he know who they were? Did they have some way of identifying each other? Was he supposed to approach them or wait for them to come to him? Master Peider had not lived long enough for him to find out. Frisha seemed to know a lot about it, though, so maybe he could just leave it to her to identify his *friends* for him.

By now the trio had reached the docks and set about finding the riverboat offices. They wandered down to one of the piers and asked a dockworker for directions. Once they knew where to go, the three found the office easily. It was a short, wooden building with faded, peeling blue paint. The sign above the door was a small mural of a riverboat. The door and windows stood open, but upon entering, they had to wait a moment for their eyes to adjust to the dimness. An old man with a worn face sat smoking a pipe as he shuffled through a stack of parchments on his desk.

"What ken I do fer ye?" the old man asked.

Tam took the lead. "Greetings, sir. We seek passage to Kaibain. Is there space available on any of the riverboats leaving in the next day or two?" he asked.

"This be all of ye?" asked the man out of the side of his mouth.

"Yes," said Tam.

"And my horse," Rezkin interjected.

Frisha glanced at Rezkin. "You have a horse?" she asked.

"How else would I have gotten to the city?" he remarked.

"Um ... walked?" she said, her own voice filled with doubt.

Rezkin shook his head. "That would have been a long walk." Frisha was about to ask where he was from when the old man interrupted.

"I ain't got all day, now. Things ta do," he griped. "There be a boat leavin' in two days. Ye ken bring yer 'orse, but ye'll be carin' fer and cleanin' up after 'im yerself. There be a stall onboard fer 'im. It'll be two and a 'alf golds fer the each o' ya an' fer the 'orse."

Frisha gasped. "So much?"

Tam stepped forward. "The two of us,"—he motioned to Rezkin—"can share a room."

The old curmudgeon laughed, "Oh, ye be sharin' a berth a'right. Ain't got room fer each o' ye ta be 'avin yer own. I've got one berth 'vailable ye be sharin'.

Anger suffused Frisha, and she huffed with disdain. "You expect me to share a room with two men!?"

The old man donned a crooked smile. "Ain't no more wenches aboard. Might 'ave ta put more folk with ye if they be comin' 'round, too."

Rezkin had heard enough. He took two large strides forward to stand glaring down at the old man over his desk. The man bit his pipe as his smile fell. "We will pay one gold for each of us and forty silver for the horse. You will also receive another twenty-five silver to ensure that no one else shares our berth.

The old sailor scowled and said, "Now see 'ere, young man. I be givin' ye a deal."

Rezkin leaned over the desk, his hands on the hilts of his swords and said, "*That* is the deal. We both know you are trying to swindle these good people. I suggest you take my offer."

The old man narrowed his eyes and replied, "Done this afore 'ave ye? One and a 'alf gold fer each o' ye, one fer the 'orse, and one ta make sure no one else stays wi' ye."

The sailor watched as the towering young man's eyes darkened, and he straightened with a cool demeanor that was somehow all the more frightening. The old man's Adam's apple bobbed up and down as he gulped.

"Twenty-five silver for each of us and the horse, and you generously make sure no one shares our berth. In return, I will *not* take your slight personally, I will *not* hurt you for your attempt at robbery, and I will *not* inform the River Transport Licensing Board of your attempts to rob decent travelers blind. I will *not* have to report how your *business practices* hinder travel between capital cities, effectively stymieing trade, nor how you would make it nearly impossible for a new recruit to afford passage so that he can report to the army recruitment board." He said this last with a nod toward Tam. "How much would your business suffer if an embargo was placed on your transportation of soldiers and supplies?"

The old sailor, who was now sweating, jumped to his feet and stuttered anxiously, "M-my apologies, M-me Lord. I didn't mean nothin' pers'nal, ye see. Jus' business, it be. Ah, ye offer a fair rate, ye do. I be 'appy ta book yer passage as ye ask. Please, don' be talkin' ta no 'fficials, now. Ain't no need fer that."

Rezkin narrowed his eyes at the old man who shifted nervously and would not meet his stare. "I might feel inclined to keep an eye on the riverboat trade. It might interest me to ask around every so often to see if people are satisfied with their service."

The old man nodded vigorously, "Aye, I understand, Me Lord. Ye won't get no complaints from me passengers. I promise ye that."

"I take promises very seriously," Rezkin stated.

The anxious sailor cringed. "That be well, Me Lord."

Rezkin nodded and then motioned Tam to step forward. Tam stood gaping after the exchange. He was not sure if he should be impressed or appalled. Watching Rezkin throw his weight around like that unnerved him, and he could not quite make himself support Rezkin's methods. He felt guilty for his part in bullying the man into compliance.

Tam gave the old man their information and obtained a writ of passage. They handed over half the money in deposit and left the timeworn, musty office. All three took a whiff of fresh air tinged with the smell of fish.

After walking for a while in silence, Rezkin noticed his two companions had not said one word to him since they left the office, although they had muttered quietly to each other a bit. He would not have been concerned except that this was uncharacteristic behavior based on what he knew of them. When they reached a location of relative safety, he came to a halt and turned to them. Neither companion would meet his eye.

"What is it?" Rezkin asked.

They both shifted uncomfortably and glanced at each other. Frisha started to speak and then shut her mouth nodding toward Tam.

"Rez, it's just … we don't really feel right about what happened back there," Tam finally managed to say.

Rez nodded in understanding, "You have to be prepared for this kind of thing. People will take advantage of you when they can." At least, that is what the masters had taught him.

The young man and woman glanced at each other again, and Tam rubbed the back of his neck. "Is that what you did? Took advantage of him?" he asked.

Rezkin was surprised to say the least. "*Me?*"

"You were pretty forceful back there, and I can't help but think we're robbing the guy," Tam said as Frisha nodded in agreement.

Rezkin frowned as he felt that tightness in his chest, again. He was becoming concerned that there might be something wrong with his heart or lungs. He put the thought aside to address his *friends'* issues.

"The man was blatantly attempting to rob us. Riverboat passage to Kaibain from here should *never* cost more than a gold and a half and that is for a private berth—the kind a highborn lord or lady would require. My first offer was quite generous considering the service he was offering. Still, he tried to take advantage, hoping I did not know any better and was just haggling the price. My final offer of payment is only slightly less than what the king pays for transportation of his soldiers. That old man is not put out in the least."

His words were firm, but his voice was calm and unemotional. "Do you realize that he could actually be thrown in the dungeon for what he was attempting? At the very least, he would lose his boats and licenses and receive a hefty fine. I am still mulling over the decision *not* to report him, and you are taking offense to *my* actions?"

Rezkin shook his head, turned, and continued the walk back to the inn. Not wanting to think about the whole incident, he tried to keep his full attention on his surroundings to avoid any troubles with the locals. It seemed these two were still unwilling to trust him. He could not really blame them since they had not known him for even a day, but it seemed they were constantly expecting the worst from him. Just because he *could* force people to submit to his will did not mean he *would*. He was not a cruel man, the kind who took pleasure in intimidating or hurting others.

In truth, he was most disappointed with himself since he was trying his best to adhere to *Rule 1*, and he seemed to be constantly failing. He knew he had the *Skills* to protect his *friends*, but honoring them at the same time seemed beyond his abilities. They were not happy with anything he did. He mentally sighed. The whole situation was completely new. As they became accustomed to each other and engaged in more tasks, they would gain an understanding of each other's *Skills* and dependability in following the *Rules*.

It had been so with the strikers at the fortress. The team had been extremely effective after training together for so many years. Rezkin unconsciously rubbed at the tightness in his chest once again. Given time, he could have that with his new *friends*.

Rezkin escorted his two companions back to the inn in silence and then left without a word for the main guardhouse. He bought a meat pie and an apple from a couple of vendors on the way. For a few hours he pored over the previous week's entry records. As he expected, he found nothing concerning Farson, but he did make a mental note of the comings and goings of a number of nobles, successful merchants, and other people of interest.

Leaving the guardhouse, he headed back to the market district. He would need to restock a few supplies for the voyage. He had never been on a boat, but he had learned about them in his studies. His masters had said that some people became ill with the motion of the vessel, and a few of the strikers had confirmed this. Apparently, even well-trained warriors could be vulnerable to the effects of water. He stopped in an herbalist's shop and purchased a small amount of fennel, horehound, and ginger, in compliance with *Rule 96—Always be prepared*.

Rezkin stopped at a few more stalls and was heading back toward the inn when a rainbow of fluttering fabric caught his eye. Rezkin suddenly remembered his master telling him that the wind could be quite cool on a boat. He thought that he should probably make sure Frisha had something to keep her warm. It would not do for her to catch a chill.

Rezkin selected a soft green scarf that reminded him of the pale green tunic she had been wearing last night when they met. He was halfway back to the inn when he realized he had not gotten a scarf for Tam. He was perplexed as to why he had not even thought of it when he purchased the scarf for Frisha. He decided Tam would just have to figure something out for himself.

For the rest of the way back, Rezkin decided to practice some of his *City Stalking Skills*. Taking care not to be seen, he scaled walls, jumped gates, and slinked across rooftops. He took a wide, circuitous route so that he could get a little more practice. While he had trained extensively all over the fort and the few outbuildings, this was the first time he actually had the opportunity to put these *Skills* to use in a city. He found that it felt liberating to traverse the city over the rooftops. Not used to the almost overwhelming confines of over-crowded streets and towering structures, he felt some of the tension in his shoulders slip away with the openness of the rooftops.

He slipped over a balcony railing and down into a darkening alley before stepping back into the main thoroughfare. The few vendors along this street were pressing their wares with more intensity as the final light of day faded. Several crates were stacked at the mouth of an alley to his right. He heard the hiss of frantic whispers when someone warned, "No, Ash. Not that one!" It was unfortunate for these people that they had not learned that whispers often carry further than quietly spoken words.

Rezkin's hand swept out and snatched the grubby little fingers that were reaching for his purse. Without slowing his stride, he hauled the young small-man into the alley and rounded on his comrades, effectively blocking their escape. The eldest small-man looked to have perhaps eleven years, although the undernourished body may have hidden a few. The second was a couple of years younger, while the third, still squirming in Rezkin's grip, was closer to six.

"Your *Skills* are practiced but still poor," Rezkin said.

"Let me go!" the youngest yelled as he attempted to kick Rezkin in the shin.

"Silence," Rezkin ordered with an icy glare. The young one whimpered but ceased his struggling as tears began streaming down his cheeks.

Rezkin turned his attention to the older two and said, "Even if the young one had not been caught on his own, the two of you gave him away. You are not *Skilled* enough to be placed in a supervisory role."

"You don't know nothing!" shouted the eldest. "If it'd been me, you wouldn't never know'd I was there." His dirty brown hair barely hid soft hazel eyes too filled with anger.

"What is your name?" Rezkin asked.

"Um … they call me Broken," the eldest said. "He's Cracker," he said motioning the middle small-man. He nodded to the youngest and said, "That's Ash."

Rezkin's cold, blue gaze bored into the young man called Broken as he said, "I knew you were here before I came within five paces of the alley. Your presence was hidden for that long only because of the noise emanating from that cantaloupe merchant. You warned the young one not to target me. Why?"

The oldest boy's mouth formed an *o* in surprise. "Ah, you've got too many sharpees … ah, I mean blades," he said motioning to the swords at Rezkin's waist. "An' you look like you can use 'em. You're a *Red*," Broken said, referring to the color-coded system the thieves used to rate the threat of a target.

Rezkin turned his attention to the one called Ash who was trembling in fear with wide eyes bouncing back and forth between the frightening warrior and his overconfident cohort. "Why did you choose to target me?"

The little one's mouth flapped silently a few times before he finally managed to speak. "I like the ones with swords. They're always lookin' for big trouble. They think they're too good to rob. They ain't lookin' for little *me*."

Shaking his head, Rezkin said, "Your assessment of the arrogance of many sword-bearing targets may have merit, but it is not always the case, and the consequences of failure are too great. Commoners who carry blades openly usually know how to use them, and anyone who does not is most likely a noble. What is the sentence for robbing a noble?"

The young one's lip quivered again, and he squeaked, "You dangle."

Rezkin nodded once. "That is correct. You hang by the noose." He looked back at eldest boy and said, "You were incorrect in your assessment, as well. I am most certainly *not* a Red. *I* am a *Black*." Broken's eyes widened in fear, and Cracker whimpered as he lost his bladder, evidenced by the darkening of his trousers. "Do you know what that means?"

Broken gulped and nodded. "Yeah. It means we're dead."

Rezkin cocked his head thoughtfully and said, "I believe this to be a short-coming in your training. Ultimately, I hold your guildmaster responsible. Perhaps we shall see what he has to say."

"The guildmaster? But, we don't know the guildmaster," Cracker stammered in a panic.

"Shut up, Cracker!" Broken said with a hard elbow to the ribs. "Ah, ya see, we don't know the guildmaster, but we can take you to Thorn."

"This Thorn is your leader?" Rezkin asked.

"Yeah, he's the denleader," Broken replied.

"Very well. Let us go to Thorn," Rezkin nodded. He released the youngest, who stumbled forward to be caught by his comrades. Rezkin stepped aside, and the three immediately took off running as though a fire had been lit under their feet. They darted down the alley and made several sharp turns before ducking through a hole where a couple of slats had broken away from a wooden fence. No doubt the three were hoping to lose their pursuer, but Rezkin kept up with them easily. Without slowing, he leapt up, bounded off a stone wall, and slipped over the rickety fence. Eventually, the boys stopped beneath a window boarded over with broken shutters. The window belonged to a small, unused storehouse near the docks. The paint was chipped, and the roof bowed dangerously in the middle, but the door was solid and locked.

The boys glanced at each other and then at the formidable mark that managed to keep up with them in their mad dash. Broken rapped a series of coded taps on the door. A heavy bolt slid to the side with a *thunk*. Before the sentry could get it open a crack, Rezkin had shoved his way past. The heavy door knocked the unseen man to the side, but two more waited in his place, each with drawn weapons. One bulky behemoth held a rusted butcher's cleaver while a shorter man with a wicked scar running from the corner of his mouth to his ear wielded a gnarled wooden club.

The behemoth attempted an overhand chop at Rezkin's head, which he easily knocked aside. Rezkin punched the man in the throat and then elbowed him in the temple. Scarface took a swing at Rezkin's exposed back, but he ducked as the club passed over his crouching form. He reached out and grabbed the club, yanking it from the man's grasp. Rezkin then proceeded to bash the man in the skull, knocking him unconscious. Behemoth stumbled to his feet just before Rezkin swept them back out from under him, landing the man on his back. He slammed the club down on the man's chest leaving him gasping for breath.

The third man who had fallen over a pile of broken crates and other refuse, came at Rezkin with a long serrated dagger and a disgruntled roar. Rezkin blocked with the club, lodging the blade in the length of wood. He thrust an open palm at the man's chest as he simultaneously swept his foot behind the man's legs. The man fell backward, and Rezkin stomped on his windpipe. The entire incident took only a matter of seconds, and the small-men were too stunned to consider running away. Rezkin pointed at them and, with a thumb over his shoulder, indicated they should lead the way.

The boys scrambled forward with haste. They lead Rezkin through a doorway into a larger, dimly lit space. Rezkin stood in the entrance and peered at the dirty, startled faces that stared back at him, an intruder in their midst. The debris-scattered chamber held about twenty small-men and small-women of varying ages, all of whom were wearing old, faded, and torn clothing, much of which was probably held together by dirt rather than thread.

Two grown men and a grown woman shoved past a couple of older small-men. One of the grown men was dressed in clean, nondescript clothing of good quality, and he was obviously well-fed if his round paunch was any indicator. The woman had long, raven hair, large green-brown eyes, sharp features and thin, pink lips that turned up in a perpetual smirk. Her tunic and leggings were tight over a toned figure and cut low at the bosom to expose quite a bit of skin. Based on Rezkin's study of the arts, she was not what most people would consider beautiful, but some might call her stunning.

The best dressed of the three was a rough man in his late twenties. He wore a good quality black coat that was worn but clean and was held closed with a gold chain. His hair was dirty and greasy but neatly tied back, and his face was partially hidden by a few days' worth of growth. The gleam in his eyes was angry and defiant as he stalked toward the intruder.

When the man passed Rezkin's reluctant guides, he thrust a hand out and socked Broken with a full-fisted punch to the nose. Broken stumbled back, and the man reached over and grabbed Cracker by his tunic, backhanding him across his face. The man's ring caught the small-man's cheek and left a vicious gash. He kicked Ash in the stomach, and the young one doubled over as he lost the vestiges of whatever food he had been able to scrounge all over the floor.

The denleader's two henchmen glared at Rezkin as their leader abused the young small-men. Rezkin watched as the small-men cowered under the older man's assault. He cocked his head curiously as he considered the dynamic. The denleader, who the small-men had called Thorn, was obviously punishing the younger small-men, but there did not seem to be any expectation that they would defend themselves. What good was a man trained to cower in fear? If the small-men at least attempted to defend themselves, they would learn from their mistakes and improve in their *Skills*.

Turning from his underlings, the denleader stalked forward. He carried a slightly warped and pitted sword and waved it around as he talked. He pointed the blade at Rezkin, who was still a good ten paces away, and barked, "Who are you? What do you think you're doin' comin' in my den uninvited?"

Rezkin had seen enough of this man's idiocy. He did not deserve to be in any position of authority. "Your recruits are dirty, underfed, and untrained, and I doubt you have the *Skills* to train them properly. I am taking it upon myself to remove you from your undeserved position."

"Who sent you? Did Draphus put you up to this?" the denleader asked hesitantly.

Rezkin did not know this Draphus, but he guessed the man was a higher-ranking member of the guild. He shook his head slightly and said, "I do not work for the thieves' guild."

"Is that so? What makes you think you can get rid of me so easy?" The man sneered.

"A strong leader needs strong warriors. Only a weak leader would intentionally keep his men weak," Rezkin replied.

Thorn raised the sword as if he was holding a club. He positioned his arms awkwardly out to the side like a chicken attempting to appear larger and more intimidating. "Are you callin' me weak?"

"Obviously," Rezkin drawled.

The denleader took a step forward and then paused. He waved his henchmen forward and said, "Kill him."

The hefty male henchman glanced uncertainly back and forth between his boss and the intruder. The woman's smirk deepened with a lift of one brow. Her eyes roamed up and down his body with interest.

"Uh, I don't know, boss. He seems pretty sure of himself. Maybe we should send for Draphus," the man argued.

The denleader rounded on the larger man shouting, "Are you questioning me?"

"No, boss. I'm just sayin'. He don't look scared, does he? Maybe he knows somethin' we don't," the big man said.

Thorn scowled with fury. Without taking his eyes off the bigger man, he snapped at the woman. "Attica, take care of him!"

Attica grinned and said, "I don't think I can. It sounded like he was challenging you for your position. Can't interfere in a challenge, can I?"

"What?" the denleader exclaimed. "It weren't no challenge." The man's poor attempt at sounding educated dissolved as his back alley burr bled through. "He ain't even in the guild!"

The bigger man, who was not as ignorant as he looked, caught on to the woman's machinations and nodded as he said, "It sounded like a challenge to me." Several of the older, small-men who had gathered at a reasonable distance started muttering to each other about the challenge and nodding along.

Thorn gripped his sword so tightly his knuckles turned white. "Fine!" he barked as he shrugged out of his coat and threw it at the rotund henchman. He raised his sword and set his feet in a poor parody of a dueling stance.

Rezkin shook his head. "Your left foot is too far forward, and your right shoulder is too high. You need to loosen your grip and shift it higher on the hilt, not that it will make much of a difference with such a poor blade. Also, you are staring at my hands when you should be looking at my shoulders or even my feet at this distance."

"Just draw your sword and get on with it. I ain't got all day," Thorn snapped.

Rezkin shrugged and said, "I did not realize you were in such a hurry to die. I will not kill you with my sword, though. I will kill you with yours." Almost as soon as he finished speaking, he had covered the distance between them. Thorn's swing was too slow and weak, and Rezkin caught the man's sword hand easily. Rezkin slammed his other hand into the crook of the denleader's elbow and twisted the man's arm. The sword came free, and Rezkin plucked it out of the air as it started to fall. With a flick of his wrist, he thrust the dull blade into the man's gut at such an angle that the tip of the short blade protruded from between Thorn's shoulder blades. With wide eyes and a blood tainted wheeze, the denleader slumped to the ground lifeless.

Rezkin stepped back and checked his clothing as he kept an eye on the former denleader's henchmen. Both were staring at the corpse in surprise. The entire *challenge* was over in the blink of any eye. Satisfied that he had managed to avoid getting blood on his apparel, he asked, "Do we have a problem?"

"No, not at all, boss," the bigger man quickly replied.

"Problems with you seem to be poor for the health," remarked the woman. "We're good, but … ah … Draphus might have somethin' to say about it, and for that matter, so might the guildmaster."

"Who is Draphus?" Rezkin asked.

The woman's smirk returned as she replied, "The Diamond Claws' second."

Rezkin tapped his hilt as he thought. "Then Borgout is dead?" That had been the name of the second for the Diamond Claw Thieves' Guild last he had heard.

The woman chuckled. "You're a bit behind. Martius is the Guildmaster, now. Greld and Borgout were killed three weeks ago."

Rezkin grunted. "I have been busy. Which one of you is second of this den?" he asked.

The big man gulped nervously and said, "That'd be me. The name's Cratz."

"What is your weapon of choice, Cratz?" Rezkin asked.

Cratz cracked his knuckled and crossed his arms over his protruding gut. "I use my fists," the meaty man replied. Several of the small-men cringed as though remembering those fists.

Rezkin turned his attention to the woman. "And, you, Attica?"

"I tend to avoid confrontation all together. My marks either don't see me or they're too busy seeing enough of me not to notice when I lift something," she said suggestively.

Rezkin frowned. Posing the question to both of them, he said, "How do you expect to overcome your enemies without any *Skills*?"

Attica lost her smirk for the briefest moment as she replied, "We're street thieves. It's not like we're going up against the Guard. If anyone serious tries to do business in our territory, Martius sends in the enforcers."

Rezkin was familiar with the thieves' guild enforcers. They were usually ex-mercenaries, soldiers, or house guards who were lucky enough to be dishonorably discharged rather than killed, and lifelong criminals and smugglers with some martial training.

"Martius'll be sendin' his enforcers after you, I reckon'," Cratz commented.

"It would be a waste of personnel," Rezkin replied. "Very well. Take me to Martius."

"You *want* to go to the guildmaster? He'll gut you!" the big man exclaimed.

Rezkin did not like the idea of entering into a confrontation with a master of a thieves' guild without reconnaissance. This, however, was the most opportune time since he had been blocking the doorway and no one could have gotten out to warn the guildmaster that someone was causing trouble in his territory. When he first became involved, Rezkin had simply wanted to correct a problem with the small-men's training. After seeing the miserable state of affairs at the den, though, he found himself in deeper than expected. Logically, he knew, it was probably good that the thieves' guild was not more successful, but his years of training and ingrained desire for efficiency drove him to seek more for the young small-men in whom he had seen untapped potential.

"A'right, I'll take you to him," said Cratz.

"No," Rezkin replied. "I need you to stay here and make sure no one leaves this room until I say otherwise. Attica will take me."

"I've never actually met the guildmaster," said the woman, her voice wavering slightly.

"But you know where to find him." Rezkin stated rather than questioned.

The woman nodded and said, "Well, yes, but—"

"Lead the way," Rezkin interrupted.

5

Rezkin followed the frilly, sheer lavender cloak through the streets and down dark alleys. The cloak would have looked fine on any number of ladies but was at complete odds with the appearance of the female thief. It was her hasty attempt to appear as anything other than what she was to the *normal* folk and city guards. Attica had wrapped the diaphanous material tightly around her to cover her unladylike appearance, and walked with a sway in her hips. Although it was still light, the sun had sunk below the horizon, and one could not immediately see that she was not wearing full skirts beneath the cloak.

The woman stopped at a door behind a seedy tavern and glanced around. She rapped on the door in a pattern similar to the one the small-men had used at the den, and the door opened a moment later. Rezkin stood to one side in the shadows as she spoke.

"The Slink's new denleader wants to meet with the guildmaster," the woman said in a forceful rush.

The guard at the door was a bit shorter than Rezkin, which was still quite tall, and built like a mercenary. He carried a dagger and a long hunting knife at his waist and wore gloves fitted with brass knobs over his knuckles. He grunted and said, "The boss didn't assign the Slinks a new leader."

"He won by challenge," the woman replied with her usual smirk. "If you could call that a *challenge*. He didn't seem to have any trouble from where I stood."

"A tough guy, eh? Well, bring 'im in, and if he gives us any trouble, he'll not be leavin'," replied the merc.

Rezkin slipped out of the shadow, and the man's surprise was evident. Along the way, he had acquired a plain, dark brown cloak, which now hid his features. The effect was hardly intimidating for the gruff merc since most thieves tended to hide themselves in a similar fashion, but it did provide the doorman with an image he expected to see. A quick perusal of Rezkin's person, and the man noted the two sword hilts at Rezkin's waist with a shake of his head. The door guard grunted and spit off to the side in derision, obviously having found Rezkin lacking.

"Draphus *might* see you, but don't think you'll be gettin' to the Master. He ain't got time to be meetin' with the likes of you," the spitwad remarked.

Rezkin kept his daggers palmed as he stalked past the doorman. He slouched a bit, bringing his height closer to the man's level. He focused on appearing less intimidating, hoping the act would get him closer to the guildmaster before he had to start killing people. He was nearly certain there *would* be killing. A truly intelligent guildmaster would accept the deal Rezkin intended to offer. These were thieves, however, and the position of guildmaster tended to attract the insatiably ambitious. It was highly unlikely the man would bow to Rezkin's demands.

The back of the tavern was the *business* end, and it took up the majority of the space. Rezkin could see through the single door opposite him that the front area, presumably open to any patrons brave or stupid enough to enter, consisted only of a long bar with a few wobbly stools. This back area, however, held numerous tables around which gamblers, drinkers, and otherwise unsavory characters gathered. While several of the women were like Attica and appeared to be just as rough as the men, others were scantily clad and buried under too much makeup. These women giggled and hooted at the men as they tossed around their coin and called for more drinks.

Rezkin focused on appearing as unimportant and inconspicuous as possible. It must have worked, because the guild members did not acknowledge his existence. Spitwad led Rezkin and Attica to a small office in front of which stood another merc who looked quite similar to and just as bored as Spitwad. He simply leaned against the wall and grunted as Spitwad and the others entered the office. An average-looking man with brown hair, brown eyes, and plain clothes sat behind an ordinary brown desk. To look at him, there was absolutely nothing noteworthy about the man, which Rezkin immediatcly noted. It was an advantageous look for a thief.

"The new denleader, here, wants to see the Master," Spitwad grunted.

The plain man leaned back and said, "Is that so? I don't recall assigning a new denleader." He looked over Attica and remarked, "The Slink Den, I presume?"

"Yes, sir," Attica said. She tilted her head toward Rezkin and said, "He defeated Thorn in challenge."

The man's lips twitched as he looked Rezkin over and said, "Not a difficult feat, I should think. The man was an idiot who shouldn't have been allowed to wield a butter knife, much less carry around that scrap metal he called a sword. Who are you, then?"

Ignoring the question, Rezkin asked, "Why did you put him in charge if you knew he was incompetent?"

The unassuming man barked a brief laugh when he replied, "Oh, he was competent enough to keep track of the street rats. He was also too stupid to calculate his *taxes* properly. He was always willing to pay more when we told him he was short. You haven't answered *my* question, though. Who are *you*?"

"I am the man who's taking over," stated Rezkin.

"Oh, I can see that, but why do you want to be a denleader?" the man asked. "You don't look like you're hurting for money, and I can't see a man like you hanging around the gutter rats."

"I do not wish to be a denleader. I am taking over the guild," Rezkin replied.

Another short burst of laughter, and then the man was leaning over his desk with fire in his eyes. "I don't take kindly to talk like that, and you can bet the guildmaster doesn't either."

Rezkin cocked his head to the side and said, "You would have me believe you are the second named Draphus, yet I know you are the guildmaster and therefore must be Martius. I have a proposal for you." Martius leaned back in his chair again and tapped the desk with one finger in contemplation. Rezkin shook his head slightly and said, "You can reach for that crossbow, but it will be the last thing you do before I take your head."

Martius's wandering hand stopped. He grinned showing a full set of yellow teeth. Actually, at least two of the teeth looked to be replacements carved from bone. "You think to intimidate me in my own guildhouse? I have an entire room of men just behind you at my beck and call, not to mention Tyre and Barclay in this very room."

Ah, Spitwad had a name, and it was Tyre. Barclay had to be the other bored guard. Both men grinned showing several broken and rotting teeth of their own. Rezkin nodded pleasantly to each of the men and then turned his attention back to the guildmaster. "If your guards wish to remain breathing, they will not interfere. You, however, have a decision to make, and you have not even heard my proposition."

The guildmaster rested his elbows on the desk as he grinned over his intertwined fingers. "Very well. I'll hear this proposition. Let no man say I'm not a gracious host, even to those who are obviously lacking in intelligence or sanity."

Rezkin drummed his fingers on the hilt of his sword. He was conditioned against such ticks, but the masters had impressed upon him that showing them at opportune times would make him appear more human, or more menacing, depending on the desired outcome. Choosing the right tick at the right time was a difficult skill, and it had taken years of observing the prisoners and other "visitors" to the fortress to use them effectively. Now, he realized those visitors were prisoners just as any of the others. It seemed that everyone who ever set foot in that fortress was destined to die there—except him.

"I know how your operation works, and I have seen enough to find it lacking. In addition, I have decided that I have a use for your personnel. Therefore, you have two choices. You will serve me or you will die," Rezkin stated succinctly.

The guildmaster frowned. "I tire of this. I thought you would at least come up with something more creative. Kill him," he said waving at the mercs to get on with it.

Tyre came at Rezkin immediately. He pulled his hunting knife from his belt and slashed at Rezkin. Rezkin easily dodged and ducked behind the man. Twisting the merc's knife-wielding wrist, he bent the man's arm straight back and shoved at his shoulders. The merc lost hold of his weapon and careened head first into the wall.

Barclay took a swing at Rezkin's head from behind, but his fist met only air. Rezkin ducked and spun, shoving his shoulder into the man's gut and causing him to double over. Rezkin grabbed the man just below the hips and stood, tossing the rugged guard into the air. Barclay landed on his back with a *whomp*, and Rezkin kicked him in the head hard enough for him to hear a crack. He did not know if it was the man's skull or neck that broke. The first guard, Tyre, was just attempting to sit up with a moan when Rezkin lobbed a throwing dagger into his throat. Blood spurted between the merc's fingers and poured down his jerkin as the man lay thrashing and clutching at his neck.

Rezkin twisted and threw himself behind the open door just as a crossbow bolt dug into the old wooden slab. A shout rang out from the adjacent room, and he knew he was running out of time. He flitted across the room faster than the guildmaster could reload. Whipping Bladesunder from its sheath, he whirled as he leapt over the desk and took Guildmaster Martius's head clean off his body. Just as the head smacked into the floor, several more men piled into the room. Rezkin whipped his blade around, splattering the men with the guildmaster's blood. He held the sword slightly behind him so it was covered by his cloak. The sword bearer did not desire for these men to know he carried a Sheyalin, but he wanted to keep his weapon at the ready.

The men paused as the guildmaster's head rolled to the center of the room. They took in the additional bloody carnage of the two top guards and then looked at Attica questioningly. The woman stood to one side of the door where she had stood upon entering the room. She had her arms wrapped around herself tightly as though doing so could protect her from the violence. Her face was pale as alabaster, and her eyes were wide with surprise, but when she noticed the attention of the newcomers she managed a smirk.

Attica tilted her head toward Rezkin and said, "He's the new guildmaster."

This did not sit well with any of the men, and the shifty one in the center narrowed his eyes as he asked, "Says who?"

The woman nonchalantly leaned against the wall with a shrug, although Rezkin thought she looked a little weak in the knees and probably needed the support. With a lift of a brow, she said, "Well, I'm not going to argue with him, but please feel free to do so. I'm sure he'll make his point the same way he did with the others."

"He can't take on all of us—" Shifty was saying when his words were abruptly cut off due to the small matter of the dagger lodged into his brain through his eye socket.

The men startled, and several even jumped back a step. No one had seen the killer move, and the strange man still stood exactly as he had moments before, the only evidence of movement being the slight sway of his worn brown cloak.

"Does anyone else care to protest the matter?" Rezkin asked. By now a few more men had shoved their way into the room to investigate the commotion. The angry shouts and sounds of dying men and falling bodies had not been difficult to interpret. Several of the men were muttering quietly and making all-too-obvious hand motions in a very poorly disguised attempt to plot some plan of attack. Rezkin could not believe these men were supposed to be the experienced *elite* of the Diamond Claw Guild.

"Okay, let us do things a little differently," Rezkin said. "Anyone who opposes me will die. That being said, all who wish to live and are willing to serve me, stand to this side of the room," he instructed as he motioned to his left. "All who think they have the *Skills* to defeat me, stay where you are."

Some of the men glanced around anxiously while several others drew weapons or crossed their arms in defiance, rooting their feet to the ground. Attica had played witness to the intruder's defeat of a number of men at this point and weighed the odds carefully. She moved several paces to her right and stood as the lone supporter of the interloper. She turned and faced the small mob of thieves with a knowing smirk. One of the larger men, who was bald with deep-set eyes, scratched at the stubble on his chin thoughtfully.

"You stand with *him*, Attica?" he asked.

Attica huffed and said, "If you're smart, then you will, too." Baldy nodded and took a few loping steps to stand beside Attica and then turned to face the other guild members. A younger man of maybe sixteen years scurried over and stood slightly behind the bigger man.

A blonde man with blue eyes and a bushy mustache eloquently expressed his disbelief. "What in the bloody, blazing hells are you doin', Rom? You don't even know this guttersucking prick. He just came in 'ere and bloody well killed Martius, Tyre, Barclay, and Meso …"

"And Dirge, Quip, and Thorn … and maybe Pratt," Attica added, thinking of the men who had been killed or seriously injured back at the den.

The man stared at her slack jawed before picking up where he left off. "He's bloody tapping our guild members, and you're just gonna to let 'im get away with it?"

The bald man named Rom eyed the intruder wearily and then shrugged and said, "Don't wanna join 'em, do I? Me thinks he'll be tapping you, too, if you don't shut it."

"For all we know this could be a bloody takeover by the Serpents!" said an exasperated Blondie.

Rezkin cocked his head and said, "I assure you, I am not a member of the

Serpent Guild … or the Wolf Pack … or the Diggers, Blood Hawks, Crimson Blades, Razor Edges, or any other guild in any city." Only three guilds actually operated in Justain, but anyone who played in the dark would know the names of the others. Like the Diamond Claws, they were the powerful *patron* guilds that operated in the other capital cities to which all smaller guilds in the other cities and towns had to pay tribute in order to continue operating—and breathing. "None of that matters, however, because in the next thirty seconds, everyone who is not on that side of the room is going to die. It will be very disappointing to have to kill all of my personnel at the start, but we do what we must," he said nonchalantly.

A couple of the younger men and an older merc moved to the side of the room where stood Attica and Rom. "Even if you *could* kill us all, you wouldn't. What good would it do you? You wouldn't have a guild left," Blondie protested.

Rezkin nodded and with an empty, icy stare replied, "That is true, but the news would spread, and the next guildmaster I approach will be more likely to accept my proposal. Now, your time is up." Just as he said this, another man scurried over to join Rezkin's supporters. "It seems the count is now six of mine against … five of yours."

Blondie and his cohorts glanced around and noticed their numbers had dwindled far more than the few who had defected to Rezkin's side. Several men and women had obviously realized the imminence of additional bloodshed and escaped out the back. Rezkin caught the eyes of his followers. "Kill them," he ordered with a nod.

A moment of stunned confusion fell over Rezkin's new followers as their eyes went wide in surprise, but it was too late. The order had been given, and Blondie and his comrades reacted instantly. Rezkin stood in place as the two sides collided. Fists smacked against flesh, daggers slashed and plunged as they slid through meat and collided with bone, and bones cracked and broke as men called out in clipped death wails.

Attica hung back behind the men gripping a small belt dagger with white knuckles. No matter how hard she gripped the thing, the hilt felt loose and slippery with sweat. One of Blondie's followers ducked past Rom as the bigger man's fist collided with Blondie's jaw. The grungy former merchant guard stumbled toward her with a feral grin tainted by the stench of cheap whiskey and rotting meat. The young woman backed up until her back hit the wall. Her fear-addled brain remembered her dagger just as the foul man reached for her.

She lashed out and scored the man across the face, opening a deep gash from cheek to mouth.

The man she knew as Yarl released an agonized howl that quickly morphed into a bestial growl of anger. The drunken glint in the man's eyes was filled with pain and fury as he grasped her with two meaty fists around her neck. Yarl squeezed her throat so tightly she quickly felt as though her face would pop from the pressure of the blood trapped within. Her lungs began to burn with the need for air. The whole room was filled with bright stars as an inky blackness closed in from the sides. In a final moment of clarity, she thought to herself how stupid she must have been to drop her dagger as she beat futilely at thick, hairy arms.

Attica's arms dropped limply to her sides, and then she was on the floor staring through a pink haze at a bloody corpse. Painfully gasping, air that felt like fire and winter's frost flooded her lungs. She coughed and tried to swallow, but the muscles in her throat were not cooperating, and she ended up gagging. As her vision cleared, she saw the corpse was Yarl. He was lying on his side staring back lifelessly into her eyes. A silver throwing dagger protruded from his neck, the image of a raven in flight etched along the finished tang.

Her muscles felt like jelly, but she managed to push herself to a seated position slumped against the wall. She looked around as she coughed and gulped. Dead men lay everywhere like a macabre carpet of flesh, blood and bone. Three still stood before her—her cohorts Rom, sixteen-year-old Benni, and middle-aged former merc, Kendt. Attica's neck muscles protested as she forced her head to turn. There she spied the man who had caused all of this bloodshed and had nearly gotten her killed. He still stood exactly as he had before the bloody battle ensued. She could not help the anger that clawed at her as the reality of her brush with death sunk in and tears began to flood her eyes. All of this was *his* fault. Life was not easy before he arrived, but it made sense. She knew her place and could depend on her day-to-day survival unless she really screwed up.

With a start, Attica realized the mysterious stranger was moving closer. He flowed like the crimson blood that spilled across the floor. She began to wonder if her ears were damaged for she could hear no evidence of the heavy boots that stopped in front of her. She looked up at him through wet lashes, but he was not looking at her. His icy-blue eyes were constantly roaming and assessing the room and its occupants, both living and dead.

The young woman jerked back as the dreadful killer bent and plucked the dagger from Yarl's neck with a wet *s-s-schlick*. Attica's stomach heaved, but her throat was too swollen to allow anything through. The young man—for she now took the moment to observe that he was, in fact, very young—wiped the scarlet-stained silver blade on Yarl's tunic and then slid the raven-etched weapon up his sleeve. Attica was shocked by the sudden revelation. It was the killer who had saved her life. He did not have to do so. Two others who had stood for the invader were dead on the floor, and as far as she could tell, he had not otherwise participated in the battle. She wondered if maybe he had a soft spot for women. That notion was quickly put at rest when she saw what he did next.

Rezkin slowly stalked around the room observing the carnage. He bent and checked to see if a few of the men with more questionable injuries were truly dead. He found one man who was unconscious but still alive and a woman who was feigning death in an attempt to save herself. Rezkin plunged a dagger into both their hearts with cold indifference. These people were criminals, and they had stood against him. Others would learn that, if they wanted to live, they would heed his wishes. They would learn to fear him. Compliance and respect by means of fear was not his preferred method of leadership, but it was the reigning system of government among thieves, assassins, and other criminal elements. The deaths of half a dozen or so enemies now would mean fewer enemies and fewer deaths later.

The final circuit of the room brought Rezkin to stand before the large, bald man the others had called Rom. Rom was still breathing heavily and clutching at a large gash that ran from his bicep to mid-forearm. The big man, who was actually about Rezkin's height, ducked his head in subservience and backed away. The body that lay at Rezkin's feet was that of Blondie. Rezkin noted the man was still breathing and appeared to be rousing into consciousness.

The young man slapped Blondie's face a few times and jerked him by the tunic to a sitting position. The man's eyelids fluttered open, and it took a moment for his pupils to focus on the cold, blue eyes that stared back at him. Rezkin could tell the moment realization struck the blonde man that his people had lost and he was now at Rezkin's mercy.

"Hold his arms," Rezkin ordered. The middle-aged thief scurried forward and gripped Blondie's arms behind his back.

"No, wait!" Blondie pleaded as he pushed to his knees. "I ... I can be of use to you! I have contacts, business deals ... I can fight!"

"Not very well, it would seem," Rezkin replied as he moved to stand over the young woman who was still slumped against the wall. The woman looked up at him with bloodshot, hazel eyes. Rezkin held out a hand to indicate she should rise. To his surprise, she reached out and grasped the proffered hand and used him for support as she pulled herself to her feet. She quickly pulled back as soon as she regained her balance.

"Your dagger," the mysterious young man said. Attica was confused at first and then realized what he was saying. She glanced around and found her dagger lying on the ground not far from Yarl's body. She bent and retrieved the small weapon with barely a sway. The young woman moved to sheath the dagger, but the stranger quickly gripped her wrist. He caught her surprised eyes in his icy, cold stare and said, "Kill him."

Attica's mouth dropped. "What?" she croaked. At first, she could not tear her eyes from his. That icy-blue was mesmerizing in a terrible, awe-inspiring way. The man squeezed her wrist slightly and returned her attention to his command. She glanced around and saw the three men standing not far away. Kendt was holding Marson's arms behind his back as the blonde man knelt on the floor. "Y-you want *me* to kill Marson?" she squeaked. Attica shook her head as furiously as she could with her injured neck and protested, "I-I'm not a killer! I'm just a thief! I have other means of getting what I want. I've never killed anyone!"

"This man led a resistance against me—against *you*. One of his men left you with those bruises around your neck when he nearly killed you." Attica's hand strayed to her sore neck as she thought about how she must look. "Do not think for a moment that this man ... Marson ... would not have done the same if he had been in the other's place," the frightening stranger replied.

"Please ... I don't want to be a killer," Attica pleaded.

"This is war, Attica. People die in war," the new guildmaster replied.

"But *this*," she said as she waved a hand at the restrained, kneeling man, "is not battle. *This* is an execution! He can't even fight back," Attica replied, her throat constricting to clip her words at the end.

"If he *could* fight back, you would die. You have no fighting *Skills*, a condition that must be corrected if you are to work for me. You are a thief. You work in a city where thieves who are caught are strung up from the bridge or sent to the gallows. Rival guilds battle for territory, and members of your own guild compete for position and will stop at nothing if they believe you are in their way. Victims of thievery occasionally fight back and are killed by accident or intentionally from the thief's fear of being caught. Death is inevitable in your line of work, Attica —yours or someone else's by your hand. It was just a matter of time. That time is now. You will kill *him* or you will leave the guild," Rezkin ordered as he indicated the cowering man on the floor. Marson's gaze darted back and forth changing from fear as he looked at the new guildmaster to pleading as he looked at her.

Attica knew the truth of the guildmaster's words. She had always known that eventually she would end up killing someone, or she would die. Everyone she knew who managed to survive long enough to bear children had either directly or indirectly killed someone. Guild members liked to think they were above the guttertrash that begged in the streets, but in reality they were the worst of it. They were the ones who had become so desperate that they sold their own souls in hopes of having something better. Attica would be nothing without the guild. The guild was all she knew, and every other dream had died away with each passing year of hardship and the knowledge that, with the black guild tattoo that had been forced upon her, no one of worth would ever accept her.

Starting with her hand, Attica's whole body began to shake as she took several steps toward her intended victim. She glanced up questioningly at Rom with tearful eyes. The big man had been almost like a surrogate father to her at times—as if she had any idea what a father was. When she was younger and truly starving, he would sometimes give her food. On cold nights, he occasionally allowed her to sleep on the floor near his hearth. He did not provide for her all the time, for he said he did not want her developing an attachment. He had no desire to be a father to some orphan girl.

Attica had always scorned a man's touch, so much that she would not consider becoming a whore, but Rom had convinced Madame Terly to teach her to seduce a man into lowering his guard long enough for her to lift his purse. No one had ever confirmed her suspicions, but Attica believed the reason most of the other guild members left her alone was because they feared Rom's wrath.

As Rom met her gaze now, though, she saw none of that protectiveness. He looked resigned. After a brief moment, the big man simply looked away without a word. Attica gripped her dagger tighter and turned her attention back to the man kneeling at her feet. She realized that he had been speaking, begging, and pleading, but she had heard none it. Attica felt like she was in a different room—*alone*—looking in on this one through panes of glass. Even the sounds seemed to be muffled. Then, in an instant, it was as if there was a *pop,* and everything was clear and crisp again. The stench of body waste, blood, and death filled the air, her face was cold and damp with sweat, her chest and throat burned, and Marson was blubbering at her feet.

"Please! You don't have to do this! I'll serve you! I'll be loyal, I swear it!" Marson howled.

The new guildmaster was suddenly at her side, although she had not seen him move. "Here." He pointed to a place at Marson's neck.

Without giving herself a chance to think about what she was doing, Attica plunged the dagger forward with perhaps more force than was necessary. She pulled her hand back quickly, terrified of what she had done. The dagger had not quite hit the correct angle at the spot the guildmaster had indicated, and Marson yowled and struggled in Kendt's grip.

The guildmaster frowned. "That was poorly executed. It will take a long time for him to die. Withdraw the blade and draw it across his throat at an angle this time," he said as though he was explaining how to carve a bird for supper.

Tears fell from Attica's eyes, and she gritted her teeth and gripped the dagger hilt. She did as the guildmaster bade, and blood sprayed across her chest as it gushed from the dying man's throat. No, not *a* man. *Marson.* She knew his name. She had spoken to him once or twice. She would not forget the man she killed in cold blood.

"If you leave your enemies behind alive, they will return to stab you in the back," the guildmaster stated. His words were cold, but his voice carried a hint of sympathy. She glanced up to meet his crystal blue stare. Somehow the icy coldness had thawed, and the man who looked back at her seemed almost human. This invader had destroyed the hierarchy she depended on for safety and survival. The men he had killed and those who had died in this room had not exactly been friends, but they had been a family of sorts—members of the guild. He had turned her into a killer, as well. At least, that is what she told herself. Deep down she knew it had been her choice. But, he had also saved her life, and the way he looked at her showed no hint of potentially lecherous reasons for doing so.

"Why?" she asked in a choked whisper. The man cocked his head questioningly. She swallowed hard and said, "Why did you save me?"

"I gave you the chance to protect yourself, and you failed. I had to intercede, or he would have killed you," the guildmaster stated with indifference.

"No, but *why* did you save *me*?" Attica said. "You did not save *them*," she said nodding toward the two men who had fought on his side.

"You had already proven yourself. I protect those who are loyal to me and avenge those I cannot. But, make no mistake. This man's death,"—he looked at Marson—"was a kindness compared to what I will do to those who betray me." With that statement, the young man's eyes turned cold and hard as stone leaving nothing of the slight softness she had seen moments ago.

"You are the new guildmaster, Attica," the stranger announced suddenly as he continued to stare into her eyes.

Attica blinked a few times as her mind struggled to catch up. "W-what?"

"Rom will be your second, and this man …" he paused as he looked at the third man questioningly.

"K-Kendt," the middle-aged man said uncertainly.

"Kendt will be third," Rezkin said.

"But, I thought *you* were the new guildmaster!" Attica blurted in protest.

"I have no time to be guildmaster. I do not care for the position in any case. I only care that the guildmaster heed my wishes. If Martius had accepted my proposition, he would still be guildmaster. It was inevitable, though, that he would be killed. I could not depend on his loyalty. I think *you*, Attica, understand the consequences of betrayal and the benefits of loyalty. Am I wrong?" Rezkin asked.

"No, I mean, I understand what you're saying. But, I'm no guildmaster. I don't even know what to do. I'm only twenty-seven," the young woman added.

Rezkin was a little surprised. She looked younger than her twenty-seven years, and she must have been doing something right to last that long in the guild, especially without killing anyone. "Age has nothing to do with this. Intelligence and loyalty are what I desire, and I believe you have both. There are others with more experience who can assist you with the day-to-day operations. Your primary job is to ensure that *my* objectives are carried out without question."

"Yes, Master," she replied with a seriousness that lacked her usual smirk. Rezkin noted the woman's sincerity and nodded once. "Um … what do we call you?"

"I do not care what you call me as long as you follow orders," Rezkin replied as he turned toward the door. He stepped carefully over the carnage as he went. "Take the bodies to the river. Line them up along the bank, and make sure their marks show," Rezkin said, referring to the emblem tattooed on the forearm of every Diamond Claw member. Some members had multiple tattoos indicating their den memberships or former guilds. Those former guilds would be the smaller ones that paid tribute to the Diamond Claws or guilds that had been consumed and destroyed by the larger one. None of the major guilds would accept a traitor from another major guild. They all recognized the stark reality: once a traitor, always a traitor. "Everyone will know what happens when they defy me."

When he reached the door, Rezkin turned and assessed the young man who had been keeping quiet behind the others. The young man appeared startled when he realized he had caught Rezkin's attention. He looked as though he was unused to being noticed by others.

"What are you called?"

"Uh … Benni, Master," the young man replied. He was a nice looking young man, clean and of clear complexion with a full set of teeth, as far as Rezkin could tell. His face was still a bit round with youth and did not look as though it required shaving often. He was of slightly less than average height, but he looked as though he had a bit more growth in his future.

Rezkin cocked his head thoughtfully and asked, "What are your *Skills,* Benni?"

Benni shifted uncomfortably and glanced at Rom for confirmation or assurance. Rom, being a smart man, gave neither and declined to meet Benni's questioning eyes. Benni swallowed and said, "I, uh, I'm a *sneak.*"

Rezkin nodded in understanding. *Sneak* was the thieves' guild term for those who specialized in stealth and were assigned jobs that required breaking and entering businesses, homes, and offices without being detected. It made sense that someone with that specialty would be accustomed to going unnoticed. "You must be *Skilled* to be holed up in the guildhouse rather than a den."

"Y-Yes, Master. I'm the best in the guild," he said with a slight flush as he ducked his head.

"You also took down two of these men with your daggers," Rezkin said, pointing at the two bodies in question. "You have had combat training."

"A bit, Master. Rom and Carduk been teachin' me," Benni replied.

"Where is this Carduk?" Rezkin asked.

"He's out on a mission," Benni said quickly. "The Master … uh … Martius sent 'im out two days ago. He's s'posed to return tomorrow."

"Is this Carduk going to be a problem?" Rezkin asked, the hardness returning to his voice.

"No, Master," Rom interrupted. "We'll explain things to 'im. He's a smart man. He'll understand."

"See that he does," Rezkin ordered. "You and Carduck are to begin training Attica in combat." Rezkin cocked his head thoughtfully and then said to Attica, "I will also be sending someone else to train you in the sword. Begin gathering the members who were not a part of this resistance and familiarize yourselves with the guild business. I will return tomorrow, and you will inform me of any problems you cannot handle. Benni, you are with me tonight."

Attica's brows rose and a thought occurred to her as to why the frightful invader had not seemed to notice her feminine attributes. She knew she was not a beautiful woman, but she had received enough looks from men to know they found her form appealing. Benni's face paled, and he appeared to have forgotten how to move his feet. It was obvious he had no desire for the advances of another man, even if that man *was* one of the most enticing men Attica had ever seen. Rom looked at the young man sympathetically, and Kendt would not meet the boy's fear filled eyes.

"M-Master?" Benni asked with a whimper.

"Bring whatever gear you require," Rezkin stated as he turned toward the open doorway, oblivious to the assumptions the group had made about his intentions. "I will be evaluating your *Stealth Skills*," he said as he disappeared into the common room.

Benni's breath left him in a *whoosh*, and Rom and Kendt chuckled as they released the tension that had built up over the last … half mark. Only half a mark had passed since the invader entered their sanctuary? Benni laughed a little with the other men, but Attica was rattled. The stranger had come in almost on a whim and quite literally decapitated the guild. Now, *she* was at its head with absolutely no idea how to run a major thieves' guild, and she feared it was only a matter of time before her head rolled like the rest. Maybe if she proved her loyalty, she would not end up lining the riverbank with the other corpses.

Benni followed the master into the common room and came to an abrupt halt. The room was completely empty, but the backdoor was barred from the inside. He turned and checked the door leading to the front of the *tavern,* and it too was barred from the inside. The young man spun in a quick circle surveying all of the tables and scattered chairs, some of which had been overturned in the earlier commotion. The master had disappeared, and the only people in the Guildhouse were the three in the room behind him—aside from the corpses, of course. The young man anxiously backpedaled toward the office where he had left his comrades, but instead of an open doorway, he collided with a solid figure. Benni nearly jumped out of his boots as he yelped and twisted, falling over his own feet.

Rezkin looked down at the young man sprawled on the floor with a frown. "You may or may not possess sufficient *Stealth Skills*, but your observational *Skills* need work. You must not only be able to move invisibly, but you must also detect others who are attempting to evade *your* notice."

"But … there was no one 'ere! I looked everywhere! You were gone!" the young man protested shakily as he got to his feet.

"Obviously not," Rezkin drawled. "Come. I have a task for you, and we will see how well you perform." He critically eyed the young man whose frame was too thin and clothes were too tight and too short. "Have you eaten?"

"What?" Benni was surprised by the question. He could not remember a time when anyone cared to ask whether or not he had eaten. "I mean, yeah, I guess. I ate yesterday," he said with a shrug.

"Night has fallen, and you have not eaten since yesterday?" Rezkin asked with disgust.

Benni shrugged and said, "Well, I was hopin' the master would 'ave a task for me tonight, and then I could get a meal, but, well …" he said, shrugging again as he let the statement hang.

"If you are such a capable sneak, why did you not obtain your own food?" Rezkin asked.

"Well, ah, the master didn't like us doing our own jobs, 'specially the Sneaks. He says … ah … *said* we're too valuable to get caught stealin' bread," the young thief replied.

Rezkin raised a brow and said, "If he did not wish for you to steal your meals, then he should have provided you with sustenance, no?"

The young man shrugged and said, "If we finish our tasks, we get fed. It's 'ow it always is. It's bloody 'ell when the master ain't got nothin' for us to do, though." Benni suddenly seemed to remember to whom he was speaking and began to stutter, "I mean … not that you … well, whatever you think is best, of course, M-master."

Rezkin did not want people to call him Master, but it was necessary to maintain respect and authority within the thieves' guild. It also meant that he did not have to provide a name. It was just easier this way. "We will get you something to eat before your task. I will not have you giving us away when your stomach rumbles, nor do I desire for you to make careless mistakes or lose consciousness from hunger."

"Oh, yeah, I only done that a couple times. Lucky for me, I was already on the roof when I passed out, and no one found me," Benni said as though it was a normal occurrence to black out from lack of sustenance. Looking at the scrawny young man, Rezkin decided it probably *was* normal for Benni.

Rezkin had been taught that thievery was simply another aspect of society to which he must learn to acclimate under necessary circumstances. As in the wild there were predators and prey, so, too, did they exist among men in towns and cities. The hardworking peasants were the grazers, and the thieves were the starving coyotes. The metaphorical coyotes were not the largest predators in the hierarchy of society, though. Amongst the nobles, mages, and royals were wolves, lions, and even the occasional dragon. Rezkin wondered, though, with so many predators, how could the common folk ever hope to survive? He thought of young Benni, who was actually not much younger than Rezkin, and wondered what the young man could hope to achieve if he were not a thief. Perhaps he could become a soldier and die on a worthless battlefield defending a few hundred acres from "invasion" by a neighboring lord's peasant farmers.

Rezkin stopped at a vendor's stand to purchase a meat pie for the young thief, and Benni seemed particularly surprised to see that the new guildmaster was actually paying with coin. The Master promised the young man another pie after completion of the assignment since Rezkin did not want the young man going into the task with a heavy stomach. If the young sneak truly ate so infrequently, filling his stomach too full now could only lead to upset later.

Benni, however, was genuinely grateful for the warm, fresh food that contained actual meat. It was a rare luxury indeed.

Rezkin thought of the young small-men he had left in the wrecked storehouse. Broken, Cracker, and Ash were seriously underfed and poorly clothed, as were the other small-men he had seen. Rezkin began contemplating ways he could properly care for and train the underprivileged of the thieves' guild while *not* emptying the pockets and clearing the tables of the hardworking people of Justain. He told himself he was only doing what was necessary to extend his influence and gain the upper hand. Although he did not know for what he was preparing, he felt that having as many resources as possible would be in his best interest. The thieves' guilds would provide those resources.

Rezkin led the sneak to an upscale inn where many of the more affluent nobles resided when they were traveling through the great trade city. He pointed to a dark second floor window and informed Benni that the young man's job was to collect any correspondence he could find within the room. He was to enter and leave without being detected.

Rezkin monitored the young man as he scaled the building and pried the window open. Benni was in the room for several minutes before he reappeared in the same window. He made his way down the building and crossed back over the dark road to where the master waited. What the young sneak did not know was that his new master had followed him up the building and had observed his every move. Rezkin spent the next several minutes detailing the thief's mistakes and giving him the opportunity to suggest ways he might improve.

He looked over the documents the young man had obtained, made several mental notes, and then sent him back into the building to replace the documents whence they came. Rezkin also instructed Benni to correct the mistakes he had made within the room, ensuring that it was put back in order, so that no one would ever suspect the room had been compromised.

The young man was a decent sneak, Rezkin supposed, but far from a master. He would make a good apprentice and had the potential to one day become a master in his own right. Rezkin did not have the time to teach the young man, however.

"How is it that you are the best sneak the guild possesses?" Rezkin inquired.

Benni ducked his head in embarrassment that he had not lived up to the master's standards. He was still astonished at the master's knowledge and abilities. He had never seen anyone so skilled—or rather, *not* seen him. "Well, it's the guild, Master. The Diamond Claws ain't known for Sneaks. We're more of a 'business enterprise,' as the old master always said. You know, the enforcers … they go 'round collectin' 'taxes' from the shop owners and such. The really skilled Sneaks is in the Serpents."

"Yet, you belong to the Diamond Claws," Rezkin said.

"Well, yeah. They got me and marked me when I could barely walk," he said as he pulled up his sleeve. The tattoo was faded and slightly stretched and distorted from Benni's growth. "I've always been small. Weren't no good for bein' an enforcer. I was always runnin' and hidin' from the bigger boys. Turned out it did me some good. Rom convinced that master I'd make a good sneak."

Rezkin nodded in understanding. It seemed Rom had a soft spot for the underdogs. He had taken an awkward girl and a scrawny runt under his wing and helped them find a place in the guild where they would be relatively protected from the violence and terror the others endured—those like Broken, Cracker, and Ash.

It was quite late, and Rezkin had only a day before he was scheduled to leave Justain—one day to secure his power over the underworld of Justain. Rezkin handed Benni a few coppers to cover the cost of another meat pie and ordered the young man to meet him at dawn at a designated location on the docks.

When Rezkin returned to the inn late in the night, his innocuous roommate, Tamarin Blackwater, was sound asleep. He decided that Tam must have a very poor survival instinct to sleep so soundly, especially knowing a stranger would be sharing his room. The young man could probably sleep through a stampede of northern bison. Luckily for Tam, Rezkin held no ill intent toward him. In fact, Rezkin had every intention of providing Tam and Frisha both, with the protection he had promised, the protection he was obliged to extend under *Rule 1.*

6

The following morning, Rezkin rose early, as usual. He cut his morning training routine short, only practicing his various combat techniques and weapons skills for an hour. He fed and watered Pride and then rinsed the sweat from his body and donned his armor, securing as many concealed weapons as he could fit. He departed before Tam awoke, leaving only a note indicating that Tam and Frisha should stay together at all times and remain near the inn. He mentioned that he had heard rumor of a war breaking out amongst the criminal elements of the city, and implored his two *friends* to remain safe while he secured their travel supplies and arrangements.

When Tam read the missive, he was more than happy to remain at the inn and was once again grateful that he and Frisha had found someone so capable with whom to travel. Frisha was a little disappointed because she wanted to see more of the city. She had heard that several of the gardens near the governor's grand estate were quite lovely. While the two travelers were taking their breakfast in the common room, however, a town crier stopped not far from the open windows. From their vantage, Frisha and Tam were able to see and hear the crier clearly. He was telling of a large number of corpses belonging to members of one of the larger thieves' guilds being lined up along the river.

The other patrons at the surrounding tables quickly took to gossiping and speculation. Most agreed that it must be a war between guilds. Some of the more optimistic flibbertigibbets wanted to believe it was the governor or even the king's doing. What all agreed upon, though, was that it seemed someone was sending a message. Some said the message was a warning, and others claimed it a promise.

What the patrons discussed only in fear-filled whispers was the fact that each of the victims wore a fresh tattoo upon his or her forehead, a black raven. In myth and legend, the raven was the symbol of the deliverer of the dead. The winged creatures collected the souls of the deceased and delivered them to the Afterlife. Although the birds were often referred to as scavengers, anyone who had seen them hunt knew they were just as effective as kites and hawks. While most agreed the stories of their collecting souls were mere superstition, almost everyone secretly harbored wariness for the dark birds—just as most men scoffed at the idea of ghosts and trembled in the dark when alone.

After hearing the news, Frisha made no more complaints about staying at the inn for the day. She and Tam could only wonder about how Rezkin had heard the news before the crier had delivered it. They had decided their mysterious companion had probably spoken to one of the city guards before heading out for supplies. Tam and Frisha were both still anxious about having offended their new friend the previous day. They had not seen him since their confrontation regarding his treatment of the riverboat manager.

Frisha, in particular, hoped to apologize soon. She truly did not wish for the object of all of her latest fantasies to change his mind about traveling with them.

Rezkin arrived at the docks slightly before dawn. He had observed the guild's handiwork lying along the riverbank and was curious about the marks left on the foreheads of the bodies. When Benni arrived, though, Rezkin had thoughts only for the mission. This morning, they would visit the Serpents' Guild. Rezkin had donned the worn brown cloak over his armor, and he pulled the hood low over his face as he approached the abandoned storehouse that the Serpents' Guild currently used as its headquarters. The guilds moved their headquarters every few weeks to prevent the city guard from organizing against them. Many of the city guard members were actually on the various guilds' payrolls, though, so it was unlikely anyone would develop an effective antitheft initiative.

Benni stood several paces from the master as he approached their rival guild's hall. He could not believe the master would be so reckless as to show up in the open at the Serpents' headquarters basically alone. The young sneak knew he would be essentially no help if things went bad.

Rezkin strode up to the guildhouse where two sentries, brawlers by the looks of them, lounged casually against the weathered wooden planks of the storehouse. They gave the appearance that they were simply standing around bored with nothing better to do, but Rezkin knew otherwise. He also noted the crossbowman on the roof. It seemed the Serpents were taking no chances after the attack and takeover of the Diamond Claw Guild the previous night. The cloaked warrior stopped several paces from the steps leading into the storehouse and waited.

"Who are you? What do ya want?" asked the scruffier man as he clutched the handle of a dagger at his waist.

"I am here to see the guildmaster," Rezkin stated.

"Yeah, and who're you ta be askin' ta see the Master?" the thinner guard asked.

"My name is unimportant. I have a proposition for the guildmaster," Rezkin replied.

"Well, I gotta proposition fer yer mamma!" said *Scruffy* as he grabbed his crotch in a crude gesture.

"Your words mean nothing to me. I *will* see the guildmaster. Whether or not you live to witness it is up to you," Rezkin responded.

"Ain't nobody getting' in 'ere without our say so, so you best bug off, you gutter-bred bastard," said *Thinman*.

Rezkin cocked his head and replied, "Perhaps you should inform the guildmaster that I am here before you make your demands … or do you believe that *you* speak for your master?"

Scruffy scowled angrily, but Thinman looked unsure as he glanced to his partner for reassurance. Scruffy made a slight flicking motion with his finger just before the crossbowman on the roof released a bolt. Rezkin felt a flood of the familiar battle energy he usually experienced before serious combat. He spun with the speed of the bolt, snatching it out of the air. On the return spin, he lobbed the bolt back at its sender, striking the man in the throat. The young crossbowman reached up and grabbed at the protruding object as he struggled for breath. Losing his balance, he fell over the lip of the roof and struck the cobbled street with a crunch. With the guards' attention on the dead man only a few paces away, Rezkin flicked two daggers into his hands. He took several steps forward and spun the daggers for no other reason than to make their presence known and intimidate the offensive men.

"Would you like to join him, or will you be informing the guildmaster of my presence?" Rezkin asked, his voice deepening to a dangerous pitch.

Thinman did not even glance at his partner before he jerked the door open and disappeared into the dark interior of the storehouse.

Benni was stunned when he saw the ease with which the Master dealt with the rooftop crossbowman. He had thought for certain their lives were forfeit when he saw the ranged weapon pointed at them.

Scruffy stood with his sword half drawn as he fumed with anger, his nostrils flaring and jaw clenched. He took a step forward and then seemed to think better of the action and stepped back again. It was obvious he wanted to attack Rezkin but feared the odds of surviving.

A sensibly dressed man, who looked more like a profitable businessman than a thief, emerged from the door followed quickly by the second guard. He was of average height and well-groomed with smooth features and a sturdy build. He wore a dark grey and charcoal colored suit with silver buckles. Overall, he looked completely out of place in the broken-down dockside storehouse.

"So, are you he? You are the one they call the Raven?" he asked in a well-bred accent.

Rezkin raised a brow and answered, "Am I? Perhaps. You are?"

The well-dressed man stood with one hand clutching his lapel in gentlemanly fashion and the other arm casually resting behind his back, no doubt holding a weapon of some sort. "I am Adsden, second of the Serpent Guild."

Rezkin nodded politely in greeting and replied, "I have come to speak with the guildmaster. I have a proposition for him."

Adsden smirked ever so slightly. "This would not happen to be the same proposition you offered the Diamond Claw Guild, would it?"

Rezkin smiled cordially and replied, "The very same."

"Many of their highest members now line the riverbank," Adsden remarked.

"They rejected my offer. I was forced to ensure the Diamond Claw Guild's compliance. Things need not get messy here provided the Serpent Guild proves to be more … accommodating," Rezkin replied cordially.

"You do not appear to be the rabid killer of whom I have heard tell," the second remarked.

"A killer, yes. Rabid, no," Rezkin replied without hint of guilt or remorse.

"I respect a man who acknowledges his own dark deeds without excuse.

Martius was never the kind of man from whom one could expect even a semblance of refinement. I am afraid you will find Urek to be much the same, despite his upbringing. Please, come with me. I guarantee your safety at least as far as Urek's study. After that, you are on your own," explained Adsden.

Rezkin was not about to trust the man, but at least he would be permitted entry into the guildhouse. He did not relish the idea of fighting his way into the facility just to reach the guildmaster. Thus far, it seemed his newly minted reputation had fostered the kind of reaction he desired. "Come, Benni. You are with me."

Benni now shook harder than he ever had in his sixteen years of living amongst thieves, brutes, and murderers. He could barely move his feet as he ambled forward. When he reached the steps where stood the Serpent Guild guards, he thought he might lose his bladder. He was literally entering the serpent's den, and he was certain he would not be leaving alive. The young man did not imagine the master would look kindly on his failure to comply with orders. If he failed to do as the master commanded, he would likewise die.

Although at times the master seemed friendly and perhaps even compassionate, Benni had seen the man deliver death with cold indifference. Even if the Master had a plan to survive this encounter, he doubted the man cared enough to ensure that Benni, too, would make it. With heavy boots and an even heavier heart, Benni stepped through the doorway into the Serpents' lair.

Rezkin walked beside Adsden through the dark storehouse. It was not unlike the storehouse inhabited by the Slink Den except that this one was larger and actually contained goods and supplies, presumably black market goods pilfered from cargo ships and caravans. This one lacked the dirty, smelly small-men and women. Behind a large stack of crates sat several large men around a table. They were chewing crass root and rolling dice as they shouted and grumbled over the results. All action stopped as the hooded stranger and the young man were led through their midst.

Benni shrunk into himself as he passed the table. He wished he could slip into the shadows and disappear. The young sneak had always hoped to catch the guildmaster's attention and attain a higher position in the guild, but he had never thought it would lead to this. This was complete insanity, and he was not entirely sure, at this point, that the new master was not insane as well.

Beyond a temporary partition were a number of rough looking men wielding sharp weapons. Every one of them was on edge, no doubt having heard by now that the so-called Raven was in their midst. They all watched the brown-cloaked figure as lions would assess their king's rival. Each one was sizing him up and essentially ignoring Benni, to the young sneak's apparent relief. Rezkin's masters had impressed upon him the need to *live* each role he played. He had to believe the ruse before others would. Once he held the belief in his mind, he exuded confidence and practically willed others to accept him for the image he portrayed. In this case, he was a man to be feared, a man to be obeyed without question.

Benni shifted anxiously as Adsden stopped beside an open door and the armed men surrounded them. The young sneak could not believe how calm and unconcerned the Master appeared while surrounded by homicidal enemies. The master passed through the doorway, leaving the men behind, and strode to the center of the room as he surveyed the surroundings. Benni entered and immediately slid along the back wall in hopes of being forgotten. Adsden stood in the doorway leaning nonchalantly against the frame. He looked surprisingly pleased, which made Benni all the more anxious.

The study was larger than Rezkin expected. It easily comprised a quarter of the storehouse. The vast space was filled with luxury items to rival any lord. The desk was hard kendlewood imported from Ferélle. Crystal bottles, no doubt containing expensive spirits, lined silver trays upon which also sat several crystal goblets. Thick silk and velvet drapes covered paintings hung to look like windows through which one could view ethereal landscapes, and a plush woven Channerían rug covered the fatigued floorboards. In fact, the only element that was out of place was the man sitting behind the desk.

Guildmaster Urek leaned back in a plush reclining chair with his muddy boots discourteously propped up on the opulent desk. He was a disgusting man. Nearing fifty, what was left of his greasy hair was combed over in a futile attempt to cover his bald pate. His outdated, once luxurious coat strained at the seams where it struggled to contain his rotund belly, and his jowls and multiple chins jiggled with every movement of his full-lipped mouth. Beady grey eyes glared hatefully at the intruders who threatened his inglorious reign over the Serpent Guild.

Even with the infamous company in his midst, it seemed Urek could not bring himself to sit properly. Rezkin thought the man simply was incapable of moving without assistance. He honestly could not fathom how the fat man managed to work himself into such a position in the first place.

Urek eyed the visitors as he took another bite of his sweet pastry, flakes of dough and glaze raining down onto his chins and chest. He plucked a goblet from his desk and gulped half its contents before he had even swallowed the dessert. The unpleasant man slammed the crystal goblet back onto the desk with a threatening *clink* and followed it with the *clunk* of a meaty fist. At first, Rezkin was simply disgusted with the man's complete lack of fitness and utter disregard for the *Rules*, but after seeing the poor excuse for threatening gestures, he realized he was experiencing an unfamiliar feeling—amusement.

"You expect me to believe this *boy* took out half the high members of the Diamond Claw guild and that he did it by himself?" Urek scoffed, his question directed at Adsden who remained in the doorway.

The second stood leaning against the frame with his hands casually tucked into his pockets as though this was nothing more than a leisurely visit among trusted companions. He wore a relaxed smile as he shrugged and said, "So I have been told."

"Well, I don't buy it!" Urek barked. "You think you can come in here to *my* House and make demands?"

"I come with a proposition," Rezkin stated succinctly.

Urek huffed in annoyance. "You think I'll simply hand over the guild? You're delusional. And, don't even think about trying to pull that gutterspit you somehow pulled off with the Diamond Claws. There's a reason I've been guildmaster here for over six years!"

"Yes, and that reason has nothing to do with your capabilities as a guildmaster," Rezkin said.

The guildmaster sputtered with indignation. "You insolent little whelp! You'll regret making an enemy of me! I have resources, and everyone knows not to mess with Lord Urek!"

"I am familiar with your *resources*. Your cousin's patronage will do you no good here. You have no right to the noble title of *lord* since your father disavowed you, and your title was revoked. The fact that the current head of your former house, Marquis Addercroft, is your cousin and that he placed you in this position with promises of suffering and death for any who would see you deposed is inconsequential."

"So, you're not ignorant. You're just an imbecile or insane. Either way you'll regret crossing my path! Addercroft will make you suffer, if my men don't kill you first!" Urek growled as his chair lurched forward, and his heavy boots struck the floor. Using the acquired momentum, he rolled out of the chair as it righted itself with a deep groan. The guildmaster stomped around the desk moving faster than Rezkin would have thought possible for such a large man. In truth, Urek was rather short, all of his mass seeming to spread out from the middle. The guildmaster came to a halt only a few feet from where Rezkin stood.

Urek raised a pudgy finger and thrust it toward Rezkin's face. "I'll tell you what's going to happen," he said. "My men are going to kill you and your little friend, and then we're going over to the Diamond Claw Guild and putting it under *proper* management. I'll have my men dump your bodies at the river with the rest of the Diamond Claws, and by next week, no one will even remember you existed!"

Rezkin cocked his head as he considered the scenario. Of course, it was ridiculous, but he could see how the narcissist in front of him would believe it so. "Let me make myself perfectly clear, Urek. I care not about making any enemy of your cousin. Even if I did, I would have no cause for concern. You see, I know *why* he put you in this position," Rezkin said. The guildmaster's bulbous face went ashen. "The threat of blackmail from one such as myself far outweighs his concern for threats from a man disgraced, such as *you*. You have already caused him far too much trouble as it is. I assure you, by now, the marquis would rather see your body tossed in an anonymous grave than make an enemy of *me*."

The man's jowls swayed as his mouth opened and closed soundlessly, reminding Rezkin of an overfed codfish. "Kill him!" Urek screamed as soon as he found his voice.

Benni jumped at the command, looking for anything behind which he could hide. He knew it was futile, but his survival instincts demanded he at least try to stay alive for a few more minutes. His furiously pounding heartbeat was loud in his ears when he realized no one was even moving, much less aiming for him.

Rezkin stood perfectly still, his eyes staring at the furious guildmaster while his attention focused on his periphery. He had combined what he already knew of the Serpent Guild with a quick assessment of the atmosphere at the guildhouse and the sentiments of Urek's men and then gambled with his little speech about the marquis's involvement. Although it was all true, everything Rezkin said was for the benefit of the guild members surrounding him.

Rezkin had quite a bit of information on the guildmaster and the marquis, all of which had been provided to him by the strikers and his masters. Since Urek took over, no one had made claim to his position because they feared the marquis's wrath, and the marquis had provided Urek with the position as payment for his silence. Rezkin, however, knew the marquis's secret, and even though Urek was oblivious, Rezkin had just secured his place.

"Your men do not seem to have heard you, Urek. Perhaps you should yell louder. The crossbowman in the rafters has failed to load his weapon, the guard behind the drapery seems reluctant to reveal himself, and your second … well, he looks quite comfortable where he is," Rezkin observed.

"What are you doing? I said kill him!" Urek shouted as he frantically glanced around at his men. His face flushed a deeper red, and sweat broke out across his forehead. The crossbowman leaned back against a support as he looked down on the scene, and the man behind the curtains stepped into the open holding his hands out and away from the hilt of his sword.

In a moment of confused, angry desperation, Urek decided to take matters into his own hands. He attempted to reach across his body to draw the sword strapped to his hip, but it must have been some time since the man attempted the feat because he could not reach. He pulled the sword partially out using his left hand until he could grab the hilt with his sword hand. He then jerked at it a few times as it caught in the scabbard at an awkward angle. Once the sword was finally free, he swung the weapon recklessly at Rezkin.

Rezkin barely had to move to avoid the poorly aimed swing. Before Urek had even completed the arc, Rezkin's sword flashed through the air severing the carotid arteries and windpipe of the heavy man. Rezkin flicked the blood from the blade and sheathed the sword in one fluid motion. Urek's eyes widened as realization struck, and he gasped for breath. The heavy man dropped his sword and clutched at his neck. His legs gave out, and he tumbled to the ground gracelessly, rolling and flailing about as he gasped and gurgled.

Rezkin stepped around the dying man without the least acknowledgement and strode to the desk. He flicked a hand at the guard near the drapes who was grinning like he had just received the best naming day gift. The man's smile drowned in concern when he received Rezkin's notice. He nodded and took up position across the room next to the second who stood staring blankly at the now lifeless former guildmaster that was bleeding out on the carpet.

Rezkin stood behind the desk and shuffled through the few papers as he casually called out to the man above. "Come down from there before I decide you are a threat and end you." The man quickly began climbing down and Rezkin finally looked up at the second and the swordsman.

"Do we have a problem?" he asked.

Adsden smiled graciously. "On the contrary," he replied, "you have just rid us of a long-standing thorn in our side. You told the Diamond Claws that you do not to desire the position of guildmaster, yes? That woman, Attica, is now in the position from what I am told. Assuming you are offering us the same proposition, I believe we could come to an arrangement of mutual benefit."

"You are well-informed of the Diamond Claw's business," Rezkin observed.

Adsden pleasantly replied, "I have many resources, and cultivating them amongst my rivals is worth the effort."

Rezkin nodded once and said, "I care not about your informants in the Diamond Claws, except that their existence proves your capability. It is to my benefit that the Serpents and the Diamond Claws have developed separate specialties. As you know, the Serpents are largely composed of sneaks and specialize in invasion and opportunistic collection of valuable goods or contracted acquisitions. The Diamond Claws, on the other hand, primarily focus on extortion, fraud, and racketeering. I do not care that the two guilds remain independent and competitive. I will benefit from both services. However, what you say is true. I have no desire to undertake the day-to-day operations of the guild. I only require that you provide me with the results and resources I demand."

"So, it is business as usual?" Adsden asked. The man was obviously pleased that the long-standing barrier between him and the position of guild-master had been removed through no effort of his own.

"Not precisely. Thus far, the Serpents have been largely unfocused. Targets are essentially random, based solely on opportunity and immediate profitabil-ity. I have a larger agenda. I will provide a list of acceptable targets and your intended acquisitions. You will also receive a list of those that are absolutely to be left alone. Outside of those lists, you are free to make your own decisions as long as they adhere to my guidelines. If you are satisfied with these conditions, you are welcome to the position of Guildmaster."

"And these guidelines?" the second asked skeptically.

"As I said, I have an agenda, which does not accommodate anarchy. Attacks and theft of hardworking common folk and *respectable* upper class and nobles will not be tolerated. Personnel are to conduct business with honor."

Adsden scoffed. "We are *thieves*. Surely you have heard the adage, *No honor among thieves*. It is said for a reason."

"*I* am not a thief, and *my* business will be conducted per my guidelines," Rezkin declared. "If your men lack honor, then they will conduct business under *my* honor, and *you* will make sure *my* honor is preserved. A prosperous economy is dependent upon the men and women who produce goods and services. I will not have them hindered. A prosperous economy means more business being conducted, more deals being made, more goods being moved, more luxuries being purchased, and more scandalous behavior among happy and celebratory socialites. Overall, this means generous profits for the guild."

The second raised his brows. "You are thinking long term," he observed. "What is this plan?"

"Foremost, your primary acquisitions are no longer liquid assets," Rezkin said.

"You are saying the *thieves'* guild will not be stealing?" Adsden asked with a slight chuckle. The usurper did not smile. In fact, Adsden did not think the young man's facial expression had changed even once during the entire visit—not even when he slaughtered the old guildmaster. The thought was sobering.

"I did not say that. I said only that your primary acquisitions would not be material goods. Instead, you will collect information. Information is far more valuable, particularly in the long run. If you break into an estate and steal goods, you only have the income from the black market sale of the goods. If you steal *information*, particularly information that others would prefer to keep hidden, you may profit indefinitely."

Adsden smiled broadly. "You mean blackmail."

Rezkin nodded. "In part. Of course, knowing about affairs, illegitimate children, and murder plots is profitable, but much of the information I require will not lend itself to blackmail. It may, however, reveal trade deals, pending contracts, merchant price manipulation, and economic engineering. Even potential marriages, foreknowledge of council votes or a particular lord's wine preference may prove advantageous to someone who knows how to put the knowledge to use."

The second's brows rose in surprise. "You want a guild of common thieves to become *spies*?"

"Of course. In the eyes of the affluent, common folk are incapable of organized, long-term economic, political, and sociological manipulation. If a spy is discovered in a noble house, for example, the residents will never suspect the spy of belonging to a larger independent network. They will assume the spy is simply collecting a few extra coins from some other house. Every house has spies in the other houses. It is expected. They all know it occurs, and they usually attempt to discover the spies and feed them misinformation or simply dismiss them. The Serpents will be especially well suited to this task. With your invasion *Skills*, you can enter places that are not meant to be breached without being seen."

Adsden rubbed his chin thoughtfully as he considered the unusual proposal. "I am not sure this will work the way you expect. You may be giving our men too much credit," he mused with a glance at the swordsman and crossbowman. Both shrugged unashamedly. "While most of them are excellent sneaks, often contracted for high profile jobs, they are not the most educated bunch. Many of them cannot even read. I doubt they would have the knowledge or mental faculties to recognize what might be important."

Rezkin shook his head. "It does not matter if they think it is important so long as they *observe*. When I need information, someone will have it. As far as reading ability, they will learn. The fact that many of them cannot read at the moment may actually be of benefit. They will be accustomed to memorization, which is a *Skill* not as easily developed. Besides, you seem like a knowledgeable man—more so than I would have expected from the second of a thieves' guild," Rezkin replied.

Adsden nodded with a pleased smile and pushed off the doorframe. The swordsman who had been standing beside him looked on anxiously as the second crossed the room. "That is true," Adsden said as he stopped by the silver tray containing the crystal goblets and decanters and poured himself a drink. He lifted the glass in question toward Rezkin, which he declined.

Adsden felt an atypical desire to impress this dangerous young man. "Apparently, one of my ancestors was a scribe or clerk or something of the sort, who learned to read," Adsden explained. "The skill has been passed down to each generation since, with varying degrees of success. My own father was not a very good reader, to be honest.

"When I was a young boy, I was fascinated by books. The unfathomable knowledge contained within a single bookseller's shop was remarkable. Breaking into that shop every night so that I could hide in the attic and read to my heart's content was how I began my career as a sneak. Eventually, the shop was not enough. I wanted more. So, I practiced sneaking into building after building until I had enough skill to gain access to the library. I certainly never had the gold to *pay* for a membership, nor did I have a sponsor. The librarians and archivists are highly protective of their books. Security is surprisingly tight. Anyway, I eventually started sneaking into the homes of the nobility to check out their private collections as well." Adsden shrugged and said, "Maybe I grabbed a few things of value on my way out. It is not a particularly exciting tale, but I did become a highly skilled sneak."

Rezkin nodded. "You have the *talent*?"

Adsden looked into the swirling burgundy rose wine and considered his answer. Finally, he looked up and confirmed Rezkin's suspicions. "Not enough to become a mage, but it is specialized. I have a small amount of skill in manipulating wards, although not enough to actually produce or break them."

"A valuable skill for a sneak. I take it few are aware of your abilities?" Rezkin asked.

"No, it is not something I share. These two," he said, nodding to the men by the door, "I have worked with often and are aware of my *talent*. A few others do, as well, but not many."

"I may have use for your *Skills* as a sneak at some point," the newcomer stated, "but right now I have more need of your education and refinement. What I am proposing for the Serpent Guild will be most successful under the leadership of an intelligent, educated man. It will be *your* job to make sure things are running according to plan."

Adsden grimaced. "About that … you said you did not want us targeting *respectable* people. With all due respect, I find it difficult to comprehend exactly what *you* would find respectable." This last he said with a noticeable glance at the body on the floor. Taking a deep breath and steadying his nerves, he forged ahead.

"You speak of honor and respectability, yet you seek to build a criminal empire and slaughter any who stand in your way. You do not act like the average thief. You have the knowledge of a businessman, the plans of a criminal mastermind, the actions of a cold-blooded killer, and the words of honor like those of a knight. In short, you are a conundrum, and I am not at all confident in my ability to predict your desires." As he said this, he palmed a dagger from his sleeve in preparation for defending himself from reprisal for the offensive remarks.

"Your assessment is apt," the young man stated, surprising the second. "I am many things. You can put away the dagger, but please feel free to continue holding it if it makes you feel safer. It is a false sense of security, I assure you."

A flash of heat and excitement flooded the second at the newcomer's unconcealed threat, and he suddenly felt the need to rise to the challenge. He did not want to be seen as weak before this young man. His voice dropped in dark defiance as he asked, "And, what if we decide to simply continue doing things as we have been?" A slight tendril of fear mixed with the excitement surging in his veins. It was a feeling to which Adsden was unaccustomed. He was typically one of the most skilled men in the room and the most intelligent, as well. This strange man's confidence and utter lack of concern for Adsden's actions, which would be considered hostile by any sane man, chilled Adsden to the bone.

"I may have overestimated your intelligence, Adsden. I thought I already made myself clear on this point," Rezkin replied with a raised brow.

The interloper's calm demeanor unnerved the second. He appeared to have absolutely no compunctions with leveling threats in the middle of the Serpents' Guildhouse with nothing but a terrified boy for support. "And, you have," Adsden quickly assured the new leader. "But, you understand, I have to ask," he said with a nod toward the men standing at the door. Both men shifted nervously as they glanced back and forth between the second and the stranger. "If I do not at least make an effort, the others will talk, and people will question my decision to acknowledge you as leader."

"Either of you two care to protest?" Rezkin asked.

The swordsman glanced at his companion. "No, sir. If Adsden says we follow you, then we'll follow you. Don't matter to me whether it's you or him," he said with a lift of his chin toward the dead man. "Seein' as how I don't know you, I can't say you'll be better, but at least you seem to have some skill to back you up. You didn't have no problem dealing with Urek, but that ain't sayin' much. The only reason we didn't do something sooner was cause of the marquis. What do you plan to do about *him*?"

Rezkin shrugged off the man's concern. "The marquis is not a problem. I have everything I need to keep him in line. Let us get to business."

"Might I suggest that for our first order of business we take care of *him*," Adsden said, indicating the corpse. In truth, Adsden was very concerned about the marquis's reaction. Urek had never shared with Adsden how exactly he kept in the marquis's good graces, but he was not surprised to hear the stranger's earlier assertion that it was some sort of blackmail. That the young man claimed to know the secret did surprise him.

"Fine. Have him removed," Rezkin ordered. "In fact, deliver him to the marquis. Put him in a wagon with a wreath."

"A wreath, sir?" asked the swordsman. "Like … flowers?"

"Yes, a large arrangement of white lilies with a single crimson rose in the center," Rezkin stated.

"That is very … specific," observed Adsden. "Does it have some meaning?"

"The marquis will get the message. If he is smart, he will stay out of our way."

"If he is not?" asked the second.

"Then he will be dead. I have no problem with removing the marquis. In fact, I may still do so. His son is a far better man and would do the position justice. For now, though, Addercroft may be of use to us," Rezkin explained.

The three guild members glanced at each other in astonishment. Finally, Adsden cleared his throat and attempted to broach the concern lightly. "You speak of killing the marquis as if it is nothing more than culling a diseased horse from a herd. A *marquis*!"

"Do not concern yourself with the marquis. I am leaving soon, and I need to make sure things are running smoothly," Rezkin replied.

"Wait. You just took over five minutes ago, and you are leaving?" Adsden asked.

"I told you that I do not have the time or desire to be guildmaster. I leave that in your capable hands."

"But, how will you know we are doing as you ask?" asked the new guildmaster.

"Because you know if you do not, it will be the end of you," Rezkin said as he held Adsden's gaze in a deadly stare so cold Adsden thought for certain he could see his breath in the air.

"Today, you were smart enough to be accommodating," Rezkin continued. "You wanted something from me, and I provided. I was able to walk in and assert my authority. Do not delude yourself into thinking I could not have done so without your cooperation. If you turn on me, you *will* suffer—each and every one of you," Rezkin said as he met each man's eyes.

Adsden had to focus to stop his hand from shaking so that he would not spill the wine from his goblet. He mentally derided himself for such foolishness. Never had any man gotten to him in such a way. It was terrifying and enthralling, and Adsden realized he did not want the alluring young warrior to leave. The new guildmaster's eyes slid over to the younger Diamond Claw who was still trying to blend in with the wall. He glanced back at the new leader and wondered about their relationship.

Rezkin caught Adsden's questioning glance at the young sneak. "Ah, yes. Perhaps I should introduce you to the young man over there. That is Benni. He is to apprentice with the Serpents. Choose someone *Skilled* who is also capable of teaching."

Adsden glanced back at Rezkin in surprise. "But, he is a Diamond Claw!"

"He is one of *my* personnel," Rezkin replied with a pointed look that warned the man against challenging him further. When the challenge did not come, he continued. "He has excellent potential as a sneak, but his advancement in the *Skill* has been limited since he has surpassed his guild mates' abilities."

"I see. I will see to his training myself," Adsden replied with a slight, courteous bow. Poor Benni looked like a doe caught in the hunter's sights. His face had gone pale, and Rezkin thought the young man might have forgotten to breathe. In truth, Adsden was simply relieved that the young man's accompaniment of the new leader was of an official capacity and not because he was the warrior's *companion*.

The new guildmaster looked back at the stranger known as the Raven and decided that *warrior* was indeed an apt description, but only in part. The stunning, yet imposing, young man was so much more than that. He wanted to pursue the line of thought further. He wanted to find out if the Raven would be receptive to him, but this was not the time. Adsden had never revealed those particular proclivities to his guild mates, and doing so now would only cause undue upset.

Rezkin pulled a folded parchment from his tunic and held it in offering to the new guildmaster. Adsden strolled forward curiously and collected the proffered article while maintaining steady eye contact with the Raven. He made no effort to conceal his interest as he did so. Either the man would feel the same and return his sentiments or he would not. Adsden walked a razor's edge every time he revealed himself to a subject of interest, and this was perhaps the sharpest, but he knew from experience that even dull blades could cut deep.

Adsden wondered if there might be some information or personal connections he could exploit to gain the young man's compliance. The young warrior looked to be maybe three or four years younger than Adsden's twenty-eight, although he did not appear to be the least bit impressionable. The thief was not above using coercion to gain what he wanted, though, and maybe by doing so he could claim the upper hand from the younger man.

The Raven's cold, stoic gaze was unchanged, and Adsden saw neither acceptance nor rejection in the younger man's eyes. Pulling his eyes from the man's icy gaze, he unfolded the paper and read through several lists written in impeccable script. One was a list of targets, a second for material goods to be *obtained*, and a third for specific information he desired. The fourth was the shortest and contained a few names of individuals and houses that were not to be touched. Perhaps these were the personal connection, Adsden thought.

The guildmaster was curious about those under the Raven's protection, but he was even more considerate of the targets. He would never have even considered attempting several of them. The old adage, *Don't bite off more than you can chew*, applied to thieves as well as anyone. Some of these were very high houses, indeed, and would surely have wards. In fact …

"You want us to rob a Temple of the Maker?" he asked in shock before he could stop himself. For a man who spoke of respectability and honor, this made no sense. Adsden was once again confronted with the terrifying possibility that this homicidal man was insane.

"You do not strike me as a particularly religious man," the Raven observed.

"And, you would be right, but there are limits to what any man will do," Adsden argued.

The Raven looked thoughtful, as if he was actually trying to think of what his own limits might be. For the first time in his life, Adsden considered that the sentiment might not be true. Finally, the Raven released a slight breath of exasperation as he said, "Do not concern yourself with the morality of the act. It is not a true temple. It is a front. Its true purpose is to serve as a processing and distribution center for *ink*."

Adsden's brows shot up. Of course, the Raven was not referring to the ink wielded by scribes to battle their pages. *Ink* was the street name for the costliest and most rampant intoxicating and energizing drug. The cities had been overrun with the stuff for the past five years. The poorest wretches would simply drink a watered down version of the dark purple fluid that truly had the look of ink. The effects would last for less than a day. Those with the money and dedication to the substance, however, would use the purer compound to tattoo intricate designs on their bodies. The effects of the drug would last as long as the color, fading gradually over a week or so. It was not uncommon to see people with multiple tattoos in various stages of *fade*. The more one *inked*, the more one needed.

"So, you want us to steal the *ink?*" Adsden inquired. He eyed the impressive warrior again and was certain this man could not be an addict.

"No, I want you to steal the parabata leaves from which the ink is made. I have no use for the substance after it is processed. I have other uses for the leaves," Rezkin explained. "But, let me make this very clear. No one is to *use* the substance. I will *not* have my guild fall to its destruction due to drugs. Do I make myself clear? Anyone *inking* will be *dismissed,*" he said firmly.

"Of course, Master," Adsden said, and he could not prevent the slight thrill he felt with the use of the title. He had never seen himself as the subservient type, always dominating over his partners, but the power this young man commanded called to him in ways he had never experienced. He imagined it was nearly as intoxicating as the *ink* he had always avoided.

"How much do you require?" Adsden asked.

"All of it," the Raven replied.

"Do you know how much they have in stock?" the guildmaster inquired.

"You misunderstand me. I want you to steal *all* of it—from *every* shipment —*indefinitely.*"

Adsden's brows rose once again in surprise. This man was full of them. "That will be a major undertaking. It is sure to gain serious notice by whoever is manufacturing the goods."

"You are to put them out of business. They will run out of parabata leaves and will be unable to make more *ink.* Rumor will be spread that no additional *ink* supplies will be available in Justain. You will steal the remainder of the processed drug and hand it over to the Diamond Claws. They will sell the drug to those who are already addicted, while enforcing a systematic rationing. None will be hoarded."

Adsden looked at the Raven in confusion. "What is the point in that?"

"You should know that long-term addicts cannot simply stop *inking.* The withdrawals can be deadly. If the people know they will be receiving no more, they will have to wean themselves from it. If they choose not to, they will suffer the consequences for their own folly."

The Guildmaster ran a hand over his face. "Okay, I understand, but that is a hefty profit from the sale. Why the Diamond Claws? Especially since we will be doing the dangerous work of stealing it."

"The Diamond Claws are better suited for brute enforcement. Besides, you will be busy with other tasks. The two guilds will split the profits from the sales. I will ensure the split is fair," Rezkin said.

"What about the Wolf Pack?" the swordsman said from the doorway.

The Raven grinned with unparalleled cunning alight in his eyes. It was an unnatural, feral grin and more frightening than the man's former cold stoicism. Adsden nearly groaned at its masculine beauty. "Surely two unified guilds can work together to undermine a third. The Serpents and Diamond Claws will make it clear that the Wolves will either concede to my authority or they will be crushed between you. Absorb their personnel if you like, but leave no question as to who is in charge."

The swordsman smiled in return, although his was one of genuine excitement. "We can do that." Adsden knew his guild mate harbored no love for the Wolf Pack. Neither did the rest of the guild, for that matter. This was one task they would undertake with satisfaction.

The new guildmaster looked down at the lists in his hand and swallowed tightly. "This is all very complex, and some of these targets are nearly impossible," he said. The undertaking was ambitious and intricate, and Adsden could not even speculate as to the overall plan.

"Then you had better be up for the challenge," the Raven replied.

7

Rezkin left the Serpents' Guildhouse with Benni close on his heels. The young man was clearly shaken but could not contain his excitement. "Am I really gonna train with Adsden? I mean Guildmaster Adsden? He's a legend!" Rezkin glanced at the young man with raised brow but did not reply. "So … what now?" the young man inquired as he bounced along. Somehow in his excitement, it seemed, Benni had forgotten his fear of *the Master*.

"Now, you will report back to your guildmaster. I am sure she will want to know everything you observed. I hope you were paying attention," Rezkin replied.

Benni's face dropped. "Oh. Yeah, I guess she would. Um … I think I got most of it, but I can't say as I understand what's goin' on."

"Nor should you. That is for me alone to know for now. Go. I have other business to which I must attend," Rezkin stated. Benni responded with a *Yes, Master*, and bounded off, scurrying down an alley and out of sight.

Rezkin rounded a corner and then ducked through an abandoned building. He eventually made his way to the rooftops. He had been followed out of the Serpent Guildhouse, as he would have expected with any decent nefarious organization. His pursuer was reasonably *Skilled*, but the more qualified warrior easily lost him after a few moments. Rezkin had yet to encounter anyone in this city who was a Master in any *Skill*, although from the rumors and reports, Adsden may be close to mastery of Stealth Invasion, especially with his particularly advantageous *talent* with ward manipulation.

The silent warrior slipped over rooftops and through alleys. He was now in Wolf Pack territory, but since it was near midday, most of the guild would be pick pocketing in the market or sleeping—not that Rezkin was particularly concerned. It was time for him to check up on the progress with the marquis, and to do that he had to make his way to the more affluent part of the city, where the noble kept a grandiose estate.

Marquis Addercroft spent far more time in the city than many of his counterparts who preferred to maintain their own lands. Addercroft preferred the luxuries provided by the constant influx of migrants and trade goods. His affection for young, beautiful women was what got him into trouble in the first place. While most noblemen steered clear of causing too many problems with the young women of the peerage, preferring to *encourage* maids, tavern wenches, and other desperate or impressionable commoners into their beds, Addercroft had been unable to keep his hands off the daughter of another marquis.

The young woman, a mere fifteen years of age, had stayed as a guest in his home, about six years prior, when the marquis forced himself on the virginal girl. The poor girl did not succumb to the older man's advances willingly, and the marquis was a bit too rough. In the end, young Lillian—Lilly to her family —was secretly buried in her snow-white nightgown stained with the blood of her deflowering and the slice across her throat.

The panicked marquis entrusted his loyal cousin, Urek, to take care of the body, along with a few guards who conveniently disappeared not long after. The ever-ambitious Urek took advantage of the opportunity to bury the body in a secret location clad in the nightgown she had worn when she disappeared, along with the marquis's dagger. With the abundance of evidence preserved in the grave, any mage worth his *talent* would be able to point a finger at the marquis.

Such was Urek's hold over his illustrious cousin. A common maid might have been overlooked, but the daughter of another marquis would be a major scandal with deadly consequences. The former guildmaster was not as clever as he thought, however, and one of the northern fortress's strikers discovered the marquis's secret. Rezkin knew the location of the body.

Finally slipping over the estate wall and across the small, private courtyard, Rezkin hid himself behind a decorative topiary that flanked a waist-high sectional wall. He had a perfect view of the servants' entrance where the wagon containing Urek's body would be dropped. Since it was close to noon, his shadow fell beneath him, and Rezkin was careful to ensure he was down-wind of the entrance, since the marquis was known to keep his hunting dogs with him most of the time. The man seemed to have an obsession with the animals, even going so far as to invite them to share his bed. Rezkin pondered the possibility that it was a ploy to keep his wife from the bed so he could enjoy his extramarital pleasures. The marchioness kept to her own chambers, but that might have been due to her understandable hatred of her husband.

About a quarter of a mark later, a bell chimed from the back gate. A liveried servant came scurrying out the back door from the kitchen. The servant pulled the gate open slightly and engaged in a brief conversation with whoever stood on the other side. A few moments later, the servant drew the gate wide and then turned and ran quickly into the house. An average sized man hidden deep within his cowl drove the cart into the courtyard. He leapt from the driver's seat and ran from the courtyard, disappearing back into the anonymity of the city beyond.

Shouts and a thundering crash could be heard through the open windows somewhere above. A moment later, two dogs streamed from the back entrance and ran straight for the corpse-laden cart. The marquis followed not far behind with several of his retainers hurrying after him adorned with panic-stricken faces.

The frantic dogs barked and yelped as they ran around the cart startling the donkey that began to bray and stomp, nearly upsetting the cart. The marquis must have been particularly furious as he batted at his beloved dogs, going so far as to actually kick one in the ribs. The dog cried out pathetically and cowered away under the cart. The servants held back in an anxious huddle as they whispered amongst themselves, and the marquis's guards finally caught up with the commotion as they surrounded the small wagon. The marquis had been hasty in beating his guards through the door, especially since he was receiving a delivery from a killer. Rezkin shook his head in disgust at these outworlders' disregard for the *Rules*.

Marquis Addercroft stomped furiously into the cart where he leaned over the putrid body and gazed at its bloated, pasty face. The death was too fresh to account for most of the smell and appearance. The marquis grimaced in disgust and then finally took notice of the flowers sitting atop the mound of the former guildmaster's belly. The blood drained from the marquis's face, and even from the distance, Rezkin thought he could see the glisten of sweat break out on the man's brow. Addercroft's eyes darted around as though expecting to see the assailant watching him, which might have seemed paranoid except that Rezkin *was* watching.

Reaching into his coat, Addercroft pulled out a white handkerchief, which he used to mop his lip and brow. He then stretched forward with a shaky hand to pluck a parchment from the wreath. Curious. Rezkin had not instructed the men to leave a message with the corpse. He wondered what the missive said. His curiosity was satisfied a moment later when a sudden, unexpected gust of wind snatched the small parchment from the older man's wary hand. It fluttered in the breeze as it danced right past Rezkin's topiary. No one was paying any attention to the small piece of paper, so Rezkin snagged it as it passed. *Compliments of the Raven*, was all it said. Rezkin nearly rolled his eyes. Thieves were so melodramatic.

Finally noticing the waiting crowd, the marquis collected himself and stood straight. "It seems my cousin has had an unfortunate accident," he stated loudly.

"An accident, my lord? His throat is slit," protested the captain of the Addercroft House Guard.

Addercroft gave the man a look that could cut and said, "Yes, he must have ridden into a line. Have him prepared for burial immediately." The marquis glanced around at all the confused faces and shrieked, "*Now!*"

A flurry of motion ensued as the marquis dropped down from the cart, and his retainers surged forward to collect the corpse and make burial arrangements. The captain of the guard followed Addercroft a short distance for a private conversation, which happened to take place just on the other side of Rezkin's hiding spot.

"What do you desire of us, my lord. Shall we raid the Serpents? We can have their new guildmaster in a noose before mid-afternoon," he said. Rezkin thought the man a little too optimistic. Thieves did not tend to stick around for raiding parties. As soon as they caught wind of the incoming force, they would flee to their next safe house.

"No, absolutely not," Addercroft answered as he shifted on his feet anxiously. "Whoever this Raven is, he *knows*. He must have tortured the information out of Urek." The man ruminated.

"Raven, my lord?" the captain asked.

Addercroft waved his hand dismissively, only replying, "The note."

The captain glanced around looking for the fallen parchment and then dismissed the issue. "Urek did not appear to have been tortured. The only injury I saw on the body was to his throat," the captain said.

"No, you are correct. Urek was stubborn and hotheaded, but he did not give up easily. We have to assume the Raven knows, though. You saw the flowers," the marquis said with a bit of trepidation bleeding into his voice. Rezkin thought it interesting that the captain also knew the marquis's secret. He would have thought for sure the man would have been put to death for the crime of knowing too much.

"Maybe he only knows what happened. Maybe he does not know where the … evidence … is located," the captain proposed. "Did he make any demands?"

Addercroft answered through a clenched jaw. "No. For now, we will not interfere. I want you to find out who he is and where he can be found. Find out everything about him. I want to know where he came from, what he plans, and the names and locations of each and every one of his relatives and friends."

Rezkin tensed at Addercroft's last words. He was not overly concerned about the man finding out any details about him since no one knew anything. He had always been warned of the dangers of developing any close ties to anyone, which was one of the many reasons *Rule 1* seemed rather odd. Since he had been assigned *friends* to protect, he had to take Addercroft's words seriously. He would have to rethink letting Addercroft live. The man did not deserve the air he breathed, and he might get in Rezkin's way after all.

Rezkin considered his options. He could kill Addercroft now, making it look like an accident or suicide. A suicide would be particularly convenient because he could leave behind a letter of confession that finally solved the mystery of young Lillian's disappearance. That would leave House Addercroft in disgrace and could even lead to its dissolution. The marquis's son was a good man, from all accounts, and could do the position justice.

Another option was to do nothing at all. Urek had hidden a letter in a safe deposit box at the Golden Trust Bank. The letter contained Urek's knowledge of the crime and the whereabouts of the grave. The former guildmaster had left orders for the letter to be delivered to Lillian's family upon his untimely death. All Rezkin had to do was to ensure bank officials received word of the death, and the judicial system would take care of Addercroft—if Lillian's father and brothers did not do so themselves. But, that would have the same effect as the former option.

The third option it was then. Rezkin consumed a quick meal of pheasant and nut bread and then returned to the Diamond Claw Guildhouse to give them their new orders.

8

By the time Rezkin finally returned to the inn, he was satisfied with the progress he had made and his personnel's supposed eagerness to please him. He knew it was not a true loyalty—not yet. Everyone was too afraid to question the Raven. No one could find any information about him, some even whispered that he was a demon incarnate. He silently scoffed at the idea. Of all the people Rezkin had met thus far, he was the *only* one who followed the *Rules*; and demons, being creatures of chaos, were not known for adherence to any kind of order. Rezkin was not even certain such beings existed.

Rezkin requested that his meal and a bath be brought to the room. He did not feel like eating in the common room where he had to maintain constant vigilance. This city wound his nerves and muscles up tightly, being constantly surrounded by people. When he reached the room, Tam lay on his mattress reading a book.

Rezkin nodded a greeting but was saved from any discussion when Roxie and Pot showed up with the tub. Pot grinned and greeted him while Roxie smiled demurely. The two scurried out of the room to fetch the water, and Rezkin noticed his laundered tunic was folded neatly in the bottom of the tub alongside the basket of bathing essentials.

Laying his book aside, Tam broke the silence first. "Look, Rez, I'm sorry about yesterday. I … I didn't know it was like that. I mean, I don't know anything about riverboats, and well, you were just so … *scary.*"

Rezkin furrowed his brow and cocked his head in thought. "I made no threats of violence, and I drew no weapons. I allowed you to take the lead, but when I could see the man was trying to take advantage of you, I had to intercede. I tried to be more than fair, and when it did not work, I simply told him how it was going to be. If you were to ask the old man now, you would probably find that he is more grateful than upset since I have not turned him in to the authorities."

"I know," Tam huffed in impatience and threw his hands in the air. "Nothing you did was *wrong*. In fact, you were impeccable ... as always. It's just ... you don't even *know*, do you?"

"Know what?" asked Rezkin, completely at a loss.

"What you *do* to people. In here," he said, pointing to his head. "You're so calm and self-assured, and your eyes ..." He shook his head, struggling to get his point across. "You're so intimidating, just your very presence. It's like you're *more* than a man," he said and then stared at Rezkin as though seeing him for the first time. A small smile graced his lips as he continued. "But, you're not, are you? No, of course not. You haven't hurt anyone. It's just in our heads—all that fear." His look grew curious. "How old are you, Rez?"

Rezkin's brow furrowed. He did not know what his age had to do with the conversation, but he answered anyway. "Nineteen."

Tam barked a hearty laugh. "No way! I don't believe you."

Rezkin shrugged. "I am."

Shaking his head in amazement, Tam replied, "I think we had you all wrong, Rez. You're really kind of a softy wrapped in a scary package."

Now, Rezkin was really confused. He had never thought anyone would ever call him *soft*. Nothing Tam was saying made any sense. How could he seem like more than a man? Before he could reply, Roxie and Pot returned with buckets of water and then hurried out to retrieve more.

Not wanting to return to the confusing conversation, Rezkin changed the subject. "What are you reading?" he asked, nodding toward the book on Tam's bed.

"Oh, it's the *Tales of the Shadow Knight*," Tam said with a wide grin, as though he was laughing at some unsaid joke.

"It sounds like a book of fiction. Is it good?" asked Rez curiously.

Tam's face fell, and he exclaimed, "Surely you've read it?"

Rezkin frowned and shook his head. "No, I have never heard of it."

"But ..." Tam started to protest but was once again interrupted by the water bearers. A moment after they left, there was a soft tap at the door. Tam answered to Frisha standing out in the hall.

"Are you coming to dinner?" she asked her companion.

"Yes, I'm coming, now," he replied.

Frisha then noticed Rezkin standing by his bed unbuckling his swords. She lowered her voice to a whisper and asked, "Is he mad?"

Tam looked uncertain as he shrugged and whispered back, "How can you tell? He doesn't show it, but he didn't really say."

Frisha pushed her way past Tam and asked in a tentative voice, "Um, Rez, will you be joining us for dinner?"

Rezkin did not look up as he was removing his boots. "No, I asked for my meal to be brought up."

"Oh. Are you angry?" she asked as she worried at her bottom lip.

"Do I have cause to be angry?" he asked, finally looking at her. He could not think of a reason to be angry. No one had attacked him or his *friends*, so far. He supposed he could be angry with the riverboat manager, but it would be pointless anger. Perhaps something had happened to Tam and Frisha in his absence. He waited for the young woman to inform him of what should be upsetting him.

Frisha could tell, now, that Rezkin was more upset than she realized. His cold demeanor was obviously a defensive mechanism to deal with their poor treatment of him the previous day. She felt terrible. All he had done was try to help while asking for nothing in return. Rez had been consistently polite and courteous, and she and Tam had treated him with suspicion and accusations. If it had been her instead of Rez, she would have been crying or screaming or both.

"I'm really sorry, Rez," she said. "We shouldn't have accused you of … well … *anything*. You deserve our thanks, and we have treated you with scorn. I am very ashamed of my actions."

Rezkin cocked his head as he looked at her curiously. "You had a limited understanding of the proceedings. Based on the knowledge you had at the time and the conclusions you drew from said knowledge, which were not completely unreasonable, your response is understandable. You reacted with regard to your morals and the law. For that, I must commend you. Had you a full understanding of the circumstances at the time, I am sure you would have reacted differently."

Frisha blinked at him several times. "Is it really that easy for you? You just

… look at it from *our* perspective and accept it?" Rezkin was looking at her with complete sincerity, she could tell. He really did not hold a grudge against her. "You have to be the most compassionate and understanding man I have ever met, Rezkin. I don't think I could be so forgiving in your position."

Compassionate? Understanding, maybe, but compassionate? It was Rezkin's turn to blink in confusion. What was she talking about? He mentally reviewed everything he'd just said and could not think of a single statement that could fit the definition of compassion. He was not even sure he was capable of compassion. It seemed like a feeling with little practical application.

Roxie and Pot returned just then with the last buckets of water. Roxie fixed Frisha with a dirty look behind her back, and Pot snickered. Rezkin only wondered for a moment what all that might be about and then put it from his mind. His bath was getting cold. He looked back at Frisha and said, "If you intend to stay for my bath, would you please shut and bar the door? I do not like the idea of people coming and going while I bathe."

Frisha's face flushed bright red as she turned and fled from the room. Tam burst into laughter as he shut the door behind them. Rezkin slipped the bar into place and then began removing the arsenal of weapons he had hidden about his person. Rezkin stripped off his clothes and settled into the bath. The heat of the water soaked deep into his muscles as he allowed himself to relax bit by bit.

Down in the common room, Tam caught Frisha's attention and asked, "You're falling for him, aren't you?"

Frisha's face flushed, "Don't be silly. We just met two nights ago, and we didn't even see him all day."

Tam nodded, "I know, but I've never seen you like this with anyone else. Even Lord Byron's son, Dornell, who *all* the girls swooned over, couldn't catch your attention. And, if I remember correctly, he *tried*."

Frisha sighed, "It's just that he's so open and genuine. It's like there's no deceit or cunning in him. He just met us, and he's totally dedicated to our protection and welfare. I think it really upsets him when we seem disappointed or accuse him of pushing his weight around … which we've done *twice*."

Nodding in agreement, Tam said, "I know. Just before you arrived, I was talking to him and realized he's like a bear on the outside and a sweet puppy on the inside. I think we've been judging him all wrong based on his appearance. You know they always say don't judge a book by its cover." Tam's eyes sparked with mirth at the recollection of his conversation with Rezkin only moments before. "Speaking of which, do you know he's never read *Tales of the Shadow Knight*? He said he's never even heard of it!"

Frisha burst out laughing, "No way! I don't see how that's possible."

Tam laughed and shook his head before sobering and saying, "I do feel really bad for treating him the way we have. I know he looks and sometimes acts scary, but I'm not sure he could hurt a fly … unless maybe it was attacking one of us." He grinned. "I do think he's sincere about that, you know. I think he would do what he could to help us, although I still don't understand why."

"He lives by a code," Frisha said. "You know, everyone keeps calling him 'my lord' even when he discourages it. I think it's because, deep down, we all recognize true nobility. That's how he acts—being a gentleman, protecting people, setting crooks to rights."

Tam grunted. "I think it's just because he scares the crap out of people and orders them around like it's his prerogative. Only a lord acts like that and gets away with it, and he doesn't look too scared about getting called out for it. I think you should consider the possibility that he might actually *be* a noble. I don't know, maybe a landless minor lord or a fifth son or something."

"How would *you* know how the fifth son of a noble acts?" Frisha asked in challenge.

"I don't," Tam replied, "but I know commoners, and he doesn't act or speak like any commoner I've ever met."

Frisha nodded and said, "I have to agree with that."

Rezkin finished bathing and dressed in his dark night stealth gear. He decided he was fortunate that Roxie was so dedicated to her job, or as often as he had to change, Rezkin would have nothing to wear. These outworlders were sensitive to the sight of blood, and Rezkin had to maintain the appearance of an average outworlder. Every time he turned around, the young woman was practically begging to perform some chore for him.

He strapped on his dark, lightweight, leather armor and secreted his weapons about his body. Rather than donning a full cloak, he pulled a deep, charcoal-grey hood over his head, the ends of which attached to his tunic with ties. The material was waxed and formed to stand away from his face, leaving his field of view relatively clear and his visage in shadow. It also had the advantage of resisting rain.

He unbarred the door, but not wanting to attract attention, Rezkin slipped out the window into the adjacent alley and dropped to the ground with a soft, barely audible thud. He made his way through the encroaching darkness to the Golden Trust Bank. All of the bank's proprietors would have left for the day, and whatever security forces they had would be less likely to expect an infiltration at the beginning of their shift. Most thieves tended to attempt high profile robberies in the darkest hours of the night.

The Golden Trust Bank was the largest banking chain in the kingdom, having branches in all of the capital cities and in many of the smaller ones as well. More importantly, though, while the bank was independently owned and operated by the Banker's Guild, it was sanctioned by the Crown. It was not the kind of place the average commoner kept his money. In fact, the average commoner, if he had any money to save, would most likely keep it in a box under the floorboards. The banks were used by the very wealthy for the safe-keeping of important items and documents. Nobles and merchants who traveled could hold accounts with the bank, as well, so they could access the money from any of the cities rather than carry large amounts of coin with them. The bank had its own system of mage relays to keep track of the funds being deposited and withdrawn from the various branches.

If he had more time, Rezkin would simply have entered the bank as a customer and asked to secure some item in a safe deposit box, allowing him easier access to the room. Unfortunately, he had to leave in the morning, so that was not an option. At least this way he could take his time. If tonight's excursion went well, he might even root around in a few of the other boxes to see what secrets he could unearth.

The bank was located in a central square surrounded by guildhouses. The Merchant Guild was located directly to the north, adjacent to the Craftsmen's Guild. To the bank's east were the Scriveners' and Accountants' Guilds, and to the west was the Bankers' Guild. Most of the other guildhouses were located within a few blocks of the bank, the greatest exception being the Mage Guild, which could be found to the north at the farthest edge of the town. The mages preferred to keep to themselves and reminded others of their inequality often. Most people preferred the mages to keep their distance anyway, out of concern that some spell might go awry and wreak havoc on those around them.

Needless to say, the area was crawling with security as though someone had kicked an anthill. After dark, everything would be covered in blackness, and the guards' attention could easily be drawn to movement as the starlight glanced off the curves of the human figure. The evening shadows, with their mottled transitions from light to dark, helped to disguise the burglar better than the near absolute darkness of night. As Rezkin approached one side of the bank, the air buzzed with the power of mage wards.

The bank was surrounded on all sides by streets and was inaccessible by the roof unless someone could manage to scale the smooth stone walls. Even then, it would have been virtually useless since the slate tiles on the roof were secured by both mundane cement and mage bonds. No windows were located on the first floor, nor the third floor. The only windows were located where the second floor would have been had there been a second floor. In fact, there was none, only an open space over the first with a twenty-foot drop to the ground. In addition, the windowsills were warded to repel anything that came within a foot of them.

Rezkin stood in the shadow of the carved figure of a lion (*Rule 57— Remain in the shadows when possible*) as one of the guards passed by on his patrol. It was likely that several of these guards possessed some amount of *talent*. Guarding the Golden Trust Bank of Justain would be a coveted position with both high honor and pay. Low-level mages specializing in wards and security would be ideal candidates. Although he lacked the *talent*, Rezkin was trained to deal with such obstacles. Therefore, he was in compliance with *Rule 47—Have the necessary* Skills *for the task.*

After the roaming guard passed, Rezkin sprinted to the covered alcove in front of the building. A stationary guard stood approximately ten paces from him, but the man was looking away from the building watching for anyone coming toward it rather than someone who was already within the perimeter. Ironically, the best plan at this juncture was to simply walk through the front door.

Approaching from the shadows, Rezkin sensed the buzz of energy surrounding the entrance. The ward was strong, and he had the sense that it was intended to discourage anyone from approaching. If that failed, it would incapacitate the target and alert security officials. Rezkin had no intention of being caught, though (*Rule 117—Do not get captured*). He focused his mind and pushed his *will* at the ward. Although he had no power of his own, he had been instructed in such techniques, a *Skill* that had been difficult to master. Magic, or the *talent*, was all about *will.*

He had only another minute or two until the next roaming guard came into view. With his *will* focused, Rezkin pressed his hands through the invisible ward, the crawling tingles of power shuddering up his arms. Sliding the thin needles into the lock, he manipulated the complex mechanism with expert efficiency. The bolt slid from its niche with a soft *clunk* that sounded like thunder in the quiet night. Without delay, he nudged the door open just wide enough to allow him to slip through, shutting and bolting the door behind him.

The greatest challenge in this situation was maintaining the constant focus of his *will* on the wards. The bank was drenched in so many spells, Rezkin had no idea how the mages kept them from unintentionally interacting. With his *will* focused, he passed over, around, and through the wards and enchantments, each one sliding over his skin and leaving his flesh tingling and jittery.

The mundane, or non-*talent*-based, security was surprisingly poor inside the bank. Considering all they had to protect, he found it presumptuous that they did not bother with posting any guards within the building; but perhaps they wanted to avoid problems resulting from guards tangling with the wards. This was always an issue with the upper class, though. They were too dependent on their spells and enchantments, fully expecting them to stop intruders. It was a weakness of which Rezkin intended to take full advantage.

The cavernous first floor was relatively empty with only a few desks and chairs aligned neatly along the tiled floor. Rezkin passed these by without concern and made his way up the winding staircase. The wards were particularly strong here, almost as if he was pushing through water rather than air. Still, his *will* was strong, the hardest steel tempered with a lifetime of training in which failure was painful and unacceptable.

The massive vault door at the top of the stairs was composed of a singular carved slab of granite, which sat atop an even more massive stone pillar built into the structure of the building. Presumably, the heavy granite door could only be moved by one with the *talent* who knew the proper spell structure, perhaps even an incantation. Rezkin had none of these, and he had no intention of opening the door.

While the bank proprietors were abundantly concerned with the security of the vault, and they *did* overly depend on the wards to protect it, the Bankers' Guild members were equally concerned with their own comfort. For this reason, Rezkin would be able to go through the wall. The bank, like many of the more costly constructions, had a basement with a boiler. During colder months, the boiler heated water that was pumped under the floor of the building. The heat would rise through the stone tiles keeping the lower level warm. In addition, hot air was vented through a conduit in the central wall of the building, providing heat for both the upper and lower levels. This central wall happened to be the front wall of the vault. That meant the central wall was hollow, having only one set of stones on each side of the empty conduit.

Having come prepared, Rezkin set to work with a small hammer and chisel, quietly tapping out the mortar between the stones in the wall beside the vault door. Since no one was in the bank, it was unlikely anyone would hear him, but he still paused every so often to listen for any signs of another's presence.

Rezkin pried out the last stone from a gap just large enough for him to squeeze through. In all, he had to remove only six stones to accommodate his muscular frame and armor. Once through, he leaned over the deep conduit, which ran the length of the wall all the way to the basement level, a drop of at least forty feet, and began prying at the stones in the inner vault wall. The work was tedious and required him to lean over in such a way that even his well-developed muscles began to ache.

Finally finished with the stone removal, Rezkin carefully slipped through one gap, over the conduit, and into the vault beyond. He pulled a thumb-sized mage stone from his pocket. Held in the palm of his hand, the stone released a soft, blue glow, its light bright enough to illuminate the room but not so much that it would traveled far.

The vault was comprised of three rooms in all, one in the center with two branching from each side. They were about the size of an average sitting room, and heavy wooden doors, complete with large locks and massive bolts, blocked entrance to the two side rooms. Rezkin was not interested in the other two rooms, which contained all the wealth and treasures of the bank. His object of interest was in the central room where he stood. This was the room that contained the safe deposit boxes and was the only one accessible to bank patrons during banking hours.

A large oak table sat in the center of the vault, upon which someone had conveniently left the vault ledger. After flipping through the ledger, Rezkin found the record of the box that belonged to Urek—*Urek* with no family name because he had been excommunicated from his House. After that, it was a simple matter of picking the warded lock on the box and removing its contents, which consisted of not one, but two letters. The first, as expected, was addressed to Lillian's family. The second was addressed to a Lord Montaq, Count of Vesterfield in the Kingdom of Sandea.

Pocketing the letters, Rezkin locked the box and then shuffled through a few of the other boxes belonging to persons of interest, spying but not taking anything. He surveyed the room to make sure no evidence of his presence was left behind and then retreated back through the holes he had made in the walls. He very carefully replaced the stones and resealed them with grout made from local sources so that it would match the rest of the wall. By morning, it would be dry, and no one would be able to tell the stones had been removed. Sweeping the floor with a small horsehair brush, he removed the ruined grout, pocketing it in a small sack for disposal.

Eventually, someone might note the difference in the grout on the inside of the vault, since he could not stay in the room to smooth it, but such fine details were often overlooked when no one would even consider that someone might have gone through the *wall*. The bank proprietors would know the vault had been breached and something had been taken. Vaults such as this had enchantments that kept count of the number of items stored within at all times. Rezkin could have left behind a couple of blank parchments to make up for the difference in number, but he wanted it known that someone had succeeded in stealing from the Golden Trust Bank, particularly during this time when the city's thieves' guilds were being overtaken by a mysterious overlord.

Rezkin made his way out of the bank in similar fashion to his entrance, relocking the front door as he left. It was fully dark now, and he had to take extra care to avoid the spying eyes of the guards patrolling the perimeter. For someone who had grown up avoiding detection by the elite strikers, going unnoticed by these guards was simple. He remained vigilant and kept in mind *Rule 9—Never underestimate your opponents*. He would not be foiled by a careless mistake.

Rezkin paused only long enough to read the letters he had retrieved from the vault and was careful to avoid breaking the wax seals. The first was the expected confession regarding the marquis's daughter and her whereabouts. The second was of little consequence to him at this time, but may be of some use in the future.

It was time to take care of the current problem. He did not have far to travel. The marquis's estate was only half a dozen blocks from the bank. He did not go to the marquis's room, instead he entered the chambers of the son, Ruald. A window opened into the man's sleeping chamber, but Rezkin could hear the man speaking to someone in the sitting room beyond. The door was slightly ajar, so Rezkin peered into the occupied room to see that Ruald was speaking to his manservant. Apparently, the marquis wanted his son to attend to some business that the younger man found distasteful. Rezkin had only to wait a few moments before the manservant left.

Ruald saw the older man to the door and then barred it from the inside. He sighed heavily as he leaned forward and rested his head against the polished wood. When Ruald finally straightened and turned around, an intruder was leaning casually by his hearth as though he had been there all night. Ruald jumped back with a choked cry.

"What! Who are you? How did you get in here?" he stammered.

Rezkin inwardly groaned. If *he* had turned around to find a heavily armed, hooded figure standing behind him, the last thing he might do would be to pause for a chat. These outworlders had somehow grown to big-men and big-women, but they had not learned the *Rules* and *Skills* as they should have.

Ensuring that his face was hidden both by cowl and silhouette, Rezkin growled, "Please, have a seat, Lord Addercroft. We have business to discuss."

Ruald's eyes darted to the door, and he looked as if he would run. The intruder casually patted the hilt of a sword at his hip. The young lord swallowed hard and shifted anxiously. "Ruald," he croaked. After clearing his throat, he repeated. "It's Ruald. Addercroft is my father. Everyone just calls me Lord Ruald."

Rezkin waved a hand dismissively and said, "A small matter that will be remedied shortly. Please, sit down. I would not have you passing out and striking your head."

Ruald shook off the wave of dizziness that had clearly overcome him in his fright and straightened his spine. With a lift of his chin he replied, "I do not take orders from you, and I assure you my constitution is made of stronger stuff. What do you want? Have you come to kill me? I will not go quietly, if that is your wish." This last he said with resolve as his hand grazed his own sword hilt.

Rezkin cocked his head curiously. He was glad to see that Ruald was not so easily cowed. It gave him hope for his cause. "No, I am not a threat to you. Quite the opposite, actually. But, we *do* have important business to discuss, and I am afraid we have little time. Perhaps you would care for a drink to steady yourself?" Rezkin would never imbibe enough to feel its effects, nor would he drink at all in a situation such as this, but he had been instructed that many outworlders seek such comfort to steady their nerves in stressful situations.

The young lord scowled and said, "I do not need steadying. What I need is for you to leave immediately. You have come into my home uninvited and now make demands of my time."

"I am sure that was quite rude of me," Rezkin replied, "but once you hear the nature of my visit, I think you will agree that it is best kept between us."

"What exactly *is* the nature of your visit, then?" Ruald asked with impatience.

"Tonight, I am going to kill your father, and I need you prepared to take his place."

Ruald's jaw dropped at the frank admission. "You *what*? You cannot be serious. Why would you tell me that?" He shook his head furiously and said, "Do you actually believe that I would simply *allow* you to kill my father?"

"Your father has forfeit his life through his own actions. I am here to carry out his sentence. *You*, however, have a vested interest in what happens next," Rezkin said.

"That is preposterous!" Ruald shouted. "My father may be devious, crude, arrogant, and a terrible philanderer, but nothing he has done would warrant death. And, who are you to carry out such an act? You have no such authority!"

"Unfortunately for your father, you are wrong on both accounts." Rezkin drew a sealed letter from the tunic beneath his armor—expensive, quality armor, from what the young lord could see. He held the letter out for the young lord to take.

Ruald hesitated for several moments, his eyes captivated by the small paper. Dread filled him as he realized that this letter must contain some proof of his father's alleged misdeeds. Finally, he forced his feet to move across the seemingly endless expanse of the sitting room and gingerly accepted the proffered missive. The letter was warm and innocuous from the outside, but he feared the demons that must lie within its crisp folds.

As he read through the message, Ruald's face drained of color and his stomach lurched. He stumbled back until his legs struck a chair, into which he dropped like a stone. Rezkin strode to the sidebar and poured the man a drink, passing it to him as he returned to stand before the hearth. Ruald seemed barely to notice as he absently accepted the snifter.

"I ... I did not ..." the young lord stammered. His confused and distant gaze found the shadowed face of the intruder as he whispered, "Lillian." He gulped and averted his eyes, returning to the words on the page, but this time he did not see them. He could not through the tears that threatened to fall. "She came here for *me*. He said … he said he wanted to see if she and I were a match. He spoke of a possible betrothal."

Rezkin waited a few minutes before speaking. Eventually, he said, "Your father is going to die tonight. There will be no debate on that issue." Pausing, he watched for the young lord's reaction. Ruald looked up at him and swallowed but did not argue.

"I am here to present you with a choice," Rezkin said. "By all accounts, you are a good man, Ruald—nothing like your father. Once your father is dead, you may, in good faith, approach Marquis DeWinter with that letter and provide him closure for his daughter's disappearance. You may offer reparations for your father's actions on your family's behalf, and hopefully, such forthright actions will enable you to uphold the honor of your house. Or … you may burn that letter, and the secret of Lilly's death will stay between you, me, the captain of your house guard, and anyone else he may have told. Assuming all parties keep their peace, your family's honor will still be preserved. This does not guarantee that someone will not blackmail you."

"And you? You are here as some deliverer of justice? Would you not kill me, as well, for trying to keep such a secret?" Ruald inquired, not even sure why he would ask such a thing. Of course he had to tell Lilly's family, but he had to know what this strange intruder intended.

"Do not mistake me. In this matter, I am no deliverer of justice. Your father made the mistake of threatening me, and I cannot allow such a threat to exist. You have heard something about the thieves' guild wars?" Rezkin asked.

Taken aback by the sudden non sequitur, his mouth worked silently for a second, his brain trying to catch up through his roiling emotions. He was almost angry with the man for changing the subject. "What? Yes, I suppose so." The young lord suddenly reached up and pulled at his hair in frustration. "That is what my father wanted of me tonight! He wanted me to go into the Dead District and purchase a *whore*! As if I would do such a thing! He thought I could get information out of her about the Raven—the fellow who has been taking over the thieves' guilds and lining the banks of the Straei with bodies."

"I am actually surprised he would choose *you* for such an endeavor," Rezkin remarked.

Ruald took a large gulp of the dark liquid and grimaced. "He said I need to learn how to lead a house, and that means leading its dark side as well as the light. He wants me to be like *him*. But, I didn't know …" he said as his words trailed off, and he stared blankly at the letter in his grip.

Without looking up, he said in an empty voice, "You are he, are you not? The Raven?"

Rezkin inclined his head in the affirmative and said, "I am."

"After what you have done in the past two days alone, you now lead probably the largest criminal organization in any of the capital cities. I cannot believe you would give me this much without a cost. Is it to be blackmail? Extortion? I am not the kind of man who would sell his soul to a demon to ensure his own survival."

"That is exactly why you will live and your father will die. The only cost is that you cease looking for me. I desire anonymity and do not take kindly to threats against those under my protection."

"You would have me look the other way while thieves, thugs, and murderers run rampant in the streets?" asked the young lord.

"Obviously not. You are a lord, soon to be head of your house. You are responsible for the welfare of your people, a people who have been largely neglected under your father's reign. I am not asking you to turn your back on the criminals. In fact, technically, I am not a criminal at all. You said earlier that I do not have the authority to execute your father. That is not true."

The intruder suddenly whipped his blade from its scabbard faster than Ruald could blink. He leapt to his feet as he reached for his own hilt, knocking the snifter to the floor with a crash. Just before he drew, his gaze landed on the silvery blue swirls dancing in the firelight. His eyes widened and darted back to the hidden face. Rezkin stood in stasis with his sword held out to the side allowing for an unobstructed view of the magnificent blade.

"Y-you are sword bearer!" he exclaimed in shock.

"It is so. I am granted my authority by the crown, and by the authority granted to me, I have the right to claim your father's life. In addition, all my actions and those of my personnel by my command are equally lawful," Rezkin replied.

"You are granted such authority?" Ruald questioned in awe.

"I am. You see, I do not need your compliance to carry out my affairs."

"You were granted this great authority by the king as a position of honor and recognition, yet you use it to rule a criminal empire!" Ruald protested.

Rezkin sheathed the weapon as quickly as he had drawn it and replied, "The thieves are not aware of my status as sword bearer. I have commandeered the thieves' guilds as part of a larger agenda, one I am not inclined to share with you at this time. If all goes as I have instructed, though, you will see a change in the activities of the criminal element in this city soon. I *do* require that you keep the fact that I am a sword bearer to yourself. It would not be advantageous for my personnel to think I work for the king."

"Personnel," Ruald said flatly. "You mean thieves. I have heard of sword bearers presiding over a trial or helping to put down some civil unrest in a village, but I have never heard of one *commandeering* an entire city's worth of criminals to satisfy some agenda."

"It was the quickest, most efficient way to gain the necessary resources and people with the *Skills* I require. They were doing nothing of value, anyway, so I am not causing any respectable citizens undue hardship."

"But who *does* that? No one can take over a city's criminal element in less than two days, and you are only one man!" Ruald said. "Who would even consider such an ambitious and fool-hardy endeavor? Oh, forgive me. I did not mean to imply that you are a fool. Obviously, you are not, and you somehow *did* manage to accomplish just such a task."

Rezkin paused in his thoughts. Had it been ambitious? It seemed like a good idea at the time. Now that he no longer had the strikers to feed him information, he needed a new spy network. The thieves, with their *Skills* and connections throughout the kingdom, seemed like the perfect candidates. And, it was accomplished easy enough. He had barely killed anyone, only a little over a dozen corpses to show for it. It had not seemed as complicated as Ruald was making it out to be. Perhaps if the man had mastered some of his *Skills* and followed the *Rules*, the task would not seem quite as daunting.

"Back to the subject at hand, Ruald. You will keep what you know of me to yourself?" Rezkin asked.

"Of course. If you order it, then so shall it be, Sword Bearer," Ruald stated formally.

Ah, this was much easier. "Then, I order it to be so. What will you do about the letter?" Rezkin asked.

Ruald looked down with a heavy breath as if he had just remembered its contents. "I … I will have to inform the Marquis DeWinter. It is only right. I do not know what will come of it, though. My house could be ruined."

"DeWinter is a reasonable man, if not a kind one. He has long sought closure in his daughter's disappearance, and the fact that she disappeared while a guest here was already a black mark on your house. If you reveal the truth before anyone else, and do so with sincerity, I think it will do more good than harm—especially since your father will be dead."

"About that …" Ruald started.

"I told you, that is nonnegotiable. If he lives, and this information is revealed, your house will be disgraced and very likely dissolved. Your father will continue his lecherous exploits, possibly doing the same to another young lady, and last but not least, he will get in my way," Rezkin stated.

Ruald winced and said, "Yes, I understand, but how will you …"

"I think a suicide will work best. You will claim the letter was delivered to you by an unknown source. You were appalled when you read its contents and confronted your father. You informed him that you would reveal his secret if he did not come forward. Rather than face the king's justice or attempt to escape as a pauper, he chose to take his own life," Rezkin explained.

Ruald stared at the hooded figure in amazement. The man talked of killing another human being as though discussing the planned progression of the evening meal. In fact, his mother had shown a million times more emotion over the evening meal than this man did when discussing killing Ruald's own father. But, his father was a terrible rapist and murderer of a young girl who had been a guest in his home—a young girl who might have become Ruald's wife had his father not sent her screaming to an early grave.

Finally, the young lord nodded his acceptance with a heavy heart and a roiling conscience. In so many ways and for so many reasons he hated his father, but the man was still his father. After tonight, Ruald would be Head of his House—a House with a dark secret that simply *had* to be revealed.

Rezkin departed the Addercroft estate that night with the satisfaction of having accomplished his goal. In the end, the marquis left a hastily scrawled note stating that he would not be condemned and then jumped from the window, breaking his neck in the fall. Defenestration was messy but believable. The captain of the house guard had been standing outside Addercroft's chambers, so when he rushed in at the sound of the commotion, he knew the marquis had been alone. Ruald would not be suspected of any wrongdoing.

9

The next morning, the mood between the three travelers was very different. Frisha and Tam seemed to feel much better now that they realized their erstwhile friend was not as frightening or dangerous as they first believed. The previous night's conclusions had gone a long way in soothing away their worries. Rezkin was just glad they were packed and ready to go on time. The riverboat was scheduled to depart an hour past dawn, and if they were not aboard, it would leave without them.

Rezkin had gotten up earlier than the others, as usual, and set about practicing his sword forms. Afterward, he had gone back to his room and packed and dressed, which woke Tam. Finally, he ate a quick breakfast and headed to the stables to prepare Pride while he waited for the others to break their fast. When he had finished with Pride and his pack had been secured on the horse's back, he led the anxious battle charger to the front of the inn. Dropping the reins so that the horse knew not to move, he headed back inside to retrieve his companions. He had little fear that anyone would steal from his horse, since the aggressive steed would probably bite off the would-be thief's head.

When he entered the common room, Frisha and Tam had just finished their meal and were busy gathering their packs. Rezkin thought they were carrying a bit too much for travel to Kaibain, but he had never asked Frisha why she was going to the city. Rezkin shook his head. There was no way those two would be carrying all of that to the docks. He would have to strap some of it to his horse. Some people might have thought it amusing to see a battle charger used as packhorse. Any decent military man would see it as sacrilege.

Upon exiting the inn, Frisha stopped and gasped, *"That* is your horse?"

Rezkin looked back and forth between horse and woman. "Yes?"

"But, it's huge!" she exclaimed.

"And scary," added a slack-jawed Tam.

Rezkin nodded and said, "He is supposed to be. Give me some of your packs. I will strap them onto his back. Do not go near him, though. He will kick and bite."

Frisha asked, "Is he so mean?"

"No, not mean. It is just his training. He acts like he is supposed to," Rezkin replied. Remembering how Pot had said horses should have a name, Rezkin added, "His name is Pride."

Frisha crossed her arms and said, "It suits him."

As the young travelers left the inn, Roxie came to stand on the front stoop wiping away tears. Rezkin did not bother to concern himself with it since the woman did not appear to be injured, but Frisha hid a smug grin. She felt for the girl because it was so obvious that she liked Rez, but Frisha had to admit she had been a little jealous of the girl's constant ministrations and hovering around the handsome warrior. Frisha was glad that *she* did not have to say goodbye to Rez.

The docks were quite busy already, even though the sun had just crested the horizon. The trio found the riverboat at one end of a long pier. The captain took their writ of passage and eyed the horse doubtfully. He did not know much about horses, but that one looked a bit worrisome. *Not unlike his owner*, he thought dryly. Initially, Pride balked at crossing the ramp onto the swaying riverboat, but Rezkin took him in hand as one must with the stubborn beasts, and pretty soon they were all aboard.

As it turned out, the other passengers were all soldiers who were also heading to Kaibain. The first couple of soldiers Rezkin encountered abruptly stood to attention and performed a stiff salute, placing a fist over their hearts. "Good morning, sir," they intoned in unison.

Rezkin shook his head, and said, "There is no need for that. I am not in the army, much less an officer."

The two eyed his armor and weapons and then the magnificent battle charger. Both sets of eyes turned back to his, the disbelief clear in their minds, and they remained at attention. Rezkin shook his head and waved them off. "As you were," he said.

The men nodded and said in unison, "Yes, sir!" They went back to their tasks.

As Rezkin led the horse to the stall the captain had assigned, the entire process was repeated with each soldier he passed. As he unloaded the packs and removed the tack, Frisha and Tam stood on deck speaking in hushed voices.

"I *told* you he's a noble," said Tam. "He's obviously an officer."

"You said he's nineteen. He's not old enough to be an officer," Frisha said.

Tam waved at the soldiers milling about. "These soldiers seem to know what he is."

"Oh, Tam, they're just assuming, same as we were before. They don't know what he is, and he *told* them he's not in the army. Why would he lie about that?"

"I don't know." Sighing, he said, "Fine, you're right. I was just assuming, again. Just because he *looks* like an officer doesn't mean that he *is* one."

Rezkin rejoined his companions after getting Pride situated. He was carrying several packs, and a deckhand had the rest. Tam took a couple of the packs from Rezkin and thanked him. The deckhand led the three into the hold where they were assigned a berth. Frisha froze upon entering the tiny space and seeing her expected living conditions.

The room was long and narrow with three mattresses only slightly raised above the floor. The bunks were lined up in a row practically touching. The legs of the bunks were locked by hooks through metal rings set into the floorboards. Several additional bunks stood on end lashed against the wall closest to the door with thick, sturdy ropes. Two golden lanterns swung from hooks on the rafters. Tam exchanged nervous glances with Frisha. This was not at all an appropriate arrangement.

The deckhand unceremoniously dropped their packs and strode forward. "I see what the lass be thinkin'," he said. "I'll put yer mind at ease a bit. Ye see this 'ere?"—he tugged on an off-white canvas that had been strapped to the wall—"This be a partition fer seperatin' the bunks." The canvas slid stutteringly along a gnarled rope that crossed the ceiling. "Ye bring it out like so an' hook it into the floor 'ere. Gives the women folk some privacy, see?"

The curtain made the living arrangements only slightly better. The canvas lit up in the lamplight like a golden wall, and every shape and movement on the other side could be seen in silhouette.

Rezkin considered the sleeping arrangements. For his own safety, he would prefer the bunk closest to the far wall, but if he wanted to protect his *friends* it would be best to take the one closest to the entrance. He decided to let the other two sort out their own bunks as he plopped his pack down and set about checking the room for traps and other dangers.

The deckhand said, "We be shovin' off soon enough. Ye be careful, then. The boat ain't movin' much now since we be strapped to the pier, but once we be away, she'll be rockin' pretty."

"What's your name?" Frisha asked.

The deckhand was a little taken aback that the woman would bother to ask. His return smile was missing a few teeth but was friendly enough. "I be Nate, ma'am."

"It's a pleasure to meet you, Nate. I'm Frisha, this is Tam, and that's Rez. Do you mind if I ask where you're from? Your way of speaking is ... different."

Nate laughed. "Aye, that it be. I be from Downfest, but don't ye be thinkin' all of 'em talk like me. Only the seafolk do, ye know—those of us raised as sailors. Got it from me pappy, I did."

"So you've sailed the sea?" she asked. "What's it like?"

"Oh, I do love the sea. Ain't nothing more beautiful or fright'nin. She ken hold ye in 'er grasp, nurture ye, care fer ye. She gives ye yer food and livelihood and soothes ye with her song. But, she can be a fierce mistress, that she be. When she be angry, she'll destroy all in 'er path and ain't nothin' ken stop 'er. Ye gotta be 'umble ta survive on the sea."

Frisha's gaze fell on Rez as the old man spoke. His movements were smooth and sure with catlike grace. The lamplight glinted off the crossbar of his sword and she was reminded of its deadly edge. He caught her staring and graced her with a beatific smile. "Yes," she replied absently to the sailor, "I think I understand perfectly."

Tam spied Frisha while she was absorbed with watching Rez. He knew Frisha was completely enamored with their new friend, and he only hoped it did not end in heartache for her. He was reminded, again, that neither had discovered Rez's purpose for traveling to Kaibain and resolved to ask him at his first opportunity. For all they knew, Rez was on his way to claim his bride.

He was fairly sure, though, that Rez was not the type to string Frisha along and probably would not encourage Frisha's attentions if he did not feel something in return. As it was, he doubted the warrior realized how smitten the girl was. Tam decided not to intervene unless it really became necessary.

A loud shout sounded from above, and the floor lurched, as did the walls and ceiling. The boat was moving. Tam stumbled and caught Frisha as she fell into him. Rezkin merely lowered his center of gravity while he adjusted to the movements. It felt much like balancing on the teeter logs during his training. The strikers would impale a log on a stake and made him stand upon it and maintain his balance as they pushed it from side to side and up and down. The practice eventually evolved to include weapons forms and combat. He had thought at the time that it was simply for strength and balance training, but he now realized it was perfect preparation for travel by water. So far this was much gentler than the teeter logs.

Nate chuckled. "Ye'll get yer sea legs in no time, don't ye worry. This be nothin' compared to the sea. Aye, the river's goin' swiftly in one direction, an' it do rock a bit from side ta side, but there not be much o' the ups and downs. Ye should come a'deck an' watch the banks while ye get adjusted. Don't want ye gettin' sick."

That reminded Rezkin of the herbs he brought for just such an event. He pulled them from his pack and stuffed them into a belt pouch. He would need to find some hot water to prepare a tea if someone got sick. After he was satisfied that all was in order in the room, he nodded to the others who followed him to the deck.

The boat was picking up speed, and it was amazing to see the trees on the banks pass by so quickly. Even Pride at a full out run could not make such speed. The river was wide and deep. He looked across the murky, black water and could barely make out individual trees on the far shore. The riverboat itself was not large. It held four berths below deck and the captain's cabin and kitchen (the men called a galley) on top. The riverboat did not require a full crew to sail downstream, apparently, so the deckhands all fit into one berth. They would not all be sleeping at the same time, so they shared the bunks in shifts. The other two berths were filled with soldiers, a dozen in all. The ship's hull was shallow, but there was still room for a small cargo hold below the berths. The boat was currently carrying weapons and armor, for which the soldiers were playing escort.

Rezkin was admiring the way the early morning light cast a glow across the water and lit up the trees on the far side when he sensed a soldier's approach. The man was of average height with a lean build and skin darkened from long days in the sun. His dark blue uniform was clean and crisp, and his walk was precise, despite the rocking of the boat. The man paused uncertainly and then, coming to some resolution, saluted before speaking.

"Sir, I am Lieutenant Jimson. I just wanted to introduce myself and let you know that my men and I are at your service, assuming it does not interfere with our other duties."

Frisha and Tam were standing off to one side holding on to the deck rail and snickering. Having worked through their own misconceptions regarding Rezkin, they now found it humorous to see the same fault in others.

Rezkin caught the soldier's gaze and said firmly, "Thank you, Lieutenant. However, I am not in the military and therefore have no claim to your service. I am Rezkin."

The lieutenant glanced around surreptitiously then leaned in and lowered his voice. "I understand, sir. You are an average civilian as far as anyone else is concerned, but if you *do* find yourself in need of us, we are with you." The lieutenant nodded once, and then, deciding he should not wait for a dismissal since the superior officer was trying to keep a low profile, he turned and strode away. Tam and Frisha burst into laughter as Rezkin shook his head in amazement. Apparently, it was easier to usurp the authority of a military command than he thought.

The rest of the morning was spent meandering around the deck and examining all of the devices and equipment that were unique to a ship. The soldiers no longer saluted every time he passed, but they continued to nod deferentially and maintained a respectful distance. By late morning, Rezkin was becoming restless. He decided to approach the captain about finding a place to practice his *Skills*.

"Aye, me lord," said the captain. "Ye ain't the first soldier who's asked for that. Ye can use the quarterdeck, there, but mind yer feet. If ye fall off, we won't be comin' back fer ye." Captain Talwater's accent was not nearly as strong as that of the deckhand, Nate, but it was still noticeable.

Not caring to correct the captain on his assumptions, Rezkin simply thanked him and then went to find Lieutenant Jimson. As long as the lieutenant was being so amicable, he might as well use that to his advantage. He briefly explained to the lieutenant what it was he desired. At no time did he make it sound like a command, but the lieutenant interpreted it in his own way.

"Certainly, sir, but if I might ask, why do you not use your own blades?"

Rezkin did not wish to draw attention to his swords, especially by this lot, so he avoided the question.

"My *friend*, Tam, over there, wishes to join the army, which is why he is heading to Kaibain. He has no sword of his own and has not learned any techniques. I thought to instruct him on the way since we will have extra time on our hands. Naturally, we will need a couple of blades to practice with that are in the style and weight he should expect," Rezkin explained.

"I see. That makes sense. We will pull a couple of blades from the stores below. Will you require any armor or other weapons, sir?" asked Lieutenant Jimson.

"No, I think learning the sword will be enough for now, especially on this moving vessel," said Rezkin.

While the soldier was collecting the weapons, Rezkin retrieved Tam. He was sitting on a barrel talking to Frisha.

"Tam," he said. "I require your presence on the quarterdeck. It is time to begin your training."

"Training?" Tam asked in confusion.

Rezkin furrowed his brow. "You *do* wish to be a soldier, do you not? You need to learn the sword. Ideally, I would start your training with other *Skills*, but the voyage will be short, and you have little time. Come. We can spend a couple of hours before lunch working on basic techniques."

"*You're* going to train me? Are you any good?" Tam asked. Obviously, he knew Rezkin carried swords, but he had never seen him actually use them.

Rezkin shrugged. "Compared to what?"

"I want to learn," Frisha interrupted.

Rezkin was surprised but pleased. He appreciated that the woman wished to learn one of the important *Skills* that so many outworlders seemed to take for granted. If Frisha learned to protect herself, then it would make his job much easier.

He smiled in approval, and it somehow felt less forced than usual. "That is excellent, Frisha. You will come as well, then."

"What? You can't use a sword, Frisha," Tam objected. "It's dangerous, and you could get hurt."

Frisha placed her hands on her hips and turned to Tam in challenge, "I can certainly learn to use a sword as well as you. Besides, I think the idea is that I can learn to protect myself, so I *don't* get hurt."

Tam frowned and turned to Rezkin. "Don't you have some kind of rule about this? You seem to have rules about everything else."

Rez nodded. "Of course, let me think … *Rules 47, 96, 164, 233, and 239* should be sufficient," he said as he ticked them off on his fingers.

"There, see," said Tam.

Frisha pursed her lips and scowled at her young companion. "And, what are all *those* rules, then?" she asked irritably.

"*Have the necessary* Skills *for the task, always be prepared, do not depend on others, you are the weapon,* and *protect yourself before others to the exclusion of Rule 1*," he recited by rote.

Frisha turned to Tam with a smug grin, "See? He supports *me*."

Shocked, Tam exclaimed, "Rez, you were supposed to back me up!"

Rezkin shook his head. "If Frisha is willing to learn the *Skills,* then it is my duty to help her to do so. To actively try to prevent her from learning the *Skills* would mean that you are hindering her in growing to her full potential. Consider this. If you prevent her from learning to protect herself and she dies when she might have been able to save herself otherwise, then you have effectively killed her."

Tam's face paled. "I-I never thought about it like that." He glanced back and forth between Rezkin and Frisha. "Very well. Just … please don't let her get hurt."

"If she gets hurt, then she will learn her lessons more quickly. But, since there are no healers aboard, you will both have to strive to adhere to *Rule 6.*"

Tam rubbed his jaw. He thought he had heard *Rule 6* before but could not remember what it was. "And that would be …"

Rezkin looked directly into Frisha's eyes and said, "Do. Not. Get. Injured."

Both of his companions laughed as though something humorous had occurred. He did not see what was funny about getting injured. Many injuries could be life threatening, especially when they involved swords.

He led his *friends* to the quarterdeck. The riverboat was moving steadily down the center of the wide channel now, and while it was swift, it was also fairly steady. Rezkin started by showing them both the proper way to position their feet to maintain balance and had them move their arms in various motions to simulate sword techniques. He also taught them how to fall properly so that they did not get injured. When Lieutenant Jimson arrived, he saw Frisha participating in the lessons and looked at Rezkin quizzically but said nothing.

The lieutenant stood back and nodded often as Rezkin spoke and adjusted his students' motions and stances. To the lieutenant, it was obvious the young man knew what he was doing. In fact, he decided that some of his own men might benefit from the instruction. While recruits did learn basic techniques, the training period was short and left much to be desired. For the most part, most of the infantry simply learned enough not to drop their swords at the first sign of trouble. He eventually asked if a few of his men could join Rezkin in the lessons. Rezkin simply shrugged and nodded his assent. Who was he to stand in the way of men practicing their *Skills*?

By the time lunch was announced, Frisha and Tam were tired and sore. Frisha could not believe how exhausting the work was, and she had not even had the chance to hold a sword, yet! After a light lunch of fish and fruit, they broke from their training for an hour to allow the food to settle.

Rezkin examined the proffered blades and found them wanting. They were bulk quality, general issue—easy to rust, easy to break. It was what he had to work with, though, and it would suffice. For the remainder of the afternoon, Rezkin instructed his companions and a few of the younger recruits on their basic techniques.

At the end of the day, Rezkin and the other men hauled buckets of cool water out of the river and dumped them over their heads to rinse away the sweat. The cooks vacated the galley for a short while to allow Frisha to wash herself with river water in a small tub. That night, Rezkin lay down in the bunk closest to the door, while Tam insisted Frisha sleep in the bunk closest to the wall. Halfway through the night, though, Frisha ordered Tam to switch with her after the young man had already fallen out of his bunk three times. She argued that at least by the wall he would only have one direction to fall. Rezkin thought it must have been effective, because Tam did not fall out of his bunk for the rest of the night.

The next day was much the same as the previous day. At first, Tam and Frisha both complained quite loudly that they were too tired and sore to practice. Frisha was nearly incapable of lifting her arms high enough to comb her hair, much less hold a sword. Tam tried to be brave and push through the pain and fatigue, but it was apparent that he was miserable.

On the second night, Rezkin stayed on deck late to practice his own forms. There were no lanterns on the quarterdeck, so his practice was completely enclosed by the dark of night. He was used to night training, so it did not hinder him, and he did not have to worry over anyone getting a good look at his blades.

Unseen by Rezkin, many of the soldiers and sailors watched his silhouette dance about in the moonlight with unparalleled speed and grace.

When Rezkin returned to the berth, Tam and Frisha were already abed. He could hear Tam snoring softly, but Frisha was quiet as a mouse on the other side of the canvas. One of the lanterns had been left aglow for his benefit. Rezkin removed his belt and settled his swords against his bunk. He cast off his boots and stretched his arms and torso as he shucked his tunic. Finally, he removed his pants and replaced them with a pair that was clean and dry.

Frisha kept quiet as she spied on Rezkin. She knew she should not be looking, but she could only see a vague form, anyway. The warrior's dark silhouette slid across the golden canvas as he removed his clothing. His magnificent torso stretched like a giant black cat, and her mind superimposed the image of all those perfect muscles and taut skin that was burned into her memory back at the inn.

Frisha blushed furiously when he removed his pants. Although she could not see any detail through the canvas, her imagination got the best of her. She knew he would never do such a thing, but if Rezkin did ever proposition her, she was not sure she could refuse him. She briefly wondered how many women had fallen for his charm and devastatingly handsome looks. A surge of jealousy washed through her, and she put those thought out of her mind. Instead, she settled for fantasizing as Rezkin snuffed out the light.

On the third day upon the river, the wind was fierce. Rezkin's long black hair continually slipped from its queue and lashed him in the face. Frisha pulled her cloak around her, but her hood repeatedly caught in the wind. Rezkin remember the scarf he had purchased for her and retrieved it from his pack. Catching her attention, he handed it to her without a word.

Frisha took the soft, silky scarf from Rezkin's hand and stared at it for a moment as though trying to figure out what it was. She blinked a few times and then looked up into crystal blue eyes set into a perfectly sculpted face. His black hair fell around him and hovered in the wind. In that moment, she could not tell if he were truly angel or wraith, but he could not possibly be a simple man.

"This is a woman's scarf," she said in surprise.

Rezkin cocked his head, as he was wont to do when he was confused or considering. "Yes?"

"Where did you get it?" she asked.

"In Justain," he said.

Frisha blinked again. Rezkin's way of answering questions simply and without embellishment could be frustrating.

"Why?" she asked. Had this belonged to another woman? A lover, perhaps? Her stomach soured at the thought.

"As you can see, it gets windy on a boat. I did not want you to catch a chill," Rezkin replied.

"You bought this for *me?*" she asked.

Rezkin looked at the scarf and then back at the young woman. Surely she did not think he bought a woman's scarf for himself.

"Of course," he said. "For whom else would I make such a purchase?"

Frisha was suddenly exuberant. Her smile lit up her face as she caressed the delicate material. "Thank you, Rez. This is … just … you are so thoughtful. Thank you so much."

Rezkin reminded himself that women, in particular, seemed overly concerned with styles and colors and current fashion. His lessons in proper dress for various functions, and the constantly fluctuating trends in court fashion had been endlessly boring. He wanted to make sure she approved of this item in case he had to purchase such provisions for her in the future.

"Do you like it?" he inquired. "It is the same color as the tunic you were wearing the night we met, so I thought you would approve."

Frisha was elated. He actually remembered what she wore when they met, and he had shopped for her. Rezkin's concern for her comfort was nearly overwhelming. It was all so utterly romantic. "It's absolutely perfect," she said emphatically.

Alarm shot through him when Frisha unexpectedly leaned into him. He barely managed to contain his instincts to defend himself and remove her from his personal space. Her body pressed against his, and he reminded himself that physical contact was normal to outworlders, and she meant him no harm. His muscles were tense, but he forced himself to breathe calmly. It was just like grappling. Sometimes it was necessary for bodies to come into contact with each other. He was not sure why it was necessary at this moment, however. Frisha pressed her lips against his cheek and whispered, "Thank you," into his ear.

The besotted young woman returned to her berth, combed out her hair and wrapped the scarf over her head and around her neck, securing it tightly so it would not blow away. She examined herself in a small hand mirror and smiled with glee. Did this mean Rezkin wanted to court her? Something so lovely and personal could easily be considered an appropriate courting gift. Usually, the potential suitor would gift a woman with something she could wear. And, she had accepted. Frisha sighed happily. She had been swooning after Rezkin since she first saw him, but she had only fantasized that he might return her favor.

Tam entered the berth and scrutinized the smitten girl who was like a sister to him. "What do you think you're doing?" he asked.

Frisha, suddenly hauled from a most pleasant daydream, asked in surprise, "What?"

"I saw what happened out there," he said, waving toward the stairs. "If you have already decided on Rez, then what is the point in going to Kaibain. Besides, do you really think your father or uncle will approve?"

"I thought you liked Rez," Frisha said in dismay.

Tam huffed, his fists clenched in frustration. "I do like him, but that doesn't mean you can just up and accept his courtship." He shook his head as he remembered all the things he kept meaning to ask the mysterious young warrior. "We still don't know anything about him!"

"Of course we do. He's a gentleman, and he's dedicated and compassionate and an excellent teacher. He lives by a code, and he wants to protect and honor both of us," Frisha replied as her eyes sought out her fantasies in the space between them.

"But, where is he *from*, Frisha? What does he do for money? Does he have family? Why does everyone think he's a lord or soldier? Why is he going to Kaibain, and what does he plan to do once he gets there? What does he intend to do with his life afterward? Is he *married*?" Tam rattled off the questions that always seemed to visit him when he was alone but slipped his mind in Rezkin's presence.

Frisha looked momentarily uncertain as she considered Tam's questions, but then shook her head. She waved her hand around as if to wash them away and said, "I'm sure there is nothing to be concerned about. Nobody who acts like him could have anything terrible to hide. I'm sure it is all perfectly reasonable, and he doesn't seem to be hurting for money. We'll just ask him, and then you can be satisfied."

Tam reached up and pulled his hair in frustration. "But, what if you don't like what he has to say, Frisha? What if he lies?"

Frisha shrugged unconcerned. "It's just a scarf, Tam. It's not like we're betrothed. I'm sure it will all work out."

Tam watched his friend as she preened in the mirror once again and sighed. "For your sake, I truly hope so," he said before he turned and left.

10

The third day brought disaster. The ship was at a halt, and it looked like they would not be going anywhere anytime soon. They had come to a bend in the river, the captain explained, that was characterized by large, shallow sand bars. There was only a narrow channel through the middle that was deep enough to pass through. At the moment, that central channel was occupied by a partially sunken riverboat. Luckily, the river slowed at this point, so when the obstruction came into view, the crew had enough time to pull the sails around to slow the vessel and drop anchor. Several attempts at hailing the other boat failed, and the crew and soldiers were anxious to get underway.

The captain finally asked if Lieutenant Jimson was willing to send some of his men over to the other boat to investigate.

The Lieutenant scratched his scruffy chin, which was badly in need of a shave, and said, "I do not see that we have any other choice. It concerns me that we have not seen anyone, and they have not answered our hails. I believe it is either abandoned or everyone is dead."

The captain looked at the lieutenant sharply and said, "Dead? How might they all be dead? Yer thinkin' this ain't an accident."

The lieutenant rested his eyes on the downed vessel and said, "Captain, how often does a riverboat simply sink? And what are the chances that one would do so right here where our passage would be completely blocked?"

"Ye think this was done on purpose?" Captain Talwater asked.

Lieutenant Jimson nodded, "It is possible. It is a common enough ploy for bandits along the roads. They block off the road with a fallen tree or broken wagon and then attack when travelers stop to clear way."

The captain grunted, "It'd have to be one mighty gang of bandits to attack a riverboat, especially one full of soldiers."

"Perhaps it wasn't targeted at us," Tam piped up. "Maybe they just intended to attack *whomever* stopped here."

"Or maybe they are after the cargo," said Rezkin. He and the lieutenant shared a contemplating look before the captain spoke.

"Bah, I am still not convinced this is an attack. It's not common fer a riverboat to sink, but if it's goin' to, this be as good a place as any. It coulda struck somethin' in one o' these sand bars that busted a hole in the hull," the gruff man replied.

"Then, where are all the people?" asked Tam.

"They coulda gone lookin' fer help," the captain said. "It's a long way to anywhere from here."

Rezkin had made up his mind. There was no point in standing around talking about *what ifs*. "Lieutenant, I think it would be best if you kept your men here to protect this vessel in case this is an ambush. I will go investigate."

"By yourself?" asked Tam in dismay.

Rezkin ignored Tam and stared the lieutenant down. It was time to test how far the lieutenant was willing to believe he was more than he said he was.

Lieutenant Jimson finally looked away and spread his hands. "You are a civilian. You do as you please. If you want to go investigate the vessel on your own, there is nothing I can do to stop you. I think my men and I need to stay here for a bit to make sure things are secure and to strategize."

Rezkin almost felt a tug at the corners of his lips. He mentally applauded the lieutenant's creatively contrived method for discharging any responsibility for Rezkin's actions. As a result, he avoided calling Rezkin out in the open and questioning his station. Of course, the lieutenant would be completely within his rights to stop Rezkin from requisitioning the dinghy and placing his life in danger while the soldiers stayed onboard. It was the lieutenant's responsibility to investigate such situations and protect the citizens.

Rezkin nodded and went below deck where he quickly donned his padded leather armor and armed himself with more than the usual weapons he carried by default. When he returned to the deck, several people stared openly including Frisha and Tam. Rezkin realized that neither of them had seen him dressed for battle since he had forgone his armor when he was with them in the city to avoid attracting unnecessary attention. He shrugged off their surprise and boarded the dinghy.

Frisha leaned over the rail as the crew lowered the dinghy to the water. "Rez, be careful!" Frisha wanted to scream and protest that Rez could not go over to the ship alone. She did not want him anywhere near that ship if there was a danger. The only factors that had stayed her protests were Tam's tight grip on her arm and her resolve not to make an embarrassing scene in front of all the men. She could not help feeling baffled and bitter that, out of all the people on board—the grizzled old captain, the burly crew, and the kingdom's soldiers—it was Rezkin who was sent into potential danger to investigate the mystery of the sunken riverboat.

Rezkin rowed the dinghy over to the partially sunken vessel. It listed to one side, resting up against a shallower sand bar. He could not see any damage from his vantage, and his eyes continuously roved over the great wooden structure looking for any hint of danger. A slight movement from a window in the captain's quarters caught his attention. He could have easily played it off as a shadow or play of light, but given the circumstances, he was not going to take any chances.

Drawing the dinghy alongside the riverboat, he could just reach the deck rail with the tips of his fingers. He tied the dinghy to the loose end of a rope dangling from the side of the vessel and then reached up to cling to the rail with his fingers. He curled his body in on itself and swung his leg up until his foot caught the lip of the deck. From there, he easily pulled the rest of his weight onto the lip and slipped over the rail. Having donned his soft-soled, stealth boots, his footsteps were smooth and silent across the angled deck. He frowned at the sight of several score marks, but could not tell what had made them or if they were recent.

Rezkin slid Bladesunder silently from its sheath and held the short sword in his right hand while he drew a dagger from his belt. His blood heated, and his nerves tingled with the thrill of battle energy. The close confines of the ship would make sword work difficult, and it would be nearly impossible with a longer blade. He padded lightly up to the captain's quarters. Anyone inside would have seen him coming from the other ship, but now that he was aboard, the person could not know where Rezkin was unless the man poked his head out for a look. He lightly tested the latch on the door. It was not locked. He pushed the door open quickly, careful to keep it from crashing against the wall.

A man lunged forward from the dark. Rezkin twisted to the side, hooking his arm in the crook of the assailant's arm and used the man's own momentum to swing him around. He brought the pommel of his sword up into the back of the man's skull with an audible crack. Glancing around the room, he saw there were no other occupants. He lowered the man to the floor slowly, not to prevent any further injury to the man, but simply to reduce the amount of noise he made.

Rezkin tied the man with one of the many ropes available on a ship and stuffed his mouth with a wadded rag. He then took a moment to examine the assailant. The man was strong and muscled, but his skin hung loosely as though he had missed more than a few meals. He was scruffy, unkempt, and smelled as if he had not bathed in some time. The man did not look like he belonged to the former crew, and he was certainly not a soldier. He carried only a long dagger, which Rezkin had knocked away during the scuffle, and a slender boot knife, which he subsequently removed.

Leaving the foul man where he was for the time being, Rezkin slipped back out of the captain's quarters and padded to the back of the galley to peer through a small window. Hidden in shadows, he noticed someone was already at the window, presumably searching for *him*. He listened carefully from his vantage. At least two people occupied the room, and they both appeared anxious with restless motions and flustered chatter. Neither seemed keen on the idea of leaving their presumed safety to go in search of him. One of them asked if "the others" were in position yet. The other told him to shut up and wait for the signal. Now Rezkin knew for sure these were not crewmen or soldiers stuck on the downed vessel.

Rezkin could see the first man at the window and could tell fairly well where the second was by the sound of his voice. He slipped a throwing knife out of its sheath and flicked his arm forward. The knife spun through the air and sunk deeply into the man's neck. Before he hit the floor, Rezkin rushed forward and dove through the window. The galley was set up in exactly the same fashion as the boat on which he was traveling, so he did not crash into anything. With the floor tilted at such an angle, it was almost like jumping into a wall. He bounced and then swung his legs out so that he perched between the floor and wall. Immediately, he flicked another throwing knife into the chest of the man sitting at the table. Utter shock seized the man's features as blood burbled forth from his lips.

Once Rezkin retrieved his knives, he slipped out of the galley and headed for the stairs leading below deck. Applying the *Skills* he learned through years of practiced stealth, he managed to descend with barely a creak. The first two berths were ransacked, and one was covered in blood, but they were otherwise empty of brigands. As he approached the third berth from the shadows, he could hear two or more men speaking in hushed whispers. He glanced into the fourth berth to make sure no one would surprise him from behind then drew Bladesunder and his dagger as he edged closer to the other doorway.

Rezkin listened carefully to their voices to gauge their locations and then, with a running start, bounded into the room so fast the men had little time to react. He ran up the tilted floor in an arc slicing deeply into one man's back with Bladesunder. He kicked the second man in the chest, which sent him tumbling down the inclined floor. The first man fell forward as he died and slid down the floor until he crashed into his comrade. Rezkin controlled his descent down the wooden planks, and plunged his dagger into the abdomen of the second man. Not wanting to wait for the man to die, he drew the blade across the man's exposed throat.

After examining the dead men and cleaning his blades, Rezkin abandoned the berth to check the cargo hold. He was careful to inspect the berths again to make sure no one had come up already. The cargo hold was mostly under water and empty of brigands. Satisfied that the riverboat was now clear of threats, he returned to the captain's quarters. He tied a rope around the unconscious brigand's chest, lowered him into the dinghy, and then rowed against the current back to the other vessel. He knew people were watching him from the banks, and while he was too far away for a crossbow, he was still wary of arrows.

As he rowed, he checked himself for blood. Based on what he knew of Frisha, she would be upset if she saw any blood on him. He did not want to have to deal with a hysterical woman on top of an ambush. The crew lowered a rope ladder while he secured the dinghy, and he once again boarded the ship. Tam and Frisha were waiting to one side. Frisha was worrying her lip fretfully, and Tam did not look much better. He met each of them in the eye and said, "I am fine." Both of his *friends* released pent up breath and nodded.

Rezkin motioned to the captain and lieutenant to meet with him privately. "It was an ambush," he said. "I brought one of them back for questioning."

"One of them?" the lieutenant asked. "How many were there?"

"There were five aboard, but I overheard them speaking and expect more on the banks."

"And the other four? Where are they? Do they know he's missing yet?" asked the lieutenant.

Rezkin shook his head. "They are no longer a threat."

The ship's captain and the lieutenant stared at Rezkin for a moment. Both looked to him as if they were faced with a wild animal. The lieutenant slowly nodded. "Rezkin indeed," he said flatly.

Rezkin tilted his head. *What did that mean?*

The lieutenant said, "So, now we only have to worry about those on shore."

"I think not," said Captain Talwater. "I think it's time we get movin'. Ain't no point in sittin' here waitin' to get attacked."

Rezkin shrugged and said, "That is true. That vessel is not going anywhere. I am not sure what they did to the other boat, but there is a massive hole in the hull. We are going to have to abandon this boat and travel by land."

"I'll not be abandonin' my ship," the captain huffed.

Rezkin shrugged, "You do not have to, but I imagine it will be at least a week after it has been reported before anyone can pass through here. You can go back to Justain. My companions and I will continue on our way. Whatever course the lieutenant chooses is up to him."

Lieutenant Jimson rubbed his jaw in contemplation. "Our assigned duty is to guard the cargo, but our first duty is to protect the kingdom. If these brigands are willing to go to all this trouble and risk attacking kingdom soldiers, then they are aggressive." He nodded as he came to a conclusion. "I will send half my men back to Justain under Second Lieutenant Swin's command, and the rest will accompany me ashore. We will flush out the bandits, if we can, and continue to the fort at Lorelis to report. I assume you will be heading to Lorelis, as well, sir?" he said turning to look at Rezkin.

"I will discuss it with my companions, but most likely. Mine is the only horse, and the walk to Drennil would be much too long," Rezkin replied.

The lieutenant nodded, and satisfied that everyone was clear on the plan, the three went about making preparations.

Rezkin rejoined Tam and Frisha and explained the situation, leaving out the part about the dead brigands on the other vessel. Strategically, he felt it would be best if they understood the situation in its entirety, but up to this point, they had always reacted poorly when faced with fear and confrontation. During his studies on human behavior, he had learned such was a possibility but had not really understood the reaction until he had witnessed it in truth. He still did not completely understand except that it could make sense that people who were surrounded by others with *Skills* they lacked might feel intimidated.

"So, we have to walk to Kaibain?" asked Tam.

"No, we *could* walk to Drennil and obtain horses or river passage there, but it would be at least a few weeks on foot." He eyed Frisha and Tam, remembering their complaints after sword practice. "Maybe more," he added. "Lorelis is only about a week away. There, we can take the Lorelis River to Drennil and then continue via river, or we can purchase horses and travel the Lorelis Trade Route straight to Kaibain."

Tam and Frisha were nodding as he spoke. "That sounds good. I'm glad you're with us, Rez. I would be completely at a loss," Tam said. Scratching his head, he sheepishly remarked, "I'm not even sure where we are relative to any of those places. I just know we're somewhere on the river between Justain and Drennil." Frisha nodded in agreement.

Eyes widening, Frisha's next words came in a rush, "But, Rez, what about the bandits? The ones on the shore! Won't we be attacked?"

Rezkin nodded. "Probably, but I will protect you." Frisha and Tam's faces were twisted with doubt and worry. "Lieutenant Jimson and some of his men will be joining us," he added to put their minds at ease.

His *friends'* relief was evident, but the concern remained. Rezkin could not fathom how any of these outworlders lived long enough to be considered grown. How could people lacking in so many *Skills* and filled with such fear possibly function?

The captured brigand regained consciousness after about an hour, and both Rezkin and the lieutenant questioned him thoroughly. The man had little to share except that he had supposedly been approached by bandits who offered him a chance to make some gold. He did say that one of the bandits mentioned some kind of rebels, but he had little else to share. It was agreed that the captured brigand would accompany the ship back to Justain where he would be prosecuted and hanged upon being found guilty of at least a half dozen crimes.

After gathering their things and packing food and water, the three *friends* met back on deck. Rezkin had already discussed with the captain about how to get the horse ashore. It was not going to be easy. Nothing ever was with the aggressive, stubborn battle charger. Rezkin wrapped the horse in blankets to prevent chafing and then secured a number of ropes and straps around the horse's middle, across his chest and around his hindquarters. He then looped the ropes over a massive hook attached to the pulley system used to load large cargo. A number of the ship's crew hoisted the horse into the air.

With a fright, the battle charger kicked and thrashed wildly, but the apparatus held until the horse was lowered into the water. At the same time, Rezkin and his companions descended in the dinghy. Once the horse and dinghy were both in the water, Frisha and Tam steered the small boat while Rezkin disconnected the horse and guided him toward shore. The battle charger did not seem to enjoy swinging by ropes or swimming.

The group gathered on a large point bar in the curve of the western side of the river. Rezkin brushed the horse down and dried his back as best as he could before saddling him and loading up the packs. Several of the soldiers looked askance at the battle charger turned pack mule, but they had a long way to walk, and it was doubtful the horse would allow any but Rezkin to ride him. As soon as everyone was safely ashore, the riverboat raised its sails and began slowly making its way back up river. Without a full crew, the voyage would be long and tiring.

It was nearing midday when the group was finally ready to set out, and they wanted to get to a more secure location as soon as possible. They had already consumed a quick bite while going about their business on the riverboat, so they would not break for a while. Rezkin wanted to scout ahead and perhaps pick off any threats in stealth, but the lieutenant suggested the bandits might leave them alone if they simply passed through since they no longer had any cargo to steal. The lieutenant said that if he could get to Lorelis quickly, he or someone else could return to the area with a full platoon and flush out the bandits. The soldiers took up positions surrounding the three civilians, and the group moved steadily but cautiously into the trees.

After about an hour of tense travel, Rezkin patted his horse and implored him to behave before handing the reins to Tam. Tam looked at him quizzically, and Rezkin whispered that he would be back shortly. He fell to the back of the group, and none of the soldiers attempted to dissuade him. They had probably all heard about the dead brigands on the downed vessel by now and knew he could fend for himself. Rezkin had sensed someone following them ever since the river, but their pursuer was closing the distance. He decided to send the bandits a warning.

He slipped into the trees and doubled back, a silent wraith among towering giants that creaked and swayed in the breeze. His opponent apparently lacked stealth *Skills* as well as caution since Rezkin was easily able to track his whereabouts. While he was not making nearly as much noise as the people in Rezkin's party, it was easy to identify the occasional shuffling of leaves or crack of a branch under foot.

Rezkin swung himself up into a tree and waited for the bandit to pass underneath. As soon as his quarry was in position, he dropped down on top of the man. A swift twist broke the bandit's neck. Using a couple of sticks and some vines, Rezkin propped the dead man up into a kneeling position with his right arm extended so that his hand was raised in the common gesture meaning halt. Rezkin hoped the other bandits would understand the message and take it to heart. In truth, he wanted to kill all of the bandits himself, but he conceded that the lieutenant was right. He did not want to chance an all-out attack by a large force and risk his *friends'* safety if it was not necessary.

Frisha smiled at his return and asked, "What was that about?"

"I just needed to take care of something," Rezkin said.

The young woman's face flushed and she whispered, "I might need to relieve myself soon, as well."

Rezkin had not considered this problem. Frisha was the only woman in the group and the only one with whom he had ever traveled. For propriety's sake, she needed privacy, but he could not leave her alone. "If you can wait another ten or fifteen minutes, I will assist you. It is not safe at the moment."

"It will be safe in ten minutes?" asked the young woman.

"It will be saf*er*," Rezkin said.

Frisha nodded. After fifteen minutes, Rezkin called for a brief halt. He pulled Tam and Frisha aside and led them to a small clump of bushes out of view of the soldiers. He instructed Tam to keep watch in one direction while he stood sentry facing the other, each with their backs turned to Frisha.

Frisha's cheeks heated realizing she would have to do this out in the open and where Rezkin and Tam could hear everything, no less. Since there was naught to do about it, she pulled down her pants and relieved herself behind the bushes. When she was finished, the three rejoined the soldiers and the trek continued. The soldiers had also taken the opportunity to relieve themselves and rehydrate or make adjustments to their packs or boots.

About an hour before dusk, the lieutenant ordered his men to set up camp. They had left the wood behind a few hours prior and found themselves crossing through grassy hills dotted with smaller copses. It was within one of these that the group would overnight. The location consisted of only a few trees on the crest of a low hill. The higher ground would make it easier to keep watch, and one of the larger trees had long, leafy boughs that reached nearly to the ground. This would help to hide the light of a fire from the casual observer, break up the smoke, and block the wind. The other advantage to the location was a small stream that curved around the base of the hill.

The men went about making camp by gathering wood and digging a small fire pit. Rezkin went hunting for fresh meat in hopes of preserving their rations. He gathered his bow and arrows and disappeared for a short while before returning with a brace of hares and two pheasants. The group was impressed with his fortune, but it had not been difficult. These unpopulated hills were teeming with life.

Frisha helped pluck the pheasants, which was more work than she had expected. She had never had to do it before, and she now had a greater respect for her cooks. She kept some of the larger plumage thinking she could find some use for the pretty feathers. The young woman kept her mind on her task, trying not to think about the fact that she was alone in the wild with nine men. Her father would be livid at the entire turn of events. Tam was sworn to protect her, though, and she trusted Rezkin despite knowing him for such a short time.

When the animals were prepared and roasting on spits and the bedrolls had been laid out, everyone sat around the fire talking casually. Soldiers were set to watch in shifts, but of course, Rezkin would lend his *Skills* in his own way.

Lieutenant Jimson eventually turned to him and asked, "Sir, ah … Rezkin, do you duel?"

Rezkin pondered the question. He had achieved mastery of the *Skill* but did not particularly care for dueling as it was defined by the rules of engagement. A duel between an ax wielder and swordsman might prove interesting, but that was not the kind of dueling to which the lieutenant was referring.

Dueling, as defined by the kingdom's laws, was between two swordsmen and was rife with rules and protocol that were not practical in real combat. It was immensely popular among the aristocracy, nobles, and commoners alike, but it was not a particularly effective fighting style if both parties were not using similar weapons and techniques. Still, the nobles considered dueling to be a perfectly acceptable substitute for all-out war between the houses. Many lives and resources could be preserved if a disagreement were resolved between only a couple of duelers.

Finally, he nodded and said, "I do."

Tam clapped. "That explains the swords. I figured it had to be something like that since you're not a soldier." Tam was satisfied now that one mystery was solved. The young man had already realized that Rezkin was not the frightening, violent character that he sometimes seemed, but he had difficulty explaining the presence of the swords his new friend always carried. If Rezkin was a duelist, of course he would carry his sword, and he could easily see the refined young man being attracted to the graceful art form. Dueling was not considered to be a vicious sport, but rather one engaged in by gentlemen and nobles. In combination with the code by which Rezkin seemed to live, the explanation fit easily within Tam's assessment of his newest friend.

The lieutenant considered Tam with an odd look and then smiled at Rezkin as he spoke. "Good, I was hoping that you would consider practicing with me. I intend to join the King's Tournament this year. It is being held in Skutton, as you probably know. I have never been there before. I am no master, but I think I might make it into the third tier," he said with obvious pride.

"That's so exciting!" said Frisha with enthusiasm.

"What is the third tier?" Tam asked.

Jimson said, "The tournament is set up into five tiers so that duelists can compete against other duelists of similar ability. It would hardly be fair to pit a swordmaster against a man who had only been dueling for only a few years. This way, more people get the opportunity to compete, and there are prizes."

Rezkin shook his head. This entire tournament sounded like a blatant breach of *Rules 14—Do not revel in success* and *188—Do not engage in combat unless you must.*

"Competition is hardly necessary for advancement of *Skill*," Rezkin argued.

"Oh, I disagree," said Lieutenant Jimson. "I do not often meet other duelists who are of similar skill, so having the opportunity to test my abilities against them helps me measure my progress. In addition, I have participated in the tournament twice already, and each time I picked up new techniques from watching other duelists. It is quite captivating to watch a swordmaster in action, as well."

Rezkin nodded in understanding. When he had been training, he had several swordmasters available to instruct him every day. From what he knew now, it was pretty much unheard of for so many swordmasters to be gathered in one place for any length of time, a fact he would have to ponder later. Acknowledging that he had valuable resources most people would never have, he admitted to himself that the tournament did not sound as terrible as he first thought.

The spectacle, however, was unacceptable. The greatest prize of such an experience should be the opportunity to improve one's *Skills*. Fame and fortune were completely unnecessary. Rezkin wondered at why the king would allow such blatant violation of the *Rules,* but decided it was really up to the individual to comply with the *Rules* on his own accord.

"I heard that it's a scouting opportunity for the king. If you perform well, you could be invited to join the Royal Guard," Tam said. He leaned in conspiratorially and said, "I even heard that the top place winner could earn a place with the strikers."

Rezkin's ears perked. This was the first time he had heard anyone refer to the strikers since he had left the fortress. "What do you know of the strikers?" he asked casually.

Tam shrugged. "Only what everybody else says—that they are the king's elite forces. Not like the Royal Guards, but better. They are the ones he sends in for the really difficult and dirty tasks like spying or assassinations or stealth combat. That kind of thing."

One of Jimson's men, Corporal Lattery, added, "From what I heard, the king has his own assassin, but I think you're right about the rest. We've been told that if a striker ever reveals himself to us or sets foot on a battlefield, he's to be treated as a general, although they never go into any more detail than that."

"So, there will be strikers at this tournament?" asked Rezkin.

"Undoubtedly," replied Lieutenant Jimson. "You might see a few of them in uniform acting as officials, but most you would never notice." The lieutenant eyed the younger man speculatively and then continued. "They do not expose themselves except for formal occasions, and those are rare. They will be scouting for talent, most likely, and keeping the peace otherwise. I am sure you can imagine the problems that could arise when a bunch of trained swordsmen get heated up over a competition."

Rezkin nodded grimly. The gentry may accept dueling as an art, but there was nothing civilized about combat that could result in death. *Rule 14—Do not revel in success* applied to the battle itself, as well as the final outcome. One should not *enjoy* fighting another person, nor wounding or killing the opponent. *Rule 37—Separate from one's emotions* should always be observed.

Combat and killing were simply necessary tasks that should incite neither pleasure nor remorse.

Rezkin figured that if he could infiltrate the strikers by winning the tournament, then he could find out more about their purpose, and maybe shed some light on his own existence. If the strikers were so important to the kingdom and utterly secretive, why had they trained him since birth? Equally curious, why had he been ordered to kill them, and why had that order resulted in the masters killing each other? Rezkin had never really questioned the order to kill. He simply obeyed the masters (*Rule 258*). Now that the masters were dead and he was responsible for his own actions, he wanted to know what was going on, and he wanted answers about his past. Perhaps the strikers would have this information.

Rezkin briefly considered asking the strikers, but discarded the notion quickly. Since he had been ordered to kill the elite forces, they were likely his enemies. That thought took him to his next conundrum. If the strikers served the king, did that mean he was an enemy of the king and therefore of the kingdom? He mentally sighed. If that were the case, then he would never have been trained by the strikers in the first place. Something had to have changed that final day in the courtyard, and he needed to find out what that was. His best bet at getting that information was Striker Farson, but that seemed like a near impossibility at this point. Therefore, his second best option was to enter and win.

"I think, perhaps, I will join this tournament as well," Rezkin stated.

"That would be excellent!" said Lieutenant Jimson. "We could travel together from Kaibain. I already have permission for leave to participate. The army likes it when their soldiers win," he said with a smirk. "Have you participated in other tournaments?"

Rezkin shook his head. "No, I have never competed before."

"Hmm," said Lieutenant Jimson, "the tournament coordinators usually place you in a tier based on your performance in other tournaments. Since you do not have a ranking, yet, you will probably be responsible for determining your own level of skill and placing yourself appropriately. You want to join the highest possible tier for your skills, but if you place yourself too high, it will be your own fault for getting your hide handed to you."

Rezkin nodded unconcernedly. In his mind he was mulling over methods of hiding his identity. Others may deviate from the *Rules*, but he had no intention of doing so. Besides, if he really was an enemy of the kingdom, it would not do him any good for people to learn his face. From his recent observations of outsiders, he had come to recognize that his looks were a bit unusual but not completely out of the norm. Many people had black hair, although most had brown or blonde. Many people also had blue eyes, although the eyes were usually a bit darker with more grey or green. Few people seemed to sport both characteristics, though. Combined with his height and above average physique, he knew he was a memorable figure. In fact, with the combination of his looks, apparently unusual name, lack of title, and ownership of two Sheyalin blades and a battle charger, there was pretty much nothing forgettable about him.

A short time later, Rezkin and the lieutenant separated themselves from the group and found a clear, flat space in which to practice their dueling. Rezkin set his swords to the side to keep them from getting in the way and hefted the sword previously loaned to Tam.

"You do not use your own blade?" asked Lieutenant Jimson.

Rezkin shrugged as if the question was unimportant. "This is the same standard issue as your own?" he asked as if that would explain it.

"Ye-e-e-e-s," the lieutenant said as he nodded. He came to his own conclusion that the young man just wanted to place them on equal ground to start.

Rezkin adjusted his *Skill* level to match that of the lieutenant. The man would gain nothing from being defeated too quickly. At the end of the exercise, Lieutenant Jimson was sweating, and his breathing was heavy. Rezkin had barely loosened his muscles.

"You are quite good," Lieutenant Jimson observed. I think you are even better than I am. You should do well at the tournament."

Rezkin thanked him casually but politely and pointed out a few areas in which the man could improve. When they arrived in camp, they briefly continued their discussion of the dueling practice before their attention was captured by the roasted meat.

After everyone had eaten and finished their nightly ablutions, the three companions settled into their bedrolls. Frisha found herself sandwiched between Tam and Rezkin. She was at least an arm's length away from the handsome man, but she imagined she could feel his body heat soaking into her. Considering the circumstances, she felt surprisingly safe sleeping out in the open among so many men, even knowing that bandits might be lurking in the shadows.

Rezkin slept lightly, his mind constantly alert to the slightest sound or movement. At one point during the night, Frisha rolled into him and curled up against his side. He had never had anyone so close to him while he slept, and the experience was unnerving. He did not feel comfortable being in such a vulnerable position, even though he did not expect Frisha to attack him in his sleep. For one thing, it would serve no purpose. He was aiding and protecting her, so an attack on him would only hurt *her*. Likewise, she did not seem like the kind of person who would slip a knife between a sleeping man's ribs. But, did he dare put trust in that? There was a *Rule* against letting down his guard.

He tried to roll her away without waking the young woman, but Frisha simply snuggled in closer. He decided she must be cold, so he wrapped his blanket around her. After several minutes, she still had not moved, so he tried to force himself to relax into that place between sleep and awake, so he could rest.

Rezkin was startled when he suddenly awakened from a deep sleep. Rezkin was not certain he had slept that deeply before—*ever*. But, what was it that woke him? He started to rise when he realized he was entangled with Frisha who had wrapped her arms and one leg around him. Was she trying to keep him from leaving? Did she fear he would abandon her in the night? He would have to reassure her that he had no intention of shirking his duties. He carefully maneuvered out from under the sleeping woman. He had no idea how anyone could sleep so soundly. She would need to practice against such vulnerability.

Rezkin strapped his sword belt to his hips as he moved through the darkness out of the firelight, careful to avoid looking directly at the fire so he could retain his night vision. Corporal Lattery was on lookout duty and nearly shouted in surprise when Rezkin appeared beside him in the dark.

"There is movement," Rezkin whispered to the young soldier.

"I know," he replied. "I just saw. I was about to go inform the lieutenant.

Rezkin nodded. "Keep it quiet. They do not know we have seen them."

"Begging your pardon, sir, but we *haven't* seen them," the corporal replied anxiously.

"Four are coming up the rise over there in that gully. Two are crouching low in that brush over there, and five more are crawling through the tall grass twenty yards in that direction. I would guess a similar number are coming up the other side of the hill in an attempt to surround us," Rezkin said, keeping his voice low. "Go alert the others, but do not sound an alarm."

"Yes, sir!" Corporal Lattery whispered firmly with a quick salute.

Rezkin kept track of the corporal's movements in his mind and noted that someone else was moving from the campsite in his direction. Lieutenant Jimson arrived a moment later. After a few minutes, the lieutenant grunted softly and said, "Your eyes must be much better than mine. I can only make out a few movements that indicate their presence. I cannot determine any numbers, though. Five of my men are in position on the other side, and I told your friends to keep their swords on them and stay near the fire. I would not want them getting lost or killed by accident. That leaves you, me, and Corporal Lattery on this side. You think we can handle it?"

"It will have to do. When we are done here, we can go help the others," Rezkin replied.

The lieutenant frowned at him. "That was not what I meant. I meant, do you think we need more men on this side?"

"We are more than sufficient," Rezkin replied with surety. In truth, he could handle them by himself, but it would take too long, and some could slip by him. He would not turn down assistance when it was offered.

"If you do not mind, lieutenant, I will take the five on the right, you can take the four in the gully on the left, and the corporal can take the two in the bush," Rezkin said.

The lieutenant sucked in a heavy breath and tried to steady his nerves. Four was a lot, and he was not sure he could handle them all, especially if they came at him at once. For that matter, he did not think the corporal could take two at once if they were coordinated attacks. Rezkin noted the lieutenant's hesitation.

"If you both can hold them off for a few minutes, I will assist you once I have dispatched mine," he offered.

The lieutenant's breath released in a *whoosh*. He wondered at Rezkin's assertion that he could even take out all five men, much less do it quickly enough to render assistance to others. Lacking a better plan, Jimson decided to accept the offer in the face of their impending battle. He nodded once. "I think I can do that. Corporal?"

The corporal gulped. "Just hold them off? I think so. I'm sure I can take them both out if they don't come at me at once, assuming they aren't experts with the blade."

"I do not expect these to be masters of any sort if their comrades on the riverboat were anything by which to judge. You will probably be fine if you stick to the *Rules*," Rezkin said. The corporal was not sure what these rules were but nodded in agreement anyway.

"Okay, go," Rezkin said. He disappeared before either man registered his departure. Rezkin slinked through the dark, moving from shadow to shadow. The quarter moon provided just enough light by which to see, but the clouds and trees created pockets of darkness. Moving quickly but silently, he circled around behind the encroaching foes with battle energy coursing through his veins.

The bandits were spread out in the grasses in no particular fashion that he could discern. He dispatched the first without a sound, the man never even detecting his presence. Rezkin stalked silently to the rear of the second, and the bandit whipped around just as Rezkin bore down on top of him. Kingslayer sliced through the doomed man's gut, and he released a guttural moan as his intestines spilled across the grass. Rezkin drew Bladesunder across the man's throat to put him out of his misery. Red blood, black in the darkness, spurted over the ground, but Rezkin was already gone.

The noise from the last victim had alerted the next man in the line who jumped up with a shout. At just about the same time, the clash of metal and shouts resounded from other locations around the hill. Rezkin's third opponent ran at him with a growl, raising a one-handed battle-ax over his head. The man brought the ax down toward Rezkin's head, and rather than parrying the heavy weapon, Rezkin dodged and knocked it aside. The man swung his other fist around, which held a long, serrated dagger. Rezkin used his short sword to block the strike, taking the hand off at the wrist, and Kingslayer came down in an arc nearly splitting the man in two.

The other two attackers came at him at once, each wielding a two-handed longsword. Rezkin slashed at one opponent while blocking the other, keeping them both far enough away to be effective with his two weapons. Within seconds he had disarmed one and gutted the other. He dispatched them both without hesitation. The entire encounter had only taken a few minutes, and he could hear the heated exchange of metal on metal elsewhere on the hill.

Corporal Lattery was still exchanging blows with one of the two swordsmen, but he was bleeding from a deep gash at his shoulder. Rezkin slashed at the assailant's back as he ran by, and the corporal was able to finish the man. Rezkin ran toward Lieutenant Jimson's location, the corporal hot on his heels. The lieutenant was engaged with three of the bandits, while one lay dead in the gulley. Just as Rezkin and the corporal arrived, Jimson prevailed over another of the aggressors, leaving only two to eliminate. The three men made short work of these last and then sprinted toward the camp to assist those on the other side.

The fighting had spilled into the campsite, the five guards unable to hold the bandits at bay. Only four of the guards were still standing, and Rezkin could not see the fifth, so he knew not if the man lived. The guards were spread in a ring around the campfire protecting Frisha and Tam, who were both holding their swords in tight grips, wide-eyed and wild. Neither seemed to notice Rezkin's arrival, which was just as well. He did not want them doing anything senseless like abandoning the relative safety of the circle and running up to him. It seemed like something Frisha might do.

The campsite was surrounded by a dozen jeering bandits. Pride had managed to tear his reins from the branch that had had been holding him and was stomping furiously. He bit and kicked at the bandits, and after caving in one's skull, the rest of the intruders stayed clear of the enraged battle charger.

The assailants, apparently feeling secure in their numbers, were doing little to press their advantage. They satisfied themselves with terrorizing their prey for the time being. Occasionally, one or two would engage a guard briefly before backing away again into the pack. This all changed when the lieutenant, corporal, and Rezkin arrived and started laying into them on one side of the hill. Rezkin took down four of the bandits before the others around them even noticed his presence. Even so, those on the far side had yet to notice the disruption.

After thinning the number of bandits on one side of the circle, Rezkin slipped back into the darkness to flank the mass on the other side. Bandits, mostly hidden by night, fell into their final death throes as Rezkin scythed them down. He moved like a wraith among the fallen, and few challengers had enough skill to mount even a semblance of a defense.

After he defeated the final foe, Rezkin scanned the campsite to be sure no more bandits remained hidden. He noticed a sudden stillness around him and looked up to see Lieutenant Jimson staring at his swords. The other soldiers, seeming to sense their leader's alarm, gathered around and were now staring as well.

The lieutenant, whose eyes were riveted to the two magnificent swords, must have felt Rezkin's eyes on him and glanced up to meet his gaze. Jimson swallowed hard and tightened the grip on his sword. The frightening warrior's icy stare bore into him, and Lieutenant Jimson knew this was the face of death.

Noting the mounting tension, Rezkin sheathed his swords. The soldiers jumped at the sudden action. "Do you need to see my papers?" he asked in a deep, neutral tone.

The lieutenant's eyes flashed with surprise. "You have papers?" It was not possible that this young man had papers. The bestowing of a Sheyalin was a grand public spectacle, an opportunity for the bearer to receive acclamation and notoriety for his feats. Criers and news posts across the land would announce the event with almost as much reverence as crowning a new king. It was the highest honor of the land, one that had not been granted in nearly two decades.

Rezkin nodded once. "I do."

"Yes," said Lieutenant Jimson, certain he was speaking his final words at this very moment. "I am afraid I must."

Jimson tensed as Rezkin reached slowly into his chest armor, but rather than drawing the dagger the lieutenant expected, the young warrior pulled out a small metal cylinder about the width of his finger. Rezkin broke the wax sealing the cap and withdrew a rolled parchment. He held the small scroll out to the lieutenant and waited.

Lieutenant Jimson took the scroll with a shaky hand. He was not a coward by nature, but the things he had seen this night were astonishing. Never had he seen a man defeat so many with such ease. He still had not had time to process it all. If this scroll did not provide the warrior with the proper Certificate of Authority, which it surely could not, then Rezkin's life was forfeit by law, and he was required to carry out the sentence then and there. The lieutenant did not expect to survive the encounter.

But, why would the man known as Rezkin bother to provide any papers at all? Perhaps this was a forgery, or maybe he was simply giving the lieutenant a way to save face with his men and pretend he had seen a proper certificate, thereby enabling Rezkin to spare his life.

Lieutenant Jimson nervously unrolled the small scroll, anxiously pondering what he would do if such were the case. He was not sure what he would find, but he certainly did not expect what lay in his hands. His eyes widened to giant saucers, and he unconsciously let out a slow whistle. This was no forgery. He had seen the old king's hand and seal often enough for recognition, but this one was also backed by a hint of magic that forced the viewer to accept it as real—a mage certification. He glanced back into Rezkin's firm but expectant gaze and released his pent up breath.

"We're good," the lieutenant said hastily. He glanced around at his men and repeated, "We're good."

The soldiers felt such relief that they abruptly relaxed and felt happier than they probably should have considering they had just engaged in a deadly battle. Tam and Frisha were huddled together by the fire staring at the strange spectacle. They had not seen what initially caused the confrontation between Rez and the soldiers, but they were relieved that it appeared to be over.

Rezkin strode over to his *friends,* and Frisha threw herself into his arms. He stiffened, but forced himself to relax. He reminded himself that the young woman was *not* attacking him, and physical contact was normal in the outworld.

As soon as Frisha was in Rezkin's arms, the tears started flowing. She had been so frightened while they were surrounded by all those vicious bandits. When she realized Rezkin was nowhere to be seen, she nearly panicked. Only Tam's steady presence had reassured her and kept her from completely losing her wits. Tam had assured her that Rezkin must have gone to help the soldiers fight off the bandits. As a dueler, he would have enough skill to fight some of them, if he was any good. Thinking of it that way, Frisha nearly panicked all over again. What if something happened to Rez? What if he was killed?

"Don't *do* that!" She couldn't help but holler as she pounded a fist into his tight, oh so muscular chest.

"Do *what?*" Rezkin asked, utterly confused by the woman's sudden anger. If she was angry with him, why was she clinging to him?

"Run off like that! You could have been killed!" She hiccupped.

Rezkin took the woman by the shoulders and held her at arm's length as he captured her gaze. "I assure you that I am aware of my limitations. At no time did I put myself in unnecessary or overwhelming danger. At all times, I was cognizant of *Rules 8, 47, 147, 239,* and *245*. Of course, there are several other *Rules* that apply, but you understand what I am saying."

Wiping her eyes and sniffling, Frisha furrowed her brow and shook her head in confusion. "No, I don't think I do," she said quietly.

Rezkin waved away the concern. This was not the time to remind the woman of the *Rules* that should have been ingrained in her mind by now. "I was safe enough, is what I am saying." Changing the subject, he said to Tam, "You are well? You were not injured?"

"No, I'm fine, Rez. I didn't have to fight any of them. I was scared out of my mind, though. Some soldier I'll make," he said with chagrin.

"You would have fought them if one had come at you or Frisha?" Rez asked.

"Yes, of course," Tam said as though it did not actually *need* to be said.

Rezkin shrugged. "Then you will make a good soldier once you are trained. Do not mistake your ignorance or lack of skills for cowardice. It is a wise man that acknowledges his limitations. If you had attempted to engage those men at your current level of *Skill,* it would have been foolhardy. You would have gotten yourself, and maybe Frisha, killed."

Tam nodded and swallowed a sudden lump in his throat that had developed at the thought of him or Frisha dying. "Thanks. That does make me feel a little better about myself. I'm glad you're okay. I didn't see you here where the biggest group was, so I guess you caught a few stragglers?" he asked curiously. Lieutenant Jimson passed by at that moment and gave Tam another odd look.

Rezkin shrugged again and said, "Nothing I couldn't handle."

Frisha gasped and covered her mouth with a hand. "Oh, did you ... did you have to *kill* anyone?"

Rezkin looked askance and motioned around the clearing, "Of course, Frisha. These men were bandits intent on killing all of us. *Of course* I had to kill."

"I-I'm sorry, Rezkin. I didn't mean to be insensitive. It must be hard for you to go through this. I can't imagine what it would be like to kill someone. I think I would be sick if I did. I admire you for holding it together like you are. Just remember, you did it to protect us, and I'm sure it will get easier with time."

Rezkin furrowed his brow, stared hard at the woman, and then glanced around the clearing. What was she talking about? Did she think he was upset about killing the bandits? What else was he supposed to do? He could have captured them alive, some of them anyway, but then what would they do with them? The bandits would ultimately be put to death after a trial, so what would be the point in waiting? Although he was utterly confused, he lost the opportunity to respond when the lieutenant called to him. Fearing his dismay would show on his face, Rezkin chose not to look back at Frisha as he walked away.

Frisha felt terrible for Rezkin. He had probably never had to kill anyone before, and that was making it so much more difficult to talk about what happened. It was obvious he was distressed since he couldn't even bring himself to look at her. His eyes kept bouncing around the campsite as though he couldn't believe what he was seeing. He was clearly much more upset than he was admitting. He was putting on such a brave face. She sighed. She really just wanted to take him into her arms and tell him it was okay, but nothing she said would convince him at this point that what he had done was necessary. He would have to come to that conclusion on his own someday.

"Frisha," Tam said, interrupting her musings, "you really shouldn't push him like that. It's too soon. I'm sure he's trying not to think about it at the moment. Even as a duelist, he would not be used to death. It's rare that a duel is fought to the death. He's probably never even had to fight anyone outside of a dueling ring, much less a host of murderous bandits. Just give him some space. With whatever he's going through, he was still taking the time to try to make *us* feel better."

Frisha sighed. "I know, you're right, Tam. He's just such a noble man. It's hard to think of him being exposed to such terrible men on our behalf."

"There, now *you're* the one calling him a noble," Tam jibed.

Frisha huffed. "No, I didn't mean *that* kind of noble. I meant his character. Oh, you know what I mean."

Lieutenant Jimson had finally gotten up the nerve to confront Rezkin now that the adrenalin from the battle was fading. He called the strange warrior aside to talk in hopes that he could make things clear. Rezkin joined the lieutenant at the edge of camp, out of earshot of the others.

"You were going easy on me?" the lieutenant asked.

Rezkin cocked his head in confusion.

"When we were dueling. You were hardly trying," Jimson said.

"No, I was definitely trying. It is not easy to limit one's *Skill*. If I had engaged you with my full *Skills*, there would have been no practice," he stated succinctly with no hint of conceit.

The lieutenant stared at the young man, who was at least several years younger than he. "You are a swordmaster." It was a statement, not a question.

"Yes," Rezkin said.

"You are not a duelist." Again, a statement.

"Not by profession," he replied.

"Then you are …"

Rezkin simply shrugged.

Jimson, deciding not to push it, released a heavy breath. "Then, I am glad you are a friend and not foe."

Rezkin was surprised. This man was a *friend* as well? Why had he not said so when they first met? Now, he was even more grateful that he had managed to keep the man from getting himself killed. He could have failed in his purpose without even knowing he had done so. Just to be sure, though, he decided to check with Frisha about the validity of the assertion. She seemed to know about such things.

Even so, Rezkin nodded and stated, *"Rule 1—Protect and honor your friends."*

Jimson looked thoughtful and smiled as he said, "Yes, that is a decent rule by which to live." He glanced at the horizon and continued, "The sun will be up soon, and if it is alright with you, sir, we should be moving before the blood and bodies attract predators."

The group collected their belongings, and after making sure Pride was calmed, Rezkin strapped his new friends' packs to the horse's back. The battle charger was still agitated by the scent of blood, and his instincts and training made him more aggressive.

Frisha kept her distance from the beast, sure that it was possessed by a demon.

"I've never seen a horse act like that. He didn't try to run away. He was actually *attacking* people. It was terrifying," Frisha said.

Lieutenant Jimson nodded beside her. "That is the way of battle chargers. They are trained to not only carry their rider into combat but to participate, as well. Keeping one for a mount requires a firm hand and extreme dominance, characteristics that most people lack."

"*That* is a real battle charger?" Tam asked in surprise as he gaped openly at the massive steed.

The lieutenant looked at him quizzically. "Yes, they are rare outside of the upper military ranks. Even most of the cavalry do not have fully trained battle chargers, usually just the cast-offs or those that did not make the cut. The Royal Guard ride them only when escorting the king outside the palace walls, and the higher-ups in command ride them, as do the strikers." The lieutenant peered at Rezkin out of the corner of his eye. "The average commoner could not get one."

Tam, secure in his characterization of Rezkin, asked him, "Is that right, Rez? How did you get one?"

Rezkin shrugged, "I took him from my home when I left. There was no one else to keep him, and I needed a horse. I had already trained with him, so it was not a problem."

"Did you grow up in a castle, like a lord's estate?" Tam asked. This was the first time he had heard anything about Rezkin's home.

"It was more like a fort," Rezkin replied.

"Oh, that explains it—why you seem to have that military bearing even though you're not in the army," said Tam. "Did your parents work there?"

Rezkin shrugged, "I never met them."

"You're an orphan?" Frisha asked with compassion.

"I do not know. I never really considered it much. They could be alive somewhere, but I would not know who they are."

"So, who raised you?" she asked.

"The men at the fort. They trained me as well as they could so that I could one day become a grown man and fulfill my purpose. And, now I am," he said without embellishment.

"Oh, yes, you are …" Frisha sighed wistfully before catching herself. "Grown, I mean. You're obviously a grown man … and … very capable." She blushed and ducked her head. Tam snickered beside her, which she followed with an elbow to his ribs.

11

For seven more days, the weary travelers traversed the soft, grassy hills and sparsely wooded rises. No more incidents occurred, although there was much conjecture about the rather large gang of bandits they had encountered. It was unusual for so many to mass together and then employ such a well-organized, ambitious operation as they had on the river. Many hypotheses were postulated and even a few whispered of the elusive *rebels*.

By the time the companions arrived in Lorelis at midday on the eighth day, they were tired, dirty, and in want of a hot bath and soft bed. Frisha noticed her pants were a little loose around the middle and made a mental note to take them in when she had the opportunity.

After disembarking from the ferry that shuttled them across the Lorelis River, Rezkin, Tam and Frisha acquired a couple of rooms at an inn on the north side of town and waited for Lieutenant Jimson to call on them. The lieutenant and his men had reported to the fort straightaway, and he had mentioned that the commander might wish to speak with them.

After eating a hearty meal and washing, Rezkin could not sit still. He finally decided to run a few errands while the others rested. He gave his dirty laundry to an overly zealous maid and filled his coin purse before heading into the town. Since Lorelis was not a capital city, it was much smaller than Justain but still a decent size. Both the river and the north-south trade route that ran through the town were named for the city. It was a primary distribution center filled with many warehouses.

Lacking the cultural attraction and far from most influences of the nobility, the city remained largely functional. Fort Maneske was located at the edge of the city and served as the primary military post for troops west of the River Straei, so the city's culture was largely influenced by the presence of the soldiers. As such, crime was fairly low and lacked the organized guild structure that existed in the larger cities.

Rezkin made his way to the market and procured a new shirt and pants to replace the bloodstained set he had worn the night of the battle. Next, he resupplied his medical kit since he had used many of the bandages, ointments, and herbs to treat the wounded soldiers. Finally, he found a decent, serviceable, two-handed longsword to fit Tam. The weapon was not an expert blade by any means, but it far surpassed the quality of the general issue swords the soldiers had been carrying. Most importantly, the blade was perfectly balanced and held a razor sharp edge. The young man was built well enough to handle a two-handed weapon, but Rezkin had another reason for his choice. In the army, only the front lines of infantry were afforded shields, and if Tam enlisted with his own two-handed sword, it was less likely he would be placed on the front lines.

While he was examining the blade, Rezkin got an idea. He did not feel comfortable with Frisha confronting her assailants in close combat. The woman was slight and lacked the aggression and confidence necessary for a decent swordsman, or woman, as it were. It would also be considered unseemly in *polite society* for a woman to carry a sword. Rezkin did not care for such pretentiousness, but for all her talk and efforts to learn the sword, Frisha had refused to actually carry one. Rezkin inquired with the blacksmith and obtained a set of well-balanced, lightweight throwing knives. The knives were small and could easily fit in the young woman's petite hands.

Upon returning to the inn, he found his *friends* enjoying cool ale and relaxing among the few patrons who were trickling in before the dinner rush. He placed his clothing package to the side and laid the sword on the table in front of Tam.

"This is for you," he stated unceremoniously.

Tam's eyes widened, "What? Are you serious?"

"Of course," Rezkin replied. "You are in need of a weapon other than that dagger you carry. This one is the right size and weight for you and is better quality than what you will receive in the army. We can continue your training on the way to Kaibain."

Tam was speechless. He did not know what to say. He could probably have worked an entire year as an apprentice and not been able to afford this sword. The hilt was wrapped in green silk cord, and the scabbard was covered in soft brown leather. He pulled the blade partially from the sheath, since it would be considered rude to fully draw the weapon in the inn, and examined the blade. He did not know much about determining the quality of a sword, but he trusted in Rezkin's expertise.

"Rez, I don't know what to say. This gift is too grand. I don't think I can accept it." The words caught in his throat as he said them because he really wanted this sword.

Rezkin held up a hand and shook his head. He knew this would be coming since it was part of the *Polite Social Skills* he had learned. Anyone other than very close family should always attempt to reject a costly gift prior to accepting. It was now Rezkin's turn to make some placating statement. The whole exchange seemed frivolous since, in the end, the recipient was still supposed to end up with the item or risk offending the other party.

"You do not have to consider it a gift. It is more of an acquisition of necessary provisions, if you like. We still have a long way to travel, and you need a weapon. Besides, it is difficult to train someone to use a sword if he does not have one."

Frisha laid a hand on Tam's arm, "Oh, Tam, it's so nice, and you really do need one. You *must* accept Rez's gift."

"I am glad you feel that way, Frisha," Rezkin said with relief. He did not feel like having to go through the whole charade again with her. He laid a leather-wrapped bundle on the table in front of her. "These are for you."

Frisha's lips pursed in a surprised *o* as she untied the leather cord and rolled out the package. Inside were six tiny, shiny knives. The lamplight gleamed off the silvery blades as if fire elementals danced within the metal. The knives did not have a handle or hilt, but the tang was polished and smooth like the blades with the figure of a hawk in flight etched into each one. They were beautiful.

"Are these throwing knives?" Frisha asked.

"Yes, I think it will be a good weapon for you and will allow you to maintain your distance from any attackers. I will train you to use them properly so you do not hurt yourself."

"Wow, Rez, it's like Winterfest! Thank you so much," Frisha replied.

"Yes, thank you, Rez. I really do appreciate this, and I will train hard in honor of your generosity," Tam said.

Rezkin nodded once. "If I cannot protect you at all times, then I can at least make sure you can protect yourselves."

Tam glanced up and was the first to notice Lieutenant Jimson standing in the doorway. He waved the lieutenant over and invited him to join them. Lieutenant Jimson was washed and dressed in a crisp, clean uniform, all of the buttons and buckles polished to a shine. His face was shaved smooth, and his short hair was neatly combed. He was the ideal image of an officer of the king's army.

"Look what Rez gifted me," Tam said excitedly as he held the sword in front of him. The lieutenant took the weapon and examined it in much the same way Rezkin had, except he did not fully draw it in the inn.

He grunted and nodded. "This is a good weapon. Better than mine." He looked at Rez and asked, "Perhaps you would be willing to assist me in procuring a new one once we reach Kaibain. I would rather not use this one at the tournament, and I will need to practice for a while to get completely comfortable with a new one before the competition."

"Of course," Rezkin replied. "It will be no problem." The lieutenant was one of his *friends*, and he would do whatever he could to help him. He was just glad the soldier already had adequate sword training. It would be daunting if he *did* continue to find new *friends* and had to train all of them to protect themselves.

"So," said the lieutenant, "we can leave for Kaibain the day after tomorrow. That should give us a bit of time to rest. We are going to have to go by land, though. There is trouble on the Lorelis River. Colonel Simmons sent engineers to remove some kind of blockage over a week ago, and no one has heard from them. There have also been a few skirmishes with bandits. With the report I submitted of our troubles, Colonel Simmons thinks something bigger is happening. He's sending out a larger force to patrol the river and will be charging me with delivering a missive to the general in Kaibain."

"What do you mean by 'something bigger'?" asked Frisha.

"There have been rumors of some sort of rebel faction. Not everyone is satisfied with the way King Caydean is running things. Ever since King Bordran's untimely death two years ago, there has been talk. Bordran was not an old man by any means, and he had always been a strong, imposing figure.

He could have ruled for another twenty years, at least." The others nodded knowingly, and the lieutenant sighed. "There is more. It is no secret, but it is not yet widely known, that the king's brother, Prince Thresson, went missing two months ago." Lieutenant Jimson lowered his voice, "Some—not *me*, mind you, but some—are calling foul against the king."

"Why would the king want to harm his brother?" asked Frisha in hushed alarm.

The lieutenant shrugged. "The people who say this think that the king feels threatened by him. They seem to think the king might have had a hand in his father's death. They claim the king is paranoid that the same will happen to him, so he took steps to remove the threat. I am just saying what *some* people say, but I would prefer it if you do not spread it around that I said so."

"And, what do *you* think?" Frisha asked in wide-eyed amazement.

The lieutenant's face went blank, and he judiciously replied, "I think it is considered treason to speak against the king." He gave the young woman a stern look that said not to ask any more questions.

"Right, of course," Frisha whispered as she sat back in her chair.

The lieutenant raised his voice again to a normal level. "So, partly in thanks for your assistance against the bandits, and partly in hopes that you will assist me in delivering my message to Kaibain, the colonel has agreed to lend you a couple of horses. My duty is simply to deliver the message, and then I will be free to go to the tournament. I had hoped we could travel together?"

All three nodded assent as Frisha said, "Of course, lieutenant, you *must* come with us. It would make me feel so much better having you along. I can't imagine what would happen if we were attacked on the trade route."

The lieutenant glanced at Rezkin and grunted. "I imagine you would be just fine, but it is better to travel in numbers, just the same." Rezkin was listening to the conversation, but much of his attention was focused on a different young woman sitting at a table nearby. She was leaning over a little too far to be casual, and it was obvious she was listening to their conversation. He could not see her face since she was mostly turned away, but what he *could* see of her was atypical of outworlder fashion.

Frisha noticed Rezkin was staring at the girl sitting at the table next to them and could not help the surge of jealousy that heated her blood. She decided to call him out on his inattention to their conversation. "Rezkin, what do *you* think?"

Rezkin allowed his eyes to rove over the other patrons to see if anyone else was acting suspiciously but kept a close eye on the young woman. "I think it will be advantageous for all parties for the lieutenant to travel with us. As he said, it is safer to travel in numbers. In addition, he can assist in training the two of you in the use of your new weapons and help keep watch during the night. In return, I can ensure that his message is delivered per his orders. Traveling together to the tournament seems most efficient since group passage is usually cheaper, and his credentials will make our travel smoother. Most importantly, though, is that I prefer to keep my *friends* close, so having him with us means I can continue to remain dedicated to *Rule 1*."

Frisha frowned. She had not thought he was paying attention. Mostly, she just did not like him staring at another woman.

Lieutenant Jimson smiled and said, "Thank you. I do appreciate your companionship on this journey. It seems we will be traveling together for some time, and I would like to consider you all friends. Please, call me Jimson or Jim, if you prefer."

"Yes, please, let us dispense with the formalities. It does get so tiresome," Frisha said pleasantly even though her mind was still stewing over Rezkin's interest in the woman at the adjacent table.

Abruptly, and to the surprise of his *friends*, Rezkin stood and strode over to the table where the young woman sat listening to their conversation. All three of his companions were shocked. Frisha was just managing to contain her fury, poorly.

"Good evening, Mistress," Rezkin said with none of his usual charm. The woman's back stiffened, and her hands darted below the table. Without waiting to be asked, Rezkin sat in the seat across from the woman and leaned forward, holding her with his icy stare. "Since you were so intent on our conversation, I thought perhaps you would prefer to speak with one of us directly."

The woman was young. She could not be any older than Frisha. She had golden blonde hair swept up into a high tail at the back of her head. She wore a long brown tunic that went to mid-thigh over loose, dark pants. Her pants were tucked into high boots like a cavalryman might wear.

What was most unusual about the young woman was that she was wearing worn but serviceable armor. The armor looked slightly too large for her small frame and had probably once belonged to a young man. She was armed with a dagger and short sword at her belt. The sword's leather-wrapped scabbard was worn and frayed, but the leather grip on the hilt was new. On each arm was a vambrace into which was tucked a small knife. Large hazel eyes stared back at Rezkin, blinking in surprise.

"I wasn't—"

"Yes, you were. What is it that you want?" Rezkin's tone was brusque and assertive, brooking no argument.

The young woman's shoulders slumped, and she instantly looked younger than she had a moment ago. "Oh, alright. You win. I heard you talking about going to the tournament. I was going to approach you to see if I could travel with you. I want to compete."

Rezkin's brow arched in surprise. "*You* want to compete? I was beginning to think that no outworlder women learned such *Skills*."

The young woman lifted her chin in defiance. "I don't know what an *outworlder* is, but it certainly has nothing to do with being a woman. I am a warrior."

"Is that so?" he said. "Then you know how to use that sword?" He nodded toward her weapon.

She shifted uncomfortably and replied, "I do," but it was not the kind of response one would expect from someone confident in her abilities.

"What is your name?" Rezkin asked.

"I am Reaylin de Voss." She said it smugly, as if he should recognize her surname. He did not, which meant her family was not particularly wealthy, powerful, or influential.

"Well, Mistress Reaylin, if you are a warrior, why did you not join the army?" he asked.

Reaylin huffed and crossed her arms, a habit she would have to break since it left her vulnerable to attack and unable to quickly access her weapons. A fiery spark flickered in her eyes, and she snapped, "I tried. They said that I'm too small … or too weak … or not good enough … or not strong enough. What they really mean is I'm a woman." Reaylin was definitely a woman. She was petite and fit but all feminine curves.

Rezkin shook his head. "A few women have joined the army. It is rare, but it occurs."

"Yeah, well, those women are giants who might as well be men. But I can fight. It's not like all those recruits are swordmasters and strikers. If I can beat even one of them, they should let me in," she spat, her voice full of resentment.

Rezkin had to agree with her. If she could prove herself the equal of even the lowest man, she should be accepted. "So, in lieu of joining the army, you wish to compete at the tournament as a duelist?"

Reaylin shrugged and lifted her chin again. "If I make a good show at the tournament, they'll have to recognize me as a warrior and let me join the army."

"And, you felt it would be a good idea to travel on your own with a group of strangers? You have no care for this *propriety* that everyone seems to think is so important?"

For the briefest of moments, he saw a flash of uncertainty and a tinge of vulnerability in her hazel eyes, and then it was overcome by a fierce determination. "You don't look like bandits. That man,"—she gestured to the lieutenant—"is an officer, and you're already traveling with a woman, so I don't see any problem with it."

"We will be riding the trade route to Kaibain and then going on from there. Do you have a horse?" he asked.

The young woman's face flushed slightly as she shifted uncomfortably. "Um, I can get a horse."

Rezkin narrowed his eyes, knowing the statement was not as straightforward as it seemed. He shot a questioning look over the woman's shoulder at his three *friends* who were following the conversation intently. Lieutenant Jimson nodded assent, Tam shrugged, and Frisha refused to meet his gaze. She waved her hand at him as if the whole matter did not concern her. He was perplexed by Frisha's reaction. He thought she would enjoy having another woman along, especially one with whom she could spar and improve her *Skills*.

Rezkin looked back at the young blonde woman who was now turned in her seat to observe the others. "This is Lieutenant Jimson of the King's Army. This is Master Tamarin Blackwater, carpenter's apprentice and also a prospective recruit. And this is Mistress Frisha, Tamarin's charge. They are my *friends* and under my protection. I am Rezkin."

Reaylin grinned back at him. "Rezkin? Really? That's awesome."

When Reaylin stood to greet the others, he realized she really *was* small. He would almost think she was a small-woman if she was not already fully developed. She was at least half a head shorter than Frisha, which put her at just below his shoulders. He could understand why the army's initial reaction was to reject her, except that he knew size was not akin to *Skill* or the lack thereof. He had already seen that these outworlders' army training was sorely lacking, and with Reaylin's small stature, she would be at a serious disadvantage unless her *Skills* surpassed those of her male counterparts.

Lieutenant Jimson bowed slightly to the young woman in proper greeting, and Tam attempted to imitate the soldier's gesture. Frisha's polite smile did not reach her eyes, but she remained friendly, nonetheless. Rezkin gathered from Frisha's body language that she did not approve of the young woman who would be traveling with them for perhaps the next couple of months.

It would take the travelers about two weeks to arrive in Kaibain. From there, they could gain passage down the Tremadel River to Port Manai, which should take perhaps a week and a half. Due to the depth of the river, most ships traveling the Tremadel were galleons or carracks, which were much larger with deeper hulls and more sails than the smaller riverboats. The carrack could safely travel much faster and carry more passengers. Since the carracks were capable of sailing the sea and because of the high volume of travelers on the route to the upcoming tournament, it was possible they could find a ship in Kaibain traveling all the way to Skutton, but the travelers would most likely have to transfer to another ship in Port Manai.

Jimson had explained that every year the tournament was held in a different capital city. Skutton was the farthest capital city to the south, and with it being located on an island, tournament planners were concerned about a low turnout. As a result, the kingdom was offering heftier prizes this year than in years past to encourage participants to make the long voyage.

After everyone greeted the newest group member, Rezkin asked the lieutenant, "Do you think the colonel would part with another horse?"

Jimson glanced at Rezkin's Sheyalins. "I think he would be willing to provide you with anything you require should you ask."

Reaylin perked up and asked with a little too much exuberance, "Why? Are you someone important?"

"No," Rezkin stated flatly. Reaylin continued to blink at him questioningly, and the lieutenant seemed to recognize the need to appease her curiosity without causing Rezkin any problems.

"He recently helped us with a small matter, and the colonel feels indebted to him. It really is not a big deal. We will return the mounts to the army stables in Kaibain once we arrive."

"Oh," she replied cheerfully, "so I get a horse?"

Rezkin nodded and asked, "Do you know how to ride?"

"Oh, sure," she said with a grin. "I've ridden lots of times. Don't worry about me!"

Frisha and Tam were eyeing each other nervously. "Um, I've never ridden a horse," Frisha said quietly.

"Tam?" Rezkin asked, already knowing the answer.

"Well, I sat atop my master's mule a few times when I was younger. I, ah, usually drove the wagon," Tam replied, rubbing the back of his neck in embarrassment.

Rezkin simply nodded in resignation. How *did* any of these people ever grow to be big-men and big-women? "It is another *Skill* you will have to learn on the way," he stated.

Turning to Reaylin, Rezkin said, "We are leaving the morning after tomorrow. Be sure you have enough supplies. If you have any questions about what you might need, ask the lieutenant or me." He eyed her analytically. "You are suitably dressed and well-armed."

Frisha caught Rezkin's perusal of Reaylin's body and thought she might throw something at him if she had anything at hand. She had never seen Rezkin look at *her* that way. "What about me?" she asked, knowing she sounded like a petulant child.

Rezkin cocked his head at her. "You know I approve of your attire, Frisha. You have always been more practical than other women I have seen. Now that you have those,"—he pointed to the bundle of throwing knives he had given her,—"you, too, will be sufficiently armed."

Now that he had reminded her of the extraordinary gift and complimented her appearance, she felt silly for her reaction. Rez had been nothing but perfect since she met him, and here she was acting like a jealous lover. She blushed at the thought. Would she ever be able to call Rez her lover?

Tam rolled his eyes at Frisha's ridiculous distress. He asked, "Shall we all sit down and have a meal? I believe they are serving, now. I see a few people have already received their plates, and I'm famished." Jimson pulled out a chair for Reaylin to join them, and everyone retook their seats. Tam surreptitiously moved around to Rezkin's seat, so that Rezkin would be forced to sit next to Frisha.

After everyone had eaten and gone their separate ways, Frisha found Rezkin in the stables where he was checking on Pride. Tam was with him, and Rez was explaining the various pieces of tack and their purposes. Frisha listened to Rez's lesson, impressed once again at his vast knowledge and the easy way he had of explaining things. When Rez and Tam were finished speaking, Frisha found herself asking, "Um, Rez? When we *do* get to Kaibain, what are your plans?"

"My plans?" he asked curiously.

Tam was listening intently, now that they finally had the opportunity to solve this mystery. "I do not really have any plans in Kaibain. I suppose I will just resupply and ready myself to travel to Skutton."

Frisha furrowed her brow. "But, when we met, you said you were going to Kaibain. What were you planning to do there?"

"Yes, you are correct. I am looking for someone. I had thought to perhaps find information about him or his whereabouts in Kaibain, and I still may, but now I think I will have a better chance of doing so at the tournament," he explained.

"Oh, someone you knew at the fort where you grew up?"

"Yes," Rezkin confirmed without explanation.

"What about *me*—us, I mean? Tam and me?" she asked almost timidly.

"What about you?" Rezkin asked, certain he had missed something.

Frisha managed to lift her gaze from the floor to meet Rez's crystal blue eyes. "Well, I mean, will I see you again?" *That* was what he had missed. He had not even considered the fact that Tam and Frisha would not be continuing on to the tournament with him. No doubt she was concerned that he was going to abandon his purpose in protecting her and Tam.

Wanting to reassure the young woman that he would not abandon his duties and would do everything within his power to protect and honor his friends, per *Rule 1*, he replied, "Everyone has a purpose, Frisha. I know this. *You* are mine." As he said this he held her gaze in hopes that she would see his earnestness.

Frisha's heart stopped beating as her whole world lit up in a swirling mess of vibrant colors. "Oh, Rez," she breathed as she threw herself at the handsome warrior, wrapping her arms around his neck and pressing her lips against his. She knew she had surprised him with her inappropriate outburst of affection, but she just could not help it. When she finally forced herself away, his eyes were riveted on her, and they held questions. Was this a vulnerability she was seeing? Was he searching her for signs of her intentions? Surely he knew by now how she felt about him. No, his eyes did not quite look vulnerable, now. They looked … hungry.

Rezkin had no idea what had just happened. It was not the first time the young woman had crossed the acceptable barrier of personal space, but this had been so much more intense than the last. She pressed her body so close he could feel her every curve through the thin fabric of her tunic. Her body was warm and soft, and she smelled of lilacs. When she pressed her mouth to his, he froze. He had no idea what the woman was doing to his face. The only other time he had experienced anything like this had not been a pleasant experience. In fact, he had almost died.

Rezkin attempted to put the actions into context. He had just reiterated his vow to protect her per *Rule 1*, so maybe this was her way of accepting? What was more confusing was his reaction. He had *liked* it. The way her soft lips and warm breath mingled with his own, the way her breasts and body heat pressed into him, had made something stir deep within him that resulted in an unfamiliar feeling of pleasure. He was confused as to what the action meant and why she had done it, but he was certain he wanted to do it again.

Just as Rezkin thought he might grab Frisha and do just that, Tam cleared his throat. "Right, well, if you two are done kissing, maybe we should talk about Kaibain." Frisha's face turned a deep rose. She had momentarily forgotten about Tam.

Kissing? That had been kissing? He had heard the term before, but had never seen it in practice—aside from that one time, but at that time he had not known a name for the act, and it had been very different from *this*. He quite liked kissing, he decided.

Rezkin shook his head, forcing his attention back on to his surroundings. When had that happened? It was as though the moment Frisha's lips touched his everything he had ever learned just vanished. He suddenly realized kissing was *dangerous*. As much as he liked it, he did not think he could leave himself so vulnerable again. He would have to avoid it in the future … probably. Most importantly, he would have to figure out what had incited the reaction. He did not know why, but somehow he was absolutely certain he did *not* want to experience the same thing with Tam.

"What about Kaibain?" asked Rezkin, clearing his throat as he addressed Tam's question that he had almost forgotten during his musings.

"Well, do you know where you will be staying?" his friend asked.

Rezkin shrugged. "I suppose I will get a room at an inn."

"No!" Frisha said excitedly. "You will stay with me … us, I mean. At my uncle's home."

Rezkin cocked his head curiously. "You have a family in Kaibain? Your family is not in Cheswick?"

"Well, yes, my immediate family is in Cheswick, but my uncle and his wife live in Kaibain," she replied.

"And ..." Tam prompted firmly.

"And, that is why I am going to Kaibain," the young woman continued. Rezkin could tell she was skirting around the truth.

Tam crossed his arms and gave her a stern look. "Frisha, tell him *why* you're going to Kaibain."

"Well, I am ... um ..."

Rezkin was losing patience with the conversation. "What?"

"Looking for a husband," she mumbled, averting her eyes.

Rezkin frowned. "*Why?*" he asked, completely dumbfounded.

Frisha huffed with frustration. "Because I'm already twenty years old and still unmarried. My father says it's past time, and my mother actually *agreed*!"

"Ooookay," Rezkin drawled. "What does that have to do with Kaibain?"

"Well, you see, my father is a merchant, the most successful in our city. He's actually the head of the Merchant Administrators. So, he insists I marry well." She laughed and waved toward Tam as she said, "When we were growing up, we were so close that my father started to worry we would fall in love. He tried everything to teach Tam about commerce and trade, but Tam would have none of it."

"It was so terribly boring," Tam complained with a cringe.

"Anyway, he was relieved when it turned out Tam and I had no interest in that kind of thing. We were *too* close growing up."

"She's like a sister to me," he interjected.

Frisha nodded. "Exactly. So, my father decided to try to marry me into one of the Great Merchant Houses, but all their sons were too old or too young or just plain insufferable."

Rezkin was following along with the young woman's rambling but still was not sure what it had to do with Kaibain. He hoped she would get to the point soon.

"Well, then my uncle contacted my father and said he was going to name me his heir since he doesn't have any children of his own. My mother and father both jumped at the chance for me to marry into the nobility," she finished.

"Why would being named your uncle's heir help you marry into the nobility? Is he important?" Rezkin asked. He was familiar with important people and the nobility. This part might start to make sense.

Frisha sighed. "My uncle is General Marcum."

Rezkin was staggered at Frisha's revelation. He furrowed his brow in confusion as he said, "When we met, you told me you are not a lady. If you are General Marcum's niece, then you are a member of House Jebai."

Frisha wrung her hands as she answered, "Well, yes and no. You see, Uncle Marcum was the second son. His older brother, Simeon, inherited the lands and title." Rezkin nodded knowingly, and she continued. "Since he knew he would not inherit, my uncle joined the army. He worked his way up through the officer ranks, and after years of exemplary service and accomplishment, King Bordran named him general of the army."

"I am familiar with the accomplishments of General Marcum," Rezkin replied. Many of the modern battle strategies Rezkin had studied were first employed by the general during the last war between the Sandeans and Jerese to the far north and Channería to the east. Being long-time allies, Ashai had reinforced Channería, but once the Torreli joined the northern foe, the war spilled over into the northern territories of Ashai. Despite the enemies' greater numbers, the general had been able to push back the aggressors before they even reached one city in Ashai.

"Anyway, my mother is Marcum's youngest sister; and as I said, my father is a merchant but not a noble. Since my mother married a commoner against her family's wishes, she gave up her status and any children of the union are considered commoners. Since my uncle decided to name me his heir, though, I will be welcomed into House Marcum and considered nobility. Of course, if there had been land involved, no one would allow it, but I am only inheriting my uncle's personal wealth and estate."

"So you are a lady who was raised as a commoner," Rezkin mused. "The nobility will not accept you as an equal. It will be very difficult for you."

Frisha nodded sadly and replied, "Socially, yes. They will always see me as the woman with commoner blood. Between my father and my uncle, though, my dowry is substantial, so there are plenty of minor lords or second or third sons who will be willing to marry me."

"I see," Rezkin said. Where did that leave *him*? If Frisha married some noble, then she would already be well protected. She would no longer need him. Somewhere in his mind he had *known* that, as a woman, Frisha was expected to marry and bear heirs. With everything that had been happening, he had not really considered the possibility that it might occur sooner rather than later. He felt a nagging tightening in his gut. He was not comfortable with the situation, but he did not know why. Usually, his gut instincts were correct, but he could not place the feeling at the moment.

Realizing that Frisha's personal relationships were none of his concern, unless they caused her harm, Rezkin decided to simply put it from his mind. It was none of his business, and he had other matters to which he needed to attend. Without having to worry about protecting Frisha, he could focus on Tam and Jimson. Perhaps he would end up joining the army, after all.

Rezkin shook off the discomfort in his chest and said, "Thank you, Frisha, for informing me." He looked over at Tam, who was watching him closely. "Is there anything else you wished to discuss tonight? It is getting late."

"No," said Tam with a hint of empathy. "I think we're good. I'll be up soon if you want to go ahead."

Rezkin nodded and walked away into the darkness.

Tam immediately turned on Frisha. "What was that? I thought you wanted him, Frisha?"

"What? I do! I mean, what are you talking about?" Frisha asked in alarm.

"Think about it. The man just told you that you are his purpose in life, and you told him all about how much money you have and all the nobles who will want to marry you. Rezkin doesn't have any family, remember? He was raised in a fort. He probably doesn't own any property. He most likely carries everything he owns with him. You made him feel like he wasn't good enough for you. Now, he thinks you don't want him."

Frisha's hands flew to her mouth as she gasped, "What!? No! I didn't mean …" She glared at Tam in anger. "You were the one who kept pushing me to tell him!"

"I wanted you to tell him why you were going to Kaibain—that you were looking for a husband. I wanted you to let him know that you were interested. I didn't expect you to throw it in his face that he was so much less than your potential suitors!" Tam scolded before stomping out of the stable.

"Tam! Tam!" Frisha called. "You know I didn't mean it like that!"

Tam whirled on her, "You had better make this right, Frisha. Right now it looks like you've been stringing him along. He doesn't deserve this. He's a good man."

When Tam returned to the room, Rezkin was nowhere to be seen.

12

After leaving Tam and Frisha in the stables, Rezkin had returned to his room only to realize there was no way he could sleep. He was restless. He needed some action, so he decided to put his *Skills* to use. He donned his stealth gear and snuck out of the inn via the window in his room and made his way across the city by rooftop. Where the roofs were not close enough together, he descended into the shadows of the dark alleys and scurried along in secret. Once he reached Fort Manaske, he found it easy to breach. He already knew the layout and typical guard schedules and routes from his studies with the masters and strikers. Now that he knew more about the strikers, it made sense that they would have that kind of information. There had been times when some of the strikers would leave the fortress for weeks at a time and return with fresh information. The question was, *Why?*

Tonight, though, Rezkin would be the spy. He wanted to find out more about these rebels of whom the lieutenant spoke. After scaling the wall and dodging the patrol, Rezkin slipped from shadow to shadow across the yard and into a dark alcove. Intent on entering the building through a second story window, Rezkin clambered atop a sturdy barrel and launched himself into the air. He caught hold of an iron hook jutting from the wall that was meant to hold a lantern. His forward momentum and strength carried him higher still, and he flipped into the air once before catching the stone sill of the window. Rezkin pulled his body up to perch in the sill while he worked at the window catch. The glass panes swung silently inward, and Rezkin slipped into the darkness.

After closing and latching the window, Rezkin skulked through the dark office. His actual target was across the hall and one door down. He listened closely and then nudged it open. The corridor was dark and empty. Rezkin padded softly over the stones and stopped outside the colonel's office. The young spy slipped his lock picks from the pouch at his belt and easily disarmed the mechanism. *Someone really needs to upgrade the security around here*, he thought. He closed and locked the door behind him.

As a security measure, this room had no windows, but that only made Rezkin's job that much easier. He unwound some of the strips of fabric that he had wrapped around his frame. These strips served two functions. First, they held his clothes tight to his body to keep them from getting caught on things. Second, they could be removed for use in other capacities like tying or hanging objects or people or wrapping wounds, if necessary. At this moment, Rezkin stuffed them under and around the doorframe to prevent any light from leaking out when he lit the lamp.

Once the lamp was lit, he moved about the office swiftly. He carefully thumbed through papers in drawers and baskets atop the desk and found nothing but staff reports, inventory logs, and other mundane business. Lastly, he checked the sack of outgoing correspondence. Each of the messages was stamped with the colonel's seal ready to be delivered. The intruder heated a thin knife in the lamp flame and slipped it carefully under each seal so as not to disturb the wax. Rezkin read through each missive, even finding those that Lieutenant Jimson was intended to carry.

A few of the messages to other commanders mentioned the rebel threat but did not go into detail. One of the letters outlined the locations and numbers involved with attacks in the last few months. Another appeared to be a reply to a previous letter from a Striker Hendina. It briefly mentioned the missing prince and wished the captain luck in his investigation.

Two letters caught Rezkin's eye that were nearly exact duplicates. They were both about *him*. They provided his name and description and identified him as a sword bearer. The letters described his recent adventure with the bandits and his future plans. They even included the names and descriptions of his companions. One was addressed to the king's seneschal, and the other was, interestingly, addressed to General Marcum.

After only a moment's consideration, he returned the general's letter to the bag, but slipped the letter to the seneschal into his pocket with the intention of destroying it later. Then again, it was a letter addressed to the seneschal with the colonel's seal, and if he were to deliver it himself, it could easily be interpreted as a letter of introduction. Some people would pay a small fortune to have such a letter in their possession.

Making sure everything was back in order, he returned the room to darkness. Rezkin waited several moments while his eyes adjusted to the lack of light. After retrieving the strips of cloth from around the door and winding them back around his body, he slipped out of the colonel's office and back down the hall. Escaping the fort without being observed was easier than getting in since the guards were looking for people entering, not leaving. Rezkin made his way back through the city without incident, and the difference between the peaceful Lorelis and the crime riddled capital city of Justain was never more apparent.

Rezkin climbed to the second-floor window of his room, which cast a small amount of light into the alley since Tam had left a candle burning. One glance through the window, and he had to smile. Was this his first genuine smile? Perhaps.

He drew his thin dagger, nudged the window open a hair's width, and slipped the dagger into the crack between the window and the sill. Very carefully, he used his dagger to press down on the tip of the dagger Tam had placed in the sill like Rezkin had shown him. Sliding the window up the rest of the way, he quickly snatched Tam's dagger before it fell. Tam was snoring contentedly in his bed. Rezkin closed the window and replaced Tam's dagger. The door had been barred, but there was no dagger to alert Tam when Rezkin entered. Tam must have realized the bar would not hinder his entrance.

The next morning, Tam woke to see Rezkin sleeping in his bed. He had no idea when Rezkin had returned the previous night, but it had to have been very late. Tam had stayed up most of the night out of concern for his friend. When Rezkin disappeared just after his conversation with Frisha, he understood that Rezkin had been more upset than Tam previously realized. Rez was so steady and ... *solid* ... and he always acted like a gentleman, especially toward Frisha. Someone who did not know Rez might have thought him unaffected with his stoic demeanor, but Tam knew Rezkin had been devastated. He hoped that Rez had not gotten into any trouble during the night.

Dressing as quietly as he could, Tam slipped out the door and went down to the common room for breakfast. It was well past sunrise, another reason he knew Rez was not well. Frisha was drinking a cup of tea while waiting on her food to arrive. Tam joined her at the table and waited to be served.

Frisha cleared her throat. "Um …. where's Rez?"

"In bed," Tam stated shortly.

"Oh," Frisha said with surprise. "That's unusual for him. Is he unwell?"

Tam gave her a flat look. Frisha had the grace to blush, but said nothing. "He was out all night. I would not expect him to get up before noon if he were me."

The young woman gasped, "*All* night? What could he have been doing *all* night?"

Tam shrugged. "I am sure I don't want to know," he said cryptically. He knew he was being mean, but he was furious with Frisha for the way she had treated Rez. Frisha had not intended to hurt Rez, Tam understood, but he did not think that made any difference to his friend. It sounded like Rezkin had endured a hard life growing up. It did not seem like there could have been a lot of love to go around under the conditions he had described. Rezkin had somehow attached his heart to Frisha, and Tam's childhood friend had bungled it.

"Ohhh." Frisha moaned, hiding her face in her hands. "I've really messed things up, haven't I? I really didn't mean to hurt him. It all just came out wrong. How can I fix this?" she begged.

Tam shook his head. "I don't know. I guess you should just tell him how you really feel. How *do* you feel, Frisha? Do you even *want* him? Is this just a temporary fling until you find your nobleman? Would you really be willing to give up wealth and status for a man who essentially amounts to a well-mannered vagabond?"

"Tam! You know me. You know I don't care about being a lady or wealth and status. I'm fine with being a commoner. And, I think I *do* want Rez. He's everything I always dreamed a man should be. It doesn't matter to me that he owns little and has no family," Frisha said.

"So you *do* want to marry him?" Tam asked outright.

"Well, we haven't known each other long, barely a couple of weeks, but it wouldn't be any different if I were to marry a noble. If I had to say yes or no right now, I would definitely say *yes*."

"Okay, just … just don't hurt him, Frisha," Tam said. "He doesn't deserve it."

"I know," she replied softly.

Rezkin had heard Tam, who could not move quietly to save his life, moving around the room. He had been asleep only for a couple of hours and knew he would not be able to sleep much longer, despite having stayed up all night. The sunlight was streaming in the window, and people were moving about outside. Finally, he could stand it no longer. He dressed quickly in a dark blue shirt and grey pants. He strapped on his swords and secreted away his daggers but left his armor behind. When he entered the common room, Frisha and Tam were just finishing their breakfast.

Rezkin took a seat at the table with his *friends*, but the mood was somber. "What is wrong?" he asked. "Is something amiss?"

Frisha worried her lip anxiously and glanced at Tam. Tam nodded once and then said, "I'll just be up in the room."

Rezkin cocked his head as he watched the young man leave. "Is he upset?" he inquired.

"Yes, a bit," Frisha answered honestly.

"Did I fail in some way?" Rezkin asked. He did not think he had dishonored Tam in anyway, but maybe his *friend* was upset that Rezkin had not been in the room last night. Had Tam been concerned?

"No, not at all. He's actually upset with me," Frisha replied.

Rezkin did not ask why Tam was upset with Frisha. It was none of his business, and he really did not wish to get involved in a dispute between his *friends*. What if they asked him to choose a side? He would not be able to honor one without dishonoring the other.

"Rezkin, may I speak with you for a moment?" Frisha asked anxiously.

Were they not already speaking? "Of course," he replied.

"When … when we're in Kaibain," she said, "it's just … I don't want you to go. I want to be with you."

Rezkin nodded. "Then you can come with me," he replied.

Frisha's eyes widened. "Come with you?"

He nodded once again. "To the tournament," he said.

"You … you would like me to go with you?" Frisha asked in pleasant surprise.

"I want you to always be with me," he stated with resolve. It was so much easier to protect her when she was with him. He had been fretting over how to do so when he would be so far away. If she came with him, it would solve his dilemma.

"You do?" she beamed excitedly.

"Yes, of course," he said. "That is, unless you marry one of those nobles. I cannot see taking you with me after that."

Frisha was tearing up now. "Oh, Rez, I don't want to marry a noble."

"Good, then it is settled. You will come with me," Rezkin stated with finality and gave her his best smile.

Frisha swooned in happiness.

After finishing his late breakfast, Rezkin took Tam and Frisha into the courtyard where he started Frisha's training with throwing knives and continued Tam's sword lessons. After breaking for the midday meal, Frisha and Tam needed to go to the market for supplies, and Rezkin felt obliged to accompany them. On the way out of the inn, they encountered Reaylin, who made an extra effort to step into their path, effectively bringing them to a halt.

"Where are you guys going?" she asked. She had a way of speaking a little too loudly even when raised voices were not required.

Tam looked at her sideways. "We are going to the market," he replied.

"Great! Let's go," Reaylin nearly shouted. Tam scowled at the young woman's audacity. She had not even been invited, and now she was ordering them around.

The rest of the afternoon was spent perusing market stalls and collecting odds and ends. Rezkin ordered a supply of oats to be delivered to the inn for the horses. Since they were not taking any pack animals, a good amount of grazing would have to suffice. The land between Lorelis and Kaibain was much the same as that which they crossed on their trek from the river, so there would be plenty of grasses to be had. The group returned to the inn that evening so they would not have to spend additional money on a meal. After dinner, the travelers bathed and packed anything they would not need before their departure.

Lieutenant Jimson arrived with the horses just as the sun was beginning to lighten the sky. The beasts were large and sturdy, as would be expected of army horses. The smallest was a pretty palomino mare that was still a bit too large for Reaylin, but it would have to suffice. Reaylin did not seem to mind as she went about securing her pack behind the saddle.

Tam and Frisha stood cautiously at a distance not really knowing what to do with the beasts. Both were chestnuts, one gelding and one mare. Tam's mare had a white star on its head and white fetlocks. Frisha's mount was a hand or so shorter and had darker fetlocks and a nearly black mane and tail. Jimson rode a dappled grey gelding. At first, the other horses nickered and shied away from Rezkin's massive black charger, but they eventually settled to follow his lead.

Their first day on the trade route, the travelers did not get as far as Rezkin had hoped due to Tam and Frisha's inexperience and complaints of saddle sores. Reaylin had not ridden often and was also quite sore, but true to her word, she was a competent rider. Since they did not reach the village where they intended to stay, the travelers were forced to camp off the road. Many nights of camping were to be enjoyed on this journey.

Jimson went about setting up camp while Frisha and Tam gathered firewood. Reaylin and Rezkin both had bows, so they set out to hunt for fresh meat. Rezkin took the opportunity to scout the area and found that, as expected on the route, people had passed through recently. Luckily, none were in the vicinity at that time.

When everything was situated and a brace of rabbits was roasting over the fire, Reaylin sidled up to Rezkin. She stood much closer than was comfortable for him, but he made no overt moves to stop her.

Reaylin tilted her head far back and said, "Wow, you really are a big guy, huh?" She shifted her weight placing one hand on a cocked hip and grinned with a twinkle in her eye. "Are you so big *everywhere*?" she asked demurely through thick lashes.

Reaylin took a small amount of sadistic pleasure in the gasp that emanated from Frisha's throat. Frisha could not believe the audacity of the little blonde tramp, and how dare she behave so with Rezkin. Rezkin, however, was considering the question seriously. Why would the young woman be so concerned about his size? It did make a certain sense that, given her short stature and the discrimination she had received because of it from the soldiers, she would naturally focus on size as being of great importance. Rezkin, of course, disagreed.

Looking down at the petite woman he replied, "Obviously, I am large, but size is not necessarily of the most significance. What is most important is one's *Skill*."

"Oh," she said sweetly, "Have you many skills?"

Rezkin nodded in the affirmative. "I have mastered all of the *Skills*," he stated succinctly.

Reaylin grinned and reached out to stroke his arm. Rezkin withheld his instinct to thrust the young woman away or knock her unconscious. "Is that so? Perhaps you would be willing to show me some of your skills, then?" she asked suggestively.

"Certainly," Rezkin said. "You can join Tam and Frisha in their weapons training if you like." With this statement, he turned and walked away.

Tam and Frisha who had been completely shocked during the entire exchange could not possibly hold back their laughter at the look of stunned dejection on Reaylin's face. Reaylin glared at them over heated cheeks and then stormed into the dark trees. Frisha, having been furious during the last few minutes of conversation, tried to maintain her composure but could not hide the satisfied grin that graced her lips. When Rezkin glanced up from riffling his pack, she gave him a stunning smile of approval.

Tam walked over to Rez and remarked, "You really have a way with women."

"What?" Rezkin asked in confusion.

"Yeah, they all seem to flock to you. Now you have them throwing themselves at you. But, you handled Reaylin well. She was being way too forward, especially in present company. I think you managed to put her in her place. I don't see her doing that again. It's just as well. Someone needed to teach her."

Rezkin had no idea what Tam was talking about. All he had done was agree to teach her weapons *Skills*. He had attempted to dispel the misconception that her size was a limitation on her advancement as a warrior. Was that the lesson to which Tam was referring? Since Reaylin was not one of his *friends*, Rezkin did not feel truly concerned. She was not his responsibility. Rezkin shrugged and replied, "It does not matter so much to me. She will learn or she will not. It is up to her."

"I'm starting to regret letting her come with us," Tam stated as he stared in the direction Reaylin had gone.

"Why is that?" Rezkin asked, suddenly alert. Had Tam picked up on some sign Rezkin had missed that indicated the woman was a threat?

"I just … I don't trust her. I don't know why, but there is something wrong with that girl," Tam replied.

Rezkin nodded and said, "You should listen to your instincts. Sometimes your mind picks up more than your consciousness. We will keep an eye on her, and if she becomes a problem, I will take care of it."

Tam eyed Rezkin quizzically and then shrugged. "You're the expert on women. I'll leave it up to you."

Several more days passed, each nearly identical to the last. They would rise at dawn, ride until midday when they would break for lunch, and then ride until about an hour or two before sunset. In the evenings, Rezkin trained his *friends*, including Lieutenant Jimson and Reaylin, in their various weapons.

After Reaylin had stormed off the first night, she had sulked for a while and remained aloof around Rezkin. There was no end to her annoyance of Tam and Frisha, though. It was as if she was taking out her anger toward Rezkin on his *friends.* The girl was hotheaded, defensive, and prone to bragging. She went on and on about her exploits as a warrior, which were no doubt largely fictionalized. Jimson tried to maintain a distance from the whole mess. Reaylin mostly ignored his presence, probably only because he was an army officer.

One day, after the midday meal, Frisha invited Rezkin to take a stroll with her before they continued their ride. She said she needed to stretch her legs, but she really just wanted the opportunity to be alone with the handsome warrior. When they returned to the group, they were speaking amicably, and Frisha was smiling and laughing softly.

Reaylin decided she had to put aside her sore feelings and try another method if she was going to get Rezkin to notice her.

That night as the others were setting up camp, Reaylin approached Rezkin once again. "Rez?" she said sweetly. "May I speak with you a moment?"

"Of course," he replied. The two walked a few paces away from camp to speak in private.

Tam and Frisha watched Rez and Reaylin walk into the deepening shadows. Frisha scowled and huffed, "What is that hussy up to, now?"

Tam shrugged, "I don't know, but I wouldn't worry about it. Rez can handle himself."

Frisha turned her glare on her best friend, "I'm not worried about him handling *himself*. I worried about him handling *her*."

The young man sighed loudly. "Oh, come on, Frisha. You know he's totally smitten with *you*. He doesn't want Reaylin. He's probably just going to have a talk with her about how annoying she's being. I know *I* would be glad for it to stop."

Frisha was only mildly mollified. "Hmf. If she tries to steal him from me I'll … I'll …"

"You'll what?" asked Tam with a smirk.

"I don't know, but it won't be pretty!" Frisha snapped.

Lieutenant Jimson sat quietly off to the side taking in all the drama. On the one hand, he was glad he was not a part of it. On the other, he kind of wished

Reaylin would give him even a small amount of interest. He had been drawn to her from the beginning. Her petite frame and womanly curves were enticing, and he enjoyed that fiery spark that seemed to put everyone else on edge.

Jimson knew he had no chance of competing with Rezkin, though, so he would just have to bide his time until the girl realized the young man would not be swayed. It was no secret that Frisha favored Rezkin, and it appeared that the warrior returned her affections, although he was subtler in expressing his interest.

Reaylin turned to Rezkin more anxious than she expected. "Look, Rez, I just wanted to apologize for my behavior. It was inappropriate and forward. Before, I thought that maybe we could … well … but, now, I am hoping we can be friends."

Rezkin cocked his head in contemplation. She wanted to be his *friend*? Was that even possible? He was not sure how to make someone into a new *friend*. Did she have to be inducted? Did she need to contact the leader of the group and submit an application? Was there some protocol for selecting new *friends*? He really did not know how the whole process worked. It would be best to discuss it with his other *friends* before he gave her an answer.

"I do not know, Reaylin. I will consider it. I should discuss it with Frisha, but I think she is a little upset with you right now," he replied honestly.

"So, you and Frisha are … *together*?" she questioned coyly as she twisted the end of her ponytail in her fingers.

"She has agreed to stay with me," Rezkin answered.

"Oh," Reaylin said suddenly feeling very embarrassed. She had not realized Frisha and Rezkin were so serious. She could see, now, that she had never really had a chance with him, and she had offended Frisha. "I guess I've been kind of a jerk to her."

Rezkin was unfamiliar with the term *jerk*, so he just shrugged and said, "You would have to talk to her about that."

"Yeah, I guess I should," Reaylin said. "I'm just not like her, though. She acts so perfect and proper. Just like all the other women I don't get along with."

He considered her words and replied, "I do not agree. I have seen many women …"

"I bet you have," Reaylin said. She flushed as she realized her mouth had gotten away from her again.

Rezkin frowned at her in confusion but continued. "And she does not dress or act like them. She does not wear those ridiculous mounds of fabric, and she has made a significant effort to learn to protect herself with both the sword and knives. In my experience, that is unusual for most outworlders, but especially for women. She has also been traveling for weeks in the company of men under harsh conditions with little complaint. Most of the women in the cities seem too soft for such circumstances. Frisha also maintained her composure during the battle with the bandits and, although she had no fighting *Skills* at the time, she did not panic."

"There was a battle?" Reaylin gasped in disbelief.

Rezkin simply nodded once.

"You admire her, don't you?" she asked.

Rezkin considered the question. Frisha had not mastered the *Skills*, and she did not follow many of the *Rules*, but she *was* still trying despite the fact that most of the outworlders around her did not bother. She also had strength and spirit that he did not think was common based on his observations of other outworlders. Rezkin nodded once again and said, "She has many admirable qualities."

When the travelers were all once again gathered around the campfire, Frisha spent the evening glowering at Reaylin but otherwise avoided a confrontation. She did not know what had taken place between Rezkin and the offensive girl when they wandered off into the dark, but her imagination gave her plenty of fuel for her fire.

The next day as the travelers were riding, Tam caught up to Rezkin, who was in the lead at that point. Frisha and Reaylin were keeping their distance from each other in the middle, and Lieutenant Jimson brought up the rear.

"So, what did Reaylin want last night?" Tam asked.

"She said she wants to be *friends*," Rezkin replied. "Do you think it is possible?"

Tam shrugged uncomfortably. He did not particularly like their newest traveling companion. "Maybe," he said, "but Frisha is your girlfriend, and she would not like you getting too close to Reaylin."

Girlfriend? That was a new term. Neither woman was a small-one, so they could not really be considered *girls*, but he felt the term was being used loosely to indicate a female. They were both female, though, so would they both not be called *girl friends*?

"Reaylin is a woman, as well," Rezkin stated with confusion.

"Exactly," replied Tam. "So you understand that, naturally, your girlfriend would not like you spending too much time with her. You need to respect Frisha's feelings."

He thought he understood, now. Apparently, there was a hierarchy among *friends*. *Girl Friend* was actually a title issued to the superior female friend. If Frisha was his *Girl Friend*, did that make Tam his *Boy Friend*, or was it only a female distinction?

"So, if Frisha is my Girl Friend, what does that make you?" he asked.

Tam smirked and said, "Well, I'm your *best* friend, of course!"

Rezkin returned his smile, because it seemed like the thing to do, and nodded. So, Tam held the title of *Best Friend*, Frisha was his *Girl Friend*, and Jimson and possibly Reaylin were just *friends*. It all made sense, now. He could appreciate such an organized system. He just wished the masters had taken the time to explain this one. Perhaps it had simply slipped their minds among all their other teaching requirements. Since he had been teaching weapons *Skills* to his *friends*, he could now appreciate how difficult a task it was.

For several days, the ride was long, boring, and uneventful. Reaylin had yet to apologize to Frisha, her pride getting the better of her. Frisha tried to ignore Reaylin's presence as much as possible, but her simmering jealousy was reignited every time she caught the girl's longing gaze directed at Rezkin.

One afternoon, the group found a shady spot near a creek to partake of their midday meal. The sun was high and warm, as it was now into the heat of the summer, and no clouds graced the clear blue sky to block the searing rays. The horses were hot and sweaty and the traveler's clothes were damp. Frisha was gradually becoming offended by her own smell. It had been several days since they had the opportunity to bathe, since none of the streams they encountered had been large enough to submerge themselves.

Rezkin scouted the area thoroughly before he allowed anyone to relax and bathe in the creek. Still, he insisted the women stay together when they went to bathe around a slight bend where the men could not see. The sour looks with which each of the women graced him were ineffectual. Rezkin did not like the idea of leaving the women alone at all, but at least if they were together, they could watch each other's backs. When he threatened to stand guard over them while they bathed, they finally relented; although, for some reason it seemed as if both of them contemplated the option just a bit too long for propriety's sake.

Rezkin tended the horses while Tam and Jimson started a small fire and prepared the meal. After watering the beasts, he poured cool water over their nearly steaming flesh and brushed their coats to a glossy shine. Leaving the beasts to graze and nap in the shade of the trees, he decided he would take the opportunity to clean himself and some of his clothes. He retrieved a cake of soap and drying cloth from his pack and walked the short distance to the creek where he immediately stripped off his clothes and armor.

The women had gone a short distance upstream around a small bend, so Rezkin was not concerned that he would see something he should not. The cool water of the creek felt incredible on his heated skin. He walked to the center where the water was deepest, and still, it only rose to just above his hips. He washed his hair and scrubbed the sweat and grit from his skin, rinsing away several sweltering days' worth of grime.

Rezkin had just risen out of the water after rinsing away the soap when he heard a piercing scream followed by a large splash. His muscles tensed, and his eyes darted upstream in the direction of the sound. Just at the curve of the bend were two figures flailing in the water. He quickly made his way to shallower water and then charged ahead as fast as his feet would take him.

Reaylin and Frisha had bathed in silence, neither woman caring to breach the ice that had formed between them. Reaylin made it a point to finish first, just so she could get under Frisha's skin.

"Are you finished, yet?" she huffed. "By the time we get back, all of the food will be gone. Ugh! I can't believe I have to wait on you."

Frisha rolled her eyes. "Perhaps if you spent a little more time bathing it would start to wash away some of that grime that's stuck in your personality."

Reaylin scowled and replied, "At least I have a personality. You're just one among thousands … like all the rest."

Frisha tugged on a fresh tunic and pants over her clean undergarments. She strapped on the wide leather belt Rezkin had procured to carry her throwing knives. Each knife had a tiny sheath hidden on the inside of the belt. The belt covered her entire midsection from hips to ribs like a corset, ensuring that the knives could not be seen. The leather was soft, and the knives were positioned at a slight forward angle so that she could still bend and easily access the weapons. Some of the hilts pointed down so she could draw them from below, and others pointed up. The leather had been tooled with an intricate pattern of leaves and vines and stained a rich mahogany. Overall, the look was beautiful when worn over her tunic and breeches. It would not go so well with a gown.

Frisha had been surprised when Rezkin had presented the belt to her after they left one of the villages in which they had stayed the night. She knew an item of this nature would have to be custom made, and he would have had to pay a handsome fee to have it finished before they left.

Frisha began to wonder how much money Rezkin really had and where he'd gotten it. She and Tam had concluded that Rezkin probably had very little to his name. Frisha truly hoped he was not spending everything he had on her. She worried, now, that Rezkin might think he had to buy her love to try to keep her from marrying a noble.

After gathering the wet clothes they had washed in the creek, the two young women began walking along the bank back toward camp. When they came around the bend, their forward motion came to an abrupt halt. Frisha thought it had to be the most beautiful sight she had ever seen.

Thick, cut muscles curved around a graceful, fluid form. The warrior turned slightly away, and she could just barely make out the slight dip between the muscular cheeks of his backside peeking above the water. His silky black mane, now wet, clung to ridged muscles flexing beneath, and rivulets of water ran down the dips and valleys of his back. The warrior turned toward them as he scrubbed at his other side, and she could make out a light dusting of black curls across his chest that trailed a line down his carved, taut abdomen to the water. Muscles clenched and rolled as he contorted about in his ministrations, and his pale skin shone in the sun like the personification of a god carved in alabaster.

Frisha was mesmerized. Reaylin was, as well. Neither girl could take her eyes off the sight until Reaylin opened her mouth. "Now, that's something worth fighting for," the self-proclaimed warrior declared.

Frisha scowled over at her. "You stay away from him. He's not yours."

Reaylin laughed, "He's not yours, yet. Until you are married, he is fair game." The girl laughed again and said, "Actually, a man like that never really belongs to one woman. He could get any woman he wants, whether he marries or not. Do you really think he'll be satisfied with just *you*?" Reaylin gave Frisha a disdainful look that told Frisha exactly what Reaylin thought of her.

Frisha screamed and launched herself at Reaylin. Reaylin was completely unprepared for the sudden violence emanating from the pretty little pretentious prat and lost her balance. Both women tumbled into the creek, but their anger and animosity toward one another did not abate. Somehow, whether it was the circumstances leading to the fight, the mind-numbing rage, or basic female nature, neither girl remembered to employ any of the fighting techniques they had learned. The confrontation devolved into a brawl of slapping, scratching and hair pulling. Reaylin got one good shot at Frisha, socking her in the eye. Frisha scored deep gouges that stretched nearly from Reaylin's jaw to collar bone.

When Rezkin arrived at the scene of the disturbance, two of his traveling companions were engaged in a vicious … *What do I call this? Fight? Battle?* It was the strangest fighting technique he had ever seen. The women were like two wild animals scratching and ripping at each other's hair. One tangled limb, he wasn't sure whose, appeared to have teeth marks.

"What is going on here?" he shouted above the snarls and shrieks.

Both women froze instantly. When their eyes landed on Rezkin, they gaped but said nothing. They were still wrapped about each other with their hands tangled in blonde and brown strands.

Frisha's mouth worked without sound a few times before she was finally able to speak. "You're naked!"

Rezkin looked at her quizzically and then scowled. "Of course I am. I was washing. I do not bathe in my clothes." He simply held his ground unashamedly as he eyed them both. "It does not look like either of you are bathing."

Both girls flushed and began disentangling themselves. Once all of their fingers and limbs were separated they pushed apart to stand a few feet from each other. Neither woman would look him in the eye as if they were ashamed to be caught fighting like animals half submerged in the creek. Neither could seem to keep their eyes off of him, either. They kept glancing his way, each time flushing a darker red.

Rezkin heard the thrashing through the bushes and knew Tam and Lieutenant Jimson had heard the commotion as well. When the two men arrived, they barely noted the women except to see their presence in the water and the fact that they both appeared to be injured and bleeding. Tam stood gaping in shock while Jimson's face contorted in anger.

"Rezkin!" he barked. He slid his hand over the hilt of his sword and said, "What do you think you are doing? How dare you intrude on these women while they are bathing and expose yourself. If you touched a hair on either of their heads, I will beat you down even if it kills me!"

Rezkin gaped at the lieutenant. "What are you talking about? I did not …"

"I do not want to hear it! Not until you put some clothes on. Go!" the lieutenant shouted. There was no doubt that this was an order from an army officer.

For some reason, Rezkin felt anger creeping into his mind, and it was directed at the lieutenant. Nothing about this situation should have incited the emotion. No one had been killed or injured … well, beyond a few scratches and what looked to be turning into a black eye.

The angry warrior stepped into the lieutenant's personal space so that their bodies were nearly touching. He was so close the lieutenant could not possibly hope to draw his sword. Rezkin gazed over the lieutenant's shoulder as he spoke into the soldier's ear so quietly the others could not hear, including Tam who stood only a few feet away gaping like a fish on dry land.

"Make no mistake, Lieutenant Jimson. Even naked and unarmed I could kill you in seconds. Do not underestimate me. You are my *friend*, but if you ever issue that challenge, I *will* end you. Next time, it would be in your best interest to gather the facts before you make assumptions and accusations."

Rezkin stepped around the lieutenant and walked down the bank to retrieve his clothes and other belongings. He decided he needed time away from the group to think and calm himself. Rezkin was frustrated. He did not know why he had become angered with the lieutenant. The man had done and said nothing overtly threatening toward him. He had issued a warning, which was on the surface reasonable enough. If he *had* attacked the women, he would have expected the lieutenant to defend their honor and at least attempt to kill him. It could not have been what the lieutenant said, then.

Rezkin mulled over the question for quite some time before he finally thought he understood. It was the assumption and accusation, Rezkin realized. He was angry that the lieutenant thought he would actually attempt to harm the women for no reason or simply to satisfy his base needs.

Rezkin's only experience being intimate with a woman had started out pleasant enough but had ended abruptly when the woman attempted to kill him. He knew, however, what men did with women. Having never been around women until he left the fortress several weeks past, he had not considered the experience. Too many other events were happening, and he had to adjust at an uncomfortable rate to the outworld. Allowing himself to be open and vulnerable to another person for any length of time was more than he could force upon himself at this time. He understood that the intimacy was not really *necessary* unless he wanted to procreate, so the subject had not crossed his mind.

The thoughts brought Rezkin back to the source of his anger. Rezkin was not a selfish or cruel man. He killed and destroyed when he had to or when the masters ordered it; but he trusted that if they gave him an order, they had good reason to do so. He did not enjoy killing, but neither did it trouble him. He truly had no feelings about it at all.

To attack the women at the creek, though, would have been cruel and unnecessary. Rezkin was angry that the lieutenant, whom he had been traveling with day and night for several weeks, actually believed Rezkin could do something like that. He was angry that his *friend* would question his devotion to the *Rules*, *Rule 1* in particular. Most of all, he was angry because he cared what the lieutenant thought of him, and that was a new sensation.

Rezkin had never cared what anyone thought of him before—not *him*, as a person. The only people he had known before cared only that he learned the *Rules* and *Skills* and acted without emotion. So long as he was not cruel or weak, they did not care what he thought or felt. As far as he knew, no one had ever judged him based on anything other than his adherence to the *Rules*, and those men had trusted him to admit when he had broken any of them. It was a matter of honor and respect. Rezkin was angry because if the lieutenant thought those things of him, then what must the others think?

When Rezkin rejoined the group, he said nothing and avoided looking at the lieutenant all together. He had tried to distance himself from the emotion, but he was afraid that if he looked at the man he would feel inclined to kill him —or at least damage him severely, and that would violate *Rules 1, 37*, and *188* ... and possibly *2*, but he was still uncertain as to the meaning of that one.

Rezkin was confused by his own emotions. He could not remember a time when he had been angry with anyone other than himself. Every injury and damage anyone had inflicted upon him in the fortress, even the outright torture, had been for a reason—for training. Even the bandits he could excuse because, well, they were bandits. That was what bandits did. Somehow this felt different.

Rezkin saddled his horse in silence and then rummaged around in his saddlebags. He kept certain supplies in them for easy access while traveling rather than having to dig in the depths of his endless pack. He retrieved a few packets of herbs, clean swatches of fabric, and a jar of ointment. Next, he used a small metal cup to boil water and then placed the herbs in the water to steep. Finally, he soaked the rag in the water and then wrapped the herbs in the fabric to make an herbal compress.

Rezkin knelt beside Frisha, but she would not look up at him. She was sitting on a fallen tree at one side of the small clearing, hanging her head low so that her hair fell over her face. The young man gently placed his fingers beneath her chin and tilted her head up so that he could tend to her injury.

Frisha, in her shame, could not meet Rezkin's eyes. Her face was flushed, and her eyes were watery, but he did not think the bruising would be too extensive. The purpling around the eye would require several days to heal, though. Rezkin felt that recurring tightening in his chest when he realized Frisha would not look at him.

What must she think of him? He took her small delicate hand in his own, pressed the compress into her palm, and then maneuvered her hand so that she held it over her injured eye. Frisha nearly sighed with the immediate relief the now cool compress provided. Next, Rezkin dipped another swatch of fabric in the tin cup and used the herbal liquid to clean the cuts and scrapes on Frisha's face and arms. He applied a small amount of the ointment to the deeper cuts. All the while, he said nothing.

After tending to Frisha's wounds, he moved around the clearing to tend to Reaylin's. Reaylin sat on the ground with her knees pulled up to her chest and back against a tree. She had turned away from the group sulking in her own shame and self-pity. When she first noticed Rezkin's approach, he was already within a few strides of her. She tried to stand quickly to avoid him, but he grabbed her arm and pulled her back down to the ground.

Another woman was angry with him, but he would not allow her to suffer needlessly. He took another clean cloth, dipped it into the liquid in the cup, and set about cleaning her wounds. The long, deep scratches on her neck were the worst, and he made sure to apply extra ointment to those. Once he was finished, he cleaned the cup, repacked his healing supplies and sat down to eat what was left of their lunch.

13

J imson sat silently and watched as the young warrior moved about the clearing tending to the women's wounds. He was efficient with a practiced ease but surprisingly gentle. Rezkin had to have some training in the healing arts to be so proficient. Whatever training the young man had received had been quite thorough. Even a poor soldier with healer training was worth ten average soldiers, and Rezkin was so much more than the average soldier. Jimson could not see the young man's face when he treated Reaylin, but there had been a softness in his eyes when he looked upon Frisha.

After Rezkin had stormed off earlier, both young women had confessed to Jimson and Tam about what happened. Jimson felt guilty for the way he treated Rezkin now that he knew the real story. The young warrior had only come running when the shouts of alarm caught his attention, the same as he and Tam. Unfortunately, circumstances dictated that the man would arrive in the buff. Having more concern for the women's safety, he had set aside any worries over propriety.

Jimson understood, now, what happened, but it had not looked good at the time. Still, the young man had always acted the gentleman and seemed dedicated to the code by which he lived. Jimson should have known Rezkin was not attempting to take advantage of the women. If he was really honest with himself, he had to admit that some of his anger and assumptions at the time stemmed from his own jealousy and desire to protect Reaylin. He did not like the way the young woman had been staring at the warrior's body.

After Rezkin ate what he could, he went about packing the rest of the belongings. Tam strode over to help him saddle the horses for the women, but the young man sensed Rezkin's mood and wisely chose not to say anything. Rezkin kept trying to shake his foul mood, but it was as if now that the feeling had finally emerged, it refused to let go. Finally, the rest of the group claimed their mounts and the travelers were once again on their way.

Several hours had passed when Jimson decided it was time to approach the young warrior. He tried to fool himself into thinking it would be safer if they were both mounted. Catching up with the battle charger, Jimson waited a moment before speaking. When he finally did, he was appalled to hear his own voice quaking in fear. He was an officer in the King's Army, and here he was afraid of talking to a young man. He would laugh at himself if the situation were not so serious. "Rezkin, I would like to speak to you about what happened earlier."

"Go on," Rezkin replied dispassionately. Rezkin did not look at the lieutenant but kept his eyes roving around them in search of hidden dangers—at least, that was why he told himself he was doing it.

Lieutenant Jimson continued. "You have to see the scene from my perspective. I mean, there you were standing naked over two women who were in the water screaming. And, you know, it is my duty, my *honor*, to protect the innocent people of this kingdom, particularly those with whom I am traveling. Surely you can understand that."

Rezkin met the lieutenant's eyes with an icy stare. "I understand your duty, Lieutenant, and I know how the scene must have looked to you. But, I also know that I have never given you reason to doubt *my* honor. *My* duty is to protect and *honor* my *friends*, which includes at least one of those women, and until I decide about the other, I will treat her as such, as well.

"I have said it before, and I will say it again. I have little care for propriety except for that which is necessary to honor my *friends*. But, when propriety interferes with my ability to protect my *friends*, I will not hesitate to cast it aside. I heard a scream and saw people thrashing about in the water. I ran as quickly as I could to lend aid or protection. My appearance when I arrived was insignificant." Rezkin grunted. "I did not expect to arrive and find the women fighting *each other*."

Jimson shifted uncomfortably in the saddle and replied, "I know what happened. The women told me. I was out of line when I questioned your honor and threatened you. The truth is …"—he reached up and nervously rubbed the back of his neck—"well…I guess I was a little jealous. I got angry."

Rezkin looked askance. "Jealous of *what*?" he asked in dismay.

"*You*, of course," Jimson said. The look of utter confusion on Rezkin's face convinced him more than anything that the young man was oblivious to the real heart of the matter. "Do you know what the women were fighting over?" he asked.

Rezkin shook his head. "I cannot imagine. Those two have not liked each other since they met. It is strange to me since I see so many similarities between them."

Jimson shook his head and laughed. "You really do not know. The thing is, I like Reaylin."

"I like Reaylin, as well," Rezkin stated factually.

Jimson sighed and replied, "No, I mean, I am attracted to her. And, it is obvious to me … to everyone, actually … that you are attracted to Frisha. The problem is that both women want *you*."

Rezkin furrowed his brow. He was attracted to Frisha? He was not so certain of that. He thought for sure he would know if he was attracted to a woman. He was *more* interested in Frisha than Reaylin, so maybe that did mean he was attracted to her. He would have to ponder the idea another time.

"So, what was the fight about?" Rezkin asked in confusion.

Jimson rolled his eyes and stated, "You!"

"Why were they fighting about me? I did nothing to anger either of them as far as I know," Rezkin said.

"They were not fighting over something you *did*. They were fighting over *you*. They both want you, and they were fighting over who would have you," Jimson explained patiently. He was realizing that although Rezkin was an amazingly talented and intelligent warrior, he was completely oblivious when it came to women.

"Why would they fight about that? It is not as if the outcome of the fight would guarantee that I would choose the winner," Rezkin remarked.

"Maybe not, but if I were to pursue Frisha, would you not feel inclined to fight me?" Jimson asked.

Rezkin thought about it and then shrugged, "If Frisha wanted you, then I would respect her decision. In all, you are a respectable man who can provide for her. You would be a decent choice. Besides, I have no rightful claim to the woman. She is to select a husband from among the nobles."

"What?" Jimson blurted in surprise. "But, I thought … I mean, she is obviously smitten with you. I thought for certain the two of you were together."

Rezkin nodded. "We are together in that I am her *friend* and will protect her as long as I can. She agreed to travel with me, but her purpose in going to Kaibain is to select a husband. Her uncle is arranging the marriage prospects as we speak."

Jimson glanced back at the young woman in question. She was riding far enough back that she could not hear what was being said but was watching them curiously. The dark bruising around her eye stood out against her pale skin.

"I am not so sure that anything her uncle arranges will come to fruition. I am no expert, but I believe she has already made her choice," Jimson stated.

Rezkin looked at him quizzically and then turned to see what Jimson was observing. When his gaze fell on Frisha, the young woman gave a start, suddenly realizing the men must have been talking about her. She abruptly hid her face in her long brown hair. She normally wore it pulled back on the road, but she appeared to be trying to hide the bruising on her face.

Hating to do it, but needing the assurance, Jimson turned the conversation back to the original reason he had approached Rezkin. "So, are we good? You and me?" he asked tentatively.

Rezkin sighed deeply and answered, "Yes, but heed my warning. I tell you this now because you are my *friend*. As I said before, if you ever issue that challenge against me in truth, I *will* kill you because I know I will have done nothing to warrant such a challenge."

Jimson considered Rezkin for a moment. He had no doubt the young warrior would follow through with his promise. And, that is what it was—a promise. The statement was not a threat. Rezkin was truly warning him. If he ever attacked Rezkin without just cause, and Rezkin insisted he would never give just cause, then he expected Rezkin to defend himself. He also knew Rezkin would win, and he would die. It was a statement of fact—one that the soldier in him could appreciate.

Jimson gave a curt nod and said, "Fair enough."

By the next day, the mood of the group had lifted. Rezkin no longer held a grudge against Jimson, and the women had somehow developed an unspoken, tentative pact of nonaggression. Rezkin had decided not to confront the women about the incident. He knew from his studies that many disagreements, and even wars, had been fought because of jealousy. Never had he considered that *he* might be the object of such strife.

Rezkin was still not convinced the lieutenant had the right of the confrontation. The whole scenario seemed illogical at best. His masters had warned him, though, that matters of the heart were almost always illogical. The teachings had been warnings so that he would not underestimate the potential actions of a desperate man … or woman. Women could be every bit as vicious as men, and they were often subtler. They tended to use poisons and deceit rather than steel.

It was still a few days until they reached Kaibain, and the companions were weary from travel. The morning and afternoon were spent mostly in silent contemplation with the occasional conversation or story. The normally quiet Lieutenant Jimson had many interesting stories about his life as a soldier. While he had not actually seen any true battles in war, his duties in escorting military supplies meant that he had traveled over much of Ashai.

It was during one of Jimson's intriguing tales that Rezkin noticed a slight disturbance in the foliage ahead. Although he saw no movement, his instincts were telling him they were approaching danger. The energy that always preceded battle seeped through him like a fiery stream. Catching Jimson's eye, he made a few standard military hand signals to indicate the man should continue talking but be on alert and ready for action.

Jimson continued his story while allowing his horse to fall back gradually as though he was placing himself closer to his most avid listeners. Rezkin grinned and nodded in all the right places as though he was caught up in the story, as well. The lieutenant made a quick motion behind his back hoping Tam would get the message. He did not want the group strung out during an attack. Tam looked confused at first but seemed to recognize the change in his companions' behavior. He anxiously sped up to join Jimson and the women.

As soon as the travelers reached the location of the disturbance, Rezkin commanded his steed into battle, charging into the brush lining the eastern side of the road. Lieutenant Jimson reached out and unceremoniously yanked both women from their saddles just as a crossbow bolt whizzed through the air. Kicking his horse into motion, he charged into the thickets on the western side of the road straight at the exposed crossbowman. Before he could reload, Jimson was upon him. The man turned to run, but the soldier leaned over from his mount and ended the bandit with a wicked slash.

Just as Jimson turned to search out other foes, a thick, serrated dagger stabbed his thigh. Strong hands clawed at his uniform, pulling him from his horse. The lieutenant hit the ground with a painful jar to his injured leg. He scrambled to roll over, expecting the bite of steel at any moment. When he finally managed to right himself, he found his attacker bearing down on him, and Jimson knew he would not get to his sword in time.

Suddenly, a foot of bloody steel emerged from the attacker's chest. A burble of blood poured from the bandit's mouth as he collapsed to the ground. In his place stood Tam, wide-eyed and shaking. A moment passed before Tam's head cleared of panic enough to realize what he had done. He stared at the dead man, blinking repeatedly as if the act could wash away the image. Abruptly, his stomach lurched, and he fell to his knees retching. Jimson retrieved his sword and pulled himself to his feet, doing his best to ignore the searing pain in his leg. He gripped Tam's tunic by the collar and yanked the young man to his feet.

"Get up," he shouted. "It is not over, yet!"

Meanwhile, Rezkin and his mount stampeded over two of the attackers, plowing them into the hard dirt. The men were not dead, but they were injured badly and moaned in pain. After a quick assessment of the threat, he decided to allow the two to live for the time being. They might possess useful information. Rezkin dismounted and drew his swords as he faced off against the remaining bandits. He cut down the first man he encountered just as he heard the *snick* of crossbow releasing its quarrel. With inhuman reflexes, he flicked Bladesunder up in an arc and deflected the bolt before it struck.

The three remaining bandits shouted in astonishment when they saw the blades of liquid silver and azure swirls. They darted in the opposite direction in full retreat. Rezkin quickly sheathed Kingslayer and slipped the small throwing ax from his belt, launching it at nearest retreating bandit. With a sickening *squelch*, the axe head burrowed deeply into the man's back.

In quick succession, two throwing knives sliced through the air. One bandit was struck in the small of the back, but the other was too far away and was hit in the leg. Already in pursuit, Rezkin caught up to the man and removed his head in one clean swipe.

Rezkin surveyed the scene to see where he was needed most. Lieutenant Jimson was locked in battle with a bandit but seemed to have the upper hand. Tam was standing not far away as if waiting to lend aid, but his face was drawn and pale. Frisha was hiding behind her horse in the center of the road, but Reaylin was missing. Something in the trees to Frisha's side caught her attention, and she started in that direction. Rezkin took off at a sprint determined to intercept her and face whatever commotion had drawn her attention.

Rezkin arrived just ahead of Frisha and ordered her to retreat. He could now see what had drawn her away from the relative safety of the road. Reaylin was being tossed around like a rag doll by a hulking bandit who was probably double her weight. She had lost her sword but at least managed to score a hit with one of her daggers. The small blade protruded from the monster's thigh, but the injury only seemed to incite the brute's rising anger. Rezkin looked more closely. It was no surprise the man was unfazed. His arms were covered in purple-black *ink*. He grabbed Reaylin by her chest armor and threw her into a tree. She struck the trunk with a heavy thud and crumpled to the ground. Frisha screamed, drawing the man's attention. When the bandit turned, though, it was not a frightened woman he faced but Rezkin's demonic gaze.

With both swords in hand, Rezkin punched the man in the face with a fist braced by a heavy hilt. The bandit stumbled back but maintained his footing. Rezkin shoved his steel reinforced boot into the man's gut with all his might. The air exploded from the man's lungs, and he vomited as he fell to his knees. Rezkin sheathed Bladesunder, and taking Kingslayer in both hands, he held the sword high over his head with the tip pointed down. He drove the sword straight through the base of the man's skull severing the spinal cord. It was an execution, plain and simple.

"Rezkin!" Frisha screamed. She knew Rezkin had killed men in the last battle, but she had not actually seen it occur. To see it now, in such a brutal fashion after the man had already been beaten, was shocking. Rezkin ignored Frisha's scream and casually tore a strip of cloth from the dead man's soiled tunic. He wiped down his blade and slid it into the sheath. He turned and quickly strode over to where Reaylin lay gasping against the tree.

With swift fingers, Rezkin unbuckled the injured young woman's armor. Frisha stumbled forward and gripped his shoulder with one hand. With his body still surging from battle, he barely managed to avoid shoving her away.

"Rezkin, what are you doing?" Frisha shouted in alarm.

Lieutenant Jimson and Tam arrived at that moment and took hold of Frisha. While Tam held her to one side, softly whispering reassurances in her ear, Jimson stepped forward to kneel next to Reaylin.

"Is she okay?" Jimson asked with heavy concern. "I mean, of course she is not okay. Is it serious?" Reaylin's jaw was clenched in pain, and she was gasping for breath.

"She struck her back when she was thrown against the tree. She can still move her legs, but I think her ribs may be cracked or broken," Rezkin said as he finally managed to remove the constricting armor. He abruptly stopped with a sudden thought. "Did you restrain the two I left alive?"

Jimson was momentarily thrown off by the abrupt change in subject. "Ah … one had already succumbed to his injuries. I am assuming he was one of those you left alive since he had no injuries from blades. The other is alive but will not be going anywhere. His pelvis was crushed."

Rezkin nodded acknowledgement as he ran his fingers along Reaylin's torso. He carefully felt along each of her vertebrae. She sucked in a breath as he pressed on the areas that would surely bruise, but none of the vertebrae felt shattered or out of place. Next, he ran his fingers along each of her ribs. Three of them on her left side were very sensitive and probably cracked but not broken.

"How is she?" Jimson asked.

"Three cracked ribs. They will need to be wrapped. I think her spine is okay. We will need to keep an eye on the bruising to make sure there is no internal bleeding. Do you know when the next patrol is scheduled to pass through here?"

Lieutenant Jimson shook his head, "I am not sure."

"We should pile the bodies along the road for the next patrol to find. It may also deter any more bandits from attacking for a while. We will need to move at least a few miles down the road before making camp. A few hours left of daylight remain, but Reaylin will need to rest and lay still for a while. I have some herbs and salves that should help with the pain and speed the healing process," Rezkin said.

"Yes, sir," the lieutenant said automatically. He rose and turned on his heel. "Tam, you are with me." Tam jumped with a start, but nodded and followed him.

"Frisha," Rezkin said, "will you wait with Reaylin while I retrieve some supplies from my pack?"

Frisha was obviously shaken. She simply stared at Reaylin blankly for a moment as though she did not understand Ashaiian. She glanced at Rezkin when he said her name again and shook herself from her stupor.

"Y-yes, of course," she replied as she hurried over to the injured girl.

Frisha sat down beside Reaylin, laying the girl's head on her lap, and then watched Rezkin's retreating form. Without his reassuring presence and protection, she suddenly felt very vulnerable. He was only gone a few moments, but it felt like an eternity to the frightened young women.

Reaylin was reeling from her experience with the giant. She knew that if Rezkin had not arrived when he did, she would be dead. Even with her weapons and training, she had been no match for the mountain of a man. Here she thought she was a warrior, but in her first real battle she had been pulverized. Her pain and inability to move or even breathe comfortably made her feel all the more exposed and vulnerable, and with Rez's departure, her only source of comfort was *Frisha*!

Frisha kept replaying the images and sensations in her mind. Being dragged from her horse, the crossbow bolts, the ringing of steel, and the *blood*. Then, Reaylin engaged the massive bandit, but he threw her around like she was nothing more than a tiny pest. Frisha imagined it was *her* being beaten and tossed against the tree. She had been terrified watching the woman throttled nearly to death right in front of her, and there had been nothing she could do to stop it. Although she had been practicing with her knives, she had yet to stick one in a target. She had thrown a few at the brute with shaking hands, but she had missed completely.

More than anything, though, the image that played over and over in her mind was that of Rezkin standing over the bandit, poised to strike. When Rezkin had first beaten him with fist and foot, he had been clearly and understandably full of rage. As the man knelt retching on the ground, something changed. For the briefest of moments, it was as if the world stood still. Several strands of Rezkin's hair had slipped from the queue at his neck. They whipped in the wind around his face as his eyes turned to icy steel. When his wicked blade descended taking the man's life and releasing his soul, Rezkin's face and eyes were empty, devoid of all that was human. It was that brief glimpse that frightened her more than anything.

Rezkin returned with his horse and a roll of bandages. He pulled Reaylin's tunic up to just below her breasts. Frisha sucked in a deep breath. Even she was not sure if her reaction was due to Rezkin's seeing and touching so much of Reaylin's body or the deep purple and black bruising that was already setting in over the expanse of the girl's torso.

Rezkin gripped his metal cup and emptied several packets of herbs into the small vessel. He then stirred in a small amount of water from his waterskin.

Once the herbs were wet and clumped, he mixed in globs of pungent jelly to form a thick paste. He scooped the paste out with his fingers and spread it gently over Reaylin's back and sides. Although he was gentle, his ministrations elicited small whimpers from the injured woman. Finally, he wrapped a bandage tightly around her torso several times to keep the ribs from shifting or further cracking.

Rezkin gathered his things and packed them away in his saddlebags. He shook his head. It never occurred to him that he would need so many herbs and ointments in such short time; and thus far, they had all gone to the women. At this rate, he would need to start scavenging for replacements soon. He made a mental note to watch for the plants as they traveled. As carefully as he could manage, he lifted Reaylin in his arms. She released a strangled cry and whimpered. She was so tiny and light he thought he could probably carry her the few miles to the campsite if necessary.

"I apologize for your discomfort, but you cannot walk right now. Try to breathe deeply and push away the pain. When we make camp, I will brew a tea that will reduce the pain and help you sleep."

Reaylin whimpered through her tears and said in a tiny, strained voice, "Thank you, Rez."

Tam and Jimson were just finishing piling the bodies when Rezkin and the women arrived back at the road. Tam's face was ashen, and he looked like he was going to be sick, or maybe had already been sick—several times. Both men were covered in quite a bit of blood. Lieutenant Jimson's expression was grim until he saw Reaylin. His face immediately softened, and he hurried over to Rezkin as he wiped his hands on his pants and tunic.

"Jimson," Rezkin said. It was the first time the warrior had used his name in lieu of his title, a fact that the lieutenant seemed to notice. "If you mount up, I will pass Reaylin to you, and you can hold her while we head up the road. She cannot ride on her own right now."

"Of course, I will be glad to help," Jimson said hurriedly as he scrambled into the saddle. A bandage was wrapped tightly around his thigh, but the lieutenant declined Rezkin's offer of healing assistance. Rezkin lifted Reaylin up into the lieutenant's waiting arms eliciting moans and cries from the injured woman. Rezkin would not have openly acknowledged such vulnerability, but he recognized that these outworlders had not properly acclimatized themselves to pain.

Rezkin turned to Frisha and Tam who were both looking much paler than usual and asked, "Are you two okay? I did not see any injuries."

Frisha shook her head. Tam swallowed hard and said, "No, I'm fine. I wasn't injured." Rezkin had not seen everything that occurred on the other side of the road, but the haunted look in the young man's eyes told him that Tam had probably taken a life for the first time.

"We will talk later," he said. When Tam just nodded, Rezkin continued. "We are going up the road to make camp. I would not expect any more trouble, but we must stay on guard. Lieutenant Jimson is preoccupied, so Tam, you take the rear. Stay close, but glance behind you and to the sides frequently. Your eyes should never stop moving. If you see anything, anything at all, even if you think it is just a deer, unless you can say for certain, you let me know."

Tam swallowed and nodded again.

The travelers made their way along the road slowly for a couple of hours before finally finding a suitable campsite. It was located a few dozen paces from the road and nestled among dense trees whose low-hanging boughs and surrounding shrubbery would hopefully hide their fire from the casual observer.

Rezkin scouted the area and found no signs of more bandits. After catching dinner, he returned to the camp and checked on his injured traveling companion. For the rest of the evening, Lieutenant Jimson fretted over Reaylin, doing everything he could to make sure she was comfortable. Unfortunately, Reaylin only had eyes for Rezkin. The fact that the young warrior had saved her life, avenged her, and then treated her wounds had only endeared him to her all the more.

Even Rezkin could recognize the young woman's drug-induced longing gaze, although he may have been more attuned to the possibility simply because of his previous talk with the lieutenant. He was not sure why it should matter, but it made him very uncomfortable. Rezkin did not want Reaylin to desire him. He did not know exactly what his feelings were toward Frisha, if he indeed had any, but he knew he was not interested in Reaylin. The young woman was too chaotic, impulsive, and reactive. He knew he would never be comfortable being close to her, much less let his guard down long enough to be any kind of intimate with her.

14

The first distant view of the capital city, the Seat of the King, was unimpressive. The land was completely flat so all the travelers could see was the massive bridge that spanned the River Straei and a very tall, grey wall. The wall itself was supposed to be one hundred feet high and composed of stone quarried from the Zigharan Mountains. The stone had been transported by ship down the Tremadel River, and supposedly, when the sun was at just the right angle, the walls sparkled. From here, they just looked grey.

"Are you sure that's Kaibain?" Frisha asked, looking up at the monstrosity. "Maybe we took a wrong turn and ended up at Drennil."

Jimson chuckled. "Oh, I am sure all right. I have been here before, several times, in fact. I know it does not look like much from this side, but once we pass through the gate, you will be surprised."

Frisha eyed the wall doubtfully. It seemed like the King's Seat should be more grandiose.

"This wall is more functional than decorative, obviously," Jimson added. "In ages past, when war frequented this land, entire sections of the wall were repeatedly damaged or destroyed. It had to be rebuilt often and quickly. The builders did not have the time or funds to make it attractive. Besides, their hard work would have been for naught as soon as a catapult launched a boulder and shattered it."

The bridge spanning the Straei was slightly more impressive. It was massive and built high upon pillars, although not quite high enough to allow passage for most ships sporting a mast. Tam stood at the center of the bridge looking over the rail down at the rushing water below.

"How do they keep the stone up between pillars? It looks like they're floating on air," he said.

"They used iron and steel beams and girders to create a frame. It was quite an engineering feat, and the engineers and mages who worked on it were rewarded handsomely," the lieutenant replied.

"I just can't wait to get to my uncle's and have a hot bath. I am so tired of being dirty and smelly," Frisha huffed. "I really don't care about the rest of the city at this point."

"That reminds me," Jimson said. "Rezkin, where will you be staying and how long until you will be ready to leave for Skutton? I have a few messages to deliver, and I need to get the final letter of approval for my leave. Then, I will be free to go. How will I reach you?"

Just as Rezkin opened his mouth to reply, Frisha spoke instead. "He is going to be a guest at my uncle's home. You should have no problem finding it. My uncle is General Marcum."

Lieutenant Jimson and Reaylin, who was in serious pain but now able to ride her own horse, both whipped their heads around to stare at Frisha. "General Marcum is your uncle?" Jimson asked in disbelief.

"Yes, on my mother's side," Frisha replied with a slight flush at the attention.

Jimson looked over at Rezkin who was sitting as stoic as ever and realized, now, why the young warrior had been less than hopeful about his chances with the young lady. Even so, he did not see how the general could even consider rejecting the young man. Despite what Rezkin said, Jimson was certain he was nobility of some sort. With Rezkin's knightly sense of honor, Jimson could not imagine he had done something to be disowned. Most importantly, though, Rezkin was a sword bearer, the highest honor in the kingdom—perhaps *all* of the kingdoms. He was favored by the *king*. How could the general argue with that?

Rezkin noticed Jimson's questioning look and turned to Frisha. "Frisha, I am not sure the general will welcome unexpected guests. General Marcum does not know me and has no reason to trust me in his home. And, what about Reaylin? We cannot leave her alone somewhere, especially being injured as she is."

Reaylin beamed at Rezkin's thoughtfulness, but Frisha cast his worries aside. "Don't worry, Rezkin. My uncle will be thrilled to have you. You have saved our lives several times over on this journey. Tam and I are well aware that we would not have made it here if it were not for you." Frisha said this last with a dark look of acceptance typically reserved for those who knew they had done something so foolish they should have been dead from it. Almost belatedly, she gritted through her teeth. "I am sure Reaylin will be welcome to stay as well."

Tam nodded vigorously. "It's true, Rez. We both owe you our lives, and I'm sure Frisha's uncle will recognize that. I think he would probably be more upset if he did not have the opportunity to host you. I know my ma and pa would dote on you like you were a long lost son."

"Don't worry about me," Reaylin said. "I have plans to stay with some people already."

"Very well." Rezkin sighed. Returning to the lieutenant's original question, Rezkin said, "Our departure will depend on how long the general intends to keep us as his guests. How long will it be before your uncle releases you to travel again, Frisha?"

Frisha's face flushed. "I-I'm not sure. I am going to have to convince him first."

"Wait, *she* is going to Skutton, too?" Reaylin nearly shouted.

Frisha scowled at her. It was obvious from her reaction that she thought she was going to have a shot at Rezkin once she had him away from Frisha.

"I'm going, too," Tam blurted.

"I thought you were joining the army?" Rezkin inquired.

"Well, I am … I mean, I will … after the tournament," Tam replied. "Oh, come on, everyone else is going, and it will be exciting. It's not like the army is going anywhere. Besides, who knows when I'll get another chance to see the King's Tournament? And, I *did* take an Oath of Protection for Frisha. Even if she doesn't really need me with you around, Rez, I still must honor my oath."

"Your oath ends when we get to my uncle's home, Tam," Frisha remarked, "but I for one, will be glad of your company."

Lieutenant Jimson, ever efficient, brought the conversation back to the point. "When you decide upon our departure, send word to me at the main barracks. Although I look forward to the respite, I hope it will not be more than a few days. It is a long journey to Skutton, and you never know what troubles we may encounter," he stated glumly as he remembered all that had gone awry thus far.

After a few moments, Lieutenant Jimson came to a decision and called Rezkin aside for a private chat. The two rode side by side a few good paces out of earshot from the rest of the party. "Rezkin, as you know, I was given some messages to deliver upon arrival in Kaibain. One of those is addressed to General Marcum, and it is regarding *you*."

"Me?" Rezkin asked, feigning surprise. "What would it have to say about me, and how do you know what it says?"

"Colonel Simmons had me review the letter for accuracy before it was sealed. It is nothing, really. It just explains who you are and describes your actions and assistance in fighting the bandits back at the River Straei. It *does* identify you as a sword bearer, which is why I think the colonel thought the matter should be brought to the general's attention. Neither of us had heard of anyone being granted a Sheyalin in a couple of decades, so your showing up with not one but *two* was odd, especially at your age. I just thought you should know since you will be staying in the general's home. I did not want things to be too awkward for you. Your actions saved our lives. If not for you, we all would probably be dead, and Reaylin … Well, just, thank you. I will not forget."

"I appreciate you letting me know," Rezkin replied. "Of course, I would not ask you to forsake your duty and not deliver the letter, but I *will* ask that you simply wait a few days. I would like to get to know the man on my own before he starts making assumptions based on the fact that I bear these blades."

The lieutenant eyed Rezkin sideways. He was on unstable ground, here. On the one hand, even if he delayed a few days, so long as he delivered the letter, he would still be following orders. On the other, if he did not deliver the missive immediately, and something happened to the general as a result of Rezkin's actions while he was staying in the man's home, the lieutenant would be in hot water.

Jimson did not believe the warrior held any ill intent toward the general, but was he seriously willing to trust his career, may be his *life*, to those beliefs? Still, he owed the man his life at least twice over. Another thought occurred to him. Rezkin was a sword bearer of unspecified authority. Rezkin could *order* him not to deliver the message, and no one could *legally* question the lieutenant in his compliance.

Lieutenant Jimson nodded. "Very well. I will deliver the letter to him the day after tomorrow. If he asks why the delay, I will tell him I was acting on your orders," he said with an uncharacteristic cheeky grin.

Entering the city was not a problem. With the lieutenant's credentials, the traveling companions were admitted without delay. True to the lieutenant's word, the city was immeasurably more impressive on the inside. Most of the structures were built of stone, but many were constructed of wood. Wide avenues paved with smooth, flat cobblestones, crisscrossed and wound around clean walkways and trimmed hedges. At each of the major crossways was a circular intersection, in the center of which stood a statue, fountain, or topiary.

The main market street did not have the cluttered stalls with shouting merchants that Rezkin had experienced in the other cities. Instead, the path was lined with shops residing in stone buildings that had large glass windows along the fronts to display their wares. The lieutenant assured them that the regular merchant stands could still be found in other parts of the city, but the area along the main thoroughfare was reserved for the more affluent.

Lieutenant Jimson guided the travelers through the twists and turns of the upper-class district. The companions gawked at the splendor, breaking their silence with the occasional "ooh" and "ah" or "look at that!" Gardens and courtyards abounded, and tall spires peeked over the rooftops. The people in this area were dressed in fine silks and lace, and the women carried parasols and rode in fancy two-wheeled carts pulled by running servants. The lieutenant called the carts rickshaws.

Once the lieutenant knew he was in the correct area, he stopped to ask a local which estate belonged to the general. The estate was of moderate size compared to some of the ostentatious abodes they passed, but it was still grand. Standing two stories high with a white marble façade, the building's edges and trim were gilded to look like leafy vines and paisleys. Tall white marble pillars supported a balcony over the front entry, which was, itself, impressive with massive ten-foot solid kendlewood doors.

The home was set back from the street for privacy and was surrounded by a bright green lawn dotted with carved topiaries and flowering gardens. Several large oaks provided a respite from the sun and shaded the more delicate flowers from the luminous disk's punishing rays. The entire grounds were surrounded by a stone wall about eight feet in height with a heavy stylized iron gate that swung open on well-greased hinges. No one manned the gate, so Rezkin assumed it was only locked at night.

Lieutenant Jimson took his leave saying that he would send someone to collect the horses and would call on them in a few days. Reaylin insisted on handing her horse over immediately arguing that she could find her own way to wherever she was staying. Jimson wanted to escort her, but she flatly refused. As a compromise, he purchased a fare on one of the rickshaws for her. Reaylin had actually been excited to have the opportunity to ride in one, so she did not complain. She claimed she would return in a few days to find out when they were leaving for the tournament.

The horses clattered over the cobbled path that ended in a loop wide enough for a carriage or coach to turn around. As the three remaining travelers dismounted, the massive front door swung open silently. An older man in dark blue livery awaited their approach. Unsure how to address the weary travelers who were caked in road dust and damp from the summer's heat, the man bowed deferentially. Without meeting the eyes of any one person, he said, "Welcome to House Marcum. How may I assist you?"

Frisha bounded forward with a grand smile and said, "I am Frisha Souvain. My uncle is expecting me."

The steward's eyebrows nearly touched his thinning grey hairline as a friendly smile graced his face. "Ah, Lady Frisha," he said as he bowed even lower. "I am Narus, Steward of House Marcum. It is my honor to serve you. We have been eagerly awaiting your arrival. Your uncle is not here at the moment, but I will send a runner to inform him of your arrival. Please enter."

Frisha and Tam started forward, but Rezkin caught the young woman's arm. Frisha shivered at his touch and looked at him questioningly. Rezkin thumbed over his shoulder back at the horses. "I should see to Pride, first."

The observant steward said, "I assure you our stable hands will do a fine job of caring for the horses, Lord …" The statement turned question hung in the air until Frisha realized she should probably introduce her companions.

"Oh, my. I am so sorry. I should have introduced my friends. This is my long-time friend and escort from Cheswick, Tamarin Blackwater, carpenter's apprentice and future recruit of the King's Army. And, this is Rezkin, um … a dear friend and protector." Frisha blushed, realizing somehow she still did not know enough about Rezkin to introduce him properly.

Steward Narus bowed slightly toward Tam and even lower toward Rezkin and said, "It is my pleasure to meet you both." Then, to Rezkin he said, "Lord Rezkin, I will send for someone to care for the horses and retrieve your belongings."

"It would be best if I tend to Pride myself. He is a trained battle charger and can be quite aggressive," Rezkin explained.

"I see," the Steward replied, showing not a hint of surprise. "Then, I shall send for Stable Master Finnian. He has cared for General Marcum's battle charger for many years. He is quite capable of handling the stallion."

Rezkin was satisfied and nodded appreciatively. "Very well. I will entrust him to the Stable Master. Let me know if the stubborn mule gives him any trouble. Also, please tell the servants to be careful with my things. Some of them are very sharp, and I would not want anyone injured on my behalf. If they do not feel comfortable with the items, I will retrieve them myself."

Narus gave the young lord a gracious smile. It was not every day he met a noble, or anyone, for that matter, who was so concerned with the servants' welfare. "I thank you, Lord Rezkin, for your concern and patience. However, I do not think it will be necessary. This is the general's home, and the servants are accustomed to working around sharp things," he said as he led them into a sitting room and gracefully waved a hand toward the walls around them.

Indeed, the walls were filled with sharp things. It was obvious this was the general's sitting room and not that of his wife. Unusual swords, axes, daggers and bows were artfully displayed on each wall and shelf. Halberds, spears, pole axes, and other odd, long-handled weapons rested in racks along the walls. A pair of scythes with silk-wrapped, black handles and silver blades polished to a mirrored shine were mounted in a case. Those were definitely not used for hewing wheat.

Beside each weapon was a carved plaque that identified the item and its place of origin. Some even had a note about the people who used such a weapon or how it was obtained. Several plaques indicated that those particular weapons were no longer in use and were only of historical significance. Rezkin had learned about most of these weapons and even knew how to use them, but there were a few that even he had never seen. He was thoroughly impressed with the collection and hoped to spend more time examining the items.

"Wow, I've never seen so many different kinds of weapons. Do you think the general actually knows how to use all of these?" Tam asked.

"The general is very particular about these weapons. They are for display only. He does have a separate armory for functional weapons that I am sure he will be overjoyed to share. They truly are his pride and joy," replied the steward stepping back into the room after delivering instructions to the various servants. A few moments later, a young maid entered the room, curtsied, and then whispered to the steward.

"The lady of the house will be with you shortly. She is most eager to receive you all. In the meantime, if you would like to follow me to the parlor, some refreshments will be served."

This sounded like an excellent idea to all three of the parched travelers, so they enthusiastically followed the steward. The parlor was well lit having several large windows along two walls. Pale blue curtains framed the windows, which matched the embroidered blue flowers on the pearly white lounge and chairs. Rich cherry tables and cabinets were arranged throughout the room displaying a number of porcelain vases and carved statues and busts. Several of the vases contained attractive floral arrangements that cast a sweet scent on the air. All three travelers, covered in road grime, were careful not to track dirt across the intricately woven blue and grey rug that covered the dark wood floor.

Two maids delivered tea in small delicate cups with tiny silver stirring spoons. Sweet cakes, which were served on plates only slightly larger than the saucer, were to be eaten with miniature silver forks. Tam was visibly uncomfortable with the fancy fare, but Rezkin called upon his etiquette lessons to sip and stir and nibble with courtly grace. Still, he felt out of place doing so while wearing travel clothes and armor.

Not long after the three companions settled themselves in the parlor, a woman who could only be the Lady Adelina swept into the room with a brilliant smile. "Oh, my dear Frisha! I am so glad to see you. You are a sight to behold. My, you look so much like your mother. You have grown so much, and you have her eyes and bone structure," Adelina said fondly.

Lady Adelina was a tall woman whose womanly grace had not diminished with age. Her dark brown hair, streaked with grey, was wound in a loose bun atop her head, and the fine lines around her eyes and mouth gave her the look of a woman who laughed and smiled often.

"Aunt Adelina, thank you so much for having us. It is good to see you again."

"Yes, yes, you must introduce me to your companions," the matron said as her gaze finally took in the others in the room. When they landed on Rezkin, her eyes widened as though in recognition, but the look was quickly replaced with uncertainty.

"This is my lifelong friend, Tamarin Blackwater. We call him Tam. You might actually remember him from your visits with us when we were children," Frisha remarked.

"Oh, yes, Tam," Lady Adelina said, taking the young man's hands as though he were family. "I do remember you. You and Frisha were always getting into some kind of trouble or other. If I remember correctly, you may have been responsible for a frog in my wardrobe?"

Tam's face turned bright red, and he tugged at his collar. "Ah, Lady Adelina, I am truly sorry for that. I was only seven and …"

Lady Adelina laughed and swatted him playfully. "No, Tam, dear. Not to worry. You both were such energetic children, and I enjoyed every minute of it." A hint of sadness passed over her face but was gone so quickly one could not be sure it had been there at all. Despite the healer's efforts, General and Lady Marcum had not been able to have children of their own.

When the lady turned to meet Rezkin, her previous look of uncertainty returned, and she became a bit apprehensive. "This is our good friend, Rezkin. We met him in Justain."

"Rezkin?" she asked. "Not *Lord* Rezkin?"

"Just Rezkin, my lady," the young man replied with a courtly bow. Now, she believed him even less.

"You are from Justain?" the lady asked.

"No, my lady. I had only arrived in the city and was enjoying the inn's hospitality when I met the Lady Frisha and Master Tam," Rezkin replied formally. Frisha and Tam both looked askance. They were reminded of how proper he had acted that first night they met. After traveling with the man for weeks, living off the land and surviving two battles, they had forgotten how gracious and noble he behaved in a more civilized environment. Even in his travel-worn clothes and leather armor, his entire countenance said noble upbringing.

Lady Adelina stared up at the gentleman stranger with his strong jawline, chiseled cheekbones and full lips. His jet black hair and icy-blue eyes would have made anyone look twice, but his imposing figure and stately bearing made her feel like she was looking at someone else from long ago. Frisha's words brought her out of her reverie, and the lady blushed when she realized she had been staring.

"It is entirely because of Rezkin that we are even here, Aunt Adelina. It was terrible," Frisha said as she began to ramble faster and faster. "There were brigands and bandits and a sunken ship, and we had to walk for a week in the wild just to get to a city. Oh, Aunt Adelina, there were *battles*. And … and people *died*. And, poor Tam had to *kill* someone, and Rezkin, too. And Reaylin was beaten nearly to death and the lieutenant saved me from a crossbow bolt, I think, and …"

Lady Adelina's eyes were as wide as saucers as she hurried over to put her arms around her niece who was now thoroughly sobbing. "My dear, stop, stop. You are okay, now. My goodness! It sounds like you all have been through something terrible." As the lady stroked Frisha's hair, she turned to Rezkin and asked, "You are all staying here, correct?"

Rezkin's brow was furrowed as he looked upon Frisha with concern. She had remained so strong the entire journey, and it seemed now that they had reached her family safely, it was all rushing in on her. He wanted to help her somehow but did not know what to do. This was not the type of battle he could fight for her. Rezkin glanced up at the lady's question and bowed politely, "If you would have me, I would be in your debt."

The lady waved away his words. "No, I do not know what exactly has happened, but it sounds like it is we who are in your debt. Please, come with me. I will show you to your rooms where you can rest. The servants will prepare baths for each of you. You are our guests, so please, if there is anything you require, do not hesitate to ask."

Rezkin performed another slight bow and said, "You are most gracious, Lady Adelina. I am honored to partake of your hospitality."

Lady Adelina smiled and nodded. The handsome young man was fooling no one if he thought to hide his nobility. She wondered briefly to which house he belonged, but she already had her suspicions.

Adelina led the way up the stairs with her arm wrapped around Frisha, whose crying was only slightly more controlled than it had been moments ago. At the top of the stairs, the lady of the house turned to the right. She informed her guests that the rooms to the left of the stairs consisted of the solar, sewing room, and servants' quarters. She nodded to the first room on the left side of the right wing and indicated that it would be Rezkin's room. The next room on the right belonged to Tam, and the room at the end of the corridor on the left was for Frisha. The corridor ended at a larger door that she informed them was the master suite.

Rezkin entered his assigned room. He was glad it was nearest to the stairs. Not only did it allow for a quicker escape in the event of an attack or emergency, it would also enable him to better monitor anyone entering the upper floor at night. The room was spacious with a sitting area near the door. A large hearth was set into the wall to his right, and two tall bookcases stood to either side like literary sentinels. The furniture and draperies were modest in design, not nearly as ostentatious or feminine as the parlor downstairs. Greens and gold adorned the room with a plush beige carpet laid out before the fireplace. A portrait of some important couple hung above the mantle, probably Frisha's grandparents. He thought he saw a slight resemblance. Beyond the sitting area, a large bed sat upon a dais. The bed had elegantly carved posts and green and gold bed curtains tied back with golden cords. The mound of pillows called to him after such a long time traveling.

Rezkin noted that his pack and saddlebags were sitting propped against the dais. He checked the contents to confirm that nothing was broken or missing. After verifying everything was in order, he went about checking the room for traps and poisons. He knew it was highly unlikely that anyone in the household would want to harm him at this point, but years of conditioning would not be overridden so easily. A light tapping at the door interrupted him from his perusal.

"Enter," he barked.

A heavyset, middle-aged maid and a gangly young man in leathers entered the room carrying a large copper tub. Two younger maids carrying pails of steaming water followed. After setting the heavy tub down opposite the hearth, the older maid dipped a slight curtsy and rasped in a bored tone, "If you please, my lord, we will prepare your bath."

"Yes, that is most appreciated," Rezkin replied.

The servants gave him curious look, bobbed once more and hurried from the room to collect more buckets of water. The young man knew they were looking at him oddly because it was not proper protocol for a lord to thank his servants, but Rezkin was not attempting to play the part of a lord. He had decided that until it was necessary to play a role, he would just act like himself. Since he did not really know *who* he was, he just allowed them to think what they wished.

Most people seemed to want to believe he was a noble. Since Rezkin was not raised to know much about commoners and commoner *things*, being treated as a noble did make the most sense. He still could not think of himself as a noble, though. In fact, he had a difficult time thinking of himself in the context of any of the social groups or hierarchies. He could not even think of himself as a soldier since his training and education had gone far above and beyond what any soldier would be expected to know.

Luckily, the travelers had arrived around mid-afternoon. That meant that they had a few hours to clean up and rest before they were expected to appear for dinner. General Marcum sent word that he was busy taking care of important business but would join them for the evening meal. After soaking in the hot bath and scrubbing the grit and sweat from his hair and body, Rezkin took the opportunity to clean his supplies and armor. He was just settling down beside the hearth to rewrap his ax handle when another tap sounded at the door.

Since Rezkin was wearing nothing but a drying cloth wrapped around his waist he called out, "Yes? Who is it?"

"It's me, Tam," came the muffled reply.

"Enter," Rezkin responded.

Tam stepped into Rezkin's quarters, leaving the door slightly ajar. He found the man sitting practically naked by the hearth fumbling with an ax.

"What are you doing?" Tam inquired.

"I am rewrapping this handle. The leather came undone," Rezkin answered.

"No, I mean, why are you doing it in the nude?" Tam asked with a chuckle.

Rezkin motioned to the small mound of dirty clothes near the door and said, "Most of my clothes are dirty. I decided to dress closer to the dinner hour so that I do not get the others dirty as well. I hung them by the window to air out, and hopefully lose some of the wrinkles."

"Oh, right, that is why I'm here. Lady Adelina wanted to know if you needed something to wear to dinner tonight, but it seems you have it covered," Tam said tugging at his new tunic. It was made of fine quality green silk cut with simple clean lines and embroidered with white thread. The pants were of finely woven, dark brown wool. Rezkin nodded approvingly when he noted that Tam had polished his belt and strapped his sword at his hip.

Tam noticed Rezkin's appraisal and said, "Ah, the lady said it was considered *dress appropriate* to wear the sword with formal attire, especially in a soldier's home. She said the general would not be caught dead without his sword and that any man of standing keeps his sword on him at all times. It's kind of strange, really. These nobles seem backward. I think my parents would find it offensive if a guest of theirs thought he needed to wear a sword in their home."

Rezkin grunted. "You are not a noble. Nobles have different rules than commoners. They have *a lot* of rules about protocol and propriety and many of them are functionally pointless or seem to conflict with each other. A man is expected to carry a sword to dinner but not a dagger. A woman may carry a dagger but not a sword. Neither weapon is to be used or even drawn lest the man or woman offend the host. Therefore, the swords and daggers are largely decorative or ceremonial.

"Most nobles would not know how to draw their swords properly if their lives depended on it. Those who *do* learn do so solely for the purpose of showing off their superior skills to their peers and have absolutely no intention of ever using the skills in battle. *You* are a carpenter's apprentice. You learn to use a lathe because you need to use it, not so that you can show off your skills to the baker."

"An apt assessment," came a deep grumble from behind Tam. The young man nearly jumped out of his skin as he stumbled further into the room. Rezkin had heard the heavy footsteps ascend the stairs and knew a man had entered the corridor.

The man was close to the same height as Rezkin with broad shoulders and a narrow waist. He was dressed in a flawless black military uniform covered with flashy gold and silver medallions and insignia. A silver scabbard with a golden jewel encrusted hilt hung at his hip. Despite the man's age, which Rezkin knew to be about sixty-five, he was fit and moved with determination. His hair and short-cropped beard were once dark but were now mostly grey with streaks of white. Dark brown eyes sparkled with mirth at Tam's antics.

"Hello, young Tamarin. It is good to see you again, son," the general said as Tam recovered his wits.

Breathing heavily Tam chuckled and bowed to the older man. "Greetings, General Marcum. It is good to see you again, as well, and thank you for your hospitality." The lines were perfectly rehearsed and delivered. That was most likely the influence of Tam's mother ... or perhaps Frisha's father.

The general turned his attention to the young man sitting in the chair by the fire. The stranger looked completely unconcerned with the abrupt appearance of the General of the King's Army of Ashai in his bedchamber, particularly considering the young man was wearing nothing but a drying cloth about his waist. He rose with fluid grace. It was not his impressive physique or height that caught the general's attention but his eyes and face. That face was so much like ... but it could not be. Or could it?

The young man bowed courteously and said, "Greetings, General Marcum. I am Rezkin. The Lady Adelina has graciously offered your hospitality, and I hope it is not an imposition that I have accepted." This line was delivered with perfect sincerity and courtly grace. The young man might as well have been dressed in the most elegant finery for all the difference his nudity made. The man seemed to find no discomfort or shame in his lack of dress.

The general nodded in return. "Well met, Rezkin, is it? And your family name?"

"I have none, sir. I am simply Rezkin," the young man answered.

The general found that difficult to believe but did not push the issue. "Well, if my wife offered you a place here, then you are welcome, I am sure. I do apologize for intruding, but I overheard your conversation from the hall and thought to put a face to the words. I take it you are not one of these pompous nobles who cannot draw their own swords?"

"I assure you, General, I am *Skilled* in all of the weapons I wield," Rezkin stated with complete confidence.

"And that ax?" General Marcum asked nodding toward the weapon Rezkin had left on the floor near the chair.

Rezkin replied, "I would not bother to own it if I could not use it."

The general grunted. "You are a practical man, then. A soldier?"

Rezkin cocked his head in consideration. "I am a warrior but not a soldier."

"A mercenary?" asked the general with a hint of disapproval.

"Not as such," Rezkin stated. "I have taken no payment for any services, and thus far, all of my services since I left my training have been given freely to your niece and our friend, Tam, here."

Tam finally perked up at his name and added, "Rezkin provided protection and guidance for us both since we met him in Justain. If it were not for him, we would not have made it here. We had some serious trouble on the way."

"Is that so?" the general asked. "I will need to hear about this trouble and the services you provided, Rezkin. For now, I will let you get on with your business, and I will go greet my wife and niece. I will see you both at dinner." The general nodded once and departed.

Rezkin sat back down, picked up his ax and returned to rewrapping the handle just as he was before the interruption.

"I can't believe you had to meet the general in what amounts to little more than a loin cloth!" Tam laughed.

Rezkin shrugged unconcerned, "I had to meet him some time."

"Yes, but you're naked! Weren't you embarrassed or ashamed?" said Tam. "I would be."

Rezkin shook his head without looking up from his work. "I have nothing of which to be ashamed."

"No, I suppose you don't," Tam grumbled under his breath with just a hint of envy. He knew he would never measure up to Rezkin's perfect physique. It looked to him like the Maker had personally sculpted Rezkin to represent the ideal male form. While women tripped over themselves to get Rezkin's attention, they barely even glanced Tam's way. Tam could not fault the warrior, though. He was how he was, and Tam knew Rezkin worked hard to remain fit. Even more impressive, Rezkin displayed not a hint of superiority or conceit regarding his appearance.

Tam had always been fit and strong. He had to be in order to work as a carpenter, but he had never developed chiseled ridges and rippling muscles like Rez. He had to admit, though, that his own body was becoming more tone, and he was filling out since he began training with Rezkin. Maybe, given enough time, the ladies would start to notice him, as well. Tam shook the thought away. What was he thinking? He was joining the army soon. He would not have time for romance or a family.

A couple of hours later, everyone met in the formal dining room to partake of the evening meal. Rezkin dressed in his dark blue silk shirt and black breeches he had been saving for an occasion such as this. His masters had taught him that the clothes said a lot about a man, and Rezkin knew it to be true since he had been taught how to assess a man based on his attire. Master Peider said that to make the greatest impact, he should choose colors that complimented his features. He thought the dark blue and black with silver accents did just that for his smooth black hair and ice-blue eyes.

Rezkin replaced his usual worn belt with a new black one that was embossed with the images of ravens in flight along its length, and he mentally chuckled at the sight of the ravens. His scabbards and hilts were polished to a shine. On his feet were polished black boots in a dress military style. His clothes were not the ridiculously frilly garb typical of the courtiers. This was the fine dress style of a practical man of station, a man of power, a man who did not care for the opinions of others but demanded their respect instead.

Rezkin knew he should not have been, but he was surprised to see Frisha in a gown. It was a deep burgundy that brought out the hidden red highlights in her otherwise brown hair. The neckline was cut low, and her bosom was pushed up as though the two were attempting to switch places. Mounds upon mounds of silky fabric swirled around her legs, which had completely disappeared. Rezkin thought she looked lovely as usual, even if the dress was completely impractical. This was the way of nobles, though. He was not the only one who had to practice proper decorum when the situation demanded.

The Lady Adelina escorted Rezkin to the dining room, and he was seated to her right in the place of honor. This made Rezkin feel a little uncomfortable since he did not know why he was being treated so. Tam sat to Lady Adelina's left, and Frisha was to the right of the general next to Tam.

After a bit of small talk the general commented, "So, Rezkin, I take it that is your battle charger in my stable. I went out just before supper to check on my own, and imagine my surprise to find another. Wherever did you get him, might I ask?"

This was a difficult question for Rezkin to answer without going into the details of his life at the fortress, something he was not willing to do with the general considering he had been ordered to kill fifteen of the kingdom's strikers. Rezkin decided to hedge. "I sort of inherited him from my masters upon completion of my training."

"I see," the general commented neutrally. "And, where did you train?"

Frisha perked up at finally having something to share about Rez that she actually knew. "He was raised in a fort by a bunch of soldiers. I'm sorry, Rez, I cannot imagine what it would have been like to have been raised without your family," she said, looking at him with compassion.

Rezkin shrugged and replied, "It is simply how things were. I knew no different, so I missed nothing."

The general considered the information. If Rezkin was an orphan from an unknown family, it would explain his lack of family name, but then he would have taken the name of the town or region in which he was raised. "What fort was that?" the general questioned with interest.

Lady Adelina broke in, "Marcum, dear, let the young man eat. You can interrogate him later." Changing the subject, she said, "Frisha, love, I know things must be so different for you here with us. It will take some time for you to get used to being around the nobility. If you have any questions, please, do not hesitate to ask."

"Of course, Aunt Adelina, thank you," Frisha replied with relief.

"I have a question," Tam said cautiously.

"Yes, Tamarin, dear, what is it?" Lady Adelina asked. Her excitement over getting to share her knowledge was plain to see.

"Well, my name is Tamarin Blackwater. My father's and mother's and brothers' and cousins' names are all Blackwater. The general is Marcum Jebai, but you are Lady Adelina Marcum and this is House Marcum. Why are you not Jebai?"

Lady Adelina laughed softly. "Oh, I guess that would be a little confusing. You see, only the immediate family of the direct bloodline are called Jebai. Marcum's brother, Simeon, is the eldest son of Jerand Jebai and is now the Lord Jebai, Count of Glasbury. Simeon's wife is the Lady Jebai, Countess of Glasbury, and all of his children are Lords and Lady Jebai. Simeon is the head of House Jebai.

"Marcum, being a son of Jerand, is also a Jebai, but I, as his wife, am simply the Lady Marcum, and any of his children … if he had any … would be called Marcum after his given name. Therefore, Marcum is the head of House Marcum. It makes it easy to identify the direct lines of the great houses, but it creates a mess of smaller houses of which one cannot possibly keep track."

Tam thought he understood. "So, my father is a Blackwater. I have three older brothers. If we were nobles, my eldest brother, Cainith, would marry and have children who would be called Blackwater. If I married and had children, my children would be Tamarin?"

With a pleased smile the lady replied, "Yes, exactly, although I think it would be so much easier if the nobility followed the common customs in this and passed down the family name through the male line."

The general grunted. "Yes, well, I think the same can be said for many of the customs of the nobility."

Frisha asked, "What happens if the main bloodline dies? If, the Maker forbid, Uncle Simeon's line failed, then Uncle Marcum would inherit, correct? Then would you become a Jebai?"

"Yes, Marcum's descendants and I would be Jebai," Lady Adelina replied.

"What about the king?" asked Tam. "I don't think I've ever heard his family name."

The general grunted and replied, "That is because the line of kings does not carry a family name. Each king rules only by his given name, and his descendants bear no family name as well. They are simply distinguished by their titles of king, queen, prince or princess. Nieces, nephews, cousins and such all take on the family name of their other parent who married into the royal family."

"Why would they do that?" asked Tam.

"It was King Coroleus, over a thousand years ago, who started the tradition. He said the royal family belonged to all of Ashai so he would hold no family above his kingdom. That is why he was simply known as King Coroleus of Ashai," answered the general.

As a guest, Rezkin knew he was expected to add to the conversation, so he expounded on the general's statement. "King Coroleus was the first king to unite the lands of Ashai in defense against their common enemy that was, at that time, known as the Jahartan Empire. Before Coroleus, all of the lands were governed by independent lords who cared little for any people besides their own. It was purely by his strength of character, powerful bearing, and brilliant mind that he was able to unite the lands and drive off the enemy who would otherwise have decimated the lands. The lords, recognizing their strength in unity, crowned Coroleus as their king."

"That is correct and well spoken, I might add," replied the general. "But, how do you know it was the Jahartan Empire that was attacking at that time? None of the official records survived the First Rebellion, and none of the other known records of the events at the time actually name the aggressor."

Rezkin nodded and replied, "That is so, but Persilius's *Treatise on the Succession of Domains*, written during the last year of Coroleus's reign, describes the attacking Empire soldiers as wearing conical helms and riding great horses out of the desert. One ancient poem, written around eleven hundred years ago by a Penoian scholar refers to the *carasuan ej venuta coa Jaharta*, which roughly translates to the *cone-heads of Jaharta*. The Jahartan military helms were conical in shape.

"The *Colectuai Shu Dueja*, which was a text on common merchant practices from the same time period, notes that the large sleek horses we have today could only be found in Jaharta and Galathia at the time. Galathia was a *kingdom* and has never been referred to in any of the texts as an *empire*. It was described as having forested hills and grasses surrounded by mountains to the north and east.

"Jaharta, however, *was* named an empire—one that attempted to expand its borders numerous times throughout its history. It was also described as being a vast, barren desert. Therefore, it stands to reason that the great empire, against which Coroleus and the allied lands fought, was the Jahartan Empire."

Everyone was listening to Rezkin with rapt attention. They were equally surprised by Rezkin's thorough knowledge of the subject, and his own confidence in his words left no doubt in their minds that what he said was true.

"That is fascinating," General Marcum said. "Where did you read such a well-researched appraisal? I would be interested to read it, myself."

Rezkin shook his head. "I am afraid that argument has yet to be recorded. When I came to the conclusion, I admit, I had little time or interest in keeping a record. I actually never considered the possibility that others would care," he added as an afterthought.

The general was staggered with disbelief. "You mean to tell me *you* came to that conclusion on your own?"

Rezkin cocked his head at the general's unexpected reaction. "Well, it *did* take quite a bit of time to research. I think I spent a good three or four weeks poring over the texts and scrolls in the evenings. But, that was several years ago, so I suppose it could have been a little more or less."

"Three or four weeks," the general stated incredulously, "in the evenings." Marcum leaned forward and narrowed his eyes at Rezkin. "How old are you? Twenty-four? Twenty-five?"

Rezkin furrowed his brow in confusion. What did his age have to do with the conversation? Why were people always asking about it? So as not to be rude he answered, "I am nineteen."

The general sat back and tapped his fingers on the table in contemplation. Nineteen? It was much younger than he had guessed. A ridiculous thought crossed his mind, which he dismissed immediately. But maybe …

"Well, Rezkin," Lady Adelina said cheerfully, "I, for one, was very impressed with your knowledge, and you express your thoughts very well." Looking around the table she said, "I think we are all finished. Shall we retire to the study where we can continue our conversation in comfort?"

Everyone thanked the lady hostess for the delicious meal and followed her to the study. It was a warm room filled with hard woods and sturdy sofas and chairs with deep red fabric. The floor was covered with thick, woven rugs, and several portraits and tapestries hung from the walls. A few book cases and tables were arranged for actual studying in the study. It was obvious that those in House Marcum were well read. Books were uncommon and costly, and the modest estate seemed to be full of them.

General Marcum and Lady Adelina seated themselves in chairs adjacent to each other. It looked as if they were accustomed to sitting just so in the evenings. Tam claimed the remaining chair, which left Rezkin to sit either next to Frisha on the sofa or on a separate sofa farther away, which would have appeared awkward. She smiled pleasantly as he sat next to her.

Rezkin adjusted his swords when he sat and caught the general eyeing them speculatively. The man could not tell from the outward appearance that they were Sheyalins, but carrying two swords was unusual enough.

Two blades could be awkward in close battle and required more room to maneuver. In addition, keeping track of them was a skill that took an immense amount of time to develop. One had to be an expert in wielding a sword with each hand before blending them together in an altogether new technique. Someone with less than expert skill could do more harm to himself than an opponent. It was generally not a recommended technique because it was so difficult to master, and it was often ridiculed as being foolhardy and showy for amateurs and idiots who wanted to appear more dangerous.

Thus far, the general thought, *this Rezkin does not seem to be an idiot.*

General Marcum allowed his eyes to travel over the three young people before him as he spoke. "My wife tells me you had some trouble on your journey here. Please tell me all about it. Of course, I am concerned as an uncle, but I am also asking as the general."

Tam and Frisha both looked to Rez. Through his role as protector and guide, he had inadvertently become the leader. Rezkin nodded toward Frisha and said, "You go ahead and tell your aunt and uncle. Tam and I will add any additional details to satisfy the general."

Marcum grunted his approval. This was a smart young man.

"I don't really know where to start. Well, Tam and I left Cheswick …" Frisha began and continued the story through to the end. She left out little from her perspective, but Rezkin knew much was still missing, and the general suspected it as well.

General Marcum followed Frisha's story becoming angrier by the minute. "We have been receiving reports of increased bandit activity along the rivers and roads, but nothing indicated it was as frequent or widespread as this. I will definitely be looking into this Lieutenant Jimson's reports. We should also be receiving reports in a few days from the patrol on the trade route. They should have found the bodies you left unless someone claimed them. I doubt the reports will tell anything you do not already know, though." He finished with his gaze on Rezkin.

The general returned his attention to his niece and said, "Frisha, had I known circumstances were so severe, I would have insisted on an armed escort to bring you here. I know you tried your best, Tamarin, but from what I just heard, there was little you could have done." He turned to Rezkin once again. "It is truly most fortunate that you were there, Rezkin. Tell me, when you met Frisha, did you know she was my niece? Were you seeking my favor by protecting her?"

"Uncle Marcum!" Frisha gasped.

Marcum held up a hand to stall the young woman's protests as he held the stranger's gaze.

Rezkin waved away Frisha's protests indicating he was not upset by the question. "I had never seen you or Frisha, and she does not bear your family name, so I could not have known she was your niece. Additionally, I do not require or desire your favor except in that it pleases Frisha."

"Almost every man in the kingdom could come up with some reason to want the favor of the general of the army," Marcum countered.

Rezkin shrugged. "Be that as it may, I can think of none for myself. Any favor I would ask of you would only be on Frisha's behalf."

The general narrowed his eyes at the smooth-talking young man. "Did you know why she was coming here? Did you seek to claim her as your wife and thereby acquire my estate upon my death?"

"Uncle Marcum, how could you accuse him of such a thing? I can honestly say that he was genuinely surprised when I told him who you were to me and why I was coming to Kaibain … and I did not even tell him until we had already reached Lorelis. He risked his life for us and never asked for anything in return!" Frisha declared.

The general directed his hard gaze at the young woman and stated firmly, "*That* is what has me concerned, and surprise can be faked." Turning back to Rezkin, he waited for a reply.

"I doubt there is anything I could say to convince you, General, but I will say this, now. I do not now, nor have I ever had, any designs on your estate. I do not need your money or influence. My purpose all along was to protect and honor my *friends*, which I have done to the best of my abilities. If you truly have concerns about my integrity, General, I do not hold that against you since you do not know me. If you and the lady wish, I will gather my belongings and go elsewhere," Rezkin stated dispassionately.

"Now, Marcum, you have offended our guest," Lady Adelina admonished. "Please, Rezkin, forgive my husband. We do not wish you to leave."

Rezkin smiled pleasantly at the lady to show he was not upset. "Do not fret, Lady Adelina. I am not offended. The general's concerns are understandable, and I appreciate that he is protective of Frisha. I hope that he is just as discriminating when it concerns her actual suitors. I believe that for most of them, if any, her well-being will not be at the forefront of their aspirations."

Rezkin turned his attention back to the general. "And, yes, General Marcum, Frisha has already made it clear that she intends to select a husband from among your nobles when she is ready. I believe that her dowry has made her valuable enough to desire but not noble enough to respect. Surely her husband will eventually come to see her as the strong and passionate woman that she is," Rezkin said.

General Marcum was taken aback by the young man's candidness. While he did not like what Rezkin had to say about the nobles and how they would treat Frisha, he grudgingly admitted to himself that it was true. She would never be seen as an equal. The best she could probably hope for was a distant, loveless marriage where she lived in luxury but was otherwise ignored. He had hopes, though, that one of the young men he had selected would develop a genuine interest in his niece.

Tamarin broke through the general's thoughts. "I know it's not really my business, but Frisha is like a sister to me. I don't see what is so wrong with Rezkin being with Frisha even if he *was* after your estate, which for the record, I don't believe is the case. These nobles will only want her for your estate, also —sorry Frisha—at least Rezkin has already proven himself capable and willing to put his own life on the line for her protection. And, Rezkin has proven himself honorable over and again. He lives by this strict code, like a knight. I would much rather she be with Rezkin than some snotty noble who won't care for her. Uh, sorry Lady Adelina, I shouldn't have said that last part."

The general opened his mouth to retort and then realized he did not have one. Rezkin was sitting back wondering how they had come to a debate whether he should enter into a marriage contract with Frisha. Frisha sat next to Rezkin hiding her face in her hands. She was completely mortified that everyone was having this conversation about her, all around her, and she was apparently the only one who had no say. Rezkin noticed Frisha hiding herself and instinctively reached out to stroke her hair. It always helped to calm Pride when the stallion was upset.

General Marcum was watching Rezkin. The young man's concern for his niece did seem genuine enough. He still had many concerns about the young man's vague background, though. Nothing seemed to be adding up, and he had a growing suspicion he knew why.

Rezkin turned his attention back to the lord and lady of the house and stated, "We have had many long days of travel, including this day, and recounting the trials of our journey is upsetting for both Frisha and Tam. If it would not offend you both, I think it is time for us to retire."

"Oh, of course, Rezkin, dear," Lady Adelina replied. "You are completely correct. We should not have engaged in such a heated conversation when you are all so weary from your travels and trials. Please, get some rest and feel free to sleep through the morning if you wish. We will not be offended if you do not show for breakfast. I know how draining these things can be."

Rezkin stood and bowed politely as he replied, "You are a most gracious hostess, Lady Adelina."

Rezkin turned and nudged Frisha to stand. Her face was red and her eyes were puffy with unshed tears. She was trying her best to hold them at bay. He reached up to stroke her cheek. Looking into her eyes he said softly, "Do not fret, Frisha. You are safe now."

Looking into Rezkin's crystal blue eyes and being so close to his calm, reassuring presence, she realized she truly did feel safe. "I know," she said sincerely. Frisha took a deep breath and caught a whiff of Rezkin's clean, masculine scent. Suddenly, the troubles that had plagued her only moments ago were assuaged. Her face and shoulders relaxed and she smiled.

Rezkin escorted Frisha up the stairs but stopped at his door, allowing the young woman to continue down the corridor to her own room. When he entered his room, he stretched his taut muscles and set about checking the space for traps and poisons.

15

The next day, Rezkin woke early as usual. He made his way to the stables to check on Pride and then found a clear area at the rear of the property to practice his various fighting forms. He needed to keep his *Skills* honed, and he found that he could not bear the tedium of the languorous outworlder life-style. It took much less effort to maintain his *Skills* now that he had mastered each one, but he continued to feel anxious if he did not get enough practice. It was simply another one of those habits that had been conditioned into him throughout his life.

The night before, after he had returned to his room, he was agitated and needed to release some of his pent up energy. Instead of going to sleep right away, he spent a few hours crawling over the estate. He perused the extent of the outer grounds, slinked across the roof, surveyed the cellar, picked every lock and broke into each and every room. When he entered the master suite that night, the general's years of soldiering paid him service. The older man awoke sensing something amiss, but after he could not find the source from where he lay, he fell back to sleep. An inspection of the general's office revealed the man kept nothing of political or military interest in his home, and the household accounts and correspondence were typical and of little interest.

When Rezkin finished skulking about, he felt much more at ease. The spy mission did more than just expend some of his pent up energy. It had also served to allay some of his concerns about staying in the home of the general of the army for the kingdom against which he might just be a traitor. Now that he had a thorough knowledge of the property, he could formulate a number of escape routes and plan for the best positions of attack and defense.

After he finished his morning routine, he used the hand pump near the kitchen to rinse his body clean of sweat. The sun's first rays were just beginning to breach the horizon, and most of the household was asleep or just beginning to stir. He entered the home through the rear of the kitchens and procured a plate of bacon, eggs, and biscuits from the young maid who assisted the cook. Rezkin thanked her. She smiled sweetly and batted her lashes at him, and then he sat down at a small table to one side. Just as he was finishing his meal, the general entered in search of his own breakfast. Rezkin stood and performed a slight bow in greeting as the maid cleared away his dishes.

"Up early, I see. It looks as if you have already performed your physical training exercises, as well," the general commented. It was his attempt at civility, but not being much of a conversationalist, he stuck to soldier speak. The self-proclaimed warrior did not seem to mind.

Rezkin nodded once in the affirmative and said, "I have."

General Marcum grunted. "If only my soldiers were so motivated. I would have an unbeatable army."

Rezkin said nothing in response. He did not want to point out how lacking he found the soldiers. Most of the officers he had seen could hold their own, at least against each other, but the enlisted were little better than farmers whose pitchforks had been swapped for swords. The poor security he had encountered in Lorelis was quite discouraging, as well.

"So, what are your plans for today, Rezkin?" the general asked casually. His wife had insisted on a long discussion with him about his poor treatment of their guest the night before. The general was still suspicious and uncomfortable having the mysterious, and apparently dangerous, young man in his home and near his family. Adelina had been horrified when Rezkin rightfully questioned his welcome after she accepted him as a guest. Marcum received the brunt of her distress and was attempting to behave more amiably this morning, even though his opinions had not changed.

The young man replied, "Frisha and Tam will be rising soon, at which time we will conduct their daily weapons training. They expressed a desire to visit some of the shops, so I intend to accompany them afterward. I also need to restock a few of my medical supplies, having used quite a few during the journey."

"You do not appear injured," remarked the general.

"Indeed, I am not. After the first battle with the bandits I used quite a few supplies in treating the soldiers. On the second leg of the journey, a couple of incidents resulted in injuries for my companions, the worst of which were incurred by Mistress Reaylin during the second bandit attack," Rezkin explained.

"You provided all of these treatments yourself?" the general asked.

"Yes," Rezkin replied. Knowing the general expected an explanation, Rezkin continued, "During my training, I worked with several healers in sort of an apprenticeship. I mastered the healing *Skills* of treating injuries and illness, identifying and procuring healing plants and minerals, and preparing potions, draughts, antidotes, and ointments." Rezkin thought it prudent to leave out the fact that he was also a Poison Master. "I have no innate healing ability, however, so my abilities are limited to the mundane."

"You are a master healer of the mundane? At nineteen?" the general asked with incredulity.

Rezkin inclined his head in affirmation. A master healer would also possess innate healing powers like Master Peider and were rare enough to be extremely costly and in high demand. In fact, many master healers did not bother to learn the mundane healing techniques if their powers were great enough. A master healer of the mundane, uncommon in itself, had all of the skills of a healer without innate powers. Few healers reached the status of master healer and were simply referred to as healers. Being a skilled master healer of the mundane could be quite lucrative.

"You have papers to prove your claim?" the general asked.

Rezkin shook his head. "I have no need of papers. Being a healer is not my purpose in life. A lack of papers will not prevent me from using the *Skills* when I need them."

That was absurd. Why would someone spend years mastering such a difficult profession not to use it? The general did not believe Rezkin's claim for a moment.

"You said you are a warrior. I have not known many healers to take up the sword. They concern themselves with healing people rather than injuring them," the general countered.

Rezkin shrugged. "I am many things," he said cryptically. The general was a shrewd man. He would have to be to gain the position he held. Usually, Rezkin could get around people's suspicions by saying little, but General Marcum pressed him for answers.

Rezkin was saved from additional questions by Tam's arrival. "Good morning," the affable young man said with a broad smile.

"Good morning, Tam," Rezkin replied with a smile of his own.

"Tamarin." The general nodded in greeting.

"Frisha will be down in a moment," Tam said. Just as he said this, Frisha shuffled through the door. Tam looked at Rezkin apologetically. "I nearly had to drag her from the bed," he said.

"You could have slept a bit longer. You both needed the rest after the journey," Rezkin remarked.

Tam shook his head with a grin. "Your rules, Rezkin. Training at dawn. You're not the only one who can follow rules."

Frisha gave Tam a sideways look that morphed into a scowl. She was dressed in her tunic and pants and carried her belt and throwing knives in her hand.

"What is this?" the general asked, remembering Rezkin had said something about weapons training. "What are you three up to?"

Tam, still grinning, said, "Rez has been training us to fight. He started teaching us both the sword, but then he switched Frisha to throwing knives. He said something about not wanting her to get close enough to the enemy to use a sword. Plus, she refused to carry one being a woman and all … not that it stopped Reaylin." Frisha scowled at the mention of the young female warrior. Tam continued excitedly. "Look at this! He bought us weapons. Lieutenant Jimson said my sword is better than the one the army issued him."

The general grunted. "It is not difficult to find a sword better than those. The one the lieutenant carries is probably better than most since he is an officer, but those issued to the enlisted are little better than scrap metal," he remarked as he examined Tam's blade.

"Then why do you use them?" Tam asked.

"If it were up to me, we would not," General Marcum answered.

Tam furrowed his brow in confusion. "But, you're the general of the army. Isn't it up to you?"

The general shook his head. "I am in charge of the army, not the treasury.

They are the best we can afford in bulk for the average soldier based on the funds I am provided."

"So who decides how much money you can spend and what you can spend it on?" asked Tam.

"In this case, the king," said the general. "King Bordran kept the army supplied well, but since King Caydean was crowned, our funds have been significantly reduced, and in the past few months, our recruitment quota has increased."

"The king is building up the army?" Rezkin asked.

"Indeed. Makes one wonder why, does it not?" General Marcum commented.

"You don't know?" asked Tam with surprise.

The general scoffed, "Not even *I*, the general of the army, knows why. I am not sure anyone but the king, himself, knows." He handed Tam back his sword. "This is a good sword. I am glad to see you are taking the initiative to learn before you join up. If you perform well enough, you might even some day break through the barrier and become an officer."

"Commoners can do that?" Tam said excitedly.

Marcum nodded, "It is rare, but it can happen if a soldier proves himself to be a great leader of men. Of course, it generally happens during times of war. The soldier must not only prove himself in battle, but there must also be a need. In war, enemies will target the officers. If too many fall, the army must look to promote others. It is to our advantage to promote from within the seasoned veterans. Actually, I wish that I could promote all of my officers in such a way. Raising a man as a noble does not make him a soldier."

General Marcum turned to Frisha. "Young lady, you are learning knives? What have you there?" The general indicated her belt.

Frisha, clearly not ready to talk so early in the morning simply nodded and handed the belt with knives to the general. Marcum studied the fine quality of the leather and the decorative scrollwork. He examined the small knives and tested their weight and edges. "This is a very nice gift and an unusual design, I might add. I do not think I have seen the like," he remarked.

"I am still not very good," Frisha mumbled, "but I can sometimes stick them in the target, now, even if they don't hit where I want them to."

General Marcum laughed. "Frisha, my dear, do not fret. If you have achieved that, then you are doing well. These things take many years to master." Looking back to Rezkin he said, "I see that you have taken your promise of protection to the next level, Rezkin. From the story I heard last night, I can see that you have done well to protect them, but teaching them to protect themselves and making sure they have decent weapons with which to do so is most commendable."

Rezkin bowed at the unexpected compliment and said, "It is the best way to ensure their safety. I cannot be with both of them at all times. Lieutenant Jimson has improved, as well, and I expect he will make a fine showing in his tier at tournament."

"Is that so? Perhaps there is a promotion in his future, then," the general said. Glancing out of the kitchen door and noting the lightening of the sky, General Marcum said, "It is time for me to be gone. I have duties to which I must attend. Have a pleasant day."

General Marcum strode down the wide lane deep in contemplation. That *boy* could not possibly be a master healer of the mundane. At his age, he would have had to begin his apprenticeship at the age of four or five. It was absurd. He did not believe Rezkin for a moment, but at the same time, he was wary of thinking him a liar. It was a contradiction he could not resolve. Perhaps the young man had been duped. Some charlatan could have taken him under his wing for a couple of years, for a price of course, taught him a few herbs and techniques and proclaimed Rezkin a master. Marcum might have been able to convince himself of that if Rezkin did not appear to be so intelligent.

The young man was cultured, educated, well mannered, and conducted himself with both courtly grace and the elegance of a skilled warrior. Marcum had not yet seen the young man in action, but the way he moved indicated he was either a dancer or practiced fighter. Rezkin did not look like a dancer. He was a mystery the general could not solve. Every conclusion seemed to point in a different direction. The only confluence he could find was one he did not wish to consider.

Tam and Frisha worked their way through their exercises. Tam's motions grew more fluid as he became comfortable with the weight of the sword and motions of the forms. Rezkin always knew exactly when Tam had not performed correctly to the slightest nuance and was sure to correct him. In addition to memorizing the movements of the sword forms, Tam was learning to block. At first, Tam was hit nearly every time, but now he felt a growing sense of pride every time he managed to block a strike.

Frisha found that she was better able to clear her mind and focus when Rezkin was working with Tam. As soon as she caught the handsome warrior's attention, her concentration shattered, and her blades would fly wide or short of the target. This morning, Frisha was having particular difficulty clearing her mind. It was obvious that her uncle did not care for Rezkin, and she could not understand why. Rezkin was the model of perfection and had been courteous and exceptionally tolerant of her uncle's accusations the previous night. Frisha had been utterly mortified by the entire turn of events.

At first, Frisha was confused that Rezkin did not defend his desire to court her, but when he mentioned her intentions to marry one of the nobles, she was distraught. She had thought he understood after their previous conversation about going to the tournament that she really wanted *him*. Now that she thought back on it, she realized she had never actually expressed her feelings for him. She had only said that she wanted to go to the tournament and that she did not *want* to marry a noble. She had never said she *wouldn't* marry a noble or that she would choose Rezkin instead.

Rezkin, for his part, had not asked for any promises or show of interest. He had simply accepted her company for what it was and seemed happy with what he could get. On top of that, she knew from the general's reaction to her gifts that Rezkin had paid handsomely. Frisha felt terrible.

For the rest of the day, the three companions strolled along the streets and gawked at fancy things in expensive shops. Most of the shop owners were opposed to the idea of people perusing their wares without making any purchases, so they relegated themselves to peering through windows. Rezkin purchased another fine quality but serviceable tunic to replace the one that had been stained with blood from the battle with the bandits.

He saved the herbalist's shop for last since it was where he would need to procure the most items. Tam and Frisha followed him inside, wrinkling their noses at the strong scents that mingled in the small confines. Their eyes roved over the countless bottles and packets and pouches labeled with strange names that meant nothing to them. Rezkin was talking to the shop owner and seemed miffed.

"This is a ridiculous price for sparywort. I could go just outside the walls and collect bushels of the stuff," Rezkin asserted.

"But, you're paying for the *quality*. This sparywort was grown with the freshest water collected from the last winter ice in the light of the afternoon sun. The plant was then snipped with silver sheers on the eve of the full moon," the shopkeeper replied.

Rezkin scoffed. "This herb is used by apothecaries, not alchemists. None of those things matter for its healing properties, and it would be ridiculous for anyone to bother with performing those useless rituals. You most likely had your apprentice go out and gather this from the patch I saw growing near the bridge."

The shopkeeper, a sour-faced, middle-aged woman with dull, stringy blonde hair, sputtered, "I assure you, *boy*, I am a master herbalist, and I know what I am talking about. I did no such thing."

"Save your lies for someone who cares to hear them," Rezkin said with a frown. "There are quite a few things I require, but I will not be purchasing them from you. I *will* be reporting your business practices to the Healer's Guild, so we will see how *they* feel. Let *them* deal with you."

With that Rezkin motioned Tam and Frisha toward the door. As they exited the shop, the herbalist frantically called out, "My lord, wait, please. I may have been mistaken. Sparywort, did you say? My lord ..." She was cut off as the door closed behind them.

"What was that all about?" Tam asked.

"The woman was a thief and charlatan. I cannot imagine she always conducts her business in such a way, or she would not have a license to operate. Items always cost more in the city, but everything in that shop was priced at least three or four times what it should cost. I think she was trying to swindle me because of my age. She probably thought I was some struggling healer's apprentice who knows no better."

Frisha gasped, "That's even worse! That would mean she is stealing money from those who have the least and are struggling to make something of their lives."

Rezkin nodded once. "Exactly, which is why she needs to be reported."

"I agree," Frisha responded. "Do you think she does that to everyone or just *you* for some reason?"

"It is possible she thought I was a noble who could afford it," Rezkin replied.

Tam looked at him sideways, "A lot of people seem to think you're a noble. I can't say I disagree."

Rezkin shrugged but said nothing.

The trio headed to the Healer's Guild to report the herbalist's underhanded business practices. An elderly man with white hair that stuck up all over his head recorded the information Rezkin provided. The man was kind enough to give the young people the names of a few shops where they could purchase supplies at a reasonable price. After visiting one of the shops mentioned by the old healer, they returned to the general's estate. By the time they arrived it was already close to the dinner hour.

That evening at dinner, General Marcum asked, "So, Tamarin, when will you be visiting the recruiter's office?"

"I've decided to wait until after the tournament. Rezkin, Lieutenant Jimson, and Reaylin are all going to compete, and I'm going with them," Tam replied.

"Are you? I did not realize you were a duelist, Rezkin," General Marcum remarked with an underlying hint of disapproval.

"I am not," Rezkin replied, "but I am capable."

"What? I thought you were a duelist," Tam replied. "You told Jimson that you duel."

"I am proficient with the … *sport*," Rezkin replied, "but it is not my preference to compete in such a way. It is not a fighting technique that is suited to the battlefield. If you attempted to engage the enemy in such a way, you would be easily cut down. True battles are messy and lack rules of engagement. From your own experiences, I am sure you can appreciate that enemies, whether soldiers or bandits, will not adhere to any rules. Dueling is a brutal sport, but it is a sport, nonetheless. It was designed for the aristocracy to show off their *Skills* in a safe environment."

"I quite agree," stated General Marcum, "but that begs the question of why you intend to compete if you feel that way."

Rezkin considered how to answer the general's question. "Lieutenant Jimson made a few good points regarding the usefulness of such a competition. He said it was the only way he had to measure his progress relative to other duelists and claimed to have learned several new techniques from watching other combatants. The lieutenant also pointed out that the tournament is the only opportunity he had to observe a Swordmaster."

"Hmm, that is all good and well for the lieutenant, but it does not explain why *you* wish to compete," the general said.

Seeing that the general was not satisfied with his explanation, Rezkin merely shrugged and said, "I have my reasons."

"Which are?" Marcum asked.

Rezkin met the general's eyes and replied, "My own."

Frisha took that moment to jump into the conversation. "Actually, I have decided to go to this tournament as well."

"No," General Marcum said flatly.

"What?" Frisha asked in surprise.

"I said, no. You will not be traveling alone with these men any longer. It is not appropriate. The fact that you had to in order to get here can be excused, but I cannot abide you doing so simply for the adventure."

Frisha raised her chin in defiance and said, "All of my companions are honorable and most excellent protectors ... except maybe Reaylin," she remarked with repugnance, "but she is a woman, so that should not matter. One of your own lieutenants will be accompanying us. There is no reason to prevent me from joining them."

Lady Adelina decided to add her opinion to the mix. "Frisha, dear. We are supposed to be preparing you to meet with prospective husbands. We cannot have you running off with other men for extended periods of time."

"But, Aunt Adelina, I will have my entire life to be married. How many more opportunities might I have to go to the tournament? How many times have *you* gone? And *your* husband is the general of the army! Most of the noblemen will be at the competition, anyway. It will give me the opportunity to see them compete. Besides, Rezkin has offered his protection. I will be safe," she said with confidence as she crossed her arms.

General Marcum slammed his fist down on the table causing the dinnerware to clink. "I will not allow you to travel halfway across the kingdom with someone I do not know or trust."

Frisha argued, "There is no reason for you to object. Rezkin has been a perfect gentleman, he has comported himself with dignity and respect, and he has protected me and even saved my life at least twice. You know he is capable."

"I know nothing of the sort," the general stubbornly responded. Then, more softly he said, "It is unseemly, Frisha, for a young woman to go gallivanting across the countryside without a proper escort."

"What exactly would you consider a proper escort?" Frisha asked.

"My dear," Lady Adelina said, "you are among nobles, now. There are proper protocols for every occasion including one such as this. There are only three ways an unmarried lady may travel and retain her honor. Otherwise, people will question your virtue, and with your commoner blood already working against you, you really cannot afford that. I am sorry, dear. I mean no offense. It is just a statement of fact."

Frisha nodded in acknowledgement and asked, "And what are those three ways?"

"Well, the first is that you must be accompanied by an adult male blood relative. Since neither your uncle nor father can accompany you, that is not an option. The second is that you would be accompanied by your betrothed—also not an option at this point. The third is usually reserved for necessary travel only. It could still be considered acceptable, as far as your reputation is concerned, but it would damage your chances of finding a husband."

"Well, what is it?" Frisha asked, not really caring so much about finding a noble husband anymore. She already knew who she wanted, and she doubted he cared about such things.

"You would have to enter into a formal prime courtship, and then your prime suitor could accompany you," Lady Adelina replied, "but it would still be frowned upon by our peers."

Seeing the confusion written across the young woman's face, she continued, "You see, when nobles enter into a marriage it is quite complex. During a normal courtship, the young woman may court several suitors at a time to give other potential suitors the opportunity to express their interest and also so that she can decide which young man she wishes to marry. Once she and her family have decided upon a suitor, a betrothal contract must be signed. The betrothal contract outlines all of the political and financial agreements between the families of the bride and groom. After the betrothal contract is signed, the bride and groom must wait at least one year before the wedding can take place.

"As you probably already know, nobles can be a stubborn and finicky lot and coming to such agreements can take quite some time. It may take six months or more for some of the larger houses to finalize an agreement. Then, they would have to wait an entire year for the actual marriage."

"Why a year?" asked Tam.

Lady Adelina paused to sip her wine, so Rezkin answered Tam's question. "Some of the betrothal contracts between larger houses can have widespread political and economic ramifications. Waiting a year for the contract to take effect provides enough time for the news to spread and for others to make plans for the impending changes. Anyone who will be affected by the contract has the opportunity to file a protest, and the contract must then be reviewed by the king. The king has the authority to approve the contract, send it back for revisions, or dissolve it completely."

"What is a prime courtship?" Frisha pressed.

"A prime courtship was devised for two purposes. The first is when it is agreed that a couple will wed, but it will be some time, years, before they can do so. Perhaps one or both of the young people are too young, or one must go away for a time, maybe to study ..."

"Or go on campaign." The general grumbled.

Lady Adelina continued, "So forming a betrothal contract can be difficult if the houses do not know what their state of affairs will be when the time comes. This usually applies to the smaller houses, since their finances and political standing tend to fluctuate. The second application is to get around the problem of the long waiting period. A prime courtship is a simple contract that states that the lady has chosen her suitor, and the suitor has agreed to the marriage, but the terms of the betrothal agreement have not yet been agreed upon.

"The time spent in a prime courtship can be applied to the yearlong waiting period. As a condition of entering into a prime courtship, both parties must either stipulate that the terms of their betrothal agreement will have limited effect on outside parties, *or* they can publish the *potential* terms so that outside parties can respond appropriately. In that case, the financial or political impact of the published potential terms cannot be increased, only decreased, during future negotiations," Lady Adelina explained.

Frisha's shoulders sagged. "So either way, I cannot go unless I either have a relative or future husband with me."

After dinner, Tam followed Rezkin to the stables. As the young warrior was checking on his battle charger, Tam decided to broach the delicate subject.

"Rez, why don't *you* enter into a betrothal with Frisha?" he asked.

"What? Why?" Rezkin asked, genuinely bewildered.

"Oh, come on. You've been courting her for like a month, now. Don't act so surprised," Tam chuckled.

I am courting Frisha? Rezkin thought. *When did that happen?*

"It's not like she can stay your girlfriend forever, Rez," Tam huffed in exasperation. "Eventually, you will either have to marry her or move on. If you don't marry her, she needs to find someone else to marry. She can't just keep being your girlfriend."

Rezkin furrowed his brow. He had not been aware of this stipulation to the position of *Girl Friend*. The hierarchy was more complicated than he initially thought. He attempted to liken it to some other type of relationship hierarchy that he *did* understand.

"What, it is like a promotion?" Rezkin asked in confusion.

Tam laughed. "If you want to look at it that way."

If Frisha were a career officer in the military, she would be expected to work hard and receive promotions. If she were passed over for promotion too many times, she would be dismissed from service. It sounded like Tam was saying that Frisha's responsibility as his *Girl Friend* was to eventually enter into a marriage contract with him. If she failed to meet his standards for such a contract, she would lose her position.

Would whoever was in charge of his *friends* replace Frisha with a different superior female *friend* until he finally chose one? Rezkin did not want a replacement *Girl Friend*. He understood Frisha's strengths and weaknesses and knew that she would not panic in dangerous situations. In addition, he was surprised to admit, he trusted her not to stab him in his sleep. These seemed like good qualities to have in a wife, and there was no guarantee that a replacement *Girl Friend* would possess them.

Still, Rezkin was not ready to enter into a marriage contract. He had just left his training and had no need or desire for heirs at this time. Striker Farson was still out there somewhere, and Rezkin had a rising desire to solve the mystery that was his life. There was also the fact that husbands had certain responsibilities to their wives, or so he understood from his studies. He would be expected to provide Frisha and his heirs with a home in which he spent most of his time, and he would need a socially respectable position to provide a regular income. He doubted being a criminal overlord counted as such.

"I am not ready to enter into a marriage contract, Tam, and I cannot provide for a wife and offspring in the obligatory way," Rezkin replied.

Tam sighed. "But, if you don't, then General Marcum and Lady Adelina will marry her to someone else. Do you want to lose her? If you aren't ready to get married, then why not enter into one of those prime courtships instead?"

Rezkin furrowed his brow in irritation. Why did all of this have to come up so quickly? Was it part of his purpose to finish his training and immediately enter into a marriage contract? What was the point of all of his training? Still, he did not want Frisha to be replaced with a stranger.

"I will consider it," Rezkin replied.

Tam smiled broadly and slapped Rezkin on the back. He noticed that he did not tense up as much as he usually did when someone made physical contact and reminded himself not to let his guard down per *Rule 24.*

"It'll be great!" Tam exclaimed. "We'd almost be like brothers." Tam rubbed at his brow and laughed. "If I was actually related to Frisha, I mean."

16

That night, after everyone else was abed, Rezkin slipped into the night wearing his dark clothing, black armor, and deep cowl. The criminal element in the city of Kaibain was strong, highly influential, and ruthless. Far more dangers resided in this city than just a few simple thieves' guilds, and Rezkin intended to add as many of them as possible to his repertoire of resources.

First, he had to meet up with the personnel he sent separately from his own traveling party. They were supposed to have left Justain the day after he and his companions departed. The thieves would have encountered the riverboat returning to Justain with the bandit captives and learned of the change in plans. From there, the Diamond Claw members should have continued to Drennil to complete the task he had set for them. After Drennil, they would have continued on to Kaibain. A few experienced thieves would have had a relatively easy time of the rough travel and should have made it to Kaibain ahead of him. Of course, that was assuming everything went to plan, which rarely was reality.

Rezkin traveled the dark streets of the city with efficiency using the map he held in his mind. On occasion during his training, Rezkin had wondered why he was required to memorize so many maps and floor plans when he was never permitted to leave the immediate area of the fortress. At times he had been sent on longer treks into the forests and mountains of the north, but never had he ventured into civilization, so the knowledge seemed frivolous at best. Now that he knew he had a purpose and that purpose was to be undertaken in the outworld, the masters' insistence on the memorization made more sense.

When he was halfway to the safe house for the Kaibainian branch of the Diamond Claw Guild where he would meet his contacts, Rezkin decided to change directions. He had made an instantaneous decision to completely over-haul his plans having realized that he would need the element of surprise to carry out his ambitions. Once he met with his people, news would spread, and the element would be lost. His masters and the strikers had always been pleased with his ability to think quickly and change tactics in an instant. Rezkin had learned to follow his instincts, and they had saved him innumer-able times. This was one of those times when he just knew he had to adjust his strategy.

Rezkin did not know where his destination was, so he needed to find a guide. It would be a toss-up whether he ended up with the Razor Edges or the Crimson Blades, the city's two other thieves' guilds. While the Diamond Claws had branches in Justain and Kaibain, the Razor Edges could be found in Kaibain and Port Manai. The Crimson Blades were purely local, though, having been unable to gain a foothold in the other cities. Because the King's Seat had their full attention, their influence within the city was slightly stronger than the other guilds.

By now, news would have spread to most of Ashai about the takeover of the thieves' guilds in Justain. The mage relay would see to that. Guards and security officials had been notified of a major movement in the criminal element of one of the country's capital cities. He doubted anyone took the threat of the disturbance spilling into the Seat of the King seriously, though. No one had that kind of influence, surely. Rezkin needed to take advantage of their apathy and misplaced sense of security. No one would be expecting him to be here already, if at all.

After dancing across several rooftops and scanning dark alleys near the rowdy taverns and brothels, Rezkin finally found a promising lead. A young man had just stabbed an older man in the gut and grabbed the man's coin purse. The young man darted away quickly before anyone noticed, not that help was likely to come anytime soon or that it would do any good. The older man had already expired on the ground in a pool of blood. The knife must have struck something vital, or perhaps the man's heart simply gave out.

Rezkin took off in silent, secret pursuit of the young slayer. Eventually, the young man ducked into an abandoned shop that looked to have once held a chandler's workshop, if the globs of wax in the sills and across the exposed floor were any indication. Unconvinced that this was the location of the guild-house, Rezkin waited. A couple of jittery young men entered the building a brief time later but were shoved back out with a shout from the building's other occupants. After about an hour, the young killer finally emerged looking alert and excited. Dark lines crawled up the back of his neck—lines that had not been there during Rezkin's pursuit. An *inker*.

Rezkin mentally shook his head in disdain. No respectable guild would allow its members to *ink*. He was about to give up pursuit of the drug addict and find an *actual* guild member when the young man joined with a small group of equally seedy men.

The largest of the men wore clothes that were a bit too small, his trousers and tunic sleeves riding too high on his legs and arms. The guild tattoo on his inner forearm was unmistakable. Two serrated daggers stood in the shape of a *V*, the pommels nearly touching at the bottom with the blades facing outward. It was the symbol of the Razor Edges.

Finally, he was getting somewhere. Rezkin hoped the man intended to return to the guildhouse tonight. He did not have much time to get everything done before he needed to leave for the tournament. The tournament was still his best chance at finding out about the strikers—at finding Farson.

The men laughed and tossed a small jug around sharing its contents, which Rezkin surmised were most likely of an intoxicating nature. It was a wonder the Razor Edges were successful at all if their members were all drunkards and *inkers*. Perhaps these were the worst of the lot, or maybe the branch in Port Manai was more proficient.

Eventually, an older woman dressed much like the women near the brothel approached the group. She scolded them, and the men ducked their heads in submission. Some of them looked chagrined, others were angry, but no one protested the dressing down. Finally, the group dispersed.

Rezkin followed the tall man and his two companions. They turned a corner and descended a set of stone steps leading to the basement level of a slaughterhouse. He nearly cringed in spite of himself. *Who would want to live or work beneath a slaughterhouse?* The smell alone would be enough to drive one away, not to mention all the fluids and other gore that would drain down into the lower level.

In only moments, the men reemerged, one carrying a heavier purse, and

Rezkin was relieved. He had no desire to infiltrate the location, and not just because it was a slaughterhouse. The basement likely had only one entrance, and the enclosed space would make it dangerous to penetrate and escape if necessary.

Rezkin followed the men in a winding route, passing through the working district and then the merchant district. Eventually, they entered the back court-yard of a moderate but well-appointed estate house not unlike the general's home. As the young men entered, a couple of others were leaving. One raised his hand in greeting, and his sleeve fell back to expose the guild tattoo. *Interesting*. It seemed this guildmaster lived lavishly and liked his luxuries. Unfortunately, Rezkin had no information on the current Razor Edge guildmaster. The last information he received about two months ago had indicated unrest within the guild. The former guildmaster had been killed, and at the time, no one had been able to hold on to the position.

Rezkin wondered who lived here and if the current resident was the rightful owner. It was not uncommon for criminals to set up shop in an empty home while the owners were away. Perhaps they had even killed the owner and someone had yet to discover the treachery. It was even possible that some minor lord or merchant had decided to extend his influence with the darker side of society, not unlike the disgraced *Lord* Urek.

Rezkin could learn only so much from sitting outside in the shadows. He also tired of the inaction. He dropped from his perch on the low branch of a tree, silently landing within the estate courtyard. He slipped through the shadows to one side of the building that was lacking in doors but had plenty of windows, which were just as good. Actually, Rezkin preferred windows. People did not expect anyone to enter through windows, and they were often located in secluded places rather than along corridors that others used for passage. He wondered how people could feel secure at all when their sanctuary was riddled with such weaknesses.

The intruder casually pulled himself through one such weakness on the first floor. He was a little surprised to encounter a minor ward, probably one intended to discourage entry and alert the homeowner of an intruder. Rezkin was unconcerned. This ward was a negligible annoyance compared to the plethora of wards he had encountered in the bank.

The room was dark and devoid of people. Although it had been dark outside, he still waited a moment to allow his eyes to adjust to the deeper blackness. The room appeared to be a kind of catchall workroom with equipment ranging from washboards and basins to files, grinding stones and whet-stones to broken cart axles. He made his way to the door, careful not to upset any of the equipment. From the outside, this side of the house appeared to be quiet and unoccupied, and it seemed his evaluation was correct. The corridor was unlit and empty.

As Rezkin slinked down the hall, he felt the tingle of mage power slide over his skin from somewhere above. He realized that something of interest must lay up there if someone went to the trouble and expense to have it warded. For him to feel the ward down here meant it was poorly shaped and unfocused. Still, any ward was costly, even a poor one.

He reached the stairs, but rather than following them all the way up where he might be spotted, he launched himself onto the banister with silent grace and then leapt up to grasp the balcony railing. His toes touched the second floor without a sound, and he crouched low in case anyone had detected his movement. Just as he was about to stand, a door opened below and a man's voice echoed through the stairwell.

"Yes, Guildmaster, but you know people are talking. It's bad for morale. Half the men want to give in already, and the other half want to kill the first half," the voice argued.

"I don't care," replied a woman. "We have no reason to believe the Raven will come here. For all we know, this is a scheme cooked up by the authorities to throw us off. They're probably hoping we'll give ourselves away in a panic." Rezkin could not see the two since they were below him, but the woman sounded mature and confident.

"But, if he *does* come here demanding our loyalty, what do we do?" the man asked in frustration. Rezkin wanted to know the answer to that question as well. Then, more quietly the man added, "They're saying he's not *human*."

Silence ensued for a moment, and he assumed the woman was contem-plating the answer. Finally, she said, "From what we've heard, he only kills people who oppose him. So, if he comes, then we just go along with it. We'll let him think we're on board, and when he lets down his guard, we take him out. He's only one man."

Fortune favors the bold, Rezkin thought. It was by pure luck he had been present at this precise time and location to overhear their plans. Of course, he would have suspected such deceit anyway, but this way he knew for certain. The man changed the subject, and by the sound of their voices, he knew they were walking toward the stairs. Rezkin quickly padded down the walkway until he felt the tingle of the mage ward he had encountered earlier. He pressed past it with a focused *will* and tested the latch on the door the ward was intended to secure. The door was unlocked. Rezkin would never understand why people put such faith in mage wards.

The warded room was an office. It contained a plush chaise, a few lounge chairs, and a large desk. Several shelves lined the walls upon which sat record books, stacks of correspondence, and loose parchments. The hearth crackled with flame in the heat of the summer, making the air too warm and stifling. A box of incense placed near the fire suffused the room with a spicy aroma.

Rezkin quickly crossed to the side table and poured himself a beverage. It smelled strongly of spirits, but he had no intention of actually drinking it. He took a seat at the desk and shuffled through a few papers noting anything of importance. Then he leaned back, propping his legs up as Urek had done. He wanted to appear confident and unconcerned, and these thieves seemed to appreciate overly dramatic gestures. He held the drink casually but made sure his cowl hid his features. He did not want these people to recognize him when he went about town with Frisha and Tam.

The door opened and in strode a man and a woman deep in conversation. The man closed the door behind them. He was tall and broad of shoulder, his face and hair clean, and his clothes cut in the style of a servant of high station. The woman was in her early thirties and was dressed in a fine silk and velvet gown in a mustardy gold color. Layers of petticoats pushed the lower part of the gown out to completely fill the doorway as she entered. The bodice was cut low enough to show ample cleavage, and she had wrapped about her arms a burgundy shawl of crushed velvet. Her shimmering golden locks were piled atop her head in mounds of curls, and glittering jewels dangled from her ears. She might have passed for a lady if she did not appear to be trying so hard.

The woman was halfway across the room before she looked up and gasped, stumbling into the man. The startled man was so preoccupied with catching the woman that he did not notice the cause for her distress.

"Who are you? What are you doing here? How did you get in?" the woman shrieked into the man's ear. He flinched at the high-pitched sound but immediately jerked his head around to see to whom the woman was speaking.

Rezkin continued to lounge, casually swirling the amber liquid in his glass. Once the man and woman were straightened out, he said, "Which question should I address first?"

"What?" came the startled reply. "I mean, get out of here! Guards!" she shouted.

The man finally shook himself from his surprise and pulled an overly long dagger from his pants. The dagger looked far too long to have fit comfortably in its hiding place, and Rezkin wondered how the man had accomplished such a feat. He tossed the thought aside for another time and said, "I do not believe your guards will hear you since the room is surrounded by a sound-proofing ward. Although, you should know that since it is *your* room."

The woman huffed and took a step to turn toward the door. She stopped abruptly when a small dagger whisked past her shoulder and lodged in the doorframe. "You may, of course, continue to seek assistance, but you will not live long enough to accomplish the task if you do," Rezkin stated calmly.

Turning back with a pale face, the woman repeated one of her earlier questions. "Who are you?"

Rezkin smirked and said, "I think you know the answer to that one."

The man's fist clenched tighter around his dagger, and he said, "The Raven."

The intruder inclined his head and replied, "That is what they call me. I am pleased that my reputation precedes me. It makes this so much easier."

"You want my guild," the woman stated in challenge.

"Your guild is already *mine*," Rezkin replied. "You just have not accepted it, yet."

"What makes you think I'll give it up so easily?" she countered, her face sour and her lips pursed.

"Oh, I know you will not. In fact, I know you intend to betray me when you think I have let down my guard." The woman sucked in a quick breath, and the man groaned. Rezkin grinned knowing the only part of his face they could see was his mouth. "You should learn not to voice your intentions so loudly, especially when you intend to betray someone."

The man looked a bit ill. His face was ashen, and he gulped repeatedly. The woman's face burned with a pink flush that might have been attractive under different circumstances.

She shrugged and said, "What do you expect? It is my duty as guildmaster to look out for the interests of the guild."

"Are you so certain it is in the guild's best interests to defy *me*?" Rezkin asked, contempt thick and heavy in his voice.

Uncertainty slid over the woman's gaze as she replied, "One does not

271

simply hand over power because a stranger demands it. This is *my* guild. I have *earned* my place."

"Perhaps. How exactly did you *earn* this place?" Rezkin asked with a slight tilt of his head. His tone was knowing even though he had no idea how the woman came to be guildmaster.

The woman's posture shifted from stiff surprise and antagonism to one of sultry arrogance. She shrugged one shoulder and swayed her hips as she said, "My late *husband* did not exactly know what he was getting into."

Ah. The woman was a fraud. She married the poor noble to whom this estate belonged. She had probably duped him into thinking she was a lady, and he had likely overlooked certain flaws for the benefits of her physical attributes. Rezkin recognized that most men would see her as quite alluring, but he saw only the hidden teeth and claws. His one and only experience with a woman had been quite effective in curing him of the fatal weakness men had toward women, especially women like this. Actually, *this* woman reminded him quite a bit of that other woman.

He scoffed. "You take a noble House and waste its resources on common thievery. Simple plans for simple minds," he mused. He plucked a parchment off the desk and read the signature at the bottom: *Lady Hilith Gadderand*. He performed a quick mental search through the seemingly endless lists of houses he had memorized. Gadderand was a minor offshoot, by several generations, of House Ruolt, which held a countship under the authority of Duke Darning. Gadderand held no lands of its own but obviously had enough wealth to maintain an estate in the capital city of Kaibain, the Seat of the King.

"I'll have you know it's not easy getting into a noble house," Hilith replied. "Those who recognize *true* talent commend my accomplishments," she said with a proud lift of her chin.

Rezkin was out of his seat and across the room faster than either could react. He stood before the woman and gripped her jaw firmly in his right hand as he gazed at her from the shadow of his cowl. His left hand held a thin knife, the tip resting just under her partner's ribs. The woman's startled eyes stared into the shadowed recess trying to catch a glimpse of his face and understand what was happening.

"*True* talent?" he said with scorn, his deep, quiet rumble brushing softly over her ears. "You are originally from the East, Krellis, perhaps? You eventually moved to Umbrell where you began an apprenticeship with a seamstress." Rezkin had recognized the slight nuances in her speech. The tiny lilt at the end of some of her words spoke of an eastern origin, while the slight clip was particular to the river town farther south. Her long fingers were crisscrossed and dotted with tiny white lines where she had been repeatedly nicked with shears and needles, more so than was typical for a woman who was not employed in such a profession.

The woman's eyes widened further in surprise. "How—" she started but was cut off by the Raven's tight grip.

He tilted her head to the side and then back and said, "You found yourself in disgrace, hiding away in a brothel. You eventually ended up here, in Kaibain, where you began looking for an easy mark." He leaned forward, closing the distance between their faces. Hilith could not mistake his closeness for one of desire. It was completely hostile and domineering. She shivered under his control.

"Do not mistake a lonely man's willingness to overlook your flaws for a sign of *talent*. You are easy to read, *Hilith*," the Raven said. Of course, he knew her name was not Hilith. Hilith was a fictional character, a ruse.

The woman blinked several times, holding back unshed tears. The Raven's tight grip dug painfully into her jaw, but it was his words that truly stung. "You are wrong," she whispered.

Rezkin was momentarily taken aback. The last part of his assessment had been mostly conjecture based on her current *profession* and the manner in which she comported herself. It was entirely possible that he was wrong, but he doubted it. He loosened his grip slightly to allow the woman to speak. The proximity, the dominance, the taking of liberties in touching her, was all strategy, a form of psychological manipulation. Based on his calculated profile, he felt this tactic would be the most effective.

When the Raven's fingers loosened, Hilith took it as a sign that she was permitted to speak. She inhaled deeply and said, "It is never a disgrace to bear a child." The woman's eyes glistened as she spoke, revealing a hidden inner turmoil.

Rezkin searched deeply in her eyes and made another quick assessment, solely based on instinct. He released her jaw and stepped back, his knife vanishing as though it had never been. She failed to hide the briefest spark of triumph, but it was too late. He had already judged her. "You do not fool me, *Hilith*. Any child you might have borne was scraped from your womb long before it could take breath."

Hilith's jaw clamped shut, and the flicker of smug satisfaction disappeared along with the false tears. The woman was nothing if not consistent. Once a fraud …

Hilith scowled deeply with burning hatred. "What do you know of it? How did you get your information?" she said. The man next to her took a step back, a plethora of emotions flashing across his face. Rezkin was satisfied he had gotten under the façade to reveal the serpent beneath.

"I am claiming this guild, Hilith, but I am afraid there simply is no place for *you*. Unfortunately, you are the enemy that cannot be permitted to linger at my back. Tomorrow morning, the city post will report that a robbery occurred this night. Lady Hilith Gadderand, widow to the late Lord Gadderand, was killed during the home invasion. Having no heirs, Gadderand was survived only by his brother, who will inherit the property and all its wealth.

"You can't do this!" Hilith screeched. "*I* am master of this guild! My people will fight you!"

"Maybe, but it will not matter to *you*. *You* will be dead," Rezkin nonchalantly replied as he stepped back behind the desk.

"Do something, Breck! Kill the bloody gutterrat!" Hilith ordered, her accent degenerating to that of a common street urchin.

Breck's attention was not focused on the intruder, though. He was looking at *her* in horror. "You said you had a miscarriage."

"What?" the woman gasped in consternation. "That's not important! Get rid of *him*!" she shouted as she jerked her head toward the intruder.

Breck shook his head, his complete focus on the woman, as though Rezkin did not exist. "If you lied about that one, what about *ours*? Did you kill *our* child, too?" Breck asked, his voice choked but filling with anger.

"Don't be absurd. We're not talking about this right now! *Priorities*, Breck!" Hilith scolded as she attempted to redirect Breck's attention to the present threat.

Breck balled his fists as his face flushed in anger. "No, we *are* talking about this now! What about our baby, Hilith?" he shouted as he stomped toward the woman. "You killed him, didn't you? You *killed* my son!"

Hilith's face flooded with fear as she stumbled back from her furious second. "No!" she shouted. "Stop, Breck! It wasn't like that!"

Breck raised a heavy fist as he reached for the woman. "You *did*! Don't deny it!"

"No, Breck! You don't understand!" Hilith shouted as she cowered away. "I couldn't have …" she started, but Breck grabbed her arm and yanked her roughly toward him. Just as he was about to strike the crying woman she shouted, "*There was no baby*!"

Breck's hand froze midair. All was still and silent save for their heavy breathing. "What?" the man finally said on a breathy exhale.

"I-I lied." Hilith sobbed. "I wanted your support. I needed you on my side."

Breck's hand dropped, and he took several steps back. His face was pale and drawn as he stared uncomprehendingly at the woman. "I … I have been mourning the loss of a child that never *existed*? How could you?" He huffed breathlessly, his voice ending on a choked sob.

Rezkin had returned to the chair behind the desk to watch the unexpected exchange. This behavior amongst outworlders was strange and foreign. Hilith held the higher station within the guild and apparently dominated the relationship she had with her second, but he was obviously the superior fighter. As soon as he felt the bite of betrayal, he reared up to chomp at the weaker woman.

Aside from the lie, Rezkin did not understand Breck's disquiet. The man seemed truly upset that the woman had not borne him an heir, which made no sense. The two had obviously not entered into a marriage contract, especially since Hilith was married to the late Lord Gadderand, and their lifestyle was hardly conducive to rearing young.

The Raven's smooth, deep voice cut through the thick air when he spoke. "You two obviously have much to discuss, but I have no time for it. Breck, do you care to dispose of her or shall I?" Without looking at him, Breck slumped down into a high backed chair. Staring into the lively, dancing flames of the hearth, he waved a dismissive hand.

"Breck!" Hilith shouted. "You can't be serious! You're just going to sit there while he threatens me? I mean, honestly Breck, it's not like we can't still have a baby. I-I could even be pregnant now! If you let him do this, he would be killing me *and* our baby!" Hilith desperately pleaded, but her words seemed to sound hollow and crude even to her own ears.

Rezkin was amazed at his luck. These outworlders were overrun with emotions to the point that they would turn on one another even without his assistance. Adsden and the Serpent Guild had been angry and resentful of the blackmailing Urek, while Hilith had used her womanly wiles to wrap Breck around her finger. It was only a matter of time before the second realized what a monster she truly was. She most likely expected to have a much stronger hold over the guild before that day occurred, probably even to have another susceptible man at her beck and call by then, someone who would *take care* of Breck for her.

Moving around the desk, the Raven approached with smooth, calculated steps. Hilith backed away until her back struck the closed door. In a panic, she reached to the side and grabbed at the knife lodged in the frame, but it had sunk deep, and her shaking hand could not get the necessary leverage. She whimpered and cowered.

"Y-You wouldn't hurt a *lady* would you?" the woman begged. The Raven huffed his amusement at the statement, and Hilith swallowed hard, apparently understanding that she would have to use a different tactic. "You don't have to do this! I can be of use to you! I have skills that only an experienced woman could have," she said, attempting to sound seductive but utterly failing in her terror.

Crowding her against the door, the Raven leaned forward so close she thought for sure she should be able to make out his face, but somehow his features remained elusive. "I am sure you do," he said cryptically. His focus lingered on her as he reached over and easily plucked the knife from the door-frame, secreting it away as he did. The Raven's entire demeanor spoke of cool detachment that, combined with his predatory gait and the unnatural blackness beneath his hood, made Breck's earlier assertion that the man was not human seem more than plausible.

He reached up and softly stroked her cheek with feigned fondness. Hilith licked her lips salaciously, and just as her muscles began to relax, the Raven gripped her jaw forcefully once again. The woman whimpered in fear and pain, her chest heaved in a contained sob, and her eyes watered with impending tears. "Please ..." she whispered.

The Raven cocked his head curiously and said, "Perhaps you *can* be of some use to me."

"Yes," she uttered immediately, furiously attempting to nod her head that was trapped in his firm, unyielding grip. "Anything you desire ... *Master*," she whispered. Hilith's eyes flashed with renewed hope and ... *desire?*

Rezkin could see Breck watching them, now, from the corner of his eye. The man was curious and angry, although Rezkin did not know if the man's anger stemmed from jealousy or the fact that he had not yet killed the woman. Hilith believed she had managed to use her so-called *Skills* to convince the Raven to spare her life. In truth, Rezkin never intended to kill the woman—not unless she did something truly stupid like choose to be uncooperative—but allowing her to believe that she had gained even the tiniest hold over him would keep her trying to prove her worth. Even if she did not believe she could defeat him, being the kind of woman that she was, she might believe she had a chance at claiming the Raven for herself, thereby attaching herself to a most powerful, albeit terrifying, man.

Rezkin dropped his hand from her jaw and stepped away. Hilith released a heavy, relieved breath, but her eyes flashed with disappointment. What did she think might happen? That he would take her here and now, right in front of her lover? *Yes, she probably did think that*, Rezkin conceded. He was more familiar with her type than he wished, but he mentally thanked his masters for that particular lesson. It had been a terrible one to learn, but he now recognized the necessity.

"I assure you, Master," Hilith said in a rush, "that the Razor Edge Guild will serve you well."

"Yes, they will, but that will not be your concern," the Raven asserted. "You are no longer guildmaster, Hilith. I have another task for you. I will give you the opportunity to prove yourself, but make no mistake. If you are found unworthy, you will not enjoy the consequences. In fact, henceforth, there will be little joy to be had in your life."

Hilith raised a manicured brow and said smartly, "As if there ever was."

Breck growled and pounded his fist on the arm of his chair but said nothing. Hilith turned her attention to the man, her lover. Her face flushed with embarrassment, but she lifted her chin and shrugged with one shoulder as if to say she felt no shame for her actions. Breck turned his face away as he gritted his teeth and bit back any retort he might make.

Rezkin found the display to be curious. He commended the second for his adherence to *Rule 104—Meet uncertainty with silence and listen*. The man had not complied with many of the other *Rules*, but at least he had this much self-control. Still, he was not sure Breck was up to the challenge of taking on the position of guildmaster. While he had managed to attain the position of second, he had the countenance of a follower rather than a leader. Still, if he could follow Rekzin's lead and still get things accomplished, the arrangement might work.

"What of you, Breck? Are you prepared to fill the position of guildmaster?" the Raven asked, almost as if he actually cared about the response.

Before Breck could utter a word, Hilith interrupted. "*What*? You'll make *him* guildmaster?"

Rezkin turned back to the flummoxed woman. "You chose him as your second. Surely he is the most *Skilled* and strongest of the guild," he said wryly.

Hilith shrugged noncommittally while avoiding Breck's furious gaze. "Well...I had ... *other* ... reasons for choosing him."

"Then you are saying he is not worthy of the position with which you honored him?" the Raven asked calmly with unnerving patience.

Hilith risked a look at her *former* lover and then lifted her chin and said confidently, "No, he's not."

"And, who would *you* choose?" the Raven asked.

Feeling as though she were gaining ground, Hilith strutted forward. "Demky, perhaps ... or Triald," she said with a pert smile.

Again, Breck clenched his fist and gritted his teeth but said nothing. He glared furiously at the woman and then pulled his eyes away to watch for the Raven's response. The Raven nodded beneath his hood. "Hmm ... do you know what I think, Hilith? I think you are worried that the new guildmaster will hold a grudge against you, and you are hoping to secure someone of *your* choosing in his place, someone you believe you have a chance at seducing to regain a semblance of power."

Hilith's smile fell as Breck's fists unclenched. The man released a pent up breath. *Ah*, Rezkin thought. The man had been concerned that Hilith's manipulation had gained a hold over the Raven, and Breck had been biding his time until the truth was revealed. It had been a test of sorts.

Breck's voice was low and gruff as he said, "I am well prepared for the position. It would have been mine had Hilith not ..." He did not finish the sentence. They all knew, now, what Hilith had done.

"You will serve *me*?" the Raven asked, as though Breck had a choice.

"I ..." he said and then glanced at Hilith before looking back, "owe you a debt. I will serve you. You, at least, are forthright and honest in your intentions." It was a dig at the woman, but Hilith held her head high and shrugged shamelessly.

"Very well," the Raven replied. "Here are some instructions to begin with, but I will return several times over the next few days to ensure there is no *miscommunication*. Do not bother to set a trap. It will fail, and you will die."

Breck seemed to watch the highly armed shadow warrior carefully. The man's confidence in the Raven's threat was so overwhelming that if any thoughts of traps or ambushes had existed in Breck's mind, they had summarily fled. Breck nodded once in affirmation but made no other move. Rezkin was pleased with the man's self-control.

"W-What about *me*?" Hilith asked with a bit of a pout.

The Raven grinned wolfishly, the firelight highlighting the white of his perfect teeth, so discordant with the black shadows that otherwise concealed his face. "Oh, I have a task for you. I suggest you begin making preparations. The Lady Gadderand is going on a trip, and I expect she will be gone for quite some time." Hilith was struck with the realization that the Raven had planned this all along.

17

The following morning, after they finished the weapons training, Frisha, Tam, and Rezkin decided to partake of the midday meal at a small inn Lady Adelina suggested. It was located in the upscale central market district, but the lady assured them the prices were reasonable. The quaint restaurant was busy but not so busy that they had to wait long to be seated. The table they were assigned was located on a patio that overlooked the busy square. Along the wall of the building ran a trellis with flowering vines that smelled sweet and fresh. The three shared a large salad made with fresh greens and vegetables tossed with a savory marinated grilled fish. The salad was followed by roasted rosemary chicken with seasoned potatoes. Everything tasted superb.

As they ate, Frisha made polite conversation with a couple of young women who were dining at the table next to them. The two ladies, Joselia and Meriana, ostensibly bestowed all of their attention on Frisha, who was surprisingly susceptible to their doting. They complimented her dress and hair and gossiped about all of the people she was sure to meet. All the while, they were surreptitiously batting their lashes and casting eyes at Rezkin. Tam even received a brief perusal, but he was obviously a commoner, so neither gave him any additional attention.

At the end of the meal, the three stood to leave when a group of raucous young men walked by causing a commotion. The young men, who ranged from their late teens to midtwenties, were lavishly attired, the rich sons of nobles who flaunted their wealth with fine clothes and other accouterments. The young men all laughed at something and then one of them shoved another a little too hard.

The young man tripped over his own feet and stumbled toward Rezkin. Ever aware of his surroundings, Rezkin sensed the young man's uncontrolled approach and stepped out of the way. He was unable to stop the imminent collision, however. The flailing man crashed into the table upsetting the dinnerware and spilling wine over Frisha's fine dress. The other young men laughed hysterically and offered no apologies.

Rezkin strode over to confront the dominant male who had caused the disruption. "You will cease this offensive behavior and apologize to the lady," he demanded.

This particular young man looked to be about twenty-four and nearly matched Rezkin's height and breadth. He wore a gold-embroidered cream silk doublet with matching breeches. At his hip was a rapier with an ornate twisted silver handle. The silver scabbard was embellished with gold accents and gemstones. The young man's eyes traveled the length of Rezkin, apparently sizing up his opponent. Rezkin had dressed in his fine blue silk shirt and black pants for the outing. The lordling snickered when he noticed the two swords at Rezkin's waist. He ran a tanned hand through his gold-blonde hair and grinned.

"And why would I do that?" he said haughtily. His friends chuckled beside him but were decidedly more subdued.

Rezkin cocked his head as he stared with icy-blue eyes. "Through your negligence, you have upset the lady and ruined her dress. An honorable man would provide recompense and an apology."

The young lord scowled, "Are you questioning my honor?"

"Are you?" Rezkin retorted.

The man's dark blue eyes flicked over Frisha, and he smirked as he said, "I see no harm done. She would look better without the dress anyway."

Frisha gasped and flushed bright red. Lady Joselia stomped a foot and said, "Tieran, you are a cad!" To Frisha she said, "That is Tieran, eldest son of the Duke of Wellinven of House Nirius."

"Ye-e-e-e-s," Tieran drawled. "You may call me *Lord Nirius*. If you are *very* nice, you may call me Lord Tieran," he said suggestively.

"*I* am about to call you dead," said Rezkin coldly, "if you do not apologize to the lady. I will not stand for you besmirching her honor with your lewd remarks." Rezkin's muscles flexed, and he seemed to expand to fill additional space around him. His icy eyes appeared to barely hold a deep darkness in check. To the young lord's dismay, Tieran felt a sudden wash of fear. Tieran was not sure why, but this man's imposing presence had a familiarity that unsettled him. His hand immediately went to his hilt, but he stopped short of drawing the blade.

Rezkin subtly shook his head once. "We have already determined you lack honor. Let us not find that you lack intelligence as well. If you draw that sword, you do so with your last breath," he warned dispassionately.

It was that cold, emotionless assurance that got to the young lord. Nothing in the imposing man's voice or bearing said bluster. For some reason, Tieran knew he did not want to fight this man. It was like staring into the maw of a hungry wolf. Tieran continued to grasp the hilt of his sword, more for comfort than anything, as he glared at the other man.

Rezkin cocked his head curiously as he studied the noble. Tieran gripped his rapier but failed to draw the weapon, giving Rezkin ample warning and time to prepare for the imminent strike. Surely a future *duke* would have greater *Skill*, he thought, therefore there must be some other reason for continuing to grip his sword.

"I am aware that some blades are enchanted, giving their wielders extra advantage. Perhaps this is why you continue to grip yours? Does it make you more intelligent?" Rezkin inquired with a mixture of condescension and genuine curiosity.

Tieran was not about to let everyone know he had been cowed by this stranger, though. He donned his greatest smile, and with his usual brash, haughty conceit he said, "Come now, *friend*. We were just having a bit of fun. Perhaps you could do with some. Who are you? I do not believe we have met." Tieran thought he had met every one of importance, but now he was uncertain.

"I am Rezkin, and that is my *Girl Friend*, Lady Frisha Marcum, and I am still waiting to hear an apology," Rezkin responded without blinking. He was a stone, cold statue, unmovable … until the right moment.

Tieran's eyes widened. "Marcum? Well, that does change things. You must be the general's *commoner* niece. I had heard that you were coming to Kaibain to look for a husband. It seems you work quickly," Tieran remarked.

The young lord's attention turned back to Rezkin, "She is your girlfriend, eh? I can see why you are all bent out of shape, then."

"The next words out of your mouth had better be an apology or you will speak no more," Rezkin remarked, his voice low and flat as though he was simply commenting on the weather.

Tieran maintained his smile, but his eyes spoke of fear as they flicked to Rezkin's gaze. The young noble laughed boisterously and waved his hand around as if the whole incident was insignificant, "Of course, of course, friend Rezkin." His steps were masked with confidence, but inside he was shaking like a leaf. He stood before Frisha and gave an exaggerated courtly bow as he implored her. "My Lady Frisha, my most humble apologies for ruining your dress. I will, of course, compensate you for the loss. And, I do hope my comments did not offend you. My mouth does tend to run away with me when I am in the presence of such beautiful ladies." This last he said with a total lack of sincerity as his eyes fell over each of the ladies, who actually were quite lovely. Tieran considered them all to be insignificant and beneath his station.

In an effort to save face and discourage anyone from thinking Rezkin had gotten to him, he performed the same courtly bow to his friend, who had picked himself up off the ground. "My dear friend, Lord Ambry, I do apologize that your feet are so big that you could not keep them under you." Tieran then walked past Rezkin out into the street and performed a sweeping bow to the first person he saw stating, "My fellow Ashaiian, I do apologize that the sun is so unbearably hot. I will do my best to see that it behaves itself in the future." The young man motioned to his friends and then walked off bowing and apologizing for more absurdities to each person he passed.

Rezkin watched the discourteous, juvenile performance with dark eyes. His immature antics were an attempt to avoid shame in front of his friends. He was considering plans to hunt the man down that night in his bedchamber and fix the problem. With his arrogance and massive ego, Tieran was sure to become a terrible duke. The kingdom would be better off without such a man in power. Rezkin would have to check into the age of the current duke and inquire about his health. Given time, the young Tieran *might* learn some humility. He nearly grinned when he thought of all the ways he could teach the young lord.

Ladies Joselia and Meriana both ran up to Rezkin, each grabbing on to an arm. Rezkin drove off his instincts to throw the women away from him but kept a close eye on their movements. He did not want to fall victim to a dagger through the ribs.

"Rezkin, that was *amazing*," said Meriana with fluttering lashes.

"I never thought to see Tieran cowed. I have never seen *anyone* put him in his place before," Joselia tittered excitedly.

Meriana continued speaking as soon as Joselia took a breath, "I was so scared. I actually thought that you were going to kill him for a minute there!"

Shaking off the anxiety of the moments before, Tam laughed and said, "Don't worry about that. Rezkin is harmless. Well, unless he *needs* to kill someone, I guess." As he said the last, he furrowed his brow at his own contradiction.

"Oh?" Meriana said with a thrill. "Have you killed many men?"

Rezkin struggled to follow the rush of words coming from the excitable women. "I have killed many," he replied honestly.

Joselia's eyes widened. "How many? Were they all bad?"

"Of course they were all bad," Tam replied. "They were bandits who attacked us on our journey."

"Have you killed any women?" Meriana asked curiously.

Rezkin glanced over to see Frisha standing alone and pouting as though she had been forgotten. She scowled at the two ladies clinging to his arms and hanging on his every word. Extricating himself from the women, Rezkin said, "If you will excuse me, ladies, I believe Lady Frisha would like to return home to change her dress." Rezkin strode over to Frisha and bowed slightly before offering her his arm as was the proper way to escort a lady. Frisha blushed and smiled coyly.

Tam followed several paces behind Rezkin and Frisha, content to let them have some privacy. They walked in silence until Frisha asked, "Why did you call me Frisha Marcum? My surname is Souvain."

"General Marcum has named you his heir. You now have the *honor* of using his family name," Rezkin answered.

"Oh," she said. Frisha finally worked up her courage and remarked, "You called me your *girlfriend*."

Rezkin cocked his head as he looked down at her imploring brown eyes. "Well, you are, are you not?" he asked.

Frisha blushed and bit her lip before answering. "Y-Yes, if you want me to be. Are you sure you would not prefer one of *them*?"

Rezkin furrowed his brow. "One of whom?"

"Joselia or Meriana," she replied, secretly pleased that he had not instantly jumped to thoughts of the other women. "Actually, they would probably *both* agree to be your girlfriend. They'd likely be willing to share."

The young man frowned at the idea. Why would he possibly need another *Girl Friend*? Protecting one was difficult enough. Having multiple *Girl*

Friends would amount to a lot of work, and so far he had not really seen any gain from the position. Rezkin once again met Frisha's eyes and said, "I cannot possibly think of any reason I would ever want any other *Girl Friend*."

He must have said something Frisha liked because she beamed up at him as though he had just granted her the kingdom. Rezkin glanced behind him at Tam who had also heard and was grinning ear to ear.

As they neared the house, Frisha stopped Rezkin and looked up at him with concern, "Um, you know when you leave in a few days, I won't be able to go with you."

Rezkin frowned but nodded. "I am not sure that I should go to the tournament if it means leaving you here. I will not be able to protect you, as is my purpose."

Frisha's jaw fell. "You would stay for me?" she asked breathlessly.

"Of course," Rezkin replied. "I cannot fulfill my duties to you if you are not with me. It is complicated, though, because I have another duty that I must fulfill, and my best chance of furthering that is at the tournament."

"No, you should go," Frisha said regretfully. "You need to be there, and Tam and Jimson … and Reaylin … are all depending on you. Besides, whether you're here or there will make little difference to my uncle. He said he has been putting together a list of suitors that he would like me to start meeting."

"About that," Rezkin said. "I do not want you to marry another. I do not want to replace you. I cannot think that any other woman would fill your role to my satisfaction, and, frankly, I do not care to find out."

"My role?" Frisha asked.

"As my *Girl Friend*," Rezkin clarified.

Frisha smiled and nodded her understanding. She loved hearing Rezkin call her his girlfriend.

Rezkin took a deep breath and plowed ahead. *Why was this so hard?* "I am not ready for marriage," Rezkin stated.

Frisha's heart sank. She had known it was too much to hope for but could not stop her fantasies.

"I have only just come to the outworld, and I have many things I need to do before I think of taking a wife and having offspring." He did not mention that he had been warned against such things. "I cannot provide properly for them at this time."

Frisha's heart plummeted further.

"No matter what you decide," he continued, "I will always honor and protect you so long as I am permitted, but I hoped you might consider accepting me as your prime suitor. When it is time, I will make sure you have everything you need and anything you desire."

Frisha's mouth gaped like a fish a few times. As Frisha stared into Rezkin's beautiful topaz eyes, she could see that he meant every word he said. She truly believed that if she asked for it, he would find a way to give her the world. The fact that he promised to be there for her, whether she accepted him or not, told her that he sincerely loved her. "Oh Rez, yes, yes, yes, yes, yes! We'll have to convince my uncle, but I don't care what he says. I say, '*Yes!*'"

Frisha flung her arms around Rezkin's neck, and he did not even tense. He decided that he must have unconsciously anticipated the move. Rezkin released a heavy breath he did not realize he had been holding. Now that the issue was out of the way, he no longer had to worry about his *friends* replacing Frisha or her uncle marrying her off before he had a chance to promote her to wife status.

Rezkin thought he should have felt more concerned about entering into a contract of any sort at this point, but he was simply relieved that this was one less problem with which to be concerned. Now that he had a future wife lined up, he had no need to revisit the issue in the future; although, he was not certain he would have addressed the issue at all if circumstances had been different. Having a wife and offspring seemed tedious at best.

Rezkin's instincts went on alert when he noticed Tam was moving in on them quickly. Tam threw his arms around both his friends and squeezed. "Congratulations! I'm glad you two finally got that worked out. I thought I'd be an old man by the time you got through your courtship. It took you nearly a month!" Tam teased.

Frisha giggled and swatted at him. Rezkin did not understand. A month was on the lower end of decent for a courtship that had not been prearranged by family. After a moment, Rezkin realized Tam was making an attempt at humor. Rezkin was not sure he could pull off laughter at this time. He had not prepared for it since he was not playing any particular role. He settled for producing his best smile.

18

"**A**bsolutely not!" barked General Marcum. "Last night you did not even know what a prime courtship was, and now you are ready to enter into one? Well, I know *you* did not know," he said to Frisha, "but *he* knows much more than he wishes us to believe."

The three friends, the general, and Lady Adelina were gathered in the study. Rezkin and Frisha had planned to discuss the matter with her family after dinner, but the general returned home early, and Frisha just could not wait. Rezkin had approached the general and his wife asking for a word. Tam and Frisha, refusing to be left out, had joined them.

"*You* are up to something, *Rezkin*, and I will not let you dupe me or my family," the general continued as he paced angrily across the floor. Rezkin stood stoically watching the man stomp back and forth. Everyone else was seated observing with wide eyes. Even the Lady Adelina did not seem inclined to interrupt her husband's tirade.

"I assure you, general, I have no ulterior motives," Rezkin asserted.

"Ha! Like I would believe *you*," the general remarked.

Rezkin considered the situation objectively. Besides Marcum's general dislike of him, to what aspect was the general most opposed? He seemed most concerned that someone was trying to swindle him out of his estate.

Making a quick decision, Rezkin offered a concession, "General Marcum, if your greatest concern is that I am attempting to claim your estate against your wishes, then I will gladly remove it from the terms of the agreement. In fact, I do not require that Frisha come to the agreement with any kind of dowry at all. My only desire is to retain Frisha."

General Marcum stopped pacing and stared at Rezkin like he was some fantastical creature. Lady Adelina gasped and covered her mouth with her hand as her eyes darted to her young niece. Frisha had tears in her eyes and was grasping Tam's hand. Tam simply wore the biggest grin he had ever seen.

"You do not want the dowry?" the general asked uncertainly. After a moment, he collected himself, and his anger returned. "Oh, you are good. You are bluffing, though. You do not really believe I would consider sending my niece into the world without a dowry. Her father would disembowel me. Besides, I have already named her my heir. You know I will not retract that for *your* sake."

Rezkin restrained his frustration before the audience, and for all appearances, he looked steadfast and earnest with a hint of boredom. He asked, "What exactly would convince you of my sincerity, General?"

"To start with, a *name!*" the general barked.

"A name?" Rezkin asked with confusion.

"Yes, *your* name. Your family name to be specific. I do not believe for one minute that you were raised as some commoner orphan," he stated.

"I would gladly give it if I had one to give. I truly do not have a family name. If my parents had one, I would not know since I never met them," Rezkin explained, a bit of his frustration breaking through.

"Fine, then where are you from? Give me the name of this fort in which you were raised," Marcum ordered.

Rezkin rubbed at his jaw in an uncharacteristic outward expression of discomfort. This was going to be more difficult than he thought. "I am afraid it also does not have a name, or if it does, I do not know it."

Frisha gasped. "Rezkin! Just tell him!"

Rezkin looked at her apologetically.

"A fort with no name," the general stated flatly. He looked over at Frisha in exasperation, "You see? A man with no name from a place with no name."

"I have a given name. It is Rezkin," the young man replied.

The general scowled, "That is not a name! It is a character—a joke!"

Rezkin frowned. "A character?"

"I tell you this!" the general continued. "None of my forts are without a name and neither do they take to raising and training orphans!"

The light tapping at the door sounded like thunder in the booming silence that followed the general's shout.

"Enter!" he barked.

Steward Narus entered the room and announced, "General Marcum, there is a Lieutenant Jimson here to see you."

The general paused. He glanced at Rezkin and then Tam and Frisha. "He said he wishes to see *me*?"

"Yes, My Lord, shall I show him in?" Narus asked, his tone filled with boredom.

"Yes, Narus, bring him here. Perhaps he can help to straighten out some of this mess," the general muttered.

A few moments later, Lieutenant Jimson entered the study, surprised to see such a gathering. Maintaining his attention on the general, a man he never thought to meet in person, he saluted smartly and said, "General Marcum, I am Lieutenant Jimson. I have a letter for you from Colonel Simmons of Fort Maneske."

The general narrowed his eyes and said, "You carried this message yourself?"

"Yes, sir," the lieutenant replied.

"You arrived in Kaibain more than two days ago in the company of my niece, her escort, and this ... *rogue*." He motioned toward Rezkin with irritation, and Jimson's eyes briefly met those of the man in question with surprise and confusion. The general continued, "And you are just now delivering the message?"

"Yes, sir," Jimson replied anxiously but without a hint of apology.

The general huffed. "Just give it to me," he barked. The general had been in a foul mood to begin with, and this was not making it any better.

Lieutenant Jimson confidently strode forward, handed the sealed letter to the general, and then backed up a few paces to resume his stance at attention.

General Marcum checked that the seal had not been tampered with, and then opened the letter from the colonel. As he read, his brows rose higher and higher. At one point his attention flicked to Rezkin's swords, and his hands shook slightly before he steadied them. Once he finished reading the letter, he read it again. Afterward, he took his time folding the parchment, cleared his throat and, without looking up, quietly said, "You may be at ease lieutenant." Lieutenant Jimson relaxed but remained standing in place.

The general's anger had clearly dissipated, and the Lady Adelina was concerned by his reaction. "What is it dear? Are you unwell?"

Marcum looked at her as though he did not comprehend what she had asked, and then he finally turned his attention to the warrior he had been berating for the past twenty minutes. Rezkin's icy stare was arresting. The young man reached into a pouch at his waist and pulled out a small silver tube, which he held out for the general. Marcum realized that Rezkin knew exactly what was in the letter.

Marcum took the silver tube and carefully removed the cap and contents. He unfolded the parchment and read. Even without the enchanted seal, he would have known Bordran's hand. He lowered himself into a chair as he studied the familiar script of his old friend. To Marcum, Bordran had been more than a king. He had been his closest friend and confidant. Marcum, being quite a bit older, had known Bordran all of the man's life. He truly missed the man, and he missed the king. Bordran had been a king Marcum was proud to serve. When Bordran gave an order, Marcum felt confident he could follow it without reserve. Things had not been the same since Bordran died. Things were not the same with Caydean on the throne.

The general finally was able to focus his attention on the *content* of the parchment and was shocked that not only did the Certificate of Authority bestow upon the warrior *two* Sheyalin blades, but it also did not specify or limit the young man's authority in any way. The fact that Rezkin's name and description had been written in by a different hand was odd. It seemed absurd that the king would compose a nonretractable certificate of unlimited authority and leave the name of the recipient blank. Anyone could have written any name in the blank and had the authority to do whatever he wanted in the kingdom. No, that was impossible. The mage seal would have prevented it.

The other oddity was that Rezkin's name lacked not only a family name and place of origin, but also a title of any sort. By kingdom law, he truly was just *Rezkin*. He was not lying about that. A sobering thought crossed the general's mind.

Still gripping the certificate, he looked up at Rezkin and said, "You could have just claimed her all along."

Rezkin cocked his head in thought and then simply nodded once.

"Why did you not?" the general asked. "Or is that why I am receiving this now?"

"It was purely coincidence that the lieutenant chose to deliver his message to you at this time, and I would prefer to discuss any other details with you in private," Rezkin stated.

"They do not know?" General Marcum asked in surprise.

"No, and I would prefer to keep it that way for now."

Tam, Frisha, and Lady Adelina were all astonished and utterly confused by the entire spectacle. Whatever the lieutenant delivered had clearly unnerved the general, and then the note Rezkin handed the man had taken the wind right out of his sails. Now, they were talking about some secret.

Tam and Frisha shared a look. A secret *they* did not know? One about Rez? What could Rezkin be hiding, and how could it be so important as to affect the general of the army in such a way? It had to be important to Marcum in his capacity *as* the general since the missive came to him via one of his lieutenants from the colonel at Maneske. What did the general mean when he said that Rez could have claimed "*her*" all along? Was he talking about Frisha? That made no sense. People could not claim other people. Was he talking about a weapon? Sometimes men referred to their weapons as *she*.

Marcum glanced at Lady Adelina, Frisha, and Tam and said, "If you would all please excuse us, we have some business to discuss." With the strange change of mood and Rezkin's insistence on a private discussion, Frisha decided not to argue. If Rezkin could convince the general to accept him as her prime suitor, then she did not really care what was said … for now. She *really* wanted to know the secret. What was in those notes? With a questioning backward glance at Rezkin, Frisha followed Tam and Lady Adelina out of the room.

"Lieutenant, will you be staying for a while?" the general asked.

Jimson looked uncertainly at Rezkin. "I had hoped to visit for a bit. We were to discuss our travel plans."

Rezkin nodded once and said, "The lieutenant may stay. He is already aware of the contents of both of those documents."

The general realized he was still holding Rezkin's Certificate of Authority. With one last perusal, he rolled it up and replaced it in the metal tube before giving back to Rezkin. Marcum strolled over to his desk where sat a wine carafe and a set of goblets. He filled three of the goblets and then handed two of them to Rezkin and the lieutenant. "Shall we sit?"

The men seated themselves in the three high-backed chairs. Rezkin examined his goblet. Under the circumstances and having seen the general pour the wine, he decided the threat of poison was minimal. Besides, he was aware of only two poisons in existence that could dissolve that quickly, and neither were fast acting. He had antidotes for both in the pouch at his waist, along with several others.

A few moments of uncomfortable silence ensued before anyone spoke. Rezkin's Certificate of Authority was more than just a parchment bestowing the Sheyalins upon him. It was an authority that should have been outlined clearly. The general found himself in a quandary. The failure to define that authority meant the young man had both a complete lack of authority *and* an authority to rival the king—*literally*.

"I take it you are the reason I did not receive the lieutenant's message on the day of his arrival in Kaibain?" the general directed at Rezkin.

"Yes, I requested that he not deliver the message immediately. The lieutenant felt beholden to oblige." The general eyed the lieutenant attempting to discern the man's motives. Lieutenant Jimson held his head proudly and met the general's eye.

General Marcum nodded and said, "Yes, I can see that he did. I understand your difficulty, Lieutenant. We are all in a grey area, here. This young man,"— he indicated Rezkin—"has been given the right to enforce his authority within this kingdom, and yet, it seems, that he is the only one who can determine what that authority *is*. I cannot imagine what Bordran was thinking." But that was not exactly true. He had an idea. Actually, he had two, and he was not sure which was worse.

Rezkin said nothing. He had no idea what the old king had been thinking either. He was not even sure the king had meant for the swords to belong to *him* in the first place. His name had been written in a different hand, and it had not been that long ago, since the description of him was a recent one. Two years ago when the old king died, Rezkin had been several inches shorter.

Breaking the silence, General Marcum continued, "Bordran died a little over two years ago. You claim to be nineteen, so you would have been sixteen, maybe seventeen, when these were bestowed? There was no celebration. There were no announcements. Even I, the general of the army of Ashai, was not told. Whatever it is you did to earn the honor of carrying not one but *two* Sheyalins was kept in complete secrecy. Does King Caydean even know?"

Rezkin cocked his head to the side thoughtfully. "I am uncertain. Events have transpired for which I have no explanation. It is for this reason I am going to the tournament. I have no desire to prove myself before the masses, but I do need answers."

"Why do you not just go to the palace and ask?" the general asked. He was not particularly fond of the new king, but Marcum was loyal to Ashai.

Choosing his words carefully, Rezkin stated, "There may be forces in the palace working against me."

"A traitor?" the general asked. Rezkin inclined his head, not quite agreeing but not denying it either. He did not know who was responsible for the massacre at the fortress. It could have been the king for all he knew. If the king found out the strikers were traitors and issued the orders for them to die, then Rezkin had done the king's work. If someone else had ordered the deaths of the strikers, then Rezkin could be the traitor along with whoever issued the orders. With the authority granted him by the old king, though, Rezkin could not be tried openly. He would have to be dealt with in secret.

The general cleared his throat, "If a traitor is in the palace, then I must warn the king. Likewise, if he does not know about you already, then he must be told."

"Actually, I would prefer you not do that," Rezkin stated firmly.

Marcum narrowed his eyes at the young man. "And, why not?"

Rezkin leveled his gaze at the general *willing* the man to see his sincerity and authority. "We are in the midst of a conspiracy, General. People who are not involved need to remain uninvolved. I assure you this conspiracy is quite *deadly*," Rezkin stated ominously as his voice dropped. It was a warning. It held the implication that the king could be in more danger if he knew and that the general's own life was threatened if he spoke.

Jimson's face went pale with Rezkin's threatening words, and the lieutenant was glad that, so far, he had not been dragged into the conversation.

General Marcum stiffened. "Surely the king knows by now. Colonel Simmons would have sent a letter to the palace as well."

Rezkin reached into his tunic as he replied, "He did." Pulling out a sealed scroll, he waved it in front of the general. "This is the letter that was meant to be delivered to the seneschal.

General Marcum's eyes darted over to the lieutenant. "You gave it to him? That is a letter to the king!"

Lieutenant Jimson's jaw dropped as he shook his head vigorously. "No, sir! I have not seen that letter. It was not given to me to deliver. I swear it, sir!"

Stuffing the letter back into his inner pocket, Rezkin waved their concerns away. "The lieutenant is not at fault, General. I retrieved this before it ever left the colonel's desk. Lieutenant Jimson never received the letter."

"When did you see the colonel?" Lieutenant Jimson inquired with disbelief.

"I did not meet with the colonel. I said I retrieved the letter from his desk," Rezkin stated. He looked back at the general and remarked, "You really must improve the security at Fort Maneske. It was disturbingly easy to break in, go about my business, and leave. I barely had to try."

"You *stole* it?" The general gasped. "Stealing the king's correspondence is an act of treason! Yet … yet, you sit here calmly as if it is nothing more than another errand."

Rezkin shrugged. "What are you going to do about it?"

The general's jaw dropped. "Well, I will tell the king. I will have you arrested!"

"Let us dispense with the bluster, General," Rezkin replied. "Neither you nor the lieutenant will be making any attempts to arrest me. Even if you succeeded, which you would not, you could be tried for failing to comply with the authority of a sword bearer, among other crimes."

After allowing them a moment to contemplate the statement, Rezkin continued. "Aside from your own safety, you also fear for the safety of the king. Already, a part of your mind is wondering what fate could befall the king should he find out about me and the conspiracy in which I am involved, assuming a traitor is in the palace. No, General, you will not arrest me, and you will not inform the king of my existence. In fact, you will speak of me to no one except in the sense that I have been a guest in your home as your niece's friend."

The general was quiet as he considered the young man's words. Marcum was a riot of emotions. He was furious that this insolent young man would dare to give him orders, that he would finagle his way into the general's own home, that he would dare to bring his niece into this mess.

Lieutenant Jimson cleared his throat, "Rezkin, I have a question, if I may."

Rezkin's demeanor relaxed slightly as he turned his immediate attention to the lieutenant. "Of course, Lieutenant, you may ask anything."

Jimson released a breath and asked, "If you were able to retrieve the letter to the seneschal from the colonel's office, then were you not also able to intercept the one addressed to the general?" This caught the general's attention. He had been so wrapped up in his anger that he had not considered that small detail.

"Of course. I had already read the letter and knew you were carrying it. It was never my intention to conceal my identity from the general for long. I had hoped to get to know you personally, General, before you became aware of my status," Rezkin replied directing his response at both of them.

"Why?" General Marcum huffed.

"Two reasons, really," Rezkin replied. "The second was because I needed to study you. I knew, of course, about your military exploits and political maneuverings within the court, of which you have very few, by the way, for a man of your standing. What I did not know is what kind of man you are personally and where your true loyalties lie."

The general scowled, "I am the general of the army of Ashai. My loyalties are to the kingdom, of course."

"I do not doubt that, but there are many interpretations of what is best for the kingdom," Rezkin remarked.

General Marcum scoffed. "What was the first reason, then?"

"Frisha," Rezkin stated.

"What *is* your interest in my niece, Sword Bearer?" Marcum asked with hostility.

Rezkin sighed. "I have told you, General, my intentions toward Frisha are pure. She is my *friend,* and as such, I will protect and honor her. Both Frisha and her father recognize you as her guardian until the time she marries. Therefore, I must respect you as such. I had hoped to give you the opportunity to know *me* before you received that letter. Unfortunately, it seems your suspicions instilled within you an immediate dislike, which I have been unable to assuage despite my efforts to put your mind at ease."

The general laughed. "Of course I am suspicious. Anyone with any intelligence would not believe your story. You claim to be a commoner, but it is obvious you were raised as nobility. If you desire someone's trust, you should start with being honest, or at the very least become a better liar."

Rezkin cocked his head and replied, "I have never lied to you, General. While there is much I will not disclose, I have always been honest in what I *have* told you. I assure you that if I wanted to imitate some persona, whether noble or commoner, I could do so flawlessly. I never claimed to be a commoner. I simply stated that I am not a noble. Since I left my home, I have only endeavored to be myself."

"If you are neither commoner nor noble, then all that is left is royalty, and you are certainly not King Caydean or Prince Thresson," General Marcum said, but in his mind the alternatives were sprouting thick roots.

"Why must I be either?" Rezkin questioned.

"Everyone has a place. You must be *something*," the general remarked.

"You have seen my papers, General. I am Rezkin. *Just* Rezkin."

The general grunted. "So you are." After a moment's pause Marcum finally said, "Let us get to the point, Rezkin. What do you want?"

Rezkin pondered the question. "Hmm, I cannot say what I *want*, but I can say what is necessary. You see, someone in this kingdom has a very dangerous enemy, and I need to know who it is."

"Who? This *someone* or the enemy?" asked the general.

"Oh, I know who the enemy is," Rezkin replied.

"Then, who is the enemy?" Marcum asked.

"*Me*," Rezkin stated.

"Explain," the general commanded, as generals are prone to do.

Rezkin curled his fingers and tapped on the arm of the chair as he thought about how much he should divulge. "I was given orders to kill a number of people, which I did, all except for one. He managed to escape while I was dealing with the others. I question, now, why those particular people had to die. If it had been my choice, I would not have killed them."

"Yet, you killed them anyway," the general stated grimly. The truth was finally revealed, and he could see the young man for what he was. He was a killer. He murdered people on command rather than through necessity. The fact that the young man admitted his actions so casually demonstrated his cold and calculating nature.

Rezkin shrugged. "They learned of my orders at the same time as I, and after that, they really gave me no choice. Although, in truth, I cannot say I would have done differently at the time had they not attacked me first. I must follow the *Rules*."

"So your rules say you are supposed to kill innocent people?" General Marcum asked.

Rezkin cocked his head as he replied, "I did not say they were innocent, General. I am not a cruel man. In fact, if I was given orders to kill the men, then there was most certainly a good reason for it. The problem is, I do not know the reason, nor do I know who issued the orders in the first place. As such, I do not know where I stand. Since I am no longer obligated to follow anyone's orders, I am free to make my own choices. That is with one exception. My last order was to kill those people and one escaped. I must find him."

"So that you can kill him?" Marcum said.

"Perhaps," Rezkin replied honestly. "More importantly, I wish to know what he knows. Those men I killed knew much more about my orders than I."

"And what of the one who gave you the order in the first place," Lieutenant Jimson said.

Rezkin frowned. "He is dead. He was killed during the battle, but not by my hand."

"Battle? Just how many did you kill?" Lieutenant Jimson sputtered.

"There were many, but that is irrelevant. The point is the kill order would not have originated with the man who issued it. I want to know where the order came from and why it was given. And …" Rezkin paused as he worked to understand his own thoughts. "I want to know if I really must finish the job."

"You want to know if you must kill the survivor," the general stated.

Rezkin shook his head. "Not just him. There may be many more I was intended to kill with that order. It was unclear. I do not know if I was supposed to kill only those present or all others associated with them. You have seen the authority I was given, General. With my masters dead and that certificate, I am no longer beholden to anyone. Does the order still stand? If so, will someone else finish the job if I do not? What are the consequences for not completing the job? Most importantly, what are the consequences for those deaths for which I am already responsible? What I know right now is that there are at least two sides to this war, and I do not know which side I am on, if any."

"You speak of war. You think that what you are involved in is that serious?" the general asked.

"Believe me, General. Whoever ordered the deaths of the men I killed is fighting nothing less than a war," Rezkin replied.

General Marcum set his empty wine goblet down on the side table and leaned forward. "If what you are saying is true, then you have killed some very important people; yet, I have received no reports of any high profile deaths. Something of that magnitude could not have been kept from me unless it was either ordered by the king or is being kept from the king. To keep something like that from the king, it would have to be someone very high up indeed." Marcum sat back and asked, "Just how do you know it was not I who issued the orders?"

Rezkin's lips pulled into a feral grin as he replied, "Because, General, then you would have known who I was when we first met, and if you had, I can guarantee you would not have been able to sleep with me under your roof."

297

Despite the general's outward calm, his face paled at least a few shades, and Rezkin knew he had achieved the desired effect. It was not that he enjoyed frightening the general of the army. It was purely a strategic maneuver. He wanted to impress upon him just how serious it was that someone had used *him* to carry out the deaths of the high profile targets.

As he took a sip of wine, Rezkin waved his hand in the air as if to clear away the saturnine mood. He said, "Do not be overly concerned. If I intended you harm, I would not have had to maneuver my way into your home to do so. In fact, if I had intended to kill you, you would never have been aware of my existence. You have my word that as long as you do not take actions against me or interfere with my purpose, no harm will come to you or your family by my hand while I am a guest in your home."

Composing himself, the general cleared his throat and said, "That is very reassuring, especially considering the fact that if I were to ask you to leave, you would no longer be a guest in my home and no longer beholden to your oath."

Rezkin suddenly felt that strange sense of anger rise up in him, the same anger he felt previously toward Lieutenant Jimson when he questioned Rezkin's honor. "Really, General, you have had the absolute worst perception of me since we met. I do not go around murdering random people, nor do I take pleasure in the act. You, yourself, have killed many men by order of the king. In that, you are no different than I except that you knew by whom your orders were given."

"Yes, my orders are given by the king. You do not even know who was issuing your orders. It could have been an assassin's guild for all we know," the general acerbically replied.

"And your orders have always come from the king, himself?" Rezkin turned to Lieutenant Jimson who was feeling the strongest desire to flee the room. "Do you, Lieutenant, receive your orders directly from the king?"

"W-well, no. They come through the chain of command," the lieutenant replied cautiously.

Rezkin nodded once. "Exactly. The lieutenant does not always know who originally issued his orders," he said as he redirected his attention to the general. "If a superior officer issues a command to the lieutenant, and he carries out that order, is the lieutenant responsible for the outcome? Like you and the lieutenant, here, I followed a chain of command. My masters issued the orders, but those orders came from somewhere else."

"The lieutenant knows his superiors work for the kingdom," Marcum countered. "You do not seem to know whom yours worked for at all."

"What you say is true. I was raised since infancy to follow the orders of my masters, *Rule 258*. While I did not question whom my masters served, I have come to believe they, too, worked for the kingdom. More specifically, it is almost certain they worked for King Bordran, considering the certificate that you already verified is authentic. But, *he* was not the one to issue my last orders, was he? Who do you suppose replaced him in the chain of command, General?"

General Marcum stilled. If Rezkin had worked for King Bordran, then King Caydean should have seized Bordran's authority upon his death. But, Rezkin insisted that he was ordered to kill a number of secret, high profile targets. Was the king killing his own people, or had someone else usurped the authority in his stead? If the king believed the targets to be traitors, it would have been within the king's authority to have them investigated, and the general would have been informed.

Rezkin could see the general was finally beginning to realize the magnitude of the conspiracy before him. Rezkin released an audible sigh, not because he felt a need, but because he knew it to imply a change of mood in the discussion. "I know you were King Bordran's man, and although I cannot expect you to place your trust in me, I would hope that you could place your trust in *him*—to believe that he knew what he was doing when he gave me that certificate. I have mastered all the *Skills*, strictly adhere to the *Rules*, and am dedicated to my purpose."

Maintaining eye contact with the general as he spoke, Rezkin said, "I could accept your unfair judgment when you did not know me, but now we have spoken, and I have been unnecessarily candid in answering your questions. You know of my authority and, therefore, know that I am not obliged to provide you with any information. I have merely done so out of respect for both your position as general of the army and as Frisha's uncle. Since we met, you have repeatedly made unfounded accusations against my character and questioned my honor. Quite frankly, General, I am beginning to take offense."

The general's brows rose, and he actually barked out a laugh. "You are just *now* taking offense? I have been pushing your limits since you entered my home, and I swear I have never met a man with a steadier countenance. If it had been me at your age, I would have already run me through for such offenses."

"It was a test, then?" Rezkin questioned curiously.

Marcum frowned. "Not exactly. I meant what I said. I just simply made no efforts to filter my comments for the sake of common decorum, and neither did I make an attempt to play the role of hospitable host. I knew there was something wrong about you from the beginning, and now I know what it is. Oh, I believe I know what you are, and I do not want it anywhere near Frisha. She deserves better than you."

"I fail to see how any of the nobles who would not respect her would be better than I," Rezkin remarked. "What exactly is it about me that offends you?"

"You are a killer," the general spat.

"So are you," Rezkin countered.

"I have killed in battle. It is terrible but necessary. I am no assassin," the general stated.

"If the king ordered you to sneak into some lord's home and slit his throat? Would you deny your king?" Rezkin probed.

General Marcum clenched his jaw and scowled at the young man. "King Bordran would not have issued such an order."

"King Bordran did not issue my orders," Rezkin countered. "Besides, I did not assassinate the men I killed. They were fully armed masters of their respective weapons, and fifteen of them came against me alone all at once. My master gave the order for me to kill them when I was standing in the center of them all. You can hardly consider that an assassination attempt, unless you think I was the target of the assassination ..." That was a point he had not considered.

"Fifteen masters!" Lieutenant Jimson cried. "Where the hell do you find fifteen masters, and how did you manage to kill them all?" Abruptly, Jimson recognized the inappropriateness of his outburst and with chagrin calmly said, "Pardon me."

General Marcum frowned. "If that is true, which I find difficult to believe, then it sounds to me like your master did not intend for you to survive the impossible encounter."

Rezkin cocked his head in thought. "No, my masters would have been confident in my ability to prevail. I am nearly certain they expected my survival. I suspect that whoever issued the order was either likewise aware that I would succeed or completely underestimated me and expected that I would die."

He paused as he pondered the new perspective. "I was not scheduled to complete my training for another four or five years. I achieved mastery of the *Skills* far ahead of schedule. It is possible that whoever issued the order was unaware of this and truly believed that fifteen would be sufficient to end me. I had not previously considered that I could have been the target. It would have been absurd. All of the men I killed were those who had trained me for the prior nineteen years. They were aware of my *Skills* and would have known they could not succeed. I do not believe they were aware of the orders until I received mine. They did look quite shocked. It would explain why the last one ran away, as well. If they had followed the *Rules*, more of them might have survived."

"What do you mean?" asked the general.

"*Rule 245—Retreat when you cannot win*," Rezkin answered absently as his mind raced through the possibilities. Was it really *he* who was meant to die? But, why would the masters set it up in such a way that he was sure to survive? And, why had the masters killed each other?

"You killed your own trainers?" Lieutenant Jimson asked with disdain.

Rezkin cocked his head as he considered the lieutenant. "If I had not killed them, they would have killed me."

"But, they *raised* you!" the lieutenant protested.

Rezkin felt the tightening in his chest again. It was odd that it always seemed to happen when he thought of the strikers and his masters as people rather than targets or trainers. "They trained me to become a man. If they felt any sentiment toward me, it did not prevent them from trying to kill me in an attempt to protect themselves."

"But, did you not feel *anything* from killing them? No remorse? Have you no conscience?" Lieutenant Jimson questioned, his disgust obvious.

Conscience. That was the word associated with *Rule 2*. He would have to discuss the subject further with Jimson, but now was not the time. Rezkin replied, "Whether or not I have feelings regarding the deaths is irrelevant. It does not change the fact that they are dead, either directly or indirectly, through my actions. They would not have spared my life, Jimson. If you can see it no other way, then at the very least, does a man not have a right to protect himself?"

"But, you said they only attacked *after* you were given orders to kill them. They believed they were protecting themselves from *you*," the lieutenant argued.

"That is true, and they were. But, as I said before, it was not my decision. The orders were given in the presence of everyone, at which point nothing could have been done to stop it." Rezkin looked to the general and said, "Two forces were against each other. The smaller but deadlier force was surrounded. The commander yelled, 'Attack.' What do you expect to happen?"

The general nodded solemnly in understanding. "Were there others who trained with you? Other boys?" he asked.

"No, there were no boys. I was the only trainee," Rezkin answered, wondering what children had to do with anything. Why would children be asked to train? He had read of children. They were the weak and coddled offspring of a union between a man and a woman. He had never seen one, but from what he had read, he believed them to look similar to small-men and small-women. He was not exactly sure what determined whether a man and woman produced a child or a small-man like himself when he was young. Perhaps only those who had mastered the *Skills* and followed the *Rules* produced small-men.

"These men who trained you—you said they were masters of their respective weapons. How was it that fifteen masters gathered to raise and train one boy?" the general asked.

"Actually, there were seventeen, if you count my masters, and on the occasion that one of my trainers died, he was replaced with a new weapon master. But, I cannot answer your question," Rezkin replied. The truth was that he did not know the answer, but for some reason, he was hesitant to inform the general that the men had been strikers.

"Who exactly were these trainers of yours?" the general queried.

Rezkin held the general's gaze for several moments as he considered whether to answer. Finally, he said, "I do not believe it would be prudent to reveal that at this time." The general was an intelligent man, and Rezkin knew the possibilities were limited. Marcum could easily figure it out, but Rezkin had no desire to confirm his beliefs.

The general's suspicions had already grown into a budding tree. He was nearly certain of who and what Rezkin was. Of course, it should have been obvious from the beginning. Actually, it *had been* obvious, which is what raised the general's suspicions in the first place. The name alone should have been a dead giveaway. Initially, the idea had been so farfetched he had considered it to be a ridiculous flight of fancy, a bit of paranoia. As it became more realistic, he simply did not want to admit to it. Now, he could hardly deny it.

One thing was certain, though. He did not want his niece anywhere near Rezkin whether the man had Bordran's trust or not.

Aside from the king, there was only one person the general truly feared before Rezkin appeared in his life. Now, there were two. General Marcum cleared his throat and gathered his courage. "Rezkin, despite the disdain with which I have previously treated you, I do recognize both the authority and trust granted you by King Bordran. I respect you for your honesty and the gentlemanly conduct with which you have comported yourself at all times. However, given what I know about you, I cannot approve your request regarding Frisha. You have said that you recognize me as her guardian, and I hope you will respect my decision as such." The general cleared his throat and belatedly added, "Please, take no offense."

The deadly young man's icy eyes stared unremittingly at the general as though they alone could slay him where he sat. *And, perhaps they could*, Marcum thought darkly. Rezkin appeared as a statue, a silent warrior seething for the opportunity to step from its pedestal and release its wrath upon its foes like the vengeful God from which it was conceived. His gaze was that of a lion sizing up its prey, deciding if it was worth the effort it would require to take it down. Just as the general was truly regretting his words, the young man slowly, but silently nodded once.

Lieutenant Jimson watched the silent exchange with apprehension. He did not know what request Rezkin had made regarding Frisha, but he assumed it was of a personal nature. He knew the two had become close on their journey and had seen how besotted the young woman was with the warrior. Jimson had known Rezkin was dangerous, but he could never have imagined just *how* dangerous. The man was positively frightful. If he had killed fourteen weaponmasters in a single battle, then Jimson knew little could defeat Rezkin, short of an army. The young man's paranoia with checking for poisons and traps was suddenly understandable. If someone truly wanted to kill him, and it sounded like someone *did*, then the best way to do so would be via some quiet, underhanded assassination. Anyone challenging him openly was just asking for his own death.

After a few tense moments, the general turned his attention to the other occupant in the room. "Captain Jimson, it is time we addressed your involvement in my niece's journey."

Jimson was startled when suddenly addressed … and confused. "Ah, it is Lieutenant, sir."

"I think I know the ranks of my own officers. I believe a promotion is in order. I read the reports from your encounters with the bandits after first hearing of your involvement in my niece's journey. For your bravery and leadership in the face of mortal danger, you are hereby promoted to the rank of captain. The fact that you assisted in preserving the life of my own niece makes me personally beholden to you, and therefore, I am inclined to award you a gift."

"Thank you, sir! I am honored, but I must say that they were hardly battles. The first was little more than a few dozen. They were nothing like the battles of hundreds or thousands fought during times of war," Jimson argued.

General Marcum huffed. "They were battles nonetheless and more than most of your peers will have endured in these times of peace. You could have been as easily killed by those few dozen as you could have by a thousand considering your numbers and the need to protect the civilians. Yet, you prevailed, and I have my niece here today."

The lieutenant rubbed his neck anxiously. He did not want to argue with the general, but neither did he want to take credit for an accomplishment that was not his to claim. "Yes, General, thank you for your recognition, but I think we really have Rezkin to thank for our successes. Without him, we would not have made it out of either situation alive."

The general grunted. He was not yet ready to concede anything in Rezkin's favor. The idea that Rezkin and his niece meeting was purely coincidence seemed even more farfetched now than it had before. Knowing what he thought he did about the young man, he felt that very little of what Rezkin did would ever be left to chance.

General Marcum stood, and as he did, the two other men gained their feet as well. "Come, Captain. Let us see about that gift." The general led the two men to the first study that Rezkin had entered upon arriving at the house, the one filled with weapons. Captain Jimson's eyes widened at the display, and he released a soft whistle. Selecting a key from the ring in his pocket, Marcum marched over to unlock a small display cabinet. He waved the newly raised captain over and commanded, "Choose one. It will be yours."

Captain Jimson's jaw nearly dropped, but he managed barely to maintain his composure. "These are master blades?" he asked uncertainly.

"Several of them are. The others are close enough. They all are excellent weapons and are a worthy reward for the man who helped save my niece's life."

The captain's eyes unconsciously darted in Rezkin's direction. The movement was fleeting, but the general caught it, anyway. Marcum scowled as he added, "I have nothing that could rival what he already possesses." *Except Frisha*, Marcum's subconscious added sardonically.

Captain Jimson cleared his throat and focused his attention on the contents of the display case. His gaze roved over the selection of swords carefully lined up and hanging from pegs. Each was polished to a shine and sharpened to a fine edge. Jimson was familiar with swords, but he was far from an expert. All of the blades before him were beautiful, and he could not decide which he should choose. Hesitantly, he reached out and selected a longsword of similar weight and length to the one he carried. He had not yet purchased a new blade for himself, so he was still carrying the mediocre army-issued officer's blade. It looked like a child's toy compared to the one he held now. He hefted the sword and swung it a few times, but still he was uncertain as he looked back at the others.

Not wanting to anger the general, he tried not to look at his friend, but he could not help the pleading glance aimed at the young warrior.

Rezkin noted the captain's hesitation and imploring eyes and decided to help him out, despite the general's blatant dislike.

Rezkin walked over to the captain who still held the blade up questioningly. General Marcum stood back and watched the two men. He could see that somewhere along the journey the two had bonded. It was probably best for the captain's sake, as the general doubted Rezkin would have left the man alive had he desired to be rid of him. Rezkin's kind were cold-blooded killers. Even with the men's apparent friendship, he knew Rezkin would not hesitate to kill the captain if it suited him. It was in the young man's nature, or so he believed, now that he was nearly certain of Rezkin's identity.

Rezkin grasped the hilt of the blade the captain proffered and replaced the sword in the display case. He selected a sword that was slightly longer and a bit heavier than that to which the captain was accustomed. Rezkin handed the sword to the Jimson and then stepped back, allowing the man to make the decision for himself.

Captain Jimson was surprised at Rezkin's selection. This sword was larger than the one he typically carried, but he found that he could still easily maneuver the blade. When he sliced the air, he could feel the difference the added weight made in the momentum of his swing. Jimson remembered how difficult his practices had been when he had first received his old sword and realized, now, that he had gained quite a bit of strength since that time. In fact, much of his increased strength was acquired in the past month that he had been traveling with Rezkin.

General Marcum approved of the sword Rezkin had selected for the captain. It did, indeed, appear to be a proper fit for the man. He noted that it was actually one of the better master blades and wondered briefly if the young warrior had chosen it just for spite. He immediately banished the idea, as it was only fair since the general had offered any one of the blades to the captain. The general truly did want to thank the captain for his part in saving his niece's life, and as such, Marcum wanted the captain to have the best blade that suited him. Had the captain asked for *his* advice instead of Rezkin's, he might have selected a different blade for the man, but he grudgingly admitted to himself that this one was a better fit.

Captain Jimson turned back to the general with eyes filled with gratitude and pride and said, "Thank you, General. This is truly amazing. I cannot express my appreciation."

"The thanks is all mine, Captain," Marcum said with sincerity. The general stepped forward and pulled out a drawer in the bottom of the display cabinet. The drawer was lined with soft fabric and held several of the scabbards belonging to the swords displayed above. Marcum pulled out the scabbard that belonged to the blade the captain had selected and turned it over to him. The scabbard was lacquered black with red swirls scrolling along its length. A black leather strap with a dangling red silk tassel was used to attach the sword to the belt. It matched the red silk-wrapped hilt of the sword. The hilt had a gold-toned, bar-shaped cross guard and flat, gold pommel, which was inset with several small red-black garnets.

"Now, I believe it is past time for dinner," General Marcum said. "Captain, you will be joining us." It was a command rather than a request.

"Yes, sir. Thank you, sir," Jimson replied.

Marcum met Rezkin's silent gaze with a frown but said nothing. The young man's persistent silence was unnerving. The general lead the way to the dining room. He really did not like having Rezkin at his back, but it was unlikely the man would stab him under the circumstances. Besides, Rezkin *had* given his word not to harm the general so long as he remained a guest in the general's home. Marcum realized that somewhere along the line he had come to at least trust Rezkin's word, even if the young man did lack any other sense of morality.

Adelina, Frisha, and Tam were already patiently waiting in the dining room, although they had yet to be served. As soon as the others arrived, the staff began flooding the room with an aromatic feast. An extra place had been set on Rezkin's side of the table, and Rezkin took the initiative to move down a chair. This put him closer to the general, but seated Captain Jimson in the place of honor by the hostess. Marcum nodded in approval at Lady Adelina's questioning look. After the first course was served, Marcum stood and announced Jimson's recent promotion to captain. Everyone cheered and congratulated the captain, except Rezkin who remained silent but nodded meaningfully toward his *friend*.

The rest of the meal was filled with pleasant chatter about the journey and stories from back home for all those at the table except for Rezkin who remained silent throughout the meal. Frisha's curious glances in his direction were only interrupted by the occasional silent plea in Lady Adelina's direction, after which Lady Adelina would glance meaningfully between Marcum and Rezkin. Tam's eyes kept bouncing between the four trying to pick up on the unspoken current of conversation taking place beneath the audible pleasantries.

Jimson could tell that he was missing something important, but could not quite grasp what was going on and felt it was not the time to ask. General Marcum stubbornly refused to acknowledge anything abnormal and relentlessly questioned the captain when the others failed to carry the conversation.

Once the meal was finished, the lady invited her guests to join her and the general in the sitting room once again. Rezkin simply bowed politely toward the general and his wife and then left through the rear door of the kitchen without a word. Everyone else retired to the sitting room where they took their places among the chairs and couches. They were in the exact same places as the first night, except that Captain Jimson now sat where Rezkin had previously been seated.

Frisha chewed at her bottom lip anxiously. When she could not take it anymore she asked, "What's going on? Uncle Marcum, what did you say to Rezkin?" she asked accusingly.

General Marcum huffed, and Lady Adelina interrupted, "Frisha, dear, this is not the time. We have a guest."

"Nonsense! Jimson is our friend and Rezkin's, too. He knows how we feel about each other," Frisha asserted. She turned to Jimson and said with a dazzling smile, "Rezkin asked to be my prime suitor."

Jimson's eyebrows shot up in surprise. He knew the two cared for each other, but he had not known it had become so serious. "Oh," he said before turning his attention to the general. "So, that is the request you denied?" The general scowled and Jimson flushed. He had forgotten himself. It was so easy, when surrounded by the general's family who treated him as a friend, to forget that the man was the general of the army and his superior.

"What!?" Frisha shouted as she lurched to her feet. "Y-you denied it? B-but, *why?*"

"He is not right for you, Frisha. You deserve better than *him*. I will not have you bound to one such as he," General Marcum barked.

"What are you talking about? Rezkin is a *good* man! He has ever been the gentleman. He took it upon himself to protect us without asking for anything in return," Frisha said.

"Except for *you!*" the general interrupted.

"That's not the same, and you know it. It wasn't like he *planned* to fall for me. Besides, it's more than just the protection. He's *brave*. He went into that other riverboat all by himself, which I admit I didn't really care for at the time. But, he did it and he came back with the captive. And, he *cares* for people. You should have seen the way he ministered to the injured, and not just me, either! He treated all of the lieutenant's—ah, sorry—*captain's* men after the first battle. He also saved Reaylin from that huge monster of a man and treated her wounds as easily as a master healer. You should have seen him. You would never think such terrible things if you knew him!"

Captain Jimson truly wished he had *not* been present for this conversation. The general's face was flushed with anger, and never in his life had Jimson thought to see anyone stand up to the man in the way the young Frisha was at this moment.

General Marcum stood to face the hysterical young woman. "I *do* know him—better than you! I will not let you marry such a soulless creature!"

Frisha gasped in shock. "Soulless creature! Is that what those letters told you? That Rezkin is a soulless creature?"

Marcum scowled. "Of course not."

"Then what did they say? I know they were about Rezkin, and it was something important. What was it?" Frisha asked as she lifted her chin in determination.

The general ground his teeth as he glanced at the captain. Jimson sat curiously, wondering what the general would come up with to keep from exposing Rezkin's secrets, which he was obliged to conceal since Rezkin had asserted his authority on the matter. "That is none of your business, Frisha."

Frisha stomped a foot and said, "Like Hells it isn't! If you will deny me my chosen husband, then I have a right to know why!"

Lady Adelina gasped. "Frisha, dear, language!" She looked at her husband and said apologetically, "She *does* have a point, love."

Marcum huffed. "Nothing in those letters said anything negative about the man."

"Quite the opposite, really," Captain Jimson supplied. He knew he was playing with fire, but he felt that he owed a great debt to his friend.

The general turned his ire on Jimson, but before he could say anything, Frisha perked up. "Is that so? What did they say, then? How did they *not* refer to him as a soulless creature?" she asked flippantly.

"Rezkin has asked that I not divulge their contents," the general answered.

"And you are so inclined to do as he asks," Frisha remarked. "Then give me the general idea, since it is obvious they had some profound effect on you."

General Marcum growled. "Fine! Rezkin had the trust of King Bordran."

Frisha's mouth dropped as did Tam's and Adelina's. Jimson smiled slightly. It was a *very* simplistic summation of the certificate Rezkin carried. Frisha grabbed onto the boon with the tenacity of a drowning woman to a lifeline.

"I-If Rezkin had the trust of the king, then how can you say he is a soulless creature? How did he even *know* the king? If he really had the trust of the king, then how could I do any better than such a man?" The multitude of questions flying through her mind was more than she could process at the moment, and she had to stay on task if she was going to make her point.

"There is much more to that man than you know, Frisha. There is more than even *I* know, but what I do know is not good! I cannot in good conscience give you to that man. I am sorry, Frisha, but it is for your own good," General Marcum stated firmly.

"For my own good? You have told me absolutely nothing that supports your rejection of him as my prime suitor. If anything, you have made my case for me!" the young woman yelled.

"He is a killer, Frisha!" Marcum hollered back.

"So are *you!* And, so are Tam and Captain Jimson!" Frisha shouted in return. Tam winced, but Frisha's attention was solely on her uncle and did not notice.

"This is different, Frisha! He is not like us," the general stated. "He …"

"That is enough," a deep voice asserted from the other side of the room. Everyone turned to see Rezkin standing in the doorway. Rezkin met the general's eyes with an icy glare. He did not like to see Frisha so upset, and he certainly did not care for the general to say more than was permitted. The more his *friends* knew about him, the more it would place them in danger.

"Frisha," he said quietly with a slight bow, "your uncle is your guardian. He has been charged with finding you a husband by your own father. On our journey here, you made it clear that you accepted this arrangement. General Marcum has denied my request to be your prime suitor, and by my honor, I have agreed to accept his decision." The young man's face was devoid of emotion, but a dark shadow seemed to pass over his icy eyes.

"Well, I don't accept it," Frisha pouted. "I reject your rejection, Uncle, and if you won't change your mind, then I will reject my inheritance, as well."

"What?" Marcum and Adelina spoke in unison.

Frisha raised her chin and said, "That's right. Rez already said he doesn't require a dowry. He wants me either way, so I have no need of the inheritance. Without it, I can choose to marry whomever I please, just like my mother." She added the last for effect. The general had commented on several occasions that he had admired his little sister for following her heart, even if she did marry a commoner.

Rezkin strode farther into the room to stand before the young woman. He did not want to replace Frisha, and he did not like the idea of her marrying some noble who would not appreciate her, but he did not think it fair for him to take her from the family she obviously loved. It was a bond he could not comprehend but found himself envying in some small way. Besides, he could not see how forcing her into the loss of her inheritance and title could possibly be *honoring* her.

"Frisha, it is my duty to protect and *honor* you. I cannot see that this is the best way to do that. I cannot ask you to give up your title, wealth, and family for my sake," Rezkin stated as he stared into her large brown eyes.

"But, I don't care about the title. I never had one before, so why should I care for it now? As for wealth, you have said you can support us and don't need the dowry, so it's not a problem," she argued.

"And, your family?" Rezkin asked.

Frisha scowled over at her uncle as she answered, "If they cannot accept me and the man I choose, then they are hardly any family of mine."

"Frisha! You do not know what you are saying," Lady Adelina cried.

"I'm sorry, Aunt Adelina, but you heard what Uncle said. How can I accept his decision with absolutely no explanation?" Frisha inquired earnestly.

"That is true, Marcum. You have not given any reason for the denial of Rezkin's request," Lady Adelina remarked.

General Marcum scowled heatedly at Rezkin. He could not give a decent explanation without exposing Rezkin's secrets, and he was bound by Rezkin's authority not to divulge them.

Rezkin recognized the general's dilemma. While the argument did work in his favor, he felt it was a dishonorable way to win Frisha's hand. He took Frisha's hand as he had seen men do to the women they were courting and looked into her eyes. "Frisha, the general is honoring my request by not divulging his reasons for denying our courtship. There are things you do not know about me that, until speaking with the general, I had not realized were considered to be undesirable by outworlders. I have ever endeavored to live my life by the *Rules,* and in doing so, felt that I have lived as a worthy and honorable man. I am learning, now, that the *Rules* seem to be different for most outworlders.

"I cannot say that I understand it, but the general does not approve of who I am, and I believe he has your best interest at heart. I disagree with him because I believe I can provide you with a far more satisfying life than will one of the nobles who will not appreciate you. However, I have many secrets, and these are what concern your uncle. Your uncle has based his decision on what he knows of those secrets. It would be unfair to allow you to make this decision without knowing those secrets, as well. And, I am afraid I cannot, will not, divulge those secrets to you at this time and perhaps never will."

Frisha's face fell and tears came to her eyes. "So, that's it? You're just going to forget about me?"

Rezkin ran a hand through his hair, pulling a few strands from his queue, in an uncharacteristic expression of frustration. Keeping his friends close to him was more difficult that he thought it should be. He thought he had come up with the perfect solution for keeping his current *Girl Friend* with him, and it had failed miserably. *Rule 1* was by far the hardest rule he had encountered except for perhaps *Rule 2*, which he still could not even understand.

"Frisha, I have no intention of replacing you—at least, not unless you choose to marry another. But, I cannot marry you without your uncle's consent. It would dishonor you," Rezkin explained.

Frisha's eyes spilled over as she heaved a heavy sob and ran from the room. Rezkin watched her flee and then turned his fiery gaze on the general. He had no idea why the general had rejected him. He had mastered all of his *Skills* far earlier than expected and adhered to all of the *Rules* to the best of his ability. He had embraced his purpose, found his *friends*, and was doing everything possible to keep them together. Based on everything he had been taught, it was an exemplary performance.

Yet, the general *had* rejected his request and seemed to think the worst of him. Rezkin had heard Frisha's shouts, which had alerted him to the argument in the first place. He knew the general had called him a soulless creature. It seemed that nothing Rezkin could say or do would change the general's mind. Rezkin turned and strode from the room with purpose. He needed to work off some of his anger.

Captain Jimson waited a moment and then stood. He saluted the general and thanked the lady for her hospitality and then followed Rezkin. Tam quickly excused himself and followed, as well. Tam and Jimson walked slowly after agreeing that Rezkin needed time to cool off. They eventually tracked him to the far back corner of the property that was shaded by massive trees with thick boughs full of fluttering leaves that blocked the direct heat of the setting sun. Rezkin had already shed his shirt and was whipping his swords around in a fluid dance so quickly that the blades looked like shining lights extending from his palms.

Rezkin noted his *friends'* arrival and knew they wanted to speak with him. He was not yet ready to deal with them. He ignored their presence and continued his training. Eventually, the two men drew their blades and began to practice their own techniques. Tam was working on the newest series of forms Rezkin had shown him, and Jimson was getting acquainted with his new blade. He would have to work hard to be completely comfortable with the weight and length before the tournament.

Back at the house, Lady Adelina sat with her husband in silence. Eventually, she spoke her thoughts. "It was good of you to respect the young man's wishes in not divulging his secrets. I know it was difficult for you when Frisha was so upset."

Marcum sighed and replied, "In truth, Ady, I had no choice. Such was the authority given him by the old king."

Adelina's eyes widened. "What is this? How can the boy have so much power over the general of the army?"

"Yet, he does. Say nothing, Ady, to anyone. This is deadly serious," he said grimly. He rubbed his face in frustration, "I should not even have told you."

"Is that what you meant when you said that he could have taken her at any time?" Adelina asked.

"Yes," he sighed again. "If he chose to claim her, there is nothing I could do to stop him."

"And, yet, he respects your decision. He could have done so even without exposing his secrets simply by choosing not to speak up in your defense. Since you could not divulge your reasons for denying him, Frisha would never have accepted your decision. Had he said nothing, he could have won her hand, anyway," Adelina observed.

Marcum nodded, "It is true."

Adelina nodded and said softly, "He is an honorable man, then. I believe what he said about always living by that code of which he often speaks. He is ever courteous and protective of both Frisha's person and her honor. He truly does seem the embodiment of the term *noble*."

The general scoffed, "He is nothing of the sort. He is a killer, Ady."

"So are you, dear," Adelina retorted.

"It is not the same. I have killed in battle. *He* kills whomever he is order to kill," Marcum argued.

Adelina considered Marcum's statement and replied, "Does a soldier not kill due to orders? If you were not ordered to the battlefield, would you choose to go and kill? And, if you did choose to go on your own without orders, would that make you a better man or worse? Is the executioner a terrible man because he is ordered to kill the criminals? If the king asked you to kill a traitor quietly so as not to upset the public, would you do so? Is the king a terrible man for asking you to kill anyone? Was Bordran a terrible man? Rezkin may be a killer, but Bordran obviously trusted him to give him so much power. The fact that Rezkin chooses not to use his power to force your hand says a lot about him. I think most young men given that level of power would be tyrants."

Marcum could not argue with his wife. Everything she said was true, and still the general could not let it go. *Why* could he not let it go? The answer that came to him was not really a surprise. He had known it all along. *Fear*. He was afraid of the young man. It had been so long since he met anyone who could instill that kind of fear in him that the general did not know how to react except with righteous anger. Marcum feared for himself, for his family, and he feared for Frisha. He even feared for his kingdom. That dangerous, mysterious young man would be completely within his rights if he ran rampaging through the kingdom. Adelina was right. A young man his age with that amount of power and authority and his level of training could actually become the soulless creature he had accused Rezkin of being.

Marcum hung his head. He had seen it in the man's eyes, in his bearing, in his noble demeanor. He had seen it in the way he softened toward the lieutenant even when he was angry with Marcum. He had seen it with the way Rezkin took Tam under his wing and provided him with a weapon and the knowledge of how to use it. He had seen it with the way Rezkin always treated his Adelina with the respect and dignity due the lady of the house, and he had most certainly seen it when Rezkin looked at or spoke to Frisha. Rezkin was not a tyrant *or* a soulless creature. He truly seemed genuine in his intentions toward Frisha, and the fact that he was willing to accede to Marcum's authority as Frisha's guardian said much about the young man's honor.

One floor above, Frisha lay on her bed crying a terrible mess. These were no ladylike tears of sorrow. She was sobbing, her nose was running, and at one point, she developed hiccups that just would not go away. She knew she was in a miserable state, but she did not care at that moment.

How can Rezkin do this to me? I was willing to give up everything for him, and he rejects me for honor! I just cannot believe there is anything so terrible about Rezkin that I wouldn't desire him. He is the perfect man. And, somehow, he even had the trust of the king! How could Uncle Marcum reject him knowing that?

19

A warm breeze caught the reeds causing them to clack together in a chaotic percussive cadence. Liquid silver ripples danced across the black water under the cool light of the full moon, and in the distance, ship hulls creaked and thudded as they knocked against the wooden piers. Rezkin pulled his sodden feet from the thick muck of the riverbank, taking care to place them firmly so he would not slip on the muddy tract. This night had been his least favorite since leaving the fortress. Breaking into the bedchamber of the grandmaster of the Assassins' Guild without getting caught *and* without leaving a trace of his passing was not an easy feat. But, in truth, Rezkin had relished the challenge. That had not been what made this night so frustrating.

Earlier that night, after he had worked out his frustrations at the general's home, Rezkin met up with his contacts from the Diamond Claw Guild in Justain. They informed him that although the Justain branch of the guild now recognized him as their leader, he was unwelcome in Kaibain. Apparently, the guildmaster at the Kaibainian branch was just as reluctant to give up power as Martius had been. Rezkin was irritated because he had been forced to kill another twenty-six of his more experienced personnel in order to gain control of the guild. It seemed the Diamond Claws were particularly stubborn and slow to learn.

Before he arrived in the capital city, the Diamond Claws had been the least powerful of the three Kaibainian thieves' guilds. Now they were barely a guild at all. At least the Razor Edges were in line. Once the Crimson Blades heard what had happened to the others, he hoped they would be as well. He did not relish needlessly exterminating additional resources.

The man he placed in charge of the Diamond Claw Guild was not a particularly skilled thief, according to his comrades, but he was quite good with numbers. Rezkin did not care whether or not the guildmaster could steal anything. He needed someone who was intelligent and organized. He would have preferred someone more intimidating, but the second he selected could cover that ground. The man was a brute and seemed particularly eager to please the Raven. If the second could keep the guild in line, then the accountant could oversee its workings, and Rezkin would receive the resources he required. Already, he had the members of the other guilds keeping an eye out for Striker Farson. Rezkin had provided them each with a drawn likeness of the man and a few of his known habits. If every criminal in Ashai was looking for the man, Rezkin was bound to find him sooner or later, assuming the striker had not left the kingdom altogether.

Taking Pride's reins in hand, he led the horse to a slightly higher embankment with less mud and more pebbles and grass. He shucked his waterlogged clothes and boots and donned a clean, dry set from his saddlebags. He led the horse back to the main road and mounted smoothly despite the pain in his leg. He would never expose an injury or weakness with an unconscious wince or groan. Although he could have walked the short distance from the city, he knew Pride needed the exercise and change of scenery. Battle chargers were not meant to be cooped up in a stable yard. Now, he was glad for the horse's service.

Rezkin considered the plans he had set in motion over the course of the night. He had much to accomplish in the morning, and he would have to do it as quickly as possible if he was to avoid suspicion, especially from an already mistrustful general. After making it clear that the Diamond Claws were now under his authority, Rezkin had taken on the more tedious task of setting up his confrontation with the assassins. One could not brutalize and intimidate assassins into cooperating.

Men turned to thievery for survival or to improve their stations in life. They did what they did because they wanted to *live*. Assassins, on the other hand, had a different attitude toward life and death. Although they preferred to keep living, assassins knew there were often times when one was just as good as the other, and they understood that there were occasions when death was preferable. If Rezkin simply tried to push his weight around, he would be outnumbered and overpowered. The assassins would have no fear of his threats warning them against reprisal, and his *friends*, whom he was sworn to protect, would be in danger. No, if he wanted the assassins to cooperate, he would have to earn their respect and show them that he, too, could be an asset—that collaboration would be in their best interest.

It was to that end that Rezkin infiltrated the Assassin's Guild. He needed to show them that he was absolutely a threat, that he had no fear, and that he was a master of the *Skills*. The master assassins, in particular, tended to have a sense of superiority, a firm belief that they were the most *Skilled* men and women in the kingdom. They needed to know that Rezkin could get to them at anytime and anywhere, and there was nothing they could do to prepare or prevent it.

The quarters of the guildmaster were located in an underground sublevel in the center of the guildhouse, which the assassins referred to as the *Hall*, in honor of the Halls of the Afterlife. Everyone else called it the *Black Hall*. The entrance to the sublevel was visible from nearly the entire first floor of the Hall, and in order to access it, one had to pass through the training arena, which was occupied at all times by assassins of varying levels of *Skill*.

The Assassins' Guild was not large in numbers when compared to the numerous thieves throughout the cities. In fact, there was only one Assassin's Guild for all of Ashai, and they maintained a few smaller units in other king-doms that they referred to as chambers. The guild boasted only three master assassins in Ashai, including the guildmaster, whom they referred to as the grandmaster, and half a dozen assassins, more commonly referred to as slips. The remainder of the residents of the guildhouse were trainees. At any time, about two dozen young men and women were in training, starting as young as seven or eight years of age. Only a few would survive long enough to become slips.

The Hall was located in the hills to the east of the capital city across the Tremadel River in the northern Fendendril Forest. The location of the Hall was not exactly a secret in the upper echelons of society, but neither was it easy to find. The guild existed because corruption and competition amongst the houses demanded it. Therefore, the nobles whose job it was to oust such a villainous organization were its most lucrative clients. The singular tower, plain and ugly, had no windows up the sides, only a single door at the base, and a conical cap of slate for a roof. The tower itself was really just a giant, highly functional gatehouse for the extensive structure below the surface.

Getting into the Hall had been tense and tedious but not as difficult as Rezkin had anticipated. He watched and waited. After a few hours of surveillance, one of the slips who emerged from the Hall was sufficient to suit Rezkin's purposes. The man was a bit shorter than Rezkin, but his frame was similar, and the dark clothing and long cloak the man wore could conceal the discrepancy. Rezkin had tracked the man a ways into the forest before finally descending on him.

The slip detected Rezkin's presence at the last second, and the man was fast. He ducked the strike intended to render him unconscious and dove to the side. Rezkin spun, kicking out at the man, but landed only a glancing blow to the man's shoulder. As the Slip sought to regain his feet, he launched two throwing daggers at him. Rezkin deftly avoided the gleaming projectiles as he jumped to grasp a not-so-low-hanging bough. The slip seemed surprised by the attacker's agility only for a moment, shaking himself back into action as Rezkin's momentum carried him forward, straight toward the assassin. Rezkin landed steadily on his feet and immediately assaulted the assassin, preventing him from drawing any additional weapons. After a flurry of kicks and punches interrupted intermittently by swift ducks, dodges, and blocks, he finally managed to land a stunning blow to the man's temple. This was quickly followed by a strike to the back of the slip's head, rendering him unconscious.

Rezkin had gone easy on the slip. The man was *Skilled*, but not a master. Rezkin could have taken him out quickly with much less effort, but he did not want to kill or permanently damage the assassin. Likely, the Hall would not have blamed Rezkin for the death, determining it was the Slip's own fault for allowing someone to track him and failing to protect himself. With Rezkin's far superior *Skills*, though, it would have been as dishonorable an act as defeating an unskilled small-man. In fact, Rezkin wanted the slip to live to report back to his comrades and superiors about Rezkin's *Skill* and honorable mercy. Also, he did not want any blood to get on the clothes. He needed them to get into the Hall undetected.

Rezkin slumped as much as he could without appearing too awkward and kept his face hidden beneath the hood. During his training, he had learned the silent language of the assassins—a series of hand and body signals used to communicate without words. Properly used signs could convey not only meaning, but also emotional state and feelings, much like the tone and volume of voice when speaking. When questioned with these signals by the sentries, Rezkin answered fluidly and strode forward with confidence. His masters had insisted that if one *appeared* to belong somewhere, then people would assume he *did*.

Once in the main Hall, Rezkin could see the full extent of the tower's usefulness. Extending into the flame lit darkness above were a series of staggered lofts and platforms, each seemed designed for particular training exercises. He observed vague movements and distorted noises coming from a few of the upper platforms, so he knew them to be occupied, probably by older trainees.

Rezkin had to find a way to enter the sublevel. He did not want anyone to see him doing so, lest they question his motives. He needed a distraction. As he passed by a couple of trainees, Rezkin reached out and snatched a practice blade from a young man's hand. He smacked the small-man in the side of the head, and the young man shouted in alarm. Rezkin's signs expressed agitation as he admonished the stunned small-man for his loose grip, lack of focus, and the audible shout and revelation of injury and weakness. He finally instructed the small-man to perform a series of physical exercises designed to both punish and push the young man to improve his *Skills*. It was exactly the kind of interaction Rezkin would have expected from his own masters and trainers.

One of the slink trainers standing nearby watched the exchange with interest before nodding at Rezkin in acknowledgement. What happened next surprised him. He had never trained with other small-men, so he had not expected the *group* punishment and training that resulted from his actions. Instead of the single small-man running off to accept his punishment as Rezkin had commanded, the entire training class amassed at one end of the training arena and began performing the exercises. The slink trainer stood before them in verbal reproach, listing each of the young man's offenses and reminding them that when one failed, they all failed.

While the trainer's attention was focused on the class, Rezkin used the opportunity to slip away and into the underground. It was not the diversion Rezkin had intended. He had planned to use the minor distraction of admonishing the trainee to sabotage some of their equipment. When the equipment failed, he hoped it would create an even larger disruption that would gain the attention of the trainer. The strange behavior of these outworlders had surprised him, but it worked in his favor. He was not certain that punishment of the entire group for the failure of one young man was the most efficient training method. He knew, though, that it was a tactic used by instructors and supervisors over large groups, particularly when they did not have the resources or patience to deal with each student individually. He had learned much of this from his military training.

Once he was in the sublevel, Rezkin saw few people scurrying through the dark corridors. Even though he knew the layout, the darkness and solitude of the passages rendered the place a labyrinth seemingly designed to confuse the dead and keep them from escaping. Rezkin had never been the superstitious sort, although many of the soldiers and mercenaries he had met were greatly so; but, he was certain that if the spirits of the dead *did* walk the plain of the living, they would definitely inhabit these walls. After all, ripping spirits from their living bodies was the purpose for which the assassins lived.

The grandmaster's door was unguarded. Who in his right mind would consider entering the grandmaster's chambers uninvited? Rezkin checked the latch and lock for traps and then set to manipulating the mechanism. Halfway through, he realized the master assassin had engaged a synchronic alarm. If the tumblers in the lock shifted into the correct position to disengage, a mechanism *within* the room would activate and alert the inhabitant, in this case, the Grandmaster of the Assassin's Guild.

Rezkin adjusted his tactic as soon as he realized the truth. He focused his mind to picture the inner mechanisms of the lock. Even though no wards were present, his masters had explained that there was always the *potential* for a ward to exist. As such, a strong enough mind, even one with a lack of *talent*, could manipulate the potential ward. Rezkin had practiced many hours, perhaps more than all of his other *Skills*, to be able to manipulate potential wards with nothing but his un*talented will*. The concept was so simple, and yet, according to his masters, no one in the outworld practiced the technique.

Rezkin wrestled a tiny potential ward into existence, pressing it against the connection to the synchronic alarm. He wrapped the imaginary microward around the connection and then solidified it in place. Now, he could maneuver the locking mechanism without fear of setting off the alarm. The Grandmaster was clever to have employed such a device. Without Rezkin's intense *focus*, he would have missed the warning signals and alerted the assassin to his presence.

Once inside the room, Rezkin stepped over, around, and through various traps. He was pressed to the extent of his *Skill* to keep from waking the man or stumbling into the camouflaged traps in the dark. The room was organized chaos. Likely, the Grandmaster knew where every item belonged, but anyone else would think the place had been ransacked. Items were placed in illogical and incongruous places, a method sometimes employed for disrupting intruders. While fumbling in the dark, one would not expect a coatrack adorned with pewter eating utensils hung from bale wire to be standing in the center of the room, fishing hooks strung at various heights from the rafters, or a teetering waste basin to be mounted on a pedestal like a prized sculpture directly in front of an open toilet, which was oddly placed at the head of the bed.

Rezkin detected several poisons on valuable or desirable items—the kind of items that would draw a thief's attention. It seemed superfluous since no one would be insane enough to simply *rob* the Grandmaster of the Assassin's Guild. Well, anyone but Rezkin. The grandmaster's sleep was shallow and alert, as one would expect from a man in his position. Rezkin finally decided on the item he desired, and despite his careful retrieval, he found himself poisoned. At least, he *would* have been poisoned if he had not been immune to that particular toxin. The grandmaster had *earned* his place in truth, and would be a worthy adversary, at least for a time, if the only *Skills* Rezkin had to rely on were those of an assassin.

He slipped from the grandmaster's chamber, relocking the door and releasing his imaginary ward, allowing it to dissolve back into the *potential*. Rezkin passed a couple of slips in the corridor with a confident, casual gait, that of a man simply going about his business. The two were deep in hushed conversation and nodded without breaking stride.

Back on the main floor, Rezkin immediately made his way to the upper levels, slipping into the shadows as he did so. At one point, he had to duck behind a weapons rack to avoid a stray dart that missed its intended target. The trainee quietly scolded himself for the failure and collected the dart that had landed only inches from Rezkin's hiding spot. The young man failed to detect the intruder and went back to practicing. His other shots were much more accurate, although not nearly sufficient.

The upper level was unoccupied, and beyond that was nothing but a dark recess and empty rafters. The heavy slate roof tiles permitted no access from the roof, which is why Rezkin intended to use it as his escape. Eventually, the assassins would figure out how he had entered the Hall, but since he would not pass by the sentries at the entrance, they would not be able to figure out how he left. If they realized they had been infiltrated anytime before his intended meeting the following day, they would believe him still in their sanctuary.

The center of the roof was held up by a central shaft as large as a tree trunk, which Rezkin would have to scale. He wrapped his arms and legs around the beam and proceeded to shimmy his way to the top. Once there, he held on to the shaft with his legs while he worked a heavy dagger between slate tiles at the top. The blade abruptly snapped but not before he had pried the tiles far enough apart to get a firm grip. He frowned at the useless dagger hilt as he shoved it in a pouch at his waist. It was a cheap dagger he had acquired from one of the bandits during his trek to Kaibain.

Rezkin shoved the tile up and snatched the dagger blade before it could fall the hundred or so feet below where it would alert the assassins to his presence. Rezkin's entire body strained as he gripped the central shaft with his legs and hefted the heavy slate tile up and to the side. He had to maintain a firm grip on the tile that had been resting beneath the top shingle. It was poorly balanced and had become loose during his machinations. If the heavy shingle fell, it could start an avalanche of sliding shingles, perhaps even collapsing a large section of the roof. He had to remove the sword and scabbard from his back and place it on the roof, or he would not have been able to squeeze through the hole. The sword bearer did not carry his own blades, begrudgingly hiding them in the forest. Instead, he carried the assassin's blade along with the rest of his attire. He gripped the loose tile in one hand as he used his other to lift himself through the small opening.

Once on the roof, Rezkin carefully adjusted the two shingles until they once again fit snugly in their intended positions. He collected the sword and then began making his way down the vertical face of the tower. The tower was old, and the handholds and footholds were numerous where the grout had weathered away. Unfortunately, the same natural weathering applied to the stones, some of which were loose. Rezkin reached for a handhold and found the stone to be too loose to hold his weight at the same time that the stone beneath his foot crumbled away. Despite all his *Skills*, Rezkin was pitched into the air, falling freely into the darkness below. He twisted in midair so that he would strike the ground properly for such a fall. Upon impact, he pitched forward into several somersaults intended to absorb his momentum.

The ground at the base of the tower was uneven and on a slight hill. Rezkin wrenched his leg and heard an audible snap just before he struck a tree. The impact with the towering fir dislocated his shoulder and caused a searing pain in his chest. He mentally chided himself for his folly as he went about checking his injuries, although he would never give voice to his pain or self-recrimination. Rezkin braced himself and then slammed his shoulder into the trunk of the tree, shoving the appendage back into its proper socket. He prodded his ribs to find that at least one was probably broken although not dislocated. Finally, he pulled up his pant leg and checked the damage to his shin. The bone must have been fractured because he had heard the *snap*, but he could find no dislocation of that bone, either. He was lucky to have such minimal damage, even if it was all on the same side.

Holding his arm close to his body helped to keep both the arm and the ribs in place. Rezkin limped as he searched for a few strong, straight sticks. He had to use his damaged arm to strap the sticks around his leg. Finally, he traversed the track of his fall covering up any evidence of his passing. It was dark, but the pain helped him to focus. He had endured much pain in his life, and it was often used as an instructional method in maintaining focus and resisting torture.

Rezkin slowly made his way back through the woods until he found the assassin he had left behind. The man was gagged and tied, but he did not appear to have regained consciousness in Rezkin's absence. Rezkin removed the man's clothes and redressed him before lugging the assassin to the bank of the river, not an easy feat with a broken leg and injured shoulder and ribs. He dumped the man in a shallow pool, making sure his head and shoulders were above water. Hopefully, the water would erase any evidence that Rezkin had donned the man's clothes or that they had been removed at all.

Rezkin travelled a good distance upstream before attempting to cross the river. No bridge spanned the massive Tremadel for it was too vast and deep, and the way needed be clear for ships. If one wanted to cross, he had to purchase passage on a ferry or other vessel. Rezkin had ridden the ferry across with a group of day workers returning to their camp on the other side of the river, but it was much later now, and any crossing would be notable. Due to the swift current, it was impossible to swim the monstrous river. Rezkin did so anyway. Any boat passage would eventually be tracked by the assassins, and Rezkin wanted to appear as a wraith, untraceable, unstoppable. Rezkin swam the Tremadel in full gear with numerous injuries and still managed to reach the other shore not far from where he had left Pride.

The mounted warrior circled the city to approach the Eastern Gate, which was still closed. He slept for a few hours amongst some brush as he waited. An hour before dawn, the guards opened the gate to grant entry to the numerous merchants, farmers and traders who were lined up outside the gate with their carts and wagons. He steered Pride between two of the larger wagons and huddled beneath a worn brown cloak. The guards were tired and paid little attention as they passed around steaming cups of coffee. Rezkin was already a bit feverish, and he knew he would have to appear whole and hale when he implemented his plan later that day. He needed a healer.

Winding his way through the streets was not difficult atop the massive battle charger. People naturally shied away from such a beast and cleared the path. Moving through the city without drawing attention was impossible. He stayed to the smaller side streets as much as possible. When he was within two blocks of his destination, Rezkin dismounted and left Pride in a vacant alley. The horse stood patiently, not moving from his spot as Rezkin turned the corner and limped the short distance. Despite his best efforts to conceal his injuries, the ever-so slight limp was unavoidable. The average person might not notice, but to anyone with a trained eye, he was obviously lame.

Using his one good arm and leg, Rezkin leveraged himself up onto a short wall. From there, he gritted his teeth as he used much of his remaining strength to pull himself onto a second floor balcony. He studied the balcony above him. Normally, he would have no problem accessing the simple structure, but his fever had worsened, and he was nearly at a loss for energy. The icy cold Tremadel had done its best to claim his life, sucking him under and choking him over and again. In the end, he had prevailed, but he had not yet shaken the river's grip.

Rezkin let himself into the apartment before him and quickly made his way to the front door. He could hear a man and a woman arguing in the adjacent room. The woman wanted to know where her husband had been all night, and the man insisted he had simply passed out at the tavern and slept in the common room … *alone*.

Once out of the apartment, Rezkin dragged himself to the next floor. It was absurd that scaling one flight of stairs could be so demanding. He had endured far worse injuries in the past, but he conceded to himself that he had not previously spent an hour drowning and fighting an impassable monster river afterward. Rezkin allowed himself into the third floor apartment above, which to his surprise was not warded.

He crossed the room and eased himself into a chair beside a large desk strewn with papers. His eyes begged to close as his body yearned for sleep, but he forced himself to sit up and appear menacing, which at that moment was anything *but* how he felt. He nearly lost the battle over the next half mark that he waited. He roused himself as he heard the first signs of movement from the adjacent room.

A young man in skewed grey robes nearly stumbled from the bedroom. His hair was mussed, and he wearily rubbed sleep from his eyes. He dragged his slipper-covered feet over to the small woodburning stove and brought it to light. He filled an iron kettle with water from a barrel that looked to refill itself from a small pipe that ran through the ceiling to the roof. The young man turned with a massive yawn, and when his tired eyes reopened, his gaze landed on Rezkin. He blinked several times as if to clear away the inharmonious image of a strange, dark warrior sitting in his abode. The young man scratched his head and furrowed his brow before finally asking, "Who are you?"

Rezkin lifted one brow. He had to give the man credit for not panicking, but his total lack of concern was disconcerting. Anyone finding *Rezkin* in his home should surely be terrified. He knew he was not himself, though. He should have checked the other room to make sure of its occupant. This young man was not the one he was here to see. He also realized that since the unexpected resident had appeared, he had been focused on *not* causing a panic. Rezkin had been *willing* the young man to feel comfortable and perhaps curious but not frightened. It seemed his *will* had been appeased.

"I am looking for Master Healer Dronidus," Rezkin replied, his voice slightly hoarse.

The young man shrugged and then shuffled over to a counter that held a small canister. He scooped tea from the canister as he spoke. "Dronidus is dead. He died two weeks ago. Got run over by a spooked carthorse. Nasty business, but nothing could be done."

"And you are?"

"The name's Yerwey Dulse. I am … *was* … Dronidus's apprentice-journeyman, but when he died, the guild went ahead and raised me to full healer," Yerwey explained.

"Apprentice-journeyman?" Rezkin asked. He did not know if it was his fever, but the term made no sense. Either one was an apprentice or a journeyman, not both.

Yerwey grumbled in irritation as he waited for his water to heat. "*Master* Dronidus," he said with scorn, "insisted I would learn more by staying under his tutelage than by finding a position as journeyman. I suppose I did, but only because he never lifted a damned finger to do anything himself. I got stuck with all the work and almost none of the pay."

It was a common enough complaint among apprentices, but this young man looked defeated. It seemed that any love he might have had for his life's calling had been beaten from him with endless hours of toil for little gain.

"I have need of healing," Rezkin stated without preamble.

"I figured, else you would not be here," the healer replied. "Many such as you came through here. They were always showing up at odd hours with mysterious injuries—usually traumatic ones—claiming they occurred in the most mundane of ways. What is your excuse?"

"I fell after fixing a roof," Rezkin replied.

The young man snorted. "Because every thatcher carries swords and daggers and wears armor."

Rezkin pounded his fist on the desk. The fever and pain were making him irritable. "I did not say I was a thatcher, but the cause is still the same."

The young healer's face sobered. "Look, I am not Dronidus. Whatever he was involved in, I am not a part of it. I do *not* treat criminals unless it is requested by the city guard or magistrate."

"I can make it worth your while," Rezkin said as he plopped a heavy purse on the desk.

Yerwey glanced at the purse thoughtfully and then shook his head. "No, you need to leave. Find someone else."

Rezkin sighed, his fatigue getting the best of him. He upended the purse on the desk, and gleaming coins spilled out in a small mound. Yerwey's eyes nearly popped out of their sockets. "That's gold!" he exclaimed. Rezkin waited as the young man eyed the small fortune hungrily. It was probably half a year's income for a Journeyman, and only slightly less for a new healer.

"I … uh … damn. No, I cannot," the young healer said as he shook his head emphatically. "I do not treat criminals," he whispered quietly, as though it was a mantra he was repeating to convince *himself*.

Rezkin did not have the energy to find another healer. He needed this one. "I am not a criminal, and likely those men Dronidus treated were not either. They were most likely strikers."

"*What?*" Yerwey exclaimed, meeting Rezkin's fevered gaze once again.

Rezkin sighed again and said, "The strikers do not visit the healer's wards. Their business and their identities are secret, and only a few select healers would be permitted to know of them. When they are injured, they will go to a healer's safe house, like this one," he gestured to the room around them.

The young healer looked doubtful, so Rezkin continued. "Think back.

They were all likely large men, finely built with expensive, quality weapons and equipment. They would have shown little or no reaction to the pain they were in, and they would already have evaluated their wounds prior to arrival. How many criminals would you expect to meet such a standard?"

Rezkin did not know if other strikers had come to Dronidus for healing, but the strikers who had trained him had insisted he memorize this place, among many others, that he could use if ever he was injured in the outworld. It was likely that if they knew of and had vetted it, then other strikers would have as well.

Yerwey's eyes were wide, and his lips rounded in an '*o*' as understanding dawned. "And you ..." he trailed off.

Rezkin leaned back in his chair. "I am something else," he said as he unceremoniously dropped an unsheathed Bladesunder onto the desk with a *clunk*.

"A sword bearer," Yerwey sputtered. The young healer's eyes were riveted on the shiny, color-swirled blade. A high squeal and hiss sounded loudly from somewhere in the room, and it eventually drew his attention from the fantastical sword. "Oh!" he called as his grabbed a thick pad and pulled the screeching kettle from the flame. He held the kettle as he glanced back toward the Sheyalin, but the stranger had already withdrawn the magnificent weapon.

Glancing down, Yerwey realized he needed to finish pouring the tea. He filled a second cup as well and brought it to the young sword bearer. The man's face was flushed, and perspiration gathered at his brow. "I, uh, I guess I should check your injuries."

Rezkin was relieved to see that the man was going to finally cooperate. He appreciated that the healer lived by a moral code, but he did not care for the fact that it had delayed his own healing. "My left shoulder was dislocated, I have at least one broken rib on the left side, and my left tibia is fractured. I might also have fluid in my lungs."

As the young man came around to check Rezkin's injuries he remarked, "You did not get fluid in your lungs repairing a roof."

"No, after I was injured, I went for a swim," Rezkin replied.

"Of course you did," the healer muttered as he began the healing process.

20

The morning had been quiet. Frisha had not left her room, and Lady Adelina ordered the young lady's meals to be delivered to her quarters. Rezkin had not been around in the morning for their usual training, so a couple of hours after the midday meal, Tam and Rezkin found themselves training on the back lawn. Rezkin took Pride for a brisk ride around the perimeter several times so that the spirited stallion could get some exercise. No one knew that Rezkin had been out with the horse all night, although the Stable Master Finnian might have noticed. If he had, the man had said nothing.

In the late afternoon, Finnian strode into the stables announcing that a guest had arrived. Captain Jimson was not expected until closer to the dinner hour since he had duties until they left for the tournament. Unfortunately, with all the drama the night before, the would-be travelers had not had the opportunity to discuss their travel arrangements. Tam and Rezkin made their way into the house only to hear Lady Adelina fussing over someone.

"No, my lady, I had no problem traveling with the men. They were all very respectful. Of course, there was the one incident at the river … Oh, hi Rezkin!" Reaylin beamed as Rezkin and Tam entered the parlor.

"Reaylin," Rezkin said with a slight bow in greeting. "It is good to see you again." Rezkin was not quite sure of the veracity of the statement, but it was a polite greeting, anyway.

"Not going to greet me, eh, Reaylin?" Tam scoffed.

"Oh, hi Tam," Reaylin said with decidedly less enthusiasm. "I was just talking with Lady Adelina."

"Yes, we heard," Tam said. "Best not go into the river incident. I think it was embarrassing enough for everyone the first time."

Reaylin's face flushed. "Oh, right."

Lady Adelina's eyes sparkled as she asserted, "Oh, no, dear. You cannot leave off, now. You have already broached the subject, and now you simply *must* share."

Reaylin flushed again, "Oh, um, well, you see … Frisha and I went to bathe upstream, and then when we were walking back, we came upon Rezkin. He was also bathing, but you know, the water wasn't that deep, and anyway … well, then Frisha and I kind of fell in …"

Tam cleared his throat loudly, "If you're going to tell an embarrassing story, you have to tell it right!"

Reaylin's face was bright red as she darted a glance at Rezkin who was standing stoically waiting to hear the rest of the story. Actually, he had never asked what caused the fight in the first place, although Jimson had mentioned his hypothesis.

"Right, well, Frisha and I sort of got into a fight, and then we fell in the water and kept fighting … a lot," Reaylin said as Lady Adelina gasped. "Rezkin heard one of us scream, so he came running to see what the problem was. Well, you know, he had been bathing, so he was completely naked." Lady Adelina could not stop the giggle that bubbled up and had to cover her mouth to hide a smile as her eyes wandered over the handsome, well-defined young man. "So, then, all of a sudden, Tam and Jimson show up, and Jimson thinks Rezkin is trying to take advantage of us."

Adelina gasped again. "No!"

Reaylin nodded emphatically. "Well, Rezkin did not take kindly to the accusation, and things weren't so good between him and Jimson for a while, but they didn't fight or anything. When it was all over, Rezkin was sweet enough to treat our wounds, and he gave us some herbs that really helped with the pain. We were all really embarrassed. Except Rezkin, I think, who was just mad, and Tam, I guess, who didn't do anything."

Lady Adelina grinned and said, "Frisha did not tell me that story. I think I might have to mention it." Then her face fell, and she said, "Well, not right away, I suppose." She waved her hand and said, "I will let you young people visit while I go check on my dear niece. It was a pleasure to meet you Reaylin."

"Likewise, my lady," Reaylin said performing an awkward curtsy that just looked strange with her wearing pants and a sword strapped to her hip. As Adelina left, Reaylin looked back at Tam and Rezkin and asked, "So, what's wrong with Frisha? Is she ill?"

Tam glanced at Rezkin, who did not seem inclined to answer and decided to just tell her and get it over with. "Frisha's uncle rejected Rezkin's proposal."

Reaylin's eyes widened. "What?" Her attention darted to Rezkin. "You proposed? *Marriage*? And, he *rejected* you? I can't believe that! Who in their right mind would reject *you*?" Reaylin's mouth snapped shut as she realized what she had said, and her face flushed once again.

Rezkin shook his head. "It does not matter, now. The decision has been made, and he is not likely to change his mind." Changing the subject, Rezkin informed her, "Captain Jimson will be here in about an hour. We are to discuss our travel plans at that time. I assume that is why you are here."

"Captain? He got promoted, huh? That's great. Uh, yes, I came by to see when we are leaving for the tournament and how we plan to get there," Reaylin answered.

Rezkin turned to Tam. "Perhaps you would like to take Reaylin on a tour of the grounds while we await the captain's arrival?"

Tam scowled at Rezkin. He absolutely had no desire to be left alone with the neurotic female, but he replied, "Sure, that sounds great. You'll love it, Reaylin."

Rezkin was glad to be rid of the pair. He really did not like dealing with the awkward looks of mixed confusion and sympathy every time someone brought up his failed proposal. Rezkin had never been a prideful man. All of his experiences prior to leaving the fortress had to do with battle and training, which fell under the jurisdiction of *Rule 14—Do not revel in success*. He had to admit, though, that this rejection stung. The fact that the decision had been made based on the general's opinion of Rezkin's *character* actually caused that increasingly familiar tightness in his chest to return.

Rezkin wandered into the study that held the multitude of weapons. He retrieved two matching ones he had seen in his previous visits. They were identical and meant to be wielded as a set. Each one consisted of a central hardwood shaft about the length of his forearm. A curved scythe-like blade extended from the tip of each end of the shaft back toward the other end of the shaft but did not connect. They were most unusual weapons for Ashai, but he had seen them before. They were called su'carai and were used by the nomads of the mountain tribes far to the East. A foreign warrior had been brought to the fortress to train Rezkin in the use of the strange weapons, but it had been a while since he had worked with them.

He took one in each hand, placing his palms in the centers of the shafts. Then, he began spinning them in his fingers so that each looked like a bladed disk. He walked with them into the center of the room, which was kept clear presumably for this purpose, and began sweeping through the forms scoured from his memories.

As his body fell into the familiar motions, the blades spun faster until they created a whirring sound as they swept through the air. Rezkin twisted and spun all the while keeping the blades in motion. The whirring became a melodic cadence that sounded like the ebb and flow of an enormous locust swarm. When Rezkin had completed the final form, the spinning blades came to an abrupt halt, and so did the music.

Rezkin turned to the wall to replace the weapons as he said, "Good afternoon, General. You are home early, again."

General Marcum stood in the doorway in his crisp military uniform, clasping his hands behind his back. He grunted and remarked, "I have never actually seen those weapons in use. They were always fascinating to me, but I had a difficult time imagining how they could be effective. I understand, now. The man I purchased them from assured me that a true master could make them sing. It seems he was telling the truth."

"They are surely an interesting weapon—one I had not seen in quite some time," Rezkin replied.

Marcum shook his head and replied, "You speak of time as would a man two or three times your age. How long has it been since you mastered the su'carai?"

Rezkin cocked his head in thought. "Perhaps three or four years. These were a little awkward when I first picked them up. They are slightly larger than those to which I was accustomed. I imagine mine were sized to fit me at the time."

"It did not appear to be the least bit awkward from my perspective," the general commented.

"It came back quickly, and I adjusted," Rezkin replied. "I *have* practiced with them on occasion since then, just not often."

The general grunted as his eyes sought the window, where his attention lingered. Rezkin glanced out the window and saw nothing of interest. Realizing the general was lost in thought, Rezkin cleared his throat in an effort to regain the man's attention. General Marcum looked back at Rezkin and said, "I have not changed my mind about your proposal, but I have decided to allow Frisha to travel with you to the tournament. There will be some conditions, of course. Propriety must be observed."

"Why?" Rezkin asked. "Why does it matter to you if she attends the tournament?"

"Because she wishes to go," the general remarked. "And, it would give her a chance to meet the other nobles."

The astute warrior could tell the general had another reason but was disinclined to discuss it.

Rezkin grunted in disbelief, "So, you would have me escort her so that she may look for other suitors?"

General Marcum frowned while he ran the conversation through his head again. Realizing that was indeed what it had sounded like, he said, "No, that is not what I meant. I was not referring to the young men. I just meant the other nobles in general. Many of her peers, the young ones especially, will be attending the tournament, and it would be a good social opportunity for her. Plus, as she pointed out, she would get to experience the excitement of the tournament before she settles down."

Rezkin felt that sudden pang in his chest, and he realized he did not like the idea of Frisha settling down. This time Rezkin glanced away.

"Does that bother you?" the general asked.

"Is that your intent, General? Do you wish to antagonize me?" Rezkin asked.

General Marcum released a heavy sigh. "No, that was not my intent. I just find myself wondering if you are capable of feeling like the rest of us."

Rezkin frowned. "Perhaps I am, perhaps not. Are you capable of feeling in the same manner Frisha does? I heard her crying most of last night, and she has yet to show herself today. If you are incapable of feeling the way she does, does that make you less of a person?"

"I acknowledge your point. And, it is also not my intent to upset Frisha. When I decided to name her my heir, it was in hopes that I could give her a better life—not that her life was so terrible in the first place. Her father has been quite successful for a commoner. Ever since she came here, though, I have been regretting my decision. I had not imagined she would encounter so much danger on the trip here, and I certainly did not consider that she might meet the man she wished to marry during the journey. I would never have expected that it would be one such as you, but conversely, if it had not been you, then she likely would not have made it here at all."

Rezkin furrowed his brow. "To be honest, I do not know why she is so upset. She has so many other options," he stated as that tightness in his chest returned, "and aside from the protection I have provided, I have given her no evidence of my worth."

"The heart is fickle," the general grumbled. "I spoke with Tam, and from what he says, that girl has wanted you since the moment you met. But," Marcum stated as he held up a finger to make a point, "what we want is not always what is best for us."

"What one man believes is best is not always so," Rezkin countered.

"There are certain truths throughout society, and what you are, Rezkin, is not wholesome," the general stated.

Rezkin scoffed. "Name me a noble who is *wholesome*, General. For every major and minor house, I could reveal at least a handful of scandals and hidden skeletons. Men and women alike cheat and steal and even murder on occasion. Some men beat their wives, engage in extramarital affairs, and have a dozen illegitimate children running homeless in the streets. They plot and scheme against each other always seeking some new morsel of power or wealth. No house is spared, General. Not even your own."

General Marcum narrowed his eyes at the young man. If Rezkin were anyone else, he would think the man knew far too much for his own good, but this particular man could handle any problems and probably knew expertly how to use the information. He wondered just what Rezkin knew of the clandestine affairs of his own house. It was just one more thread of power the young man had over him that Rezkin refused to use against the general to get his way. Not that Rezkin really needed any more power, but it was astonishing that the man could restrain himself from taking what he wanted. This whole situation with Frisha was obviously upsetting to them both. If he were in the same situation, Marcum knew he would not be so noble. And, there it was again. The *noble* Rezkin.

Rezkin noted the general's concern and waved it away. "Do not worry yourself, General. I have no intention of blackmailing you. I have far more efficient ways of getting things done. All I am saying is that if you define your word *wholesome* by the actions of the nobles, then I want nothing to do with it, and I should think you would prefer Frisha to stay out of it as well."

A knock sounded from the front entry, and Steward Narus shuffled past the open doorway to answer. Rezkin said, "That would be Captain Jimson. He is coming by to discuss our travel plans. Since you seem to have your own ideas, I suppose you had better join us. If you are not already aware of it, Mistress Reaylin has joined us this afternoon as well."

General Marcum stepped back into the hall, and Rezkin followed at a comfortable distance. Tam and Reaylin were already greeting Jimson when they arrived. Tam introduced Reaylin to the general, who found the young woman to be eccentric and rather uncouth. Marcum invited the group into the study where they usually spent the evenings, and a maid served them tea and small cakes.

Tam shifted continually. He had come to hate being in the same room with both the general and Rezkin, and he had never particularly enjoyed Reaylin's company. Jimson also felt awkward. As a lowly lieutenant, he had never dreamed he would be spending so much time in the presence of his general, and his friendship with the general's newest unofficial enemy complicated the issue. It did not help that Reaylin was shamelessly flirting and batting her eyes at Rezkin. She had apparently taken the general's rejection of Rezkin's proposal as a sign that it was time to up her game.

General Marcum took the opportunity to start the conversation. "I was just telling Rezkin that I have decided to allow Frisha to travel to the tournament with you all; however, there are some stipulations." Tam and Jimson glanced at each other and then at Rezkin as the general continued. "As you know, for propriety's sake, I cannot allow a young woman like Frisha to travel such a distance without a proper escort." General Marcum directed a pointed look at Reaylin to show his derision for her own traveling choices.

"I have found a suitable solution," Marcum announced. "My brother Simeon, the Count of Glasbury, has two sons who have expressed an interest in participating in the tournament. As blood relations, they will serve as suitable escorts for Frisha." The general sighed and said, "I believe my nephews intend to bring a friend along as well. All the talk of Frisha going to the tournament has drawn the interest of their sister, and now she also wishes to attend."

Redirecting his attention to Captain Jimson, the general said, "I am retracting the approval for your leave." Jimson startled but settled as Marcum continued. "Your assignment is to provide escort for my nephews and nieces to and from the tournament. During the tournament, you are free to do as you please. I will assign you a couple of additional men, and Simeon will send a few of his own guard, as well."

Jimson quickly stood, saluted, and said, "Yes, sir, as you command," before reseating himself.

The general's mouth pulled into a smirk. "You should be pleased, Captain. This means you will get paid for taking the journey you would have taken otherwise, and I do not really expect you to run into much trouble on the Tremadel. It is too large to blockade in the manner you encountered on the Straei." General Marcum redirected his gaze to take in Tam, Reaylin, and Rezkin. "How the rest of you travel is up to you, although, if Rezkin is serious in his desire to protect Frisha, I expect he will wish to escort her as well.

Rezkin narrowed his eyes at the general as he said, "I did not see you resorting to extortion, General Marcum."

"Extortion? What are you going on about?" Marcum huffed.

"Considering the amount of trouble we encountered on the journey here, do you really expect me to believe you are willing to place the safety of *two* of your nieces and both your nephews, the count's heirs, in the hands of a few soldiers and house guard?" Rezkin questioned. "You expect *me* to escort this party, and you expect me to do so out of my desire to protect Frisha, despite the fact that you have already rejected my proposal."

"You think I am incapable of keeping my family safe without you?" the general sputtered. "Your arrogance knows no bounds."

"Not arrogance, General. *Reality*. If I refuse to provide escort for this party of yours, then how will your plans change? Would you not add at least a half dozen men to the guard? Or would you simply deny your nieces the opportunity to travel altogether?" Rezkin inquired with accusation. "No, General, you are counting on my choosing to provide escort once again with no benefit to myself."

"Ah, now we see your true colors. No longer the selfless protector, are we? Very well, Rezkin what is it you want? How much?" Marcum spat.

Tam and Reaylin were both confused. They knew Rezkin was a good fighter, but surely he could not be worth more than another soldier, or maybe two if you considered the value of his healing skills.

Rezkin's voice dropped and came out cold and unnerving, "I do not want your money, Marcum. I want you to reconsider my proposal." Rezkin intentionally left off the general's title.

General Marcum clenched his jaw. "Are you giving me an order, Rezkin?"

"Do I need to?" Rezkin replied with a previously unseen hardness in his icy glare.

Tam and Reaylin looked at each other in confusion. Why would Rezkin be giving the general orders? They both turned questioning eyes on the captain begging silently for answers, but Jimson was entirely focused on the rug at his feet. With a shared look, the two decided it was in their best interest to remain as unobtrusive as possible.

Marcum countered. "And, what of you respecting my decision? Have you reneged on your word?"

Rezkin stood abruptly, his hand clenching his hilt in a clear sign of warning. The motion was quickly followed by General Marcum's rising to his own feet. "I have reached the end of my patience with you questioning my honor and motives, Marcum. I have done nothing deserving of your derision, and your choices regarding Frisha are based on your own mental slander against my character, a preconception that is completely unfounded in the scope of reality. If you had a valid reason for your rejection, I would accept it, but as it is, you have none."

"And still, my decision stands," Marcum stated stubbornly as he wondered if Rezkin would hold to his word and not to do him harm.

Rezkin released his grip and completely changed his demeanor. He went from frightful and menacing to blasé and unconcerned in the space of a breath. Casually, he asked, "Have you considered, General, that Frisha may no longer wish to attend the tournament? The woman does not even wish to come down for supper. It seems unlikely she would desire to travel all the way to Skutton."

"You think she only wanted to go to the tournament for *you*?" Marcum snapped.

"I think Frisha is an independent young woman with desires of her own. You might want to consider those before you go about making important decisions for her," Rezkin replied.

"Captain," Rezkin barked without taking his eyes off the general.

"Yes, sir!" Captain Jimson replied as he rose to attention without thinking.

"A passenger ship, the *Luna Mara*, has been requisitioned in the general's name," Rezkin said just as the general interrupted him.

"I made no such arrangements!"

"It will be leaving two days hence," Rezkin continued. "A passenger manifest has already been filed, which you will find includes: you and your comrades, Sergeant Millins and Second Lieutenant Drascon; four of the Jebai House Guard—Ferrel, Guent, Maris, and Jeyet; the general's nephews, Lords Malcius and Palis; their friend, Lord Brandt of House Gerrand; the general's nieces, Lady Frisha and Lady Shiela; Lady Shiela's maid, Mistress Tami; Master Tamarin; Mistress Reaylin; and of course, myself—plus one battle charger."

General Marcum's face was pale, and his jaw sagged. How could Rezkin already know all of his plans? He had only made out the order to his men a few hours ago. Rezkin had somehow not only learned of his plans, but had also taken the initiative to make arrangements. How did Rezkin make arrangements in Marcum's name to begin with? And, how did he get the names of the Jebai House Guards? Marcum did not even have that information, yet. He had spoken to Simeon only last night, and it had not even been confirmed that the Gerrand boy was attending.

Rezkin gave the general's mind a moment to catch up. "Arrangements have been made for lodging in Skutton. Four rooms have been reserved at the Coral Cove Inn and another three at the Sun Coast Inn. The inns are located directly across from one another. You will find that space is limited due to the influx of travelers for the tournament.

"I am impressed you were able to get that," Jimson mumbled under his breath.

"You cannot possibly have made arrangements already. It is ridiculous. How would you have gotten word to Skutton, much less received a confirmation?" General Marcum scoffed.

Rezkin cocked his head and replied, "I used the Mage Relay, of course."

"What!? How did you get access to the Mage Relay?" Marcum shouted.

Rezkin raised a brow and deadpanned. "Really?"

General Marcum scowled. "I want to know exactly how you got your information. Some of what you know is only a few hours old."

"No, General, you really do not," Rezkin mused before striding out of the room.

The previous night, after following the general to his brother's home, and before going to the Diamond Claw Guild and the Assassin's Guild, Rezkin had spent a few hours sneaking into Houses Jebai and Gerrand to retrieve as much information as he could about their inhabitants. Both Houses had decent guards for what they were, and he had been unfamiliar with the layouts of the estates.

Slipping through the palace and accessing the general's office after he had left the healer's sanctuary had been less difficult. People were expected to be roaming the halls of the palace at that time, and Rezkin was *intimately* familiar with the layout. The interior of the northern fortress in which he grew up was an exact replica of the interior of the palace. It was a fact of which Rezkin had been aware, but until today had not really considered to be of interest. Now, he had to wonder why that was.

The general's office was secured with a mage lock, but Rezkin knew ways around those. The key was not to break the locks, but to simply bypass them altogether. Rezkin had read the general's correspondence prior to its delivery and then confirmed the participation of the young Lord Brandt. After corroborating the list of individuals with whom he would be journeying, Rezkin had gone to the river to make arrangements for the ship. It took little effort once he got there since he had already forged the documents in the general's hand.

Rezkin ducked into the Mage District after leaving the docks to deliver the second set of forged documents to the Mage Relay Station. Once he received confirmation of the reservations, Rezkin found himself back at the Marcum estate in time to train with Tam and exercise Pride before Reaylin's visit. It was surprising how quickly arrangements could be made when people received instructions from the general of the army of Ashai.

Rezkin wanted the general to know that he would always be a step ahead of the man, but he had made all of the arrangements only in part to make his point. By making the arrangements himself, Rezkin had the power to select the vessel, personnel, and accommodations of his choosing. Over the last few days, Rezkin had already been researching the various vessels and their captains and personnel, so he was already prepared when the time came to make arrangements. The final reason was simply because Rezkin was tired of waiting. He wanted to be gone from the general's home, and his *other* business was almost concluded.

"Captain Jimson, confirm those reservations," the general ordered distractedly. General Marcum was once again furious with the presumptuous young man who was staying as a guest in his home. How Rezkin had gotten his information in such a short amount of time was beyond him. The fact that all of the reservations had been made already was nothing short of sorcery.

Marcum now knew exactly what he must do. He would find out who

Rezkin truly was, and if he was really Bordran's man. Marcum would make contact with his source while the young man was away at the tournament and hopefully have some answers by the time of his return. It was perhaps the riskiest venture in the general's long career to involve this particular source. If the source turned out to be opposed to Rezkin, it would be like two wildfires meeting with Ashai in the center. They may snuff each other out, but everyone and everything caught between them would be destroyed. Maker forbid the two find common ground and become one.

"Yes, sir," the captain said as he marched from the room. Jimson was certain the reservations would be exactly as Rezkin had said they would be. He did not doubt the young warrior's abilities or, surprisingly, his truthfulness. If Rezkin said he did something, then it was a sure thing that he had. While Rezkin kept many secrets, what did come out of his mouth seemed to be the truth.

Rezkin had once said that he could pull off any role he chose, so the captain knew the man was capable of lying; but Rezkin had also assured them that he was playing no role at this time. Jimson frowned at his own logic. Could you ever really trust someone who claimed to be able to lie and play a false role like a master performer? Perhaps everything that Rezkin had said and done was a performance in itself. The thought did not sit well with the army captain, and he realized that despite Rezkin's admission of fraud mastery, Jimson still trusted his friend.

Rezkin, General Marcum, and Captain Jimson had all departed from the sitting room, which left Tam and Reaylin sitting in wonder and confusion.

Reaylin turned her hazel eyes toward Tam and asked, "What in the world was that?"

Tam shook his head. "I really don't understand anything that goes on between those two. General Marcum has hated Rezkin since they first met, despite the fact that he seems to agree with him most of the time on pretty much anything that doesn't involve Frisha. He even seems to respect Rezkin for his knowledge and skills, I think. The general has never trusted him, though. Every time they are in a room together, I am almost certain one of them is going to end up dead."

"But, didn't you notice? Rez didn't push it, but it seemed like *he* was the one in charge. Don't you think that's odd?" Reaylin asked.

Tam shook his head. "I don't think Rez was actually ordering the general around. I think they were both just being antagonistic. General Marcum gives orders and expects people to comply, and Rez just *doesn't*. He has always been respectful toward the general, but he doesn't recognize the man as having any authority over him." Tam scratched his head and furrowed his brow. "Which, I guess, he doesn't since Rez isn't a soldier. One thing is for sure, though. General Marcum knows something about who Rez is that we don't."

"Why do you say that?" Reaylin questioned with wide eyes.

Tam shrugged uncomfortably. "It was weird. The general got a letter delivered from the colonel at Fort Maneske, and then Rez handed him another paper, and all of a sudden things changed. The general was really ... upset ... or maybe disturbed. I'm not really sure. When Frisha finally got him to disclose something, General Marcum just said that Rezkin had King Bordran's trust."

Reaylin gasped. "Seriously?"

Tam shook his head. "That's what he said."

"How did Rezkin know the king? And, why would General Marcum hate Rezkin if King Bordran trusted him?" Reaylin questioned.

"That's exactly what I've been wondering," Tam replied. "I don't know. Maybe he met him at the fort where he was raised. Maybe King Bordran knew Rezkin's parents or mentors or something. It's really weird, though, right?"

"Sure is. Do you think he knows King Caydean?" Reaylin asked.

"I don't know, but I do know that whatever was in those letters, Rez doesn't really want getting around. He doesn't even want Frisha to know," Tam remarked. Tam looked sideways at Reaylin and said, "So don't tell anyone."

Reaylin scowled at Tam. "Who am I supposed to tell? Besides, Rez saved my life. I'm not going to go around telling people about him if it might cause him problems."

Tam shook his head and started to walk away. "I'd better go let Frisha know what's going on."

"Okay, well, I guess I'll come back tomorrow in case there's new information," Reaylin said.

Tam walked Reaylin to the door just to make sure she found her way out and did not snag anything that did not belong to her along the way. He still did not trust the girl. He then made his way up to Frisha's room where he knocked incessantly until she finally opened the door.

Frisha's eyes were puffy, her nose was red, and she looked completely worn. "What is it, Tam? I don't really feel like talking."

"I know, but I have some news. May I come in?" Tam asked as he shoved his hands in his pockets and ducked his head. Tam did not really know what to do for his childhood friend. He had never had to deal with a broken heart, and he had never seen Frisha so infatuated with a man.

"I guess, but keep it down. Aunt Adelina will get upset if she finds out you are in here with me *alone*," she said sardonically. "It just wouldn't be *proper*."

Tam ducked his head again and closed the door behind him. "We just had another one of those meetings with your uncle and Rez," he grumbled.

"I bet that was fun," Frisha moaned. "Did Rez convince him to change his mind?" she asked hopefully.

Tam sighed. "No. But, your uncle is going to let you go to the tournament with us."

"Really? How is that going to work? Oh, no! He's not planning to marry me off to someone else is he? It's not you or Jimson is it?" Frisha asked in a panic.

Tam scowled. "No, of course not. Your cousins are going."

Frisha blinked. "My cousins? You mean the Jebais?"

"Yeah," Tam replied, "*Lords* Malcius and Palis and *Lady* Shiela."

Frisha groaned. "Oh, I don't even want to go, anymore. I really only wanted to go to be with Rez. I wanted to spend more time with him and see him compete in the tournament. I was worried that if he went away I wouldn't see him again. There's no point, now, since Uncle Marcum rejected our union. It will just be that much more difficult to be around him knowing it can never happen. If my cousins go on the trip, it will just be even more miserable."

Tam shrugged. "Rez has already made all of the arrangements, but he did mention to the general that you might have changed your mind. You don't have to go if you don't want to. I was only going because it sounded exciting, and I wanted to see Rez and Jimson compete also. Now, the whole thing sounds like a lot of trouble."

Frisha kicked a pillow and growled in frustration. "Why won't Rez just accept me? I was willing to run off with him and forsake my inheritance, and he said, 'No!'"

"Oh, come on, Frisha. He's trying to do what's best for you, and I respect him for it. I know it hasn't been easy on him, either. I don't think he's quite given up on you," Tam replied.

"It certainly sounded like it to me! He didn't even fight for me. If he cares so little, then maybe I shouldn't go anyway. I don't even want him anymore!" Frisha huffed.

Tam scowled and argued, "You should hear some of the stuff he's been saying to the general. For a moment, I thought they were actually going to draw swords!"

"What?" Frisha gasped. "They wouldn't. Oh, no, what if Rezkin gets himself killed? My uncle is a swordmaster, Tam."

"Your uncle is *old*, Frisha, and truth be told, he didn't look so confident when he was faced with Rezkin's anger," Tam replied.

"All over me?" Frisha asked.

"Well, not *just* you. You know how the general has been treating him. It hasn't gotten any better, and I think Rez's patience is wearing thin," Tam answered. "Anyway, like I said, you don't have to go to Skutton. Reaylin was here earlier, and she's really excited, especially since she heard about your uncle rejecting Rez. I'm sure she and *Lady* Shiela will be happy to keep Rez company in your stead."

Frisha gaped in righteous indignation. She grabbed the pillow off the ground and lobbed it at Tam's head. "Tamarin Blackwater! I cannot believe you could be so insensitive."

"What? You were the one who said you didn't want him. It sounds to me like you're the one giving up too easily."

"Well, shut up. Of course I want him," Frisha huffed. "Fine, I'll go, and if Reaylin or Shiela even think about stealing him from me, I'll show them just how much I want him!"

Tam started laughing at Frisha's expense, and after a moment, Frisha could not help but join him.

21

Getting into another argument with General Marcum was the perfect excuse for leaving the general's home. Rezkin had made the extra effort to spend time practicing with Tam earlier not only as part of his duty toward his *friend*, but also as a method of averting suspicion for a conspicuous absence. The family might excuse a few hours here and there, but if he were gone for extended periods of time, people would start asking questions. Rezkin did not care to outright *lie* to his *friends*. That did not seem like a good way to honor them. Instead, he used half-truths, redirection and avoidance to prevent them from learning too much.

It was not that Rezkin *wanted* to mislead his *friends*, but it was safer if they were not involved in the darker maneuverings of his life. Tam and Frisha were innocent and naïve, having been sheltered all their lives by people who cared about them. Rezkin thought it was a detriment to their well-being to be oblivious to the way the world really worked, but showing them the truth too quickly could break their minds or, at the very least, their trust. They would not understand everything he had to do. Now, it was time for his most ambitious plan.

Although it was still afternoon, Rezkin donned his night stealth gear, more for disguise and dramatic effect than for stealth. The dark mottled clothing, black armor and deep cowl would make him more obvious in the daylight, but he did not intend to be seen. Rezkin moved through shadows and alleys and across rooftops. He eventually found himself not too far from the Diamond Claw Guildhouse. His Justainian contacts awaited him anxiously.

"No, Ash, I told you to put it down!" Broken snapped as he slapped something out of Ash's hand.

"But it's gross! I wanted to look at it," Ash said dejectedly.

"It's s'posed to be gross. It's a slug. The Raven will be here soon, and we don't want him thinkin' we're just a couple of silly kids. He asked for us *specifically.* Don't you get how important that is?" the older small-man prodded.

"But, he already *knows* who we are, and he asked for us *'pacifically,*" Ash said, repeating the difficult word used by his older guild mate. "If he wanted someone else, he woulda asked for 'em. He knows we're kids."

"An astute observation, Ash," Rezkin said as he emerged from the shadows.

Both small-men jumped with a squeal. These small-men were far behind not only in their *Skills* training, but also in understanding and adhering to the *Rules.* This was not a surprise considering how poorly these outworlders as a whole complied with the strictures. It was a condition he was working to remedy.

"Ah … H-Hello … I mean, Greetings Master Raven," Broken sputtered, which Ash parroted.

"Greetings to you. Where is your chaperone?" the Raven asked.

"Oh, Rom's takin' a piss," Ash replied. "He'll be right back."

Rom was, in fact, not *takin' a piss.* Rezkin had observed the man smashing in someone's head in an alley a few blocks from where they stood. The victim was obviously a regular *inker.* Nearly every inch of his exposed skin was covered in purple-black tattoos. Apparently, the big man desired to keep the small-men in the dark about what he was doing, so Rezkin left the matter alone.

A moment later, Rom rounded a corner wiping his hands on a rag that was probably what remained of the *inker*'s shirt. He threw the rag aside and then awkwardly bowed to the Raven. "Greetings, Master Raven," he said, his voice deep and confident.

Bowing was not something members of the thieves' guilds did, but they had begun developing some unusual habits with regard to the Raven. The thieves' guilds across the cities continued to operate independently and competitively, but most of them were now unified under Rezkin's rule, a unity he only enforced for a few specific purposes. Rom reported at their previous meeting that Attica had gained measurable confidence since taking over position of Guildmaster. The knowledge that the Raven favored her went a long way in solidifying her hold on the position, and she had a strong desire to impress the mysterious master.

Rezkin surveyed the three thieves before him. In truth, they did not *look* like thieves. They appeared to be a poor but strong, hardworking man and his two sons. Nodding once he simply said, "Come."

The three thieves followed the shadowy Raven out of the city. He moved swiftly, and they struggled to keep up, but the Raven was considerate enough to slow when one fell behind. Once they neared the long queue of travelers exiting the city gates, he told the thieves to meet him on the other side, and he disappeared.

When the patrol passed, Rezkin slipped over the wall and scurried down a thin mage rope. The rope was nearly as thin as thread but stronger than steel, and it cost a hundred times its length in gold. It would never break, slip its knot, or tangle. This was one of the treasures he had taken when he left the fortress—his home. It was a strange thought. He had never really thought of *home* before, but he supposed the fortress had been his. Once he reached the bottom, he gave the rope a swift tug and imposed his *will* upon it. The rope released itself from where it was tied at the top, and Rezkin quickly wound it up and placed it back in his pouch.

He quickly jogged to the river to check his preparations and found them in order. By the time he jogged back, Rom and the small-men were strolling up the road. Rezkin stepped into their path causing them to jump back once again. "This way," he said, and they followed.

When the motley group reached the river, they piled into a rowboat large enough for four or five grown men. Rezkin handed each of the thieves a packet of food wrapped in cheesecloth and passed around a waterskin. "Eat. You will need it."

Rezkin had already eaten his own meal, having skipped dinner at the general's house. His friends and the Marcums might be a bit offended, but due to his earlier exchange with the general, they would excuse his absence—in Marcum's case, appreciate it. Rezkin hated to see how scrawny and underfed the thieves were, even Rom, but he had a feeling the big man's leanness had more to do with giving away his rations to the younger boys. Rezkin instructed Attica and the other guildmasters to provide more food to the younger members, but he had few means of monitoring their compliance at this point.

Rom and Rezkin rowed the boat, and the big man repeatedly glanced at him questioningly but did not dare question the master. Rezkin finally nodded and asked, "What is it, Rom?"

"If ya don't mind me askin', Master, where are we goin'?" the dutiful second inquired.

Rezkin smirked and said, "To the Black Hall, of course." Rom's face drained of color, and Broken abruptly stopped eating to stare at the Master Raven.

Ash looked around curiously and asked, "What's the Black Hall?"

"It's *death*," Rom said without thinking.

Ash turned to Broken and shook him saying, "What's he mean, Broke? What's he mean *death*?"

Broken shoved Ash's hand away and exclaimed in a whispered shout, "It's the Assassin's Guild, twit. Ain't you never listened to the stories?"

"But, I thought that was just a story," Ash complained. "Are we really goin' there?" he asked the Raven with pleading eyes.

"Yes," he plainly answered.

"You, ah, have business with the slips?" Rom cautiously asked.

"I do, but they have yet to recognize it," Rezkin answered.

"Nobody goes to the Black Hall without an invitation," protested the second. "At least, if they do, they don't ever come out."

Rezkin shrugged. "Perhaps there have been others, but I know of one who has for certain."

Already suspecting the answer, Rom asked anyway. "Who would that be?"

Rezkin grinned in answer. "But, do not concern yourself. They are aware we are coming."

"You sent word ahead?" Rom asked with a tiny measure of relief. Perhaps the Slips would just send them away instead of killing them since they had announced their arrival ahead of time.

"Of course," Rezkin replied. "The Hall is very formal, full of rules and etiquette. It would have been considered rude to show up unannounced, so naturally I sent word informing them that I would be coming to collect their fealty."

"You *what*?!" Rom exclaimed. "You *told* them you were comin' to try to take them over? The *Assassin's Guild*?! You can't be serious," the second sputtered, momentarily forgetting to whom he was speaking.

"I am completely serious," the Raven replied with a dangerous edge to his voice. "I have need of their services and resources, and more importantly, I need to implement some restrictions on their *activities*." He said this as though he were discussing acquiring a new business.

"They're *assassins*! They'll kill us all!" Rom shouted.

"If you keep shouting, we will have more to worry about than just assassins," Rezkin remarked. A few patrols monitored the city perimeter and along the river in an attempt to help quell the rising number of bandits, but Rezkin had little concern for the patrols or bandits. As far as anyone could tell from this distance, they were just two men and a couple of small-ones in a boat crossing the river, nothing suspicious, but Rezkin did not want to attract anyone's attention. The river was very wide, though, so it was unlikely anyone had heard Rom's shouting.

"*Just* assassins? Who in the Hells is more frightening and dangerous than *assassins*?" Rom argued.

Rezkin cocked his head curiously and stared at the second. Rom finally caught the inference and swallowed hard. "Y-You don't seem too concerned."

The Raven smirked and replied, "Despite what you obviously think of me, I am not suicidal. I would not be going into this confrontation if I were not confident in my ability to prevail. That is not to say there will be no danger. There most certainly will be, and the consequences of failure are pain and death. Ash is familiar with such consequences." He looked at the younger small-man who smiled hesitantly at the Raven's morbid reminder of their first meeting. "I have maneuvered the conditions to my benefit, and I believe I have the *Skills* to prevail. That does not mean I will succeed."

"Just how do you expect us to take on the entire Black Hall?" Rom asked, praying the Raven would say he had an army hidden in the forest, but knowing the prayer would go unanswered.

"I expect to walk the Gauntlet," the Raven replied.

The second looked at him questioningly and asked, "The Gauntlet?"

"A test of sorts, although it is nearly impossible to survive, and more so since I will have you three to protect," he replied. "It is a demonstration of both *Skill* and honor," he explained.

Rom scoffed. "You keep talking as though assassins have honor. They kill people for no other reason than coin. I may be a thief, but I ain't never killed no one I robbed. They have a right to defend themselves, after all, and what I want from them ain't worth their life or mine. Anyone else was in self-defense."

Rezkin nodded and said, "I have often heard the phrase there is no honor among thieves. You may find yourself to be the exception rather than the rule. Regardless, respectable folk, those who are not criminals, would say you have no honor for taking what is not yours—for taking something you did not work to *earn*. You made your own code of honor to justify your actions, and it enables you to live the way you do."

Rom shifted uncomfortably but did not protest. The Raven continued. "The assassins are much the same. They live with a terrible burden, stealing away the very breath of life. Without strict order, they would fall into blood-lust and despair. Their code of honor establishes a limit for the depth to which they will descend. It also enables them to continue operating, and lucratively at that. Clients fear the assassins but place in them a certain level of trust."

"I don't see how anyone can trust an assassin," the second observed with scorn.

"And, yet, you came to Kaibain and got into this boat with *me*, and now we sit together in the middle of the Tremadel," the Raven replied. "You must place some level of trust in *me*."

Rom gulped. "Are you one of them?" he asked hesitantly, fearing the answer.

The Raven scoffed and said, "I am not one of *them*, nor do I follow *their* code; but I assure you, I have killed many more people than any one of them, probably more than all of them combined."

The three thieves remained silent as Rom and Rezkin rowed the rest of the way across the river. When they reached the other bank, Rom told the boys to wait a short distance away. He turned to the Raven and quietly said, "Consid-erin' where we're goin', I don't know whether to be appalled or thankful for your … um … skills, but I can say for certain that I'm terrified. Why'd you bring me and these boys with you?"

The Raven calmly answered, "*You* are here as an escort for the young ones and to play witness. If I succeed, I will need others to know of it not because I am vain, but because they need to know my power. I am sure you can guess my intent toward the small-men."

"But, they're just boys," Rom protested knowing it would do no good.

"They are small-men, wise in the ways of the world, and they are old enough," the Raven replied without a hint of remorse.

As the Raven led the thieves through the forest, he explained what was expected of them. "Rom, you will take each of their hands and hold them tight. Do not let the small-men bolt. You will walk along the path at a steady pace. Do not run. Do not stop. Do not veer from the straight path. No matter what comes at you, do not stop moving, and do not let go of their hands."

"What will you be doing?" Broken asked in a voice that reflected his name.

"I will be disposing of the assassins and protecting you," the Raven replied.

Ash released a heavy breath. "Oh, good, then we'll be okay." Broken looked like he wanted to argue with his younger mate but said nothing, and Rom simply appeared to be resolved to his death.

"Shouldn't I be helpin' you or somethin'?" Rom asked.

"No one walks the Gauntlet with charges to protect. The very few who survive at all are executed at the end. Your assistance will only ensure that happens," Rezkin replied.

"And, how're you gonna keep that from happenin'?" the second asked.

"Perhaps I will tell you after I have prevailed," Rezkin replied. The Raven suddenly stopped and gripped Rom's bicep, drawing the big man to a halt. "This is important, Rom. Absolutely at no point, for any reason at all, will you get involved. You *will not* intervene or interfere. Even if it looks like the lot of them are bearing down on you and will kill you any second, you do *nothing* but walk straight and steady."

"And if you're dead?" Rom asked.

"Then you will have nothing to worry about because you will already be dead," the Raven replied and began walking again.

After several minutes of trudging through the underbrush, over stones, dried twigs, and crunchy leaves, Rom began to notice something eerily unnatural. While he and the boys made enough noise to wake his deaf grandmother who had been buried for the last two decades, the Raven made no sound, nor did he leave any evidence of his passing. Not a single print or trail was left behind as he swept through the forest silent as a wraith. A shiver trailed down the second's spine, and for the first time, he truly believed he was in the presence of something inhuman.

Everything that had happened and everything the thief had learned of the Raven began to make sense. No human being could have brought down the

Justainian thieves' guilds in a day and then repeated the feat in Kaibain. The way he moved, the way he spoke, the deep pockets with seemingly limitless coin, the claims of mass murder beyond the scope of any man, much less one so young—they all lead to the same conclusion. The Raven was a demon.

Perhaps the Raven was not concerned about death because he was immortal; or perhaps if he were killed in this life, he would spawn again in H'khajnak, the demon realm. At this point, Rom could not care less about what happened to the Raven, except that his and the boys' lives depended on the creature. The boys may be thieves, but they had never really had a chance. They were street orphans with no other way of surviving. Right now, Rom *hated* the Raven for putting the boys in this terrifying situation that was certain to lead to their early deaths. Assassins were not known for their mercy, and he knew they would not stop at killing children.

After another hour or so of meandering between trees and bushes and traipsing over rocks and streambeds, the Raven held up a fist bringing the group to a stop. Ash started to say something, but Broken, sensing the tension in the adults, quickly threw a hand over the younger boy's mouth and shook his head. Ash squirmed in an attempt to remove the older boy's hand so that he could stubbornly make his remark, but stopped his protests when a thick, firm hand landed on his shoulder.

Turning to Rom, the smaller boy whispered, "I have to go to the bathroom."

The big man rolled his eyes with a silent sigh and looked questioningly toward the Raven. The hooded demon was surveying their surroundings, and Rom did not think the man had heard the boy, but the Raven abruptly turned and waved the boy over to a bush. The wraith came to stand beside Rom, and he spoke in a quiet voice that could not have carried further than the few inches' distance to Rom's ear. "We are surrounded. From here, the attack could come at any time."

"Attack?" Rom asked. "I thought you told them we were coming."

"Of course I did. I had to give them the opportunity to arrange the ambush," the Raven said matter-of-factly.

Rom looked askance but found no words to respond.

"Take the small-men's hands when we continue. Remember my orders. Stay the path no matter what. Do not fight back. Do not stop, and *do not* run."

Rom nodded his understanding, even though he absolutely did *not* understand. How could the Raven think that he would walk into an ambush of assassins who were trying to kill him and the boys and *not* fight back? But, the Raven knew much more about the situation than did Rom, and he did not think the demon would go to the trouble of bringing the boys all the way to Kaibain just to get them killed. He had plans for these boys. That did not mean the demon's plans extended to *Rom*, though. For all he knew, the Raven considered him to be nothing more than expendable fodder—a sacrificial lamb.

When Ash finished his business, Rom took both boys' hands in his and gripped them tightly, reminding the boys not to run from him. The Raven led the way forward until they came to a slightly worn path no more remarkable than a simple game trail. It was at this point when the attack came. A glint of steel flashed through the air, but Rom did not see if it hit its mark. His attention was drawn to the shadows suddenly dropping from trees and emerging from the underbrush. For a moment, the big man hesitated, his survival instinct screaming at him to draw a weapon or run or *something* other than hold on to the two tiny hands in his grip. Rom stumbled as he was shoved from behind.

The Raven growled, "Go," as he swept past.

The big man pulled the boys forward at a steady pace, at least as steady as his panicky legs would manage. All of his muscles were tense, and he knew he would feel at any moment the overwhelming agony of a blade impaling him through the back.

Deftly dodging the throwing knife that had been aimed at his back, Rezkin bounded to the side and collided with an attacker who landed beside him. At the same time, he noted that Rom stood in stunned stasis. Rezkin rolled backward, coming to his feet behind the thief and shoving into him with his back.

Rezkin grunted, "Go," as he lobbed a rock at an assailant's head. The rock struck true, and the slip dropped to his knees stunned. Rom finally got it together and started forward with the two small-men in tow. Broken and Ash were clutching the big guy's arms as they shouted in surprise.

Rezkin flowed around the trio as they walked the path toward the Hall. Assassins emerged from the forest as they progressed, and each time Rezkin was there to meet the attack, passing in and out of view of the scared thieves like a silent wraith with insubstantial form. His strikes and kicks were solid enough, though, as he swept one assassin's feet out from under him and then stomped on his sternum. The black-clad killer curled up around his injured torso, and the Raven kicked him soundly in the head. Then, the wraith was gone again.

Covering perhaps four times the distance of his companions, Rezkin dodged back and forth, making his way around the three. Up and down the trail he sped, always staying close enough to ward off any projectiles the assassins might pitch. A crossbow bolt launched at Rom's back was met by an expertly thrown dagger, which, through luck and skill, deflected the deadly instrument. Ash screamed and squirmed, and Rom faltered in his step when one assassin's blade descended toward the small-man's neck, but Rezkin was there to meet it.

Rezkin was relieved the assassins had elected to allow him to walk the gauntlet. If they had rejected his challenge, they would have attacked all at once instead of smaller numbers along the path. He could not afford an error, or their escape would end in failure. Death was not the only possible failure, though. Even if he lived, that did not mean he would succeed in his efforts to advance his influence over the Hall.

From the darkness of the thicket, two slips suddenly attacked at once. One came for Rezkin while the other went after his charges. Ducking and dodging a flurry of knife wielding strikes, Rezkin grabbed the woman by the tunic. The black-clad assassin expected to be pushed away and braced accordingly, but Rezkin yanked her forward, knocking her off balance. At the same time, he dropped to the ground and rolled onto his back. He thrust his feet into the slip's midsection and launched her into the air over his head. The woman collided with her cohort just as the man prepared to strike at Rom.

Rezkin continued with his momentum into a backward roll and bounded to his feet. He spun and ran full speed at the attackers, intercepting them just as they were untangling themselves to regain their feet. After blocking a punch, he smacked the male assassin in the head with a steel reinforced vambrace and then brought his clenched fists down on the back of the man's head. As the slip crumpled to the ground, the woman kicked out to the side in an attempt to strike at Rezkin while he was distracted. He caught the extended leg and brought an elbow down into the side of her knee with an audible crunch. To her credit, the woman did not cry out with the pain she was obviously experiencing. Instead, she managed a half cartwheel as she dragged her damaged leg, turning around to face him. She braced on one leg as stormy grey eyes filled with unshed tears.

The woman drew a curved sword reminiscent of a very small scimitar and swung at the hooded warrior with the icy-blue eyes. It was difficult to get a good view of the man's face while he was fighting under the cowl, but his eyes were inescapable. The man's gaze was cold and unflinching. It held nothing but hard ice and winter's stroke of death, as though the mind behind the gaze had never experienced a single ray of light. If the eyes were the windows to the soul, then naught but darkness resided in this man.

Rezkin did not have time to deal with the woman. Others were emerging along the path, and Rom and the small-men had already progressed a dozen steps farther than Rezkin would have preferred. The slip swung at him with the curved blade. He spun into the woman's defenses, grabbed the sword hilt, and used his considerable strength to yank the weapon from her grasp. At the same time, he smashed the back of his head into her face and then brought the weapon around to strike the side of her head with the flat of the blade. The slip fell to the ground atop her comrade, and Rezkin dropped the ill-gotten blade. The entire exchange with the two slips had taken less than two minutes.

The Raven caught up with the thieves just in time to fend off another wave of attacks from a couple of sword wielders and half a dozen throwing stars. That had been an interesting choice since not many people in Ashai used the small spinning blades. He doubted anyone even made or sold the weapons anywhere in Ashai. The star thrower, like the miniature scimitar-wielding assassin, had been wearing an unusual style of dress and armor uncharacter-istic of the slips of the Hall. Likewise, their faces had been covered up to the eyes, also not typical of Ashaiian assassins. Together, it was evidence of an altogether different group, which would also explain the numbers.

As they neared the end of the gauntlet, Rezkin and the three thieves experienced an increase in attacks from all sides. Rezkin tightened his circle around his companions, and while several times he used throwing knives to deflect projectiles, not once did he draw his swords or any other weapon on an opponent. Still, they fell. One by one, the ground was littered with black-clad bodies until finally they reached the steps of the Hall.

"Halt," the Raven said, and Rom and the boys abruptly stopped.

Rom managed to keep his shaking under control as he stood in the center of a cobbled yard surrounded by motionless bodies and an unscathed demon who looked no worse for wear. The demon was not even breathing heavily. The experienced thief felt only relief once again that he had stood with Attica and opted not to attack the creature on that fateful day when first they met. He gripped the boys' hands tightly with sweaty palms, but neither boy seemed anxious for release as they clung to his sides. Of all he had witnessed this day, nothing frightened the big thief more than the astonishing, brutal skill and undeniable inhuman speed of the Raven.

The Raven walked forward to stand before the small group assembled at the top of the steps leading into the Hall. At the forefront stood a striking man of average height with regal bearing. His stark white hair was pulled back into a slick queue, his black clothes and armor fit perfectly upon his solid frame, and his face, although lined with age, looked as though carved from stone. Straight planes and sharp edges defined his visage, and the hard look in his dark eyes was nearly enough to rival the coldness of the Raven. The man's eyes flicked over the thieves, but having found the trio to be of little note, he focused on the true threat.

"You have walked the gauntlet," he stated succinctly in a calm but commanding voice. "You not only survived, but you brought *guests* through as well." The observation was saturated with scorn and disgust.

The Raven inclined his head and simply stated, "It is so."

"My men?" the grandmaster asked.

"Will live," the Raven replied.

The grandmaster's eyes flicked to one of his men who came limping across the courtyard, if it could be called such. The man nodded once in affirmation and made a few nearly imperceptible hand gestures as he moved to stand at the foot of the steps facing the visitors. The grandmaster's stony face slipped for merely a moment as surprise caught in his eyes. While the slips surely had been trying to kill him and the thieves, Rezkin was not permitted to kill even one of the assassins lest he fail the gauntlet. Had that occurred, the full might of the guild would have descended on him until he was dead. Rezkin could possibly escape the encounter with his life, but his companions would surely be lost.

"You did not draw even once? Such was beyond the requirements of the test. It was only necessary to preserve their lives," the grandmaster stated.

"I might have drawn if I felt it necessary," the Raven remarked as though the task had been effortless.

"Men do not survive the gauntlet. Men do not bring along *friends*," he drawled disdainfully as his eyes flicked to the thieves again. "Men certainly do not feel it *unnecessary* to draw a weapon."

"*I* am the weapon," the Raven immediately responded, partially out of habit. "And, still, here I stand," he said spreading his hands toward the ground. With the slight motion, a number of slips who had gathered around the perimeter flinched and drew their weapons. The Raven smirked at their overreactions, none of which went unnoticed by the grandmaster. "But, this was not the usual gauntlet," the Raven commented offhandedly. "Your numbers were too great."

"And, yet, they failed to stop you," the grandmaster observed. With only the slightest tilt of his head, he indicated the woman who stood a short distance from him. "We have visitors." The woman was clad in black like her comrades —the ones Rezkin had encountered during the "walk"—except that she wore a scarlet mask that not only covered her lower face up to her eyes, but also wrapped around her neck and over her head like a hood.

"Adana'Ro," the Raven stated affecting a perfect Ferélli accent. "Do'grelah, Secrelé," he said with a slight bow in the woman's direction. Her dark eyes flashed with interest, and she inclined her head in acknowledgement of the formal greeting. The scarlet hood identified her as a secrelé, one of the leaders of her sect.

The grandmaster did not question how the Raven knew anything about the Hall's numbers, and if he was surprised the man knew of the Adana'Ro, he did not show it. "They wished to participate," the grandmaster said. "When they arrived this morning, and news of your infamous deeds reached their ears, they volunteered to enhance your experience on the gauntlet."

Enhance the man had said. Leave it to assassins to find spirituality in a deadly test of *Skill* and fortitude, which is exactly how they viewed it. The gauntlet was supposed to be not only a test of the body against an indomitable foe, but also a spiritual awakening that could be appreciated in one's death.

"I am honored by the Adana'Ro … and by the Hall that you should see me as such a worthy opponent," the Raven replied with more than a hint of sarcasm. His words were appropriate and respectful, but his tone conveyed that he did not believe the excuse for a moment. If they had truly approved of his walking the gauntlet, they would not have permitted outside interference. In truth, he knew the grandmaster desired his death all along, but since Rezkin had prevailed and done so in excess of the rules, there was nothing to be done except see it through.

"You did not arrive without incident," the secrelé commented in Ashaiian laced with a heavy, curling accent. Her eyes flicked to the red-fletched dart protruding from Rezkin's shoulder.

Without bothering a glance, the Raven reached up and plucked the dart from his arm. He sniffed it once and then flicked it aside. The red fletching and the scent of suraceous poison both indicated the dart belonged to an Adana'Ro. Rezkin had noticed the dart earlier but had not bothered to remove it since he needed a moment to study the tiny but deadly weapon. He would have to mentally review the battle later to determine when he had acquired the accessory, since he seemed to have missed it the first time—a major failure on his part. It was no matter. He was immune to suraceous poison.

"A minor inconvenience, not worth the effort of avoidance," the Raven said with a wink and a cheeky grin—a charismatic show of confidence affected after hours of practice in the mirror. It was like watching an opponent's feet, shoulders, and eyes in a battle, his masters had said. Wars could be won by attitude and expression alone. Although he could not see her face, the secrelé's eyes seemed to flash with humor.

"You seek to challenge me?" questioned the grandmaster in a flat tone. He might as well have been asking if the Raven wanted a cup of water. Actually, Rezkin would have appreciated a cup of water, but it would be poisoned.

The Raven cocked his head curiously and said, "If I must." He waited until the grandmaster opened his mouth to speak and said, "However … I propose a trade before we begin … as a show of good faith, of course."

The grandmaster was once again surprised. The Raven's stoic demeanor in the face of the gauntlet and resulting challenge were unprecedented. Even when he himself had walked the gauntlet long ago to acquire the position of grandmaster, he had not had such unwavering fortitude. "A trade? What could you have that I should desire?"

"Only this," the Raven replied as he launched a dagger at the grandmaster.

The grandmaster snatched the dagger from the air and called, "Halt!" before any of his people returned the volley. The grandmaster examined the black and blue silk-wrapped hilt and silvery blade etched with a raven in flight. "Why would I desire *this*?" he asked derisively.

A blade magically appeared in the Raven's grasp. He held the dagger by the tip, its blade and hilt standing erect for all to see. The hilt was wrapped in scarlet silk, and a giant ruby gleamed within the golden pommel. Along the blade was etched a stylized fox chasing a serpent. It was the grandmaster's dagger, a symbol of his station. "In trade for *this*," Rezkin announced.

The grandmaster's chin dropped just enough to leave his lips parted in surprise. "How did you get that?" he asked, but he already knew the answer for he never allowed the blade to leave his person.

"I took it from beneath your pillow while you slept," the Raven remarked. The secrelé's head whipped around as she practically gaped at the grandmaster with her eyes. "When did this occur?" she asked in her thickly accented Ashaiian.

"Last night," replied the grandmaster. "The dagger was missing when I awoke. It must have been someone in my house," the man grumbled.

The Raven shook his head and said in a somber, sonorous voice, "I am not sure which is more disconcerting, Grandmaster. That a perfect stranger could break into the *Black Hall*, into your very bedchamber, and steal your dagger from beneath your pillow while you slumbered no less and then leave again without anyone ever suspecting; or that one of your *own*, a lifelong member of the Hall, was not only capable of the same feat, but betrayed you to a complete stranger."

"I would have to agree with the Raven, Grandmaster," the secrelé remarked as the grandmaster's eyes swept over the potential betrayers in his courtyard.

"I will put your mind at ease, Grandmaster, and give you my solemn word that I did, in fact, commit the offense and that none of your people were involved. Although, one of your men may have been rendered unconscious for a time after an unfortunate encounter with a stranger in the forest," Rezkin added.

"Uratel, is this the man?" the grandmaster barked.

A man stepped forward from the crowd of onlookers. He held his arm close to his body, and from the awkward angle, it appeared to be either broken or dislocated. He studied the Raven critically and then bowed stiffly toward the grandmaster. "I cannot be certain, Grandmaster. It was dark, and I did not get a good look, but the techniques and skill I have witnessed this day are much like my assailant last night."

The grandmaster's jaw clenched before he replied. "Very well. You are excused for last night's failure, Uratel. It is now obvious that you were confronted by a far superior opponent," he said, his words clipped with irritation. Uratel bowed again and then nodded in respect toward the Raven. No resentment or anger resided in the man's gaze, only acceptance. He was probably just thankful that Rezkin had left him alive and whole during both of their encounters.

"What is it to be, Grandmaster? Shall we settle this?" the Raven inquired. His voice seemed but a whisper, yet it carried to all.

"If you seek leadership of the Hall, then it must be so," the grandmaster stoically replied.

"I do not challenge you for your place as grandmaster. I have no time or patience for mundane operations." The grandmaster narrowed his eyes at the stranger, no doubt taking offense to the idea that his position as the head of the entire Assassin's Guild could be called *mundane*. The Raven continued. "I have bested your slips on the gauntlet, even with your numbers swollen by a *Cueret* of the Adana'Ro," the Raven said as he bowed once again to the scarlet-hooded woman. *Cueret*, which translated to *Court* in Ashaiian, was the Ferélli term used by the Adana'Ro for a unit of their members who were sent out on special assignment. It usually consisted of four to eight members, depending on the task. In this one, Rezkin had identified six including the secrelé.

"Then what do you seek, Raven? Your message said you would come to claim the guild," the grandmaster replied.

"So I do," Rezkin answered. "I do not seek to own your place. I seek to own the Hall. I want no less than the fealty of the Black Hall. I seek the fealty of the Riel'sheng," the Raven stated with authority.

The grandmaster's eyes widened. "Few know this name, even amongst our own members. You may not seek my position, but you would have us serve you. The Black Hall serves no one but those we choose to serve for profit."

"Then profit under my rule by keeping your lives," the Raven responded.

"Then the challenge must be met. Do any here besides *the Raven* seek to challenge *me*?" the grandmaster asked the gathering. Although the slips were fairly beat at this point, a challenge for position would not be carried out until all parties were hale. No one stepped forward, though. From what Rezkin had gleaned, none of the other slips were even close to the grandmaster's *Skills*, and only one of the masters might have challenged him. But, anyone challenging the grandmaster at this point would then have to meet Rezkin's challenge, and no one seemed eager to do so.

"None within the Hall challenge me," the grandmaster stated. "All present recognize my authority. You have walked the gauntlet and prevailed. I accept your challenge, Raven, and the outcome will determine if the Riel'sheng will answer to you or if you will be dead."

The grandmaster descended the few steps to the courtyard. A couple of slips came forward to usher Rom and the small-men to the perimeter. Rom appeared to be gripping the young ones so tight Rezkin was concerned they would lose circulation in their hands. Neither was struggling against the big man, though, so they must have been fine. They were all three staring wide-eyed and anxious at the proceedings. After all, the outcome of this battle would determine whether *they* lived or died as well.

Now that Rom believed the Raven to be a demon, though, he was not sure if he should root for the grandmaster to dispatch the creature back to H'khaj-nak. It would be forfeiting his and the boys' lives, but their sacrifice would save the world from a *demon* incarnate. In the end, Rom admitted to himself that he was not so altruistic and decided he would rather live.

The grandmaster unsheathed the longsword at his side. It was of similar design to the dagger Rezkin had acquired from the grandmaster's chambers, a matching set. Made of gold and jewels, it was the flashy kind of sword used as a show of elevated station, not to be used in stealthy dispatching of contracted hits. Flashy or not, it was a magnificent master blade that was every bit fit to be wielded by the Grandmaster Assassin or a warrior king. As far as Rezkin knew, the blade had been used by every grandmaster since the guild's inception.

Rezkin allowed his hood to fall back, but he kept his will focused. His masters had always purported the power of mind over matter, even in those without the *talent*. They pressed him to always stay focused on the image he wanted others to remember of him, whether it be noble or street sweeper. In this case, he did not want to be remembered at all, so he focused his will on appearing average and unassuming. It was not enough to *want* others to believe it so, especially with individuals who had trained most of their lives to recognize faces, even of those attempting disguise. *He* had to believe it as well, and now Rezkin *knew* he looked no different than any other man in Ashai.

A few flicks of his wrists assured that no one was focused on his visage anyway. The wicked but graceful blue swirls of the Sheyalin blades reflected the amber rays of the setting sun. Audible gasps escaped the observers, and the grandmaster paused in astonishment and shocked admiration. "Sword bearer," he whispered. The man's surprise was quickly replaced with disbelief and then anger. "Where did you get those? You are no true sword bearer. We would have known had a new Bearer been raised."

Interesting. Rezkin was certain that if anyone in Ashai besides the king, the strikers, or the general of the army were to have known anything about his blades it would have been the Grandmaster of the Riel'sheng. But, the man's surprise and scorn were genuine. He knew nothing.

"They must have come from the outside," the secrelé commented. "He knows of the Adana'Ro. He is obviously well-traveled." She huffed a mirthless laugh, and Rezkin thought he saw a smirk behind the mask. "Only a man with his skills could retain *two* Sheyalin blades." Rezkin inclined his head in appreciation of the remark. He knew it was meant to be a compliment even if it was a simple statement of fact.

The grandmaster shook his head. "It does not matter. We will see how well he uses them." One did not have to be a swordmaster to be an assassin. In fact, many assassins did not use swords at all, although the masters were trained in many weapons including swords. Rezkin knew the grandmaster *was* a swordmaster. Not only that, but the older man had spent time training with masters in both Channería and Sandea in order to master multiple techniques.

The sword battle began in earnest with no additional preamble. The blades clashed and sang as they whipped through the air. It was not a duel with rules and bounds; rather, it was an outright fight to the death. Rezkin spun as the grandmaster's blade sliced through the hood that hung from his back. The man was fast and determined. Rezkin dropped to the ground to avoid another swing aimed at his head. He popped back to his feet and sliced at the grandmaster's legs, barely nicking the man's thigh as he pulled back his leg. Rezkin had scored first blood, but it was only last blood that mattered.

Rezkin thrust his body forward to ram the assassin, but the man was too fast and swept out of the way. Rezkin tucked into a roll and came to his feet, Kingslayer in his right hand whipping over his body to intercept the swipe from behind that might have separated his head from his shoulders. As the blades clashed, he twisted his form, bringing Bladesunder across the grandmaster's midsection. The blade gouged into the man's leather armor but did not pierce his flesh as the swordmaster darted aside.

The grandmaster lobbed a dagger at the Raven, which he deftly deflected with a flick of his blade. Rezkin ran at the older man, catching him in a flurry of strikes and thrusts, which the grandmaster met with determination. Ultimately, the older man was unable to contend with Rezkin's speed, agility, and dual-blade techniques. In fact, many of the techniques and combinations he had never before seen. At times, the Raven did not seem to have any technique at all, switching between beautiful, sensuous sword forms one moment and then becoming an uncouth brawler the next. The grandmaster observed steps and stances reminiscent of nearly every kingdom the assassin had seen, and yet he could not put a name to the style. The Raven was completely unpredictable, and that was the grandmaster's undoing.

The grandmaster lunged, expecting the Raven to parry or dodge, but he did neither. In an unprecedented flash of speed, he slapped one of his blades on either side of the grandmaster's, grasped both hilts in one hand and then shoved the grandmaster's sword aside, forcing him to either let go or cross his arm over his body. Opting for the latter, the grandmaster's arm was trapped when the younger man lunged forward and enwrapped the grandmaster in an iron embrace. Rezkin shifted his grip to drop one of the swords and brought the pommel of the other around into the grandmaster's temple. He struck the man with enough force to split the skin but not so hard as to knock him out completely.

The grandmaster slumped to the ground where he lay on his back in a daze as he gazed up at the darkening sky. The first stars appeared as he blinked blood out of his vision. The man lay for a minute or two as he regained his senses, during which time no one moved and some barely dared to breathe. When the grandmaster finally managed to sit up, he saw the Raven standing several paces from where he lay. The Sheyalins were sheathed at his back, and the young man held the sword of the grandmaster in a loose grip at his side as though it were just another practice blade. He supposed some might even see the magnificent master blade as such when compared to a Sheyalin.

"You have not finished the challenge," the grandmaster said as he spit a bit of bile.

The Raven clenched the gold and red hilt and then loosened his grip. "I have bested you thrice, now, Grandmaster. Once in stealth, an invasion of the Hall to retrieve a symbol of your office from beneath your sleeping head; once in battle against your army sent to defeat me on the gauntlet; and, once in rightful challenge held in the court of the Hall before your guild and witnessed by the Adana'Ro. Do you deny it?"

The grandmaster wiped blood from his eye and said, "I do not."

"Then, as acknowledged and unchallenged grandmaster of the Hall, swear to me the fealty of the Riel'sheng," the Raven commanded, and then he tossed the magnificent blade to the grandmaster as though the sword and all it represented were truly beneath him.

The grandmaster caught the weapon before it clattered to the ground. He gazed at it with reverence before he drew himself to his knees. As the grandmaster knelt, so, too, did the other assassins. He held the heavy sword before him, the hilt in both hands above his head, the tip pointed at the ground but not touching.

"As grandmaster of the Riel'sheng, I recognize thee, Raven, as the superior strength, the superior skill, and the superior honor. I plead to thee for mercy upon this Hall, such that we, the Riel'sheng, may serve thee in life and death." The grandmaster's next words were chorused by all of the assassins who were present. "We grant unto thee our fealty. To thee we offer our vessels, our minds, our souls to use as you please. Thine will is our will."

When the oath was spoken, Rezkin restrained a shiver. He did not care for anyone to offer him his or her *soul*, but such was the oath of the Riel'sheng. It was an oath they had all sworn upon indoctrination to the Hall. Now, they swore it to *him*. He had to accept the oath they offered, or all was for naught.

"I accept the fealty of the Riel'sheng. I accept the fealty of the Hall," Rezkin said as he surveyed the gathered assassins who knelt around him. He returned his attention to the grandmaster and said, "I recognize your defeat, Grandmaster, and honor you as a worthy opponent by granting you mercy—not the mercy of an assassin, which would allow you a quick death, but the mercy of a liege lord, which grants you life. I would have you continue to serve as grandmaster under *my* reign and lead *my* Hall by my command."

The grandmaster lifted the sword so that it rested flat in both hands and raised it high. Had the Raven ordered it so, he would have instead plunged it into his own abdomen to prove his fealty even in death. "I humbly accept your appointment, *Riel'gesh* Raven."

Rezkin cocked his head curiously at the title. *Riel'sheng* translated to "giver of death" and was the honored and ancient name for the Assassin's Guild, known before now only by the upper echelons of the guild. *Riel'gesh*, by contrast, meant "giver of life," and, ironically for the Assassin's Guild, was a higher honor. It meant that his power, skill, and honor were so great that he could afford to grant life to those who would threaten him; but, of course, he could retract that *gift* at his leisure.

"See to your wounds, Grandmaster. We have much to discuss and little time," Rezkin replied.

The grandmaster took a few moments to clean and patch his wounds. They were not serious, but head wounds tended to bleed profusely. The older man eyed the young warrior who had so easily bested him. "You were unscathed during our battle," he observed.

"You damaged my attire. It was a challenge," Rezkin replied.

The grandmaster could not help but respond with scorn. "A challenge for what? To survive? I think not. To remain unharmed? Perhaps. To remain un*ruffled* more like. You look as though the gauntlet and the challenge were nothing more than a heated practice session."

Rezkin threw the grandmaster a sideways glance as he motioned Rom and the small-men over to join them. The rest of the assassins had already dispersed at his command, but they did not stray far. Everyone wanted to witness these unprecedented events. "I have endured worse," he replied.

The grandmaster scoffed. "Worse than the gauntlet? We have lost more of our greatest members to the gauntlet than any other way. Only one will survive every few decades to become grandmaster. I expected Briesh to be the next, but he has shown no interest in walking the gauntlet. Although, truth be told, I think that he is not quite ready."

"Perhaps he simply has no desire to kill you, grandmaster," the Raven argued.

The grandmaster huffed humorlessly. "He has no love for me. Grudging respect, perhaps, but no love."

"I doubt any of you are capable of such a sentiment," Rezkin observed.

"Are *you*?" the grandmaster shot back. "I recognize your authority Riel'gesh, but I am an old man, and you are young. You should not be so quick to dismiss a man's soul. Even a hard man who bathes in blood can love." The grandmaster's eyes grew distant in remembrance, as though he spoke from experience, before he finally shook himself and continued. "No, I think Briesh does not care to take on the responsibility of grandmaster when there is someone else to do it. Perhaps when I have grown too old to hold my sword aloft, he will acquiesce and honor me with a worthy death."

"One can hope," Rezkin responded, "but you are still of use." It was a strange wish, to desire one's life to end in slaughter while others dreamed of dying in their sleep or surrounded by loved ones. It was a dream carried by many a warrior, and it was one Rezkin thought he would experience sooner rather than later. Few warriors lived to old age and even fewer desired it. Rezkin did not care either way except that if he were too old to perform his *Skills* or adhere to the *Rules,* then he would be of little use to anyone, especially if he lost his mind and knowledge with it as many of the elderly did. It would be a waste of resources to continue to support his useless life.

Rezkin felt three sets of eyes boring into him. He turned his attention to the three thieves that stood clutching each other beside him. When he met Rom's eyes, the big man quickly glanced away. Rezkin motioned to Broken and Ash and said, "The small-men are yours. They are to master their *Skills*. They are sadly deficient of training, and I would see them succeed."

Broken's mouth dropped, and he exclaimed, "Wait! We're s'posed to become assassins?"

Rezkin frowned at the young man who seemed rather upset. They should be thankful that Rezkin was making the effort to see to their education since no one else had. The assassins did not possess all of the necessary *Skills*, and they were unfamiliar with many of the *Rules,* but they were better than anyone else, except perhaps the strikers.

He replied, "If need be, but that is not my purpose in bringing you here. You must learn the *Skills* the Hall has to offer. In time, you may be transferred elsewhere to learn other *Skills*. I do not have the time to teach you myself. This is the only way I have at the moment to ensure you become proper grown men."

"Wha-what about Cracker?" the small-man whimpered as his lip wobbled.

"Your guild mate does not possess the countenance for this *Skill* set. He will be taught others more suited to his personality and abilities," the Raven responded.

Rom furrowed his brow and had to ask, "You mean you're just tryin' to make sure they get a chance in life? Are you sure this is the only way? I mean no offense, Master Raven, but I care about these boys. Maybe they could apprentice with a carpenter or somethin'—you know, somethin' respectable."

The Raven's face darkened, and he replied, "Are you saying a warrior is undeserving of respect?"

"No, no, of course not, Master, nothin' of the sort," Rom sputtered.

Rezkin shook his head. *What is it with carpenters?* "I know a carpenter's apprentice, and he wishes to be a warrior. I am trying to make these small-men into warriors, and you wish them to be carpenters." He was just about to make a comment about the nonsensical ways of outworlders when Ash interrupted.

"We're gonna be warriors?" the small-man asked as he bounced on his toes. "Are we gonna be like you?"

Rezkin looked at the small-man and recalled what he had been doing and how much he knew by the time he had reached the same number of years. He shook his head and said, "No, not like me. But, you will succeed to the best of your abilities, or you will not succeed at all." The small-man furrowed his brow in confusion and pondered the statement as the grown men talked. Eventually, the Raven and the grandmaster walked away to discuss matters in private.

"When did the Adana'Ro leave, Riel'gesh?" the grandmaster inquired. "I am afraid my head was not clear enough to notice."

"Directly after your oath," the Raven replied. "Why were they here?"

The grandmaster nodded in acceptance. He was not ashamed of his loss. It had been an honorable challenge, and no one who had witnessed it could argue the fact that the grandmaster had been outmatched by a man with inhuman skill.

"They have been hoping for a pact for many years, but we have never been able to come to an agreement," he answered not even attempting to hide his frustration. "They do not approve of our ways, nor do we care to live by theirs. I cannot speak to their specific purpose for this visit. We did not have the opportunity to discuss the details before your arrival."

"The two groups possess conflicting dogmas. I find it odd that they would seek a pact at all," the Raven commented.

"You seem quite familiar with the elusive Adana'Ro," the grandmaster said. The Raven gave no response.

After discussing all their other business, Rezkin finally said, "There is one last issue we must discuss, and this is most important."

"What is that, Riel'gesh?" asked the grandmaster.

"Marcum Jebai, general of the army of Ashai," the Riel'gesh replied.

22

The sun had finally completed its daily quest across the heavens, and Rezkin only hoped he had been as successful. The assassins upheld their strange version of honor, but they were still assassins. He truly hoped he would not have to return to the Hall and make his point again any time soon. He hated redundancy, especially when it was for the sake of wounded pride. Rezkin left Rom at the entrance to the city. The big man was sullen, and Rezkin knew he was upset over what he deemed the loss of the small-men. The thief simply could not see the truth of the matter. Rezkin wanted the small-men to become successful big-men, *grown* men, and in order to do that, they needed to learn the *Skills*.

Rezkin had already washed his body and belongings in the river and changed into acceptable garb when he finally entered the Marcum estate. He followed the sounds of chatter and laughter to the dining room. The general and Lady Adelina sat in their usual places and were joined by Frisha and Tam, as expected. Captain Jimson sat to the lady's right, and interestingly, Reaylin was on Jimson's other side. The young blonde had been awkwardly stuffed into a gown that did not quite fit properly on her petite but curvy frame. Her face flamed scarlet when she spied Rezkin in the doorway. Jimson noticed the young woman's reaction and followed her eyes to the source. His smile fell just a bit when he realized what had flustered his love interest, but his greeting was friendly and genuine.

"Rezkin! It is good to see you," Jimson exclaimed.

Rezkin was met with similar greetings from Tam, Frisha, and Reaylin. Marcum was unsurprisingly silent as he narrowed his eyes at the young warrior.

"Oh, my dear," said Lady Adelina. "I am afraid we just finished our dessert, but I am sure there is more in the kitchen if you like. Narus did inform us that you would not be here for dinner. I do hope you were able to finish all of your arrangements."

Rezkin bowed slightly to the lady of the house and said, "My thanks, Lady Adelina, but I could not possibly eat another bite. And, yes, I believe everything is in order so that we may travel without concern on the morrow."

"Did you find out anything about that friend of yours … er … I mean *comrade*," Frisha asked with a sweet smile.

General Marcum and Captain Jimson visibly tensed at the reference to the elusive Striker Farson. Although Rezkin had not told them that Farson was a striker, they knew Rezkin was hunting the man with intents on interrogation and possibly execution.

Rezkin smiled cordially and said, "No, Frisha, I am afraid there has been no progress on that front. I am glad to see you are feeling better, though." The young woman blushed slightly and graced him with a smile.

"Well," Marcum barked as he wadded his napkin and tossed it on the table. He stood and said, "Now that you are here, we have some important business to discuss before you leave."

"Just you and Rezkin?" Lady Adelina asked with more than a hint of anxiety. Most likely everyone was just waiting for the moment when the hostile truce would collapse and the two men would attempt to send each other to the Hells.

Marcum scowled at the implication that he could not have a civil conversation with the young man but replied, "No, this concerns all of our young travelers. Let us retire to the study."

When they entered the study, Lady Adelina took her seat in her regular chair, and Tam immediately claimed the only other lone chair besides Marcum's. Frisha resumed her usual seat on one of the couches, and then Marcum, in his infinite obstinacy, politely asked the captain to have a seat next to his niece. This left Rezkin to sit beside Reaylin, whose arms had disappeared into the too-long sleeves of the gown, while her generous bosom was practically spilling into his lap as she turned and leaned closer to him. She was a strange contradiction, as she appeared to be trying to hide the fact that she was wearing a dress and emphasize her exposed assets at the same time. Jimson, who felt both cursed and blessed to be included in the general's personal sphere for the time being, kept his eyes on the floor and refused to watch Reaylin's shameless flirting.

Frisha, on the other hand, did not reserve her glares only for Reaylin. For some reason, Rezkin received a fair share of his own, and he could not fathom the reason. It would have been obvious to a blind man that Frisha was jealous, but Rezkin had not encouraged Reaylin in any way. In fact, the abundance of cleavage the young woman was displaying only put Rezkin on edge. In his experience, women used such assets to distract men from the women's true purposes—like drawing a weapon or poisoning his drink or leading him into an ambush.

The young man had no idea why Lady Adelina had insisted Reaylin wear the dress to dinner, and he was certain it *was* Adelina's influence. He wondered if the lady regretted her decision now that she could see the mounting tension between the companions. A glance in her direction told Rezkin that, *no*, she was not regretting it, and she seemed to find the entire scenario to be quite amusing. *Of course.* Reaylin might be oblivious to the ulterior motive, but the lady was definitely using the young woman's assets for a purpose. Rezkin wondered what she had planned.

Marcum turned to speak to his niece but immediately noted the young woman's flushed cheeks, furrowed brow, and pursed lips, along with the furious glare she was directing at the young woman on the other couch. He turned his attention to the distasteful blonde and saw that she sat moon-eyed halfway into Rezkin's lap. Rezkin, to his credit, leaned far from the young woman, and his attention was on the general's own wife. It was not an appreciative gaze but one of calculation.

Marcum repressed a shiver and looked to see what was so interesting about his wife to the young man. Adelina was watching the captain with a small satisfied smile, and Jimson kept his eyes uncomfortably focused on the rug; although, Marcum did catch the man's involuntary glance at the blonde woman and the subsequent clenching of the jaw as his eyes returned to studiously examining the pattern of the carpet. Tamarin was the only one not caught in the web, and he looked as though he was ready to bolt from his chair to stop Frisha from doing something rash.

What a mess, *and half of it is of your own making*, Marcum thought to himself. Clearing his throat loudly, Marcum abruptly asked, "Rezkin, would you mind pouring us some wine?"

The young man raised a questioning brow and then practically leapt from his seat. "Of course, General." The agile young man skillfully maneuvered so that he did not have to make physical contact with the fawning woman, but she shamelessly watched his backside as he crossed the room. At least Frisha had been distracted by the sudden, almost cordial exchange between the young man and the general.

Rezkin poured wine into goblets and passed them around the room. The general's niece was so preoccupied with watching Rezkin's graceful stride and notable physique that she failed to notice the petite blonde doing the same. Jimson continued to shift uncomfortably, but he smiled and thanked Rezkin for his glass. The captain did not seem to hold it against Rezkin that the young woman he fancied was infatuated with the enigmatic warrior. Truly, Jimson seemed like a good man. Marcum wondered if he could redirect the captain's interest to Frisha. The general glanced back at the menacing sword bearer and reconsidered that notion. Such an endeavor probably would not be good for the captain's health.

Rezkin handed a goblet to the general and then took up position standing at Frisha's side, his hand resting on the back of the sofa. His fingers barely brushed her exposed neck, and she settled with a smug look in Reaylin's direction. Reaylin shrugged and leaned forward ever so slightly. Now that Rezkin was facing her from across the room, he would have a better look … and so did everyone else. Marcum lifted the goblet to his lips and then paused. Gazing into the glass, he subtly sniffed, but his actions did not go unnoticed.

"Really, Marcum, do you think I would stoop to poisoning you, and in front of your family, no less? A swordmaster of your accomplishment should at least have the honor of dying on a blade, should he not?" Rezkin asked as though in jest, but his eyes spoke a darker meaning.

Marcum cleared his throat uncomfortably. The seemingly benign questions were both a promise and a threat. It was a promise that should Rezkin decide to challenge the general, he would do so with honor, face-to-face in combat. It was also a reminder that, should that happen, the younger man would probably win.

Frisha laughed. "Oh, Uncle, that's absurd. You know Rezkin would never do something like that, and why should he? I know you two don't get along, but I'm confident you can resolve your differences," she said with pleading eyes. "Besides, where would Rezkin get poison anyway?"

Everyone stared at the young woman, including Rezkin. At this point, even Marcum could not believe that his niece could be so oblivious. Everything about Rezkin said danger, darkness, and death. All Frisha saw was an honorable knight in shining armor.

The answer came from Reaylin of all places. "Oh, *please*, Frisha. Even *I* could get poison. Besides, Rezkin has healing skills. He probably knows how to make one himself."

"Oh," Frisha said. "I hadn't thought of that." She was embarrassed to have that pointed out, especially by Reaylin of all people. She shrugged and brushed it off saying, "Well, he wouldn't do that anyway. He's not a *murderer*." The young woman gave her uncle a pointed look as if to challenge him to claim otherwise.

Marcum scowled but did not take the bait. He knew Frisha wanted to know more about the secrets he held in confidence. "That is not why I called you all here. What I have to tell you is very serious." That caught everyone's attention. "For the past few weeks, reports have been flooding in from all over northern Ashai. As you know, trouble was brewing with the local thieves' guilds in Justain while you were there. Apparently, they were overtaken by a new criminal overlord."

Captain Jimson leaned forward at the general's pause. "Which guilds?"

Marcum captured Jimson with a pointed look and said, "All of them." Sighing loudly, he continued. "Apparently, he took the first two in the span of a single day and then used them to destroy the third. You may remember the news of bodies lined up along the riverbank." Frisha, Tam, and Jimson all nodded acknowledgement, but this was news to Reaylin who had not joined them until Lorelis. "Well, that was just the first wave. The madness did not stop in Justain. It has spread to all of the larger cities in the north: Caradon, Drennil, Umbrell. There are even whispers of his name as far East as Krellis."

That was news to Rezkin. He had not specifically ordered anyone to Krellis. Actually, the general's news was much more up-to-date than what he had gathered since Marcum received the most recent news through the Mage Relay. While Rezkin could gain access and make use of the Mage Relay, his contacts could not, so he depended on messengers and information attained by his new spies in official channels.

"Cheswick?" Tam asked anxiously.

Marcum nodded, "Cheswick, too. Reports claim there was some resistance in Caradon, but now any who live swear loyalty to the Raven."

"The Raven?" Frisha asked with wide eyes. "He sounds ominous," she said with a shiver. Rezkin idly squeezed her shoulder for comfort, and she reached up to stroke his fingers with her daintier ones.

"It is, Frisha. It most certainly is. He has even made his presence known here in Kaibain. I have received multiple reports today that the Kaibainian thieves' guilds have fallen to the Raven. Bodies already line the riverbank, all marked with a raven upon their brows. We know he cannot be in all of these places at once, and it has been difficult to pinpoint his location, but this being the Seat of the King, I think there is a good chance he is here."

"I have never heard of such a thing," Captain Jimson remarked. "How can one man commandeer half a kingdom worth of criminals? The greatest advantage we have for keeping them in check is the fact that they are so greedy and unscrupulous that they will never unite. Their guild wars alone keep their numbers at bay."

"Yes, well, with the state of the kingdom, more people are turning to crime. You have already experienced the results of the rising number of countryside bandits. The cities' thieves' guilds are growing their numbers as well. Additionally, I do not believe this Raven intends to stop with the north."

"You think he will claim the other cities as well?" Jimson asked with concern.

"They are calling him the King of Thieves. I think he intends to claim every criminal guild in Ashai," Marcum stated. "Look, there are other happenings, too … kingdom business that I am not privy to discuss with you all. This is one of the reasons I convinced Simeon to let his sons and daughter go to Skutton and why I have decided to allow Frisha to attend. This city may not be safe. The Raven has changed the way the guilds are working. Astonishingly, the everyday crime against commoners has dropped to almost nil, but wealthier houses are being targeted. In fact …" Marcum sighed. He hated to tell them, but he needed to emphasize the threat. "The Golden Trust Bank in Justain was robbed."

"What!?" everyone shouted at once.

"That's impossible!" Tam said. "It's *never* been robbed. Even *I* know that, and I couldn't even afford anything worth keeping there, much less afford an account."

"How much was stolen?" Frisha asked with wide eyes.

"That is the strange part. Only two items were stolen from the safe deposit boxes. The money and treasures were not touched. It had to be the Raven, but I cannot imagine why he would go through so much trouble to break into the second most secure bank in the kingdom and not take a fortune."

"How did he get in?" Tam asked excitedly. It reminded Frisha of his excitement over those books he would read as a kid … *still* read.

"They still have no idea how he did it. Even the mages are clueless. There was absolutely no evidence of his having been there except the fact that the two items were missing." Marcum ran a frustrated hand through his hair. "We assume it was him since he was in Justain at the time, and it would have to be someone of considerable … no, *inconceivable* skill. Some are saying he did it just to prove he could. Others say those two items had to be worth a king's ransom. One thing is for certain. News of the accomplishment has significantly aided his cause. Thieves tend to flock to either the strongest, most skilled leader or the fiercest. They are all terrified of the Raven, *and* they respect him."

"What is the king doing about it?" Jimson asked.

Marcum flicked a glance at the captain but looked away when he said, "Nothing."

Jimson's jaw dropped. "Nothing?"

On the one hand, Rezkin was glad to hear that the king and his forces would not be interfering with his plans. On the other, it was disturbing that the monarch responsible for the welfare of the kingdom would not concern himself with the rise of a criminal overlord whose kingdomwide influence could undermine and destabilize the reigning institutional power structure and ultimately result in the development of an insidious demagogical paradigm that could infiltrate and overturn the entire monarchy.

The general grumbled under his breath and said, "The king has *other* things to worry about right now. He is not concerned with a 'lowly gutterrat who leads nothing but other lowly gutterrats.'"

"Marcum!" Lady Adelina gasped.

"Not *my* words, Adelina," Marcum barked. Everyone was stunned that the king would say such a thing. "Listen to me," he said as he met their gazes. "Go to Skutton. Get out of this city for a while. Maybe the Raven's influence will not cross the sea. By the time you return, hopefully, things will have settled down."

Rezkin thought it interesting to watch the reactions and conjectures of the outworlders toward his actions. They made it seem like he had devised some master plan to create a criminal empire. In fact, taking over that first guild had been an impulse. Taking over the second became necessary in order to prevent the first from becoming completely decimated, and he wanted all of the small-men and small-women to have better lives. By then, he had decided that the thieves' guilds would serve as a decent information network, which he needed since he could no longer depend on the strikers at the fortress. Thoughts of the fortress and its now-deceased inhabitants caused that odd tightening in his chest again. Rezkin thought perhaps he had developed some sort of psychological disorder related to the fortress. He would have to work to negate the weakness.

The news of the criminal overlord had been a heavy weight on the group, and the party split up shortly thereafter. Reaylin accepted Lady Adelina's offer to stay the night since they would be leaving so early in the morning. The young woman already carried her pack with her, so it was no trouble. Besides, no one really wanted her to leave in the dark, especially with the Raven *skulking about*, as Lady Adelina put it.

Captain Jimson returned to the barracks where he would meet up with the other two soldiers the general had assigned to their detail. He was to meet back at the estate for a final briefing over breakfast in the morning. The lady had requested breakfast be served an hour before dawn, far earlier than usual, but she wanted to send them off with full stomachs and a fond farewell.

When they all gathered at the table the next morning, General Marcum was pale and worn, and he had dark circles under his eyes from lack of sleep. As they were finishing the last bites of their meal and talking amiably, he rapped his knuckles on the table. "Something … something happened last night …" he trailed off before resuming. "Something happened that normally I would not share, but I feel I must for your own safety. I have no desire to cause you alarm, but you must understand the potential dangers we are facing. I received confidential information during the night. I would share it with you, but I expect none of you to speak of it."

"Oh, dear, Marcum. If the king ordered you not to speak of it, perhaps you should not," Adelina offered.

Marcum scowled. "The king gave no such order. He is not yet aware of this information. It is my prerogative to speak of it with whom I please."

"Oh, my apologies, dear," Adelina acquiesced.

"As I was saying, something occurred yesterday … something impossible.

The Black Hall fell to the Raven." The room was completely silent as every jaw dropped. Everyone had heard the rumors of the Black Hall. Bards sang the tales, authors designed fantastical thrillers around it and its inhabitants, and little boys wrapped black cloths around their faces and tumbled around with sticks in their hands playing *Slips*.

Tam was the first to work his mouth properly. "I thought the Black Hall was just a story."

Marcum grumbled. "No, the Black Hall is very real. Every assassin in Ashai, and some outside of it, now owe fealty to the Raven."

"He is taking over the entire Ashaiian underworld," Jimson remarked. "No King of Thieves … King of the Underwold, more like."

"I am curious, General," Rezkin interjected. "How did you get your information?"

Marcum gripped the edge of the table and then sighed as he released his hold. "That is the second piece of information I need to tell you. A slip came to me last night while I was returning from the stable." Even Rezkin was surprised. He had expressly ordered the slips to stay *away* from Marcum.

Lady Adelina gasped and swayed, and Captain Jimson reached out to steady the woman. "W-What did he want, Marcum?" the lady asked, her voice shaking.

"Be well, Ady, I am not dead. The slip did not bring *dark tidings* this time —the opposite, really. The Raven claims to have business with me, or so he told the Black Hall."

"Do you?" Adelina interrupted.

"Not as far as I am aware. I have no idea who he is, so I could not say for sure. I have dealings with people all over the kingdom, as is my job as general of the army. This slip said the Raven decreed that he would take care of me himself, if necessary, and that the Black Hall was to accept no contracts against me or my family," Marcum informed them with a pointed look at his wife and niece. "But, after the Raven left the Black Hall, the slips received just such a request."

Now, that *was* news to Rezkin. He had just spoken with the grandmaster about the general and then someone suddenly showed up with a kill order. Impeccable timing.

Marcum continued. "The slip was here to warn me about the hit."

"What? Why would they do that?" Adelina gasped.

"He said the Black Hall did not want to anger the Raven. Since they could not get in contact with him so quickly, the grandmaster made the decision to break with tradition and warn the intended target—*me*—that someone was trying to have me killed. The slip said it was to show the Raven that they were attempting, in good faith, to abide by his wishes, even if it meant overstepping by warning me.”

Going so far was to *warn* the general was a surprising response from the guild with regard to Rezkin’s directive not to harm Marcum and his family. Rezkin told the guild he had business with the general and would take care of the man himself simply because he did not want them thinking he had a personal interest in the general’s welfare when he told them not to assassinate the man. Rezkin preferred to reserve assassinations for those who were deserving of it, and although the general hated Rezkin, Marcum was still a good man and a great general. Rezkin also wanted to protect Frisha from the potential heartache of something untoward happening to her beloved aunt and uncle.

“You are saying that this Raven even has the Black Hall quaking in their boots?” Jimson inquired incredulously.

Marcum nodded once. “Yes. In fact, the slip called him Riel’gesh. If they have truly declared the man Riel’gesh, then *everyone* is in serious danger.”

“Why? What’s Riel’gesh?” Tam asked with more enthusiasm than the circumstances warranted.

“Riel’gesh means *giver of life*,” Marcum stated.

“Oh, well, that doesn’t sound too bad,” Frisha commented.

Marcum shook his head. “You have to remember, Frisha, this is a title issued by assassins. It means they believe this new leader is *indomitable*. They believe that no one can defeat him. He is so skilled and deadly that he can afford to allow his enemies to live. He has the ultimate power to grant life where others would require death, solely because he has no reason to fear. He is practically a *god* in their eyes.”

The general paused to gather his thoughts and then continued. “The Assassin’s Guild is just that—a guild. It is a commercial enterprise comprised of individuals selling their services for a profit. The members work for the common good of the guild. If they feel the grandmaster is failing to work toward the good of the guild, they will remove him. However, assassins have a strict set of rules and beliefs by which they live and operate. It is almost a religion in itself.

“By declaring the Raven Riel’gesh, they are essentially admitting defeat and declaring fealty to him. This changes the way they operate. Now, they function more like a cult. They will do whatever he commands of them, regardless of the outcome. He could order them to kill every man, woman, and child in Ashai; or he could order them to fall on their own blades, and it would be so. More so, Riel'gesh is a term recognized by assassins in *every* kingdom. Other assassins' guilds may not recognize him as Riel'gesh, but they will acknowledge that the Ashaiian guild *does*. He will be honored as such, but he will also be tested. I am no expert in matters of assassins, but to my knowledge, no one has ever actually held the position. For men and women who value such abilities, it was more of a theoretical or spiritual belief in a higher being, an individual with inhuman skill. They do not take the declaration of Riel'gesh lightly."

"So, Riel'gesh is like the assassins' version of the stories of demigods?" Tam asked with interest. "Like the heroes who have godlike strength or speed and go on great adventures battling beasts of myth and toppling evil armies and empires?"

"Something like that," the general conceded. "Only this one is a villain."

Rezkin had an academic understanding of the significance of the title of Riel'gesh but had not actually considered the reality of his newfound power. He did not care for power simply for its own sake. He cared only that he had the resources to do what was necessary. He needed to protect and honor his friends, and he needed to find Striker Farson. Beyond that, he cared little about the Assassins' Guild.

Rezkin *was* a little miffed that the general referred to him as a villain. Rezkin's personnel might be criminals, but all of the policies he had instituted had been for the betterment of society. He protected more people than he hurt, and the ones he did hurt were criminals in their own right. The thieves and assassins simply were not aware of his ulterior motives. He had to satisfy himself with the knowledge that the general did not know this either.

"It sounds like he may have some serious trouble if assassins from other kingdoms will seek to test him," Jimson observed.

"Indeed, but I doubt they will concern themselves with him so long as he remains in Ashai," Marcum replied.

"And, the king will do nothing about him?" the captain asked cautiously.

"I do not know. I will try to meet with him today, but there is no guarantee he will even grant *me* an audience," Marcum sighed. At their questioning looks he explained, "King Caydean keeps to himself these days when he is not holding court, and he holds court less and less often. If he seeks counsel, he does not do so from *me*, but I will see what I can do."

"Perhaps it would be wise not to mention it to the king just yet," Rezkin interrupted.

Marcum frowned. "Why would that be?"

"For one thing, the king may wonder exactly what business you have with the Raven," Rezkin said.

"I told you, I have none," Marcum argued.

"I might be inclined to believe that you *believe* you have none, but will the king?" the young man asked. Marcum narrowed his eyes. "It appears this Raven has granted you protection, or at least immunity, from the slips' designs. The king may wonder how you gained the favor of such a man."

"No one said I was in his favor. He said he would take care of me himself if it was necessary. That does not imply favor. It means he wants something from me, and whatever it is, I will not be inclined to grant it," Marcum asserted.

Rezkin glanced meaningfully at Adelina and Frisha then remarked, "Perhaps the king will believe you are compromised. At the very least, it would appear suspicious. If the rumors of Caydean's mad paranoia are true, he may not see reason. There is also the matter of who paid to have you killed. It is a great risk to place a target on the general of the army. It seems such a man would require a good amount of wealth and even more *reason* to want such a high profile target dead. It could even be someone in the palace itself."

Marcum's eyes widened, and he said, "The traitor."

Rezkin inclined his head and said, "Perhaps. But, you might think twice about letting such a person know that you are aware of the plot and that, not only has it failed, but you are in the Black Hall's confidence."

"Hmm … I see your point." Marcum glanced around at the concerned faces. "Do not worry. I did not get to be general of the army for nothing, and it would not be the first time I have faced an unseen enemy. Again, I remind you to speak of this to no one. Your lives could be in danger. I want you all out of Kaibain and away from this Raven and the Black Hall."

Marcum had considered, at one point, that Rezkin could be the Raven. The general had dismissed the idea when he realized the young man could not possibly have had enough time to take over the cities' thieves' guilds *and* the Black Hall in the brief absences when Rezkin had not been in the presence of himself or his family. Rezkin had been gone from the general's home for only a few hours the previous evening. It would have taken an immeasurable amount of time and planning to pull off such feats, and no one could topple the Black Hall in only a couple of hours. In addition, the young man did not have a mark on him, and anyone going up against the combined might of the assassins could not possibly walk away unharmed. While Marcum knew Rezkin was probably a formidable warrior, he doubted the nineteen-year-old had such inhuman abilities as were purported to belong to the Raven.

Marcum absolutely hated what he had to say next, but he was somewhat relieved that it was even an option. He held Frisha's gaze as he said, "If things go badly, I want you to stay with Rezkin no matter what."

"What? But, you *hate* Rezkin," she blurted without thinking.

Marcum sighed. "Listen to me. This is important. Absolutely, no matter what, you *Stay. With. Rezkin.* Understood?" At the girl's confused nod, he said, "Rezkin will keep you safe." She and Tam looked even more perplexed at that comment. From his periphery, Marcum could see the young warrior eyeing him speculatively. He finally met the young man's icy gaze and added, "No, I am not above using you to keep my niece safe. I doubt you will protest, though."

Rezkin inclined his head in acknowledgement but said nothing. He could not help but ponder the irony that the general was attempting to keep his niece far away and safe from the Raven when he was sending her off in the safe-keeping of the very man.

Marcum turned his attention to the captain and asked, "Are we clear?"

"Yes, sir," Captain Jimson replied with a fist over his heart.

Releasing a heavy breath, Marcum said, "Then, safe travels and good luck at the King's Tournament."

End of Book One
    Rezkin returns in *Reign of Madness (King's Dark Tidings, Book Two)*

CHARACTERS

Rezkin – A young warrior trained under mysterious circumstances

Master Jaiardun – Trainer at the mysterious northern fortress

Master Peider – Trainer at the mysterious northern fortress

Striker Farson – Striker at the northern fortress who escaped the fortress battle

Striker Adona – Striker at the northern fortress

Lord Butrand – A merchant brought to the fortress to teach Rezkin

Sheyalin – A master swordsmith who lived and died over two hundred years past

Mayor Jorge – Mayor of Perdony

Carlon – Butcher of Perdony

Pot – Stable boy at the Golden Cockerel in Justain

Master Nol – Owner of the Golden Cockerel Inn in Justain

Roxiella "Roxie" – Maid at the Golden Cockerel Inn in Justain

Frisha Souvain – Young woman from Cheswick traveling to Kaibain

Tamarin "Tam" Blackwater – Young carpenter's apprentice; Frisha's escort

Broken – 12-yr old thief (Diamond Claw Guild, Slink Den, Justain)

Cracker – 10-yr old thief (Diamond Claw Guild, Slink Den, Justain)

Thorn – Thieves' guild denleader (Diamond Claw Guild, Slink Den, Justain)

Dirge, Quip, Pratt - Diamond Claw guild members (Slink Den, Justain)

Ash – 6-yr old thief (Diamond Claw Guild, Slink Den, Justain)

Draphus – Guildmaster Martius's second (Diamond Claw Guild, Justain)

Martius – Thieves' guildmaster (Diamond Claw Guild, Justain)

Greld – Old thieves' guildmaster (Diamond Claw Guild, Justain)

Borgout – Old second to thieves' guild (Diamond Claw Guild, Justain)

Attica – Guild member (Diamond Claw Guild, Slink Den); raised to guild-master by Rezkin

Cratz – Henchman for Diamond Claw Guild (Justain)

Tyre – Diamond Claw Guildhouse guard (Justain)

Barclay - Diamond Claw Guildhouse guard (Justain)

Rom – Diamond Claw guild member, first to join Rezkin after Attica.

Yarl – Diamond Claw guild member (Justain) Rezkin killed after he tried to strangle Attica.

Benni – 16-year-old Diamond Claw guild member (Justain)

Kendt – Diamond Claw guild member (Justain)

Marson – Diamond Claw guild member (Justain); Attempted to lead a resistance

Madame Terly – brothel owner in Justain

Adsden – Second of the Serpent Guild (Justain)

Urek – Guildmaster of the Serpent Guild (Justain)

Marquis Addercroft – Urek's cousin; Placed Urek as guildmaster of the Serpent Guild

Lord Montaq – Count of Vesterfield in the Kingdom of Sandea

Ruald Addercroft – Marquis Addercroft's son

Marquis DeWinter – Lillian's father

Hilith Gadderand –Razor Edge Thieves' Guildmaster Guild, (Kaibain)

Breck –Razor Edge Thieves' Guild Second (Kaibain)

Cainith – Tam's eldest brother

Perrin – Tam's second brother

Connin – Tam's third brother

Lord Byron – Lord in Cheswick

Dornell – Lord Byron's son

Nate – Deckhand on riverboat

Lieutenant Jimson – King's Army officer; travel companion; later promoted to Captain

Captain Talwater – Riverboat captain

Second Lieutenant Swin – Soldier in Jimson's unit on the riverboat
Corporal Lattery Soldier in Jimson's unit from Justain to Lorelis
Colonel Simmons – Colonel at Fort Maneske
King Caydean – King of Ashai, First son of King Bordran
Prince Thresson – Prince of Ashai, Second son of King Bordran that went missing
General Marcum Jebai – General of the army of Ashai; Frisha's uncle
Simeon Jebai – Count of Glasbury; General Marcum's older brother
Striker Hendina – Striker investigating the disappearance of Prince Thresson
Reaylin de Voss – Young female traveling companion who wants to be a warrior
Narus – Steward of House Marcum
Finnian – Stable Master of House Marcum
Adelina Marcum – General Marcum's wife; Frisha's aunt
Jerand Jebai – Marcum and Simeon Jebai's deceased father
King Coroleus – First King of Ashai
Hilith Gadderand – Displaced guildmaster of the Razor Edge Guild in Kaibain
Breck – Second of the Razor Edge Guild in Kaibain, raised to guildmaster by Rezkin
Demky – Member of the Razor Edge Guild in Kaibain
Triald - Member of the Razor Edge Guild in Kaibain
Joselia and **Meriana** – Young noble ladies Tam, Frisha, and Rezkin met at a restaurant
Tieran Nirius – Son of Duke Wellinven; involved in a confrontation at restaurant
Lord Ambry – One of Tieran's friends in Kaibain
Master Healer Dronidus – Dead master healer; Yerwey Dulse's former master
Yerwey Dulse – Healer who helped Rezkin when he was injured in Kaibain
Malcius Jebai – Eldest son of Simeon Jebai
Palis Jebai – Youngest son of Simeon Jebai
Shiela Jebai – Daughter of Simeon Jebai
Sergeant Millins – Soldier in the Ashaiian army
Second Lieutenant Drascon – Soldier in the Ashaiian army

Ferrel – Jebai House guard

Guent – Jebai House guard

Maris – Jebai House guard

Jeyet – Jebai House guard

Tami – Shiela's maid

Brandt Gerrand – Heir to House Gerrand; friend of the Jebais

Uratel – Slip in the Black Hall

DEFINITIONS

Kingslayer – Sheyalin longsword

Bladesunder – Sheyalin shortsword

crass root – A root chewed for its slightly intoxicating and energizing effects

kendlewood – An expensive hardwood imported from Ferélle

thump – A unit of currency equal to ten silver pieces, named after the sound they make when dropped on the table.

Jahartan Empire – Ancient foe of Ashai during King Coroleus's reign

su'carai – Weapons used by the nomadic mountain tribes to the far east

Ink – Street drug made from parabata leaves

parabata leaves – Leaves used to make *ink*

Black Hall – (a.k.a. the Hall) The Assassin's Guild of Ashai

Adana'Ro – Assassin's guild of Ferélle

suraceous poison – A type of poison used by the Adana'Ro, particularly on their darts

Riel'sheng – "Giver of death"; ancient name for the Assassin's Guild

Riel'gesh – "Giver of life"; the name given to Rezkin as the liege lord of the Hall

LANGUAGES

PENOI

carasuan ej venuta coa Jaharta – "cone-heads of Jaharta"

FERÉLLI

Do'grelah – formal welcome or greeting
Secrelé – an officer or leader of the Adana'Ro

REIGN OF MADNESS

(Excerpt from *King's Dark Tidings, Book Two*)

1

The young travelers left General Marcum's estate in a mixture of excitement and apprehension. After an uninterrupted trek through the city, they met up on the docks near the *Luna Mara*. Frisha's cousins and their entourage had yet to arrive. Captain Jimson was standing to one side going over the paperwork with the dock master and ship's captain. Frisha stood huddled next to Tam, and both were staring at Rezkin who was tending to Pride several yards away. He was dressed in the most ostentatious finery they had ever seen on their companion. He wore a fine silk doublet in charcoal and silver brocade over a silver silk shirt and dark charcoal breeches. About his waist was a shiny, embossed black belt with a large silver buckle embedded with several large emeralds and sapphires.

From his belt hung his two swords, whose scabbards were now clamped within cages of silver filigree inset with a number of sapphires. Hanging from each were dark blue silk tassels that swung as he strutted about in a manner they had never seen from their friend. His high boots were made of high-quality, soft, black leather. Rezkin's hair was not pulled back into the usual queue, but rather was plaited past his shoulders and tied with a silver silk ribbon whose ends hung half way down the man's back. Rezkin was a picture of perfection if one were painting an idealized haughty noble.

Reaylin had only just arrived at the docks and was leaning over Frisha and

Tam's shoulders as she asked, "What is Rez wearing and why is he acting like that?"

Frisha shook her head and said, "I have no idea. He changed after breakfast and told us to just go with it. I can't imagine how he could even afford all that, much less why he would want to."

Reaylin's eyes roved over the young warrior, and she said, "It looks good on him, though."

Releasing a wistful sigh, Frisha said, "It really does. He looks so dashing. He's exactly how I imagine the heroic prince would look as he sweeps the princess off her feet."

Tam laughed and commented, "I'm pretty sure you both said the same thing when you saw him wearing nothing at all."

Both girls' faces flushed, and they simultaneously took to pummeling Tam. Rezkin glanced over at the raucous group with a questioning lift of his brow. The girls flushed again as they composed themselves. Just then, two fine coaches drew up at the end of the dock. The second coach was unoccupied but was filled to capacity with numerous bags and trunks. From the first coach stepped Frisha's cousins and their friend, Lord Brandt. Every one of them was dressed just as grandly as Rezkin. All three men were wearing fancy doublets and breeches with gaudy accessories, and their hair was plaited in the same manner as Rezkin's. Shiela fussed with her lavender gown that fell in waves of layer upon layer of silks and laces. Her dark brown hair was pulled over one shoulder and was curled and wound about itself within a fine lace netting. She wore short, white lace gloves and grasped a parasol that matched her gown, which she immediately opened upon stepping out of the coach.

Several servants had been crammed atop the coaches with the drivers. Two of the male servants were directing the deckhands to the luggage while another assisted a petite, timid woman in a drab servant's smock to the ground. The tiny woman promptly began patting down Shiela's gown, ensuring no wrinkles could be seen.

Once the four young nobles were satisfied that their attire had survived the short coach ride through the city, they began making their way down the dock. The servants and a number of dockworkers began unloading the luggage coach and were already passing by the strutting nobles. Shiela, who seemed to be in the lead, stopped a few paces short of Frisha and her companions. She stuck her nose in the air and sniffed disdainfully as she eyed Frisha's sensible tunic and pants.

"Frisha," she said, "*Cousin*, it is a pleasure to see you again, I am sure." Her tone made it seem like it was anything *but* a pleasure.

Lords Malcius and Palis next greeted their cousin with little more than a slight bow. They even neglected to introduce their friend. Well, Frisha would not be so rude.

"Malcius, Palis, Shiela, this is my friend Tamarin Blackwater, and this is Reaylin de Voss," Frisha announced. All three nodded vaguely and mumbled something that sounded like "pleasure" without actually acknowledging the presence of Frisha's companions. At that moment, Rezkin chose to make an appearance.

He strode up to the group with a broad smile and overly loud, cheery voice. "Greetings! It is a pleasure to finally meet you all. Ah, you must be Lord Malcius," Rezkin said as he clasped forearms with the young man in a familiar greeting between close friends and peers. Malcius and Palis both had the dark brown hair that ran in the Jebai family, but while Palis's eyes matched the warm brown of Frisha's, Malcius's were a soft grey like his mother's. The older brother had broad shoulders and was slightly taller, about six feet, while the younger brother had a leaner, wiry build.

Malcius grinned and greeted Rezkin with just as much enthusiasm, "And, you must be Lord Rezkin! I heard you would be traveling with us. Our uncle spoke highly of you." Frisha and Tam shared a surprised glance, both thinking the same thing. "Please, allow me to introduce my companions. This is my brother, Palis." The warrior-turned-noble clasped arms with Palis and exchanged pleasantries. Malcius motioned to the young woman and said, "And, this is our sister, Shiela."

Rezkin bowed low and intoned, "Lady Shiela, it is most gracious of you to bless us with your stunning presence." He gave her his best smile, the one that women seemed to prefer. Shiela blushed as Rezkin brushed a soft kiss across her hand.

"Oh, Lord Rezkin, the pleasure is mine, I am *sure*." The way she spoke most definitely made it sound like a pleasure. "You are one *fine* gentleman."

Rezkin bowed slightly, again, and said, "Thank you, Lady Shiela, that means much coming from a lovely lady such as you." Shiela actually giggled as she fanned her face with a lacy hand.

Malcius grinned and continued, "And, this is our good friend, Lord Brandt of House Gerrand."

Not having a direct connection to Lord Brandt, Rezkin gave him a more formal bow in greeting rather than the familiar one he had used with the Jebais. "It is a pleasure to meet you, Lord Brandt," Rezkin stated. "If I might be so bold, I would just like to say that I have always admired your mother's artistry."

Brandt's brows rose in surprise, "You are familiar with my mother's work?"

"Of course! Lady Gerrand has a way of capturing the light with a softness that makes one feel as if he is looking upon a dream. It is quite easy to forget that underneath the fantasy lies simple paint and canvas," Rezkin remarked.

"I had never really thought of it that way, but you are correct. I can see it, now. Which is your favorite?" Brandt asked curiously.

"I once had the pleasure of looking upon *The Lilies of the Lake*." Rezkin shifted his gaze to Shiela and grinned as he mock-lowered his voice conspiratorially. "If I did not know any better, I could swear that fairies lived among them," he confided with a wink. Shiela giggled and blushed as she batted her lashes.

Reaylin, who was standing behind the stunned Frisha and Tam, leaned forward and whispered, "Oh, he's good. I didn't know the tough warrior had *that* in him."

"Say, Lord Rezkin," Malcius spoke up, "is that your magnificent beast?" Malcius waved a manicured hand toward Pride who was standing further down the dock. The reins hung limply, brushing the ground in a silent command for the horse to remain where he was. Pride was nearly as opulent as Rezkin today. The stallion's black coat was clean and brushed to a shine. The embossed black saddle and black and silver bridle were polished, as well. The horse's mane and tail were braided and woven with silver ribbons in a parade style.

"Why, yes, he is. But, please, you may dispense with the title. I am quite sure none of you will forget who I am. Just call me Rezkin, although my friends sometimes prefer to call me Rez," the young man said with such confidence it was infectious.

"Yes, quite right, Rezkin...Rez. It would please me if you called me Malcius, as well," the noble replied. Frisha's jaw dropped. Her egotistical cousin *never* dropped his title—for *anyone*. No doubt Malcius thought he would look weak and insecure if he insisted on continuing to use his title after Rez's speech. The announcement was followed by a round of permissions by all to dispense with the titles. In only a matter of moments, Rezkin had completely disarmed the nobles of their pretentious snobbery, at least as far as *he* was concerned.

"You were speaking of the horse?" Shiela prompted demurely as she batted her lashes.

"Yes, tell us about the stallion," Palis piped up. "It is massive. I have not seen the like. The only horse I have seen that comes close is Uncle Marcum's."

"What breed is it? Is it of the Cronelis stock?" asked Brandt.

Rezkin grinned like he was holding all of the candy. "No, Palis is quite right. He is a purebred battle charger of the Augmerian line. I call him Pride."

The men's jaws were slack as glances darted back and forth between Rezkin and the horse. "But, that is the king's stock," protested Malcius.

Rezkin grinned broader as he placed his hands loosely in his pockets and rocked back on his heels in an uncharacteristic display of pride. "Indeed," was all he said. "Speaking of which, it is time I get him rigged so they can haul him aboard. You had best keep your distance. He tends to maim or kill anyone but me."

The three male lordlings followed Rezkin but kept their distance, whispering between themselves as he removed the saddle and tack and strapped the horse into the harnesses, readying him to be hoisted aboard the ship. The lords looked like children drooling over their new best friend's amazing toy. Shiela's eyes never left Rezkin, and every once in a while, he would bend or stoop, and her face would flush. Frisha had no idea what Rezkin was up to, but if he thought for one second that she was going to lose him to Shiela, then he had another thing coming.

Once everyone was aboard, they received their berth assignments. Rezkin already knew the assignments because he had made them himself. He had assigned himself to share a room with Malcius, while Palis and Brandt shared a second. For strategic reasons, Rezkin would have preferred to place Tam with Brandt, but it would have been considered unseemly for the young lord to share a room with a commoner who was not his manservant. Frisha, Reaylin, Shiela, and Shiela's maid, Tami, were assigned to share a four-person berth. Rezkin could get away with placing Reaylin in the room since she was the only other female onboard. As both officers and nobility, Captain Jimson and Lieutenant Drascon shared a berth; and Tam was left to bunk with Sergeant Millins as commoners. The four Jebai house guards shared another four-person room, while the other servants were placed with the crew.

The rooms were small and cramped since two or three of the berths could possibly fit into a single average room at an inn. When it came to the confines of a ship, it seemed the nobles preferred privacy over space. Malcius looked around and wondered, "Where are the rest of my belongings?"

Rezkin laughed, a sound that would have seemed unnatural to anyone who knew him but sounded genuine and effortless to the unsuspecting lord. "I do not know about you, but I would prefer *not* to sleep on a trunk." Rezkin waved a dismissive hand at the two trunks that had been placed at the ends of their respective beds. "I believe we only need one in here at a time. The rest are stored in the hold below. If you require something, I am sure one of those crewmen will be delighted to retrieve it for you." In order to keep up appearances, Rezkin was also traveling with several trunks. It would have looked odd for a noble of his unspecified, but presumably high, standing to be traveling with nothing more than a single pack and saddlebags. So far, no one was willing to risk offending him by questioning his place within the ranks of the nobility.

Since the crew had situated their belongings and Rezkin had already seen to Pride, there was little to do. He and the other passengers found themselves standing on the deck waiting to depart. The women approached the huddle of young men. All three wore sour expressions, but Frisha and Reaylin stood back as Shiela sidled up in exasperation.

Malcius grinned and said, "Ah, Sister, so nice of you to join us."

Shiela batted her lashes at Rezkin to whom she directed her answer. "Nothing could keep me away," she said with syrupy sweetness.

Rezkin bowed slightly and inquired with a pleasant smile, "Lady Shiela, how do you find your accommodations?"

Shiela's composure slipped as she fanned her face with a lacy hand and fluttered her eyes with overly dramatic distress. "Well, I am sure that little can be done, but it is *most* disconcerting to be sharing a room with a bunch of *commoners*." The disdain with which she said the word *commoners* made it sound as if she had been assigned a room filled with livestock.

Rezkin's smile dropped, and he directed an uncertain and disapproving frown in Malcius's direction while flicking a glance at Frisha. Malcius flushed at the unspoken rebuke. As General Marcum's heir, Frisha was due all the respect of the nobility, and to demean her publicly was unbecoming behavior for a lady. Rezkin's comportment as a nobleman of the highest standard encouraged Malcius to uphold the standard, as well. Malcius cleared his throat as he gave his sister a penetrating look. "Sister, I am sure you misspoke."

Shiela was startled by the reprimand and glanced over to see Rezkin's disapproving stare. She blushed slightly and replied, "Oh, yes. I meant *a couple* of commoners and our dear cousin. Forgive me, Frisha, I meant no offense," she said with feigned regret.

Frisha rolled her eyes and crossed her arms. "I'm sure you didn't," she remarked. "I must say, Shiela, I find myself greatly concerned for your wellbeing," she said, her brow furrowed with worry.

Shiela's eyes widened in trepidation of some unidentified threat, "Oh, why is that?"

"I had not realized your constitution was so delicate that the mere presence of other human beings could render you so senseless," Frisha remarked fretfully. "I worry that this journey could cause you an inordinate amount of stress. Perhaps you should reconsider attending."

Reaylin snickered behind her hand as she held back a giggle, but Palis and Brandt burst out laughing. Even Malcius wore a sly grin, which immediately fell when Shiela scowled in his direction. Shiela's face reddened, and she turned her attention to Rezkin. He observed the young *lady* with a somber face but a glint of laughter in his eyes. Shiela knew the handsome nobleman was watching to see how she would react. The heat slipped from her cheeks as she grinned wickedly. She sidled up to Rezkin and wrapped her arms around one of his muscular biceps as she turned to face Frisha. She then gazed up at the young warrior with doe eyes and said sweetly, "I am sure, dear Cousin, that I will be quite well during the trip. From what Uncle Marcum said, Rezkin, here, is quite capable. I will be in good hands."

Rezkin lifted a brow and cast a feral grin down at the young woman. Frisha was fuming but felt a shiver crawl up her spine at the look. Rezkin appeared as a lion that had just sighted his next prey—and not in a good way. Shiela interpreted the look as a different kind of hunger and smiled suggestively. Malcius cleared his throat just as another sound reached their ears.

"Do not drop that, now, and hurry up! We do not have all day, you know," said a familiar voice. Frisha and Tam's eyes widened as the late arrival stomped onto the deck. "Ah! I did not realize I would have the company of House Jebai. What is this? House Gerrand, too, I see."

Malcius bowed low as did Palis and Brandt. "Lord Tieran," Malcius intoned, "I did not know we would be traveling with such esteemed company." His eyes glanced at Rezkin who was mostly blocked by the others. He was pointedly *not* bowing. Malcius added, "Or, rather, *additional* esteemed company, I should say."

"Additional?" Tieran queried with a furrowed brow. His eyes fell on Rezkin as he stepped from behind the other young men. Tieran's face paled, and his jaw dropped slightly. "Oh, ah…I see. Lord Rezkin," he sputtered as he bowed slightly in greeting, "it is…ah…good to see you, again."

Malcius glanced between the two, his interest piqued by the superior lord's strange behavior. "You two already know each other?" He immediately thought better of his question and waved it off, "Of course, you do. Introductions are not necessary."

Rezkin greeted Lord Tieran wearing the same feral smile from a moment ago, only it looked decidedly more dangerous when directed at the duke's eldest son. His other prey had arrived. Rezkin had seen the Duke's request for passage for his son and had taken it upon himself to assign the young man to their ship. He had also sent a missive to the Duke, in the general's name, explaining the security that was already assigned to the vessel, so Tieran had not come with his own guard. Since the duke already had a number of men assigned to the tournament, Tieran's personal guard would be pooled from them upon his arrival in Skutton. Tieran and his manservant were to share the final room. It was not inappropriate for a manservant to share quarters with his master when traveling, and contrary to popular belief, many of those who served the upper Houses were of lesser nobility. Tieran's manservant was the fifth son of a minor landless noble.

Tieran gulped as he received the full brunt of Rezkin's heated gaze. While Rezkin played the amiable upstanding noble for the others, he kept Tieran firmly in his place through fear. "So, ah, Lord Rezkin. Does this mean your lovely girlfriend is around here as well?"

Rezkin's grin lost its edge and suddenly became as bright and pleasant as it had with the others. He brushed off Shiela's grasp and turned abruptly. With a sweeping motion he presented Frisha, "Yes, you are quite right! My sweet Lady Frisha is attending the tournament, as well, escorted by her cousins, of course." All eyes turned to the startled young woman, and she blushed at Rezkin's recognition of her as his girlfriend once again.

Shiela's jaw dropped. "*She's* your girlfriend?" The young lady's shocked inquiry was accentuated by a shrill whistle and the sudden rocking of the ship as it began drifting away from the dock.

On sure feet, Rezkin strode over to the stunned Frisha and took her in his arms as he gazed longingly into her eyes. Somehow, the performance did not seem as difficult as he thought it would be. Rezkin had spent some of his time in Kaibain studying the interactions between men and women. He even attended a few stage performances during the night that were classified as romances. The exchanges seemed strange and foreign, but he was practiced at mimicking behavior, so he was confident he could pull it off.

"How could I *not* be completely besotted by this stunning woman? She is a brilliant diamond in the rough." He paused theatrically. "Well, I suppose it is not that rough considering her father is a shrewd and extremely successful businessman. I am quite sure his acquired wealth exceeds many of the smaller Houses, in fact. Not to mention she is the heir of Lord Marcum Jebai." Rezkin intentionally referred to the general as *lord* and added his family name for emphasis.

Tieran furrowed his brow. "Really? A *commoner* has been so successful?"

"Quite." Rezkin remarked. "We must not forget, gentlemen…and ladies," Rezkin said as he bowed slightly toward Shiela and Frisha, "that, while the nobility serve as the mind and voice of the kingdom, the commoners are the kingdom's blood. Without them, the kingdom would cease to function." Rezkin then grinned smugly, "And, I, for one, prefer my blood rich and plentiful."

The duke's son narrowed his eyes suspiciously, "Yet, you would choose to bind yourself to one of common blood?"

Rezkin laughed heartily. Frisha and Tam jumped. It was the first time they had heard him laugh, and to their ears, it did not quite sound genuine. "Oh, please, Tieran," Rezkin said, waving off the lord's concern while intentionally dropping his title. "Is noble blood so weak as to be defeated by one commoner parent? Both the count and general are as strong as any noble can be," he remarked as Malcius and Palis straightened proudly. "Do not doubt that Lady Terissa is just as formidable and respectable." Frisha jerked her head to stare at Rezkin. What did *he* know of her mother? Rezkin stroked his jaw as he mused, "Considering her father's intelligence and success, I would not be surprised to find that he was actually the remnant of forgotten line from a minor house." Frisha frowned. She knew full well her father did not belong to any noble house, and she was sure Rezkin knew it, too.

All the nobles looked at Frisha appraisingly, as if seeing her for the first time. Rezkin was pleased as he observed their contemplations and lightly remarked, "It is a shame I have not been able to convince the general to accept my proposal."

Shiela's jaw dropped. "You *proposed*? For *Frisha*?" she questioned with scorn and disbelief. The young men all scoured Rezkin's appearance trying to process the information.

"Why would Uncle Marcum reject your proposal?" Palis finally asked. "He speaks so highly of you."

"Alas, you have struck on the conundrum that has become the bane of my existence," he said dramatically with a heavy sigh. He shook his head and continued, "I can tell you for certain that Marcum definitely recognizes his niece's worth. Perhaps he is holding out for someone more active in the court, perhaps a *duke*," he mentioned offhandedly as he waved in Tieran's direction. The young man shifted uncomfortably, and Frisha blushed furiously. "For all I know, he could be holding out for a *prince*! What I *do* know is that, despite my promises of wealth and power and protection, he continues to deny me." His face fell, and he looked away in heartfelt shame.

Frisha placed a hand on his arm as she gazed at him sympathetically with tears in her eyes. She knew that much of what Rezkin was saying and doing was an act, but she could see his sincere distress over his rejection. Even Shiela's face softened at the young romantic's plight.

Malcius shifted uncomfortably before he remarked, "The general is a cunning man, Rez. Perhaps he only hopes to test your resolve." Shiela scowled at her brother as she elbowed him in the ribs. Prompted by his aggressive sister, he continued, "I am positive it has nothing to do with you, personally, and I am sure that any House would be elated to join with you." Shiela gave her brother a pointed look, and he added casually, "My own included."

Frisha sent Malcius a dark look, and he winced as Shiela smiled smugly. Rezkin turned back to the group as he gathered his composure. He pretended not to catch Malcius's implication. "Yes, you are probably correct, Malcius." He straightened proudly and gripped his doublet over his heart as he said, "I shall remain steadfast and determined. The general may yet change his mind."

Rezkin glanced over at Captain Jimson who had been standing not far away eavesdropping on the conversation while presumably reviewing paper-work. He had not informed Jimson of his plans, and Jimson really had no idea what Rezkin was up to with this whole charade. The captain recognized a signal when he saw one, though. Rezkin's look was his cue to interrupt the conversation.

"Lords, Ladies, now that we are underway, the ship's captain asks that we all meet on the quarterdeck for instructions in safety and ship's protocol. If you would, please follow me," Jimson said as he turned and led the way.

Captain Crowleson spent nearly an hour explaining the layout of the ship, a bit of sailing terminology and what everyone should do in the case of an emergency. To the men, he explained where they should take up positions if the ship came under attack. Being a passenger ship, rather than a warship, the carrack had little in the way of defenses. Most of the space that would be used for weaponry had been designed as quarters for the crew and passengers. The captain explained that there had been no attacks for as long he had been sailing the Tremadel, but he wanted to be thorough.

During his speech, the captain also made it quite clear exactly *who* was in charge while they were on the ship. Tieran and Malcius sniffed in disdain, but Rezkin piped in with exuberance, assuring the captain that everyone understood the need for certain protocols when on the vessel. Chastened, the young men nodded their assurances, as well.

In the short time Rezkin had been in the presence of the nobles, he had effectively manipulated them into viewing him as the leader. He left open the implication that he was of very high standing without ever divulging his House affiliation, not a small feat among nobles. General Marcum's assurances had gone a long way in generating that trust with the Jebais. Rezkin wondered just how hard the general choked on his words when he issued such praise. Rezkin had successfully cowed the duke's son through fear during their previous encounter, but the Jebais' assumption of Rezkin's superior status encouraged Tieran to believe the same. Tieran simply assumed the Jebais knew with whom they were traveling.

Gaining control over the traveling party was only one part of Rezkin's plan, though. He could have done so through a number of different methods. The easiest would have been to simply state that the general had placed him in command and left them to wonder as to his status in the hierarchy of the kingdom. That would have done nothing to further his second goal, though, which was to aid Frisha. If Rezkin could rewrite the opinions of the young nobles of Houses Jebai, Gerrand, and especially Nirius, then Frisha would have a much higher chance of being accepted as an equal in high society. If Rezkin could not keep Frisha for himself, then he could at least help her make a smooth entrance into society and hopefully have a happier life.

Rezkin's third goal was to create an acceptable persona for himself. The general was a prime example of how suspicion and fear could turn others against him, and people feared what they did not understand. If Rezkin acted as himself, the others on this voyage would be distrustful and could turn against him. He could have played the role of a commoner and been effectively invisible, but then he would have had a difficult time guiding events according to his plans. Most people seemed to want to believe he was a noble, so he decided to let them believe as they wished. Surprisingly, allowing people to believe he had the utmost power and authority was the path of least resistance. Besides, he would need a strongly defined and accepted persona if his plans for the tournament were to succeed.

For the rest of the day, people mingled and chatted. The nobles gossiped about court and courtships. They even invited Frisha to join them when Rezkin was not present. Captain Jimson spent some time getting to know his comrades, and the Jebai House Guard kept to themselves playing dice or bones. Tam found a secluded spot near the poop deck to read his book. He was feeling out of sorts. His friends all seemed to fit into some niche, and he did not belong with any of them. Only Reaylin was in a similar position, and he was not yet desperate enough to suffer *her*.

Tam knew that Rezkin was playing a role, although he still did not understand *why*. The problem was that Tam was unable to discern how much of what Rezkin said was simple acting and how much was truth. Rezkin's speech about commoners was both complimentary and patronizing, and Tam did not know how to feel about it. On the surface, Rezkin's affable and joyous conduct seemed normal for a sociable noble, but the excessive jubilance and decorum seemed almost neurotic for *Rezkin*.

The warrior was typically defined by a solid, stoic presence that incited feelings of safety and stability. When Rezkin was around, Tam always felt like everything was under control, even when they were in the midst of chaos. The *Lord* Rezkin simply did not fill him with the same sense of assurance, even though he knew it lay just below the surface. Rezkin's almost passionate behavior somehow disturbed him.

Reaylin was just as aloof as Tam. She seemed particularly uncomfortable around the other women. Frisha had gained points with Reaylin when she snubbed Shiela, but now Frisha was spending more time with the nobles, as was Rezkin. Reaylin was astonished by Rezkin's behavior. Never had she imaged he was capable of pulling off such a flamboyant persona. It made her wonder about Rezkin's other capabilities and why he was such a skilled fraudster. Just who was Rezkin *really*, and could he be useful?

Reaylin still was not happy that Rezkin proposed to Frisha, but she was encouraged by the fact that the deal had failed. She did feel bad for him, but he was a strong man, and he would get over it. Frisha was too weak for a man like Rezkin. Reaylin could tell that he was put off by women like Shiela and thought that she, as a warrior, had a much better chance with such a man. If only she could get him away from Frisha long enough for him to see *her*.

Rezkin disappeared for a while as he secretly scrambled about the ship. He snuck about the captain's quarters, since the captain was busy on deck. He had already been there before, but he wanted to make sure there was nothing new of which he should be aware. There was not, so he continued with his search. He snuck into each of the guest's rooms and rifled through their trunks and then went through the mound of useless *necessities* in the cargo hold. Nothing of immediate import stood out, but he did find a few tidbits that he would file away for later use.

Two of the Jebai House Guards had gambling debts they were to pay off by performing some unspecified service while in Skutton. The future duke, Tieran, was to attend a clandestine meeting on behalf of his father with a man whose name Rezkin did not recognize. Tieran's manservant, Colton, had a secret lover who Rezkin was nearly certain was a man. Shiela was not as innocent as she would have her family believe. She had in her possession half a dozen parting letters from potential suitors moaning about how much they would miss her, and two actually pleaded for her to meet them for a private rendezvous while at the tournament.

When Rezkin rejoined the nobles, everyone wanted to know what he had been up to and how he managed to disappear for so long on a ship. Rezkin laughed and said, "Ah, well, you see I do enjoy a good voyage as much as the rest of you, but we did have to rise hours before dawn this morning." Frisha arched a brow. She knew full well that Rezkin always rose long before dawn. The man was incessantly restless when he was not moving in some fashion.

Malcius snickered, "You snuck off to take a nap."

Rezkin heaved an overly dramatic sigh and uttered, "You may have seen the truth, and I concede—I feel no shame for my absence."

Shiela, not deterred by Rezkin's intentions toward Frisha, said, "Oh, I wish you had said so earlier. I might have felt inclined to take a nap as well." She fluttered her lashes and eyed him suggestively.

Malcius scowled, "Shiela, know you no shame?"

Brandt chuckled, "Whatever vessel held *her* shame grew so full it shattered. She is no longer capable of carrying any."

"What would you know of shame, Brandt?" Shiela scoffed. "You are a cad."

"Better a cad than a...ow!" Brandt shouted as Malcius stomped his foot under the table.

"Yes, well," Rezkin cleared his throat, "it is probably best I found myself in seclusion. Tam tells me I snore quite loudly."

Malcius groaned, "And I am to bunk with you?"

Rezkin shrugged and grinned, "Every man must have at least one fault, no?"

"If that is your only fault, then you are a better man than the rest of us," Malcius muttered.

"Speak for yourself," said Brandt. "*I* am utter perfection," he remarked facetiously as he ran a hand through his long silky hair.

Palis punched Brandt in the arm and replied, "Yeah, perfect for using as a practice dummy."

Brandt sniffed and said, "You laugh now, but I am going to beat you in the tournament."

Palis barked a laugh and said, "You will be lucky to make it into the same tier as me."

"I placed high enough in the spring tournament," Brandt defended.

"Only because most of us were stuck at the *field training* our uncle insisted upon," Palis remarked.

Rezkin arched a brow. "Field training?"

Brandt rolled his eyes and answered, "The general got it in his head that we should all know how to survive in the wild '*just in case.*' Luckily, I got to leave early to participate in the tournament."

Malcius added, "It was supposed to be survival training for young lords, but try telling a bunch of nobles to leave their finery at home. Everyone had massive tents and soft cots, wine and bread and cheese aplenty. It was more like a three-week social gathering. Uncle Marcum was furious."

"You were there with the rest of us," Brandt chided.

Malcius shrugged, "I admit it. I like my fine things and prefer to live in comfort. Besides, it was ridiculous. When would we ever need such skills? It is not like we go wandering off into the wild. We live in the city, and we travel by ship or in a caravan of coaches and guards with people to see to our needs. I do not see why *I* need to know how to trap a rabbit or build a fire pit."

Frisha, who had been very quiet up until now, straightened and lifted her chin. "Rezkin can do all of those things. He is quite the skilled woodsman." Rezkin gave her a warning glance, but she ignored it and continued. "When we traveled the river before, much like *now*," she emphasized, "we encountered a problem with a massive gang of bandits. We were forced to abandon the ship and travel by land for a week with not much more than a single pack each. Rezkin and the soldiers hunted for food, set up camps, and battled the bandits. Rezkin even treated the soldier's wounds afterward. What do you think *you* could do if the ship went down and you lost all of your finery?"

Mouths were agape all around and Frisha felt a small satisfaction with the nobles' loss of composure. Eyes darted back and forth between Frisha and Rezkin. Rezkin cocked his head and studied Frisha curiously. It was interesting that when she finally gathered enough courage to speak with conviction, it was to do so in *his* favor.

Malcius recovered first and waved off Frisha's claim, "Yes, yes, but you had the soldiers with you to take care of things, and killing a few bandits can hardly be considered a *battle*."

Frisha scowled. "There were several *dozen* bandits and only six soldiers. Tam and I had no weapons training at the time, and we were pretty much useless. Rezkin was magnificent, though," she said as she took a note from Shiela's book and batted her lashes at him. Frisha had not really seen much of the battle, actually. She was too busy trying to keep the panic at bay, her eyes darting in every direction, seemingly all at once. She had picked up bits and pieces of the discussions between the soldiers and Jimson afterward, though. She knew Rezkin had been quite impressive but did not know to what extent. "Besides," she continued, "that was only the *first* time we battled with bandits."

The others were a mixture of confused and impressed, but Tieran was terrified. He had seen the look of death in Rezkin's eyes when they first met in Kaibain, and now he knew for certain that Rezkin was no stranger to bloodshed.

Rezkin suddenly laughed boisterously and waved away the serious mood, "You know I can never seem to sit still for long. I am always picking up some new hobby. I suppose I have acquired an odd assortment of skills here and there. Woodcraft can actually be quite intriguing and relaxing, you know. The general may be on to something, if not for the reasons you think. You can never understand the value of what you gain by depending only on yourself unless you have tried it. Things are different when you do not have servants looking after you. After you dispel such a weakness, I am telling you, the confidence you gain is simply intoxicating."

Malcius raised his brows, "You think having servants is a weakness?"

"Not *having* them. *Needing* them," Rezkin replied, holding up a finger for emphasis. "For me, servants are a luxury—a right of status, wealth and power, but they are not a *necessity*. I can survive without them, if necessary," Rezkin stated with smug pride.

"I guess I see your point," Malcius replied. He rubbed the back of his neck uncomfortably. "To tell the truth, I do not know what I would do if I were put in such a position that I needed to fend for myself. I cannot honestly say that I would survive," he added with a bit of chagrin. Palis and Tieran shifted uncomfortably, each knowing they would fail under the same circumstances.

Shiela, however, had caught onto a different strand of Frisha's story. "So, *Cousin*, am I to understand that you traveled for weeks alone with a host of *men*?" Her tone was light but filled with accusation.

Frisha lifted her chin and replied, "That's right. Tam was my escort. He is like a brother to me, and he swore an Oath of Protection to my father. Besides, Rezkin was providing his protection, as well." She left out the fact that she had only met Rezkin partway through the journey and had really known nothing about him.

"Yes, well, Master Tamarin is *not* your brother. He is not related to you in any way, and the oath of a commoner means nothing to me," she replied with disdain.

"Then, I suppose I am fortunate that *your opinion* means nothing to *me*," Frisha replied acerbically. "Besides, would you question Rezkin's honor, as well?"

Shiela huffed, "Of course not, but it is obvious *you* have done something to catch his attention. I cannot imagine any other reason he would want someone like *you*."

Rezkin stood abruptly, the chair scraping across the floor. He towered over Shiela with a disapproving gaze. It lacked violence but held the scorn of a father scolding a child.

"Lady Shiela, I take offense to your accusations and slander against *my* lady's character. Lady Frisha is and has always been a respectable woman, and she should be commended for her bravery and dignity during such trying times. You have made a number of unfounded assumptions. I also take offense in your comments against Master Tamarin, who I have the honor of calling *friend*. It matters not that *you* would question his honor since, from what I have seen, you seem to have very little. Unlike you, I actually know Master Tamarin, and *I* hold his oath in high regard. If you must belittle others to make yourself feel better, then you should do silently, in your own mind, where only you will suffer from your poison. You will certainly abstain from speaking such vileness in my presence."

Rezkin held out his hand and said, "Come, Frisha. Please join me on deck for some fresh air."

End of Chapter One

Reign of Madness (King's Dark Tidings, Book Two)

A NEW SERIES BY KEL KADE

Shroud of Prophecy

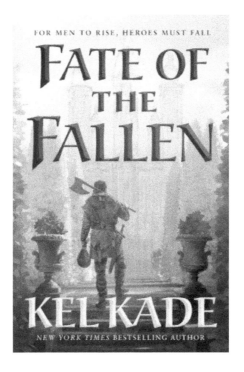

Not all stories have happy endings.

Everyone loves Mathias. Naturally, when he discovers it's his destiny to save the world, he dives in headfirst, pulling his best friend, Aaslo, along for the ride.

However, saving the world isn't as easy, or exciting, as it sounds in the stories. The going gets rough, and folks start to believe their best chance for survival is to surrender to the forces of evil, which isn't how the prophecy goes. At all. As the list of allies grows thin and the friends find themselves staring death in the face, they must decide how to become the heroes they were destined to be or, failing that, how to survive.

ABOUT THE AUTHOR

Kel Kade lives in Texas and occasionally serves as an adjunct college faculty member, inspiring young minds and introducing them to the fascinating and very real world of geosciences. Thanks to Kade's enthusiastic readers and the success of the *King's Dark Tidings* series, Kade is now able to create universes spanning space and time, develop criminal empires, plot the downfall of tyrannous rulers, and dive into fantastical mysteries full time.

Growing up, Kade lived a military lifestyle of traveling to and living in new places. These experiences with distinctive cultures and geography instilled in Kade a sense of wanderlust and opened a young mind to the knowledge that the Earth is expansive and wild. A deep interest in science, ancient history, cultural anthropology, art, music, languages, and spirituality is evidenced by the diversity and richness of the places and cultures depicted in Kade's writing.

NOTE FROM THE AUTHOR

I hope you enjoyed reading this first book in the *King's Dark Tidings* (KDT) series. Please consider leaving a review or comments so that I may continue to improve and expand upon this ongoing series. I invite you to visit my website at www.kelkade.com. The audiobook, produced by Podium Publishing, is available on iTunes and Audible.com!

Milton Keynes UK
Ingram Content Group UK Ltd.
UKHW040120111023
430332UK00003B/18/J